LOVE AFTER DARK

GANSETT ISLAND SERIES, BOOK 13

MARIE FORCE

Love After Dark
Gansett Island Series, Book 13
By: Marie Force

Published by HTJB, Inc.
Copyright 2015. HTJB, Inc.
Cover designer is Courtney Lopes
Interior Layout by Isabel Sullivan, E-book Formatting Fairies
ISBN: 978-1942295358

www.marieforce.com

The Gansett Island Series

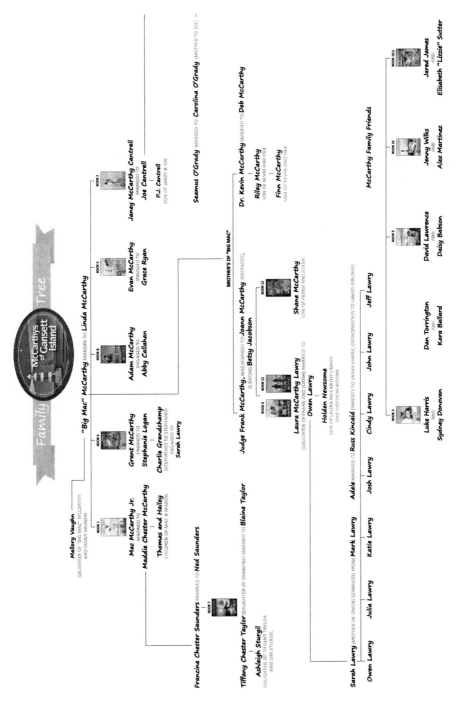

Family Tree

McCarthys of Gansett Island

Mallory Vaughn
(DAUGHTER OF "BIG MAC" MCCARTHY AND DIANA YAUGEN)

"Big Mac" McCarthy MARRIED TO **Linda McCarthy**

BOOK 1
Mac McCarthy Jr. MARRIED TO **Maddie Chester McCarthy**
Thomas and Hailey
CHILDREN OF MAC & MADDIE

BOOK 4
Grant McCarthy ENGAGED TO **Stephanie Logan**
Charlie Grandchamp STEPFATHER TO STEPHANIE ENGAGED TO **Sarah Lawry**

BOOK 8
Adam McCarthy ENGAGED TO **Abby Callahan**

BOOK 5
Evan McCarthy ENGAGED TO **Grace Ryan**

BOOK 2
Janey McCarthy Cantrell MARRIED TO **Joe Cantrell**
P.J. Cantrell
SON OF JANEY & JOE

Seamus O'Grady MARRIED TO **Carolina O'Grady** (MOTHER TO LINDA)

BROTHERS OF "BIG MAC"

Judge Frank McCarthy, WAS MARRIED TO **Joann McCarthy** (DECEASED), IS DATING **Betsy Jacobson**

BOOK 11
Laura McCarthy Lawry
(DAUGHTER OF FRANK AND JOANN) MARRIED TO **Owen Lawry**

BOOK 13
Shane McCarthy
SON OF FRANK AND JOANN

Dr. Kevin McCarthy MARRIED TO **Deb McCarthy**
Riley McCarthy
SON OF KEVIN AND DEB
Finn McCarthy
SON OF KEVIN AND DEB

Holden Newsome
SON OF LAURA MCCARTHY LAWRY AND JUSTIN NEWSOME

Francine Chester Saunders MARRIED TO **Ned Saunders**

BOOK 7

Tiffany Chester Taylor (DAUGHTER OF FRANCINE) MARRIED TO **Blaine Taylor**
Ashleigh Sturgil
DAUGHTER OF TIFFANY TAYLOR AND JIM STURGIL

Sarah Lawry (MOTHER OF OWEN) SEPARATED FROM **Mark Lawry**

Adele MARRIED TO **Russ Kincaid** (PARENTS TO SARAH LAWRY, GRANDPARENTS TO LAWRY SIBLINGS)

Owen Lawry	Julia Lawry	Katie Lawry	Josh Lawry	Cindy Lawry	John Lawry	Jeff Lawry

---

McCarthy Family Friends

BOOK 3
Luke Harris
AND
Sydney Donovan

Dan Torrington
AND
Kara Ballard

BOOK 9
David Lawrence
AND
Daisy Babson

BOOK 10
Jenny Wilks
AND
Alex Martinez

BOOK 10.5
Jared James
AND
Elisabeth "Lizzie" Sutter

CHAPTER 1

Paul Martinez loved everything about September on Gansett Island—from the cornflower-blue sky, to the cool fresh air and the quiet of the island returning to normal after another busy summer. The year-rounders got their island back in September. The tourists went home, back to school and work, after playing on Gansett all summer. During three crazy months, the island's regular population of a few hundred hardy souls swelled to thousands.

As he drove home following a long day of landscaping work, Paul appreciated that the island roads had returned to "normal," with hardly any cars, mopeds or bicycles impeding his ride. Islanders appreciated the tourists and the boost they brought to the economy. But they were also happy to see them go after Labor Day, when a collective sigh of relief greeted the cooler days and nights of September.

As the co-owner of Martinez Lawn & Garden, spring and summer were Paul's busiest time of year, followed closely by autumn, when the leaves turned brilliant colors before they dropped into yards that needed to be cleaned up before the winter set in. By the first of next month, the pumpkins would be in and ready to harvest.

A lot still had to be done before they settled in for the long, cold winter on Gansett. Other than plowing snow, their business slowed to a crawl in the winter, which was why Paul loved those months best of all. By the time the snow came, he was ready to sleep for months.

This fall promised to be extra busy with his older brother Alex's upcoming wedding to Jenny Wilks and their move into the house they'd been building on land near the house where he and Alex had grown up. Paul hadn't expected to still be living at home in his early thirties, but his mother's dementia had derailed a lot of his plans, including having a family of his own.

Alex's relationship with Jenny had given Paul hope that it might still happen for him, too, but he wasn't holding his breath waiting for Cupid to strike, even if a lot of their friends had taken the plunge in the last few months.

His future sister-in-law had gone so far as to try to fix him up with her friend Erin, the island's new lighthouse keeper. They'd hung out with Alex and Jenny a few times. He liked Erin and admired her resiliency after losing her twin brother—who had also been Jenny's fiancé—during the 9/11 attacks on New York City. But he didn't feel that spark of something extra with her, no matter how much Jenny might love to see both Martinez brothers fall for lighthouse keepers.

It wasn't going to happen between him and Erin, and she knew it as much as he did.

He'd had drinks a few times with Chelsea, the bartender at the Beachcomber. As much as he liked her and found her attractive, he didn't get the sense that she was into him that way, so he hadn't bothered to pursue it.

Every time he got his hair cut at the Curl Up & Dye salon in town, Chloe, the owner, flirted with him. Once he'd suggested they get together sometime, and she'd said she would love to, but it had never happened. Maybe he should've taken it a step further and actually asked her out, but something held him back. He suspected that flirting with guys as she cut their hair was part of her professional gig, and she probably wasn't into him at all.

Women were as vexing to him in his thirties as they'd been in middle school, when he first started to notice the way they looked at him and his brother. He'd been told on more than one occasion that they were good-looking guys. Well, he was, anyway. Alex was kind of ugly when it came right down to it.

Paul laughed at that thought. Some things never changed. He and his brother had been busting each other's balls for as long as they'd been talking. But Paul gave thanks every day to Alex for coming home to Gansett when things started to get really bad with their mom. Paul had never been so happy to see his brother, who had given up an awesome job and a satisfying life in Washington, DC, to come home to help him run the family business and manage their mother's illness.

Alex had been extremely unhappy about the changes he'd been forced to make—until he met Jenny and became the happiest bastard on the island. Not that Paul would begrudge his brother the happiness he deserved. However, he couldn't help but look on with envy from time to time, especially with the lovebirds nesting—among other things—in the room next to his until their house was finished.

Paul had never been more thankful for earplugs and headphones since Jenny moved in with them. Some things a brother just shouldn't have to hear. He'd trained himself to sleep with music blasting in his ears. The alternative was listening to the two of them go at it constantly.

He couldn't recall the last time he'd gotten laid, so that was contributing to the general malaise that gripped him lately. Living with the gleefully engaged sex fiends had only made him more aware of how long it had been since he'd had sex. How pathetic was it that he couldn't even remember the last time? Between dealing with his mom's illness, running the business and serving on the Gansett Town Council, it was all he could do to find the time to sleep and eat every day, let alone think about sex.

But it had been on his mind lately, nagging at him and reminding him that, despite his many responsibilities, he was still a healthy young man with needs. It might be time to call Chelsea or Chloe and get serious about dating again. Now that he and Alex had the help of Hope Russell, the full-time nurse they'd hired to oversee their mother's care, he was able to have a social life again.

If he'd met Hope under different circumstances, she'd be first on his list of women he'd like to date. But their dad had always hammered home the importance of not dating women who worked for them. Hope wasn't exactly in the same league as the college girls who worked in their retail store, but the last thing he or Alex needed was to give Hope a reason to leave them. So he kept their relationship friendly, not romantic. But he found himself thinking about the sexy single mom a lot more often than he should for someone who had no plans to pursue her.

As he pulled into the long driveway that led to Martinez Lawn and Garden as well as the family's home, Paul decided to make it a goal in the off-season to start dating again before he woke up one day to discover he'd missed the chance to find love and have a family. After a brief stop to make sure the retail store was locked up for the night, Paul continued on toward home, where he found Hope's seven-year-old son, Ethan, sitting on the top step waiting for him.

Paul smiled at the predictable sight of Ethan running toward him, full of excitement and energy that Paul envied. He wished he could bottle the kid's energy and keep some of it for himself. "What's the good word, my man?" Paul asked him, as he did every night.

Ethan greeted him with a fist bump that Paul returned. "The good word is school stinks, and I want summer vacation back."

"Oh, that's a tough one. Want to help me unload and we can talk about it?"

"Sure."

"Those aren't your school clothes, are they?"

"No way. I take that crap off the second I get home. Thank God it's the weekend."

Paul had to hide his grin from the boy. He had been exactly the same way when he was Ethan's age. He'd run home from school, change as fast as he could and wait for his dad to come home to pick him up so he could "help" all afternoon. Thinking about that brought a pang of sadness for the father he missed so terribly.

He and Ethan talked about everything and nothing as they unloaded the tools and equipment from Paul's truck. He was careful not to give the boy anything too heavy or sharp.

"Can we go check on the pumpkins?" Ethan asked when the truck had been unloaded and the equipment stored in the aluminum shed.

"Sure. Go tell your mom where you're going."

Ethan scampered off toward the house, running at full tilt while Paul took a seat on the tailgate of the truck to wait for him. The boy's interest in the pumpkin patch amused Paul and again reminded him of himself when he'd driven his father crazy for weeks every autumn asking when it would be time to harvest.

"I can't wait for Halloween," Ethan said a few minutes later as they crossed the yard to the fields behind the retail store. Off to the far left, Alex and Jenny's beautiful new colonial-style house was nearly ready for move-in, and not a moment too soon as far as Paul was concerned.

"What're you going to be this year?"

"I don't know. I was thinking about a Jedi warrior, but Mom said we might not be able to find a lightsaber on the island."

"I have one in the attic."

Ethan stopped short and looked up at him, agog. "*You* have a *lightsaber?*"

"Don't say that like I'm a hundred years old or something. I'll have you know that *Star Wars* belonged to my generation long before it belonged to yours."

"Huh?"

Paul laughed at the face Ethan made at him. He was a cute kid with freckles from the summer sun, dark hair that fell over his brow and big blue eyes that never missed a thing. Ethan ran ahead of him into the field where the pumpkins were growing right on schedule. With a quick glance, Paul could see they were still a dark yellow, but well on their way to the deep orange they would become in a few short weeks.

"Not quite there yet," he said. "But getting closer."

"How can you tell?"

"Size and color, my friend. They tell the story. When they're ready, they'll be bigger and orange, not yellow."

"That one there is orange." Ethan pointed to the one orange pumpkin in a sea of yellow.

"Pick it up for your mom."

"Maybe she'll let me carve it."

"Whatever you do, don't carve it by yourself. That's how kids end up at the clinic getting stitches." Paul could speak from experience about that and had the scar across his left palm to prove it. He pointed it out to Ethan.

"Wow, you got that carving a pumpkin?"

With Ethan struggling under the weight of the pumpkin he'd picked up for his mom, they started walking back toward the house. "Yep. My dad told me to wait for him, but I was in too much of a rush and sliced my hand wide open. My parents totally freaked out because there's no hospital out here."

"Was your dad mad?"

"He was after he knew I'd be okay. I got a hell of a talking-to about the dangers of knives and doing what I was told. Tough lesson learned the hard way."

"I don't have a dad anymore."

Paul tried not to show any reaction to that statement. He'd wondered about the boy's father, but neither Ethan nor Hope had volunteered any information about the guy, and Paul hadn't wanted to ask. "Neither do I."

"Yeah, but yours died. Mine's in jail."

Paul felt like he'd been sucker-punched. "Oh."

"Yeah, it sucks." Spotting his mother on the porch of the Martinez house, Ethan took off running, calling out to her about the season's first pumpkin.

Paul followed him, still reeling from what he'd just heard. He had so many questions. Why was Ethan's father in jail? What had he done? Had he hurt Hope or Ethan? God, Paul hoped it wasn't that. Why hadn't Hope disclosed the information when they hired her? Were either of them in any danger? Did he dare broach the subject with her, or did he pretend he didn't know?

Shit, what a dilemma.

Hope was still on the porch when Paul got there a few minutes behind Ethan, who'd gone inside to show the pumpkin to Paul's mother. Marion adored the boy, and they shared a special bond.

"I hope he's not driving you crazy," Hope said, as she did just about every day. She tucked a strand of her reddish-brown hair behind her ear and crossed her arms, the pose almost defensive, as if she were always waiting for disaster to strike. He'd had the thought before, but knowing what he did now, it took on new meaning.

"I enjoy hanging out with him."

"Still, feel free to tell him to leave you alone if you're busy."

"It's fine, Hope. He's a great kid."

"Yeah," she said, her smile softening her face. "He is."

"How are things here?"

"Your mom had a tough day. She's been more confused than usual."

Paul ran his fingers through his hair as he absorbed that news. "Is that even possible?"

Marion came to the door. "Is that my George home from work? George! Come see what Paul brought home. The first pumpkin of the season!"

Hope sent him a sympathetic smile. After all these weeks of working for them, she certainly knew how difficult it was when his mother regularly mistook him for his late father.

"Hi, Mom, it's me, Paul."

Like always, he had to withstand the pain of watching her face fall with disappointment when she realized it was him and not his father. That killed him a little more every day. Sometimes he was tempted to pretend to be his father just to give her a moment's reprieve, but he couldn't bring himself to do that to either of them.

"Oh, well, your father will be along soon, then. Come in and get washed up for dinner. You know how hungry Daddy is after working all day. He'll want to eat as soon as he gets home."

Paul took the stairs slowly, each step a reminder of the realities of his life.

"George? Is that you?" Marion came back to the door. "Oh, there you are! Dinner is ready! Come in and have a cold beer."

It took everything Paul had to cross the porch to the front door, to tell his mother once again that he was Paul, not George. They'd stopped telling her that George was dead, because neither he nor Alex could bear to see her relive her painful loss with every new reminder. They'd decided to let her have her illusions if they brought her comfort.

But being constantly mistaken for his late father was taking a toll on Paul—and on his brother, too.

Wearing a towel around his waist and dripping from the shower, Alex materialized out of the hallway where the bedrooms were located. "Hey, Mom," Alex said. "Come have a seat. Dinner is almost ready."

"Your dad just got home. Give him a minute to wash up."

Alex glanced at Paul. "You okay?"

"Sure," Paul said with a grim smile, "never better."

Hope followed him inside and went through the motions of getting Marion to the table and cutting her chicken into tiny bites.

Different day, same routine. Sometimes Paul wondered how much more he could take before he'd lose his own mind. But he and his brother had promised their father on his deathbed that they would take care of their mother. And that was exactly what he would do, even if their situation was slowly killing him one painful day at a time.

CHAPTER 2

After a delicious dinner of roasted chicken, potatoes and stuffing that Hope had made for them, Paul took a cold beer to the back steps that overlooked the cabin where Hope and Ethan lived. With Ethan's pumpkin successfully carved, Paul's mother in bed, Alex and Jenny gone to move a few more things into the new house, and with no meetings in town tonight, Paul found himself with a rare moment of idle time.

He liked the stargazing back here. Out front, the security lights from the store and gardens made it tough to see much of anything. But the view from the back of the house was spectacular, especially in the clear September sky.

Hope and Ethan had fallen into the habit of joining them for dinner, which made for a fun gathering at the end of every day. It was so much better to have Alex, Jenny, Hope and Ethan around to help with Marion than it had been at first, when he'd been alone with their mother's deteriorating condition.

Asking Alex to come home had been one of the most difficult phone calls Paul had ever made. But he'd needed his brother's help and support with their mother and the business he was trying to keep afloat while also trying to care for Marion.

It was better now that he had all kinds of great help, but each day was still filled with the despair that came with watching a loved one become someone you don't recognize—and who doesn't recognize you.

Now he also had a bunch of questions about what Ethan had let slip earlier. He'd hoped to get a chance to talk to Alex about it, but he hadn't had a moment alone with his brother. He'd talk to him tomorrow. Not that he thought they had anything to fear from Hope.

She was doing an amazing job with their mom, and for the first time since Marion's condition had worsened, Paul felt like they had things under control—for the most part anyway. No, he had to play this carefully. If he pried into her life and pissed her off, she might leave them, and that would be the worst thing that could happen.

Paul lived in mortal fear of driving Hope away. The thought of losing her help with their mom was unthinkable. Besides, she and Ethan had begun to seem like part of the family, and he wanted them to feel at home here.

"Beautiful night," Hope said from the porch of the cabin.

Paul hadn't realized she was there. With the lights off in the cabin, he couldn't see a thing in the darkness. "Sure is. Best time of year for stargazing."

"I love it here. It's so beautiful."

"I'm glad you like it. I was just sitting here thinking that I can't recall how we ever got by without you."

"Dementia is such a bitch."

"It certainly is. Every time she mistakes me for my dad…"

"My heart breaks for you, Paul. It's got to be so hard."

The empathy he heard in her voice wrapped around him like a warm blanket. "She and my dad were great together. Still holding hands after thirty years. Sometimes I think his death triggered her dementia. It's like she needs to forget he's gone or something."

"Grief is a complicated emotion, especially when coupled with dementia."

"Alex and I had to stop correcting her every time she asks for Dad. We can't stand breaking the news to her over and over again. It's like she loses him every time."

"You guys have done such an admirable job of dealing with it for so long."

"We've done the best we could, but we were just getting by until you came along."

"I'm glad to be able to help. And I have to thank you, as well, for the time you spend with Ethan. He's really blossomed here, and a lot of that is thanks to you."

"It's certainly no hardship to hang out with him. He reminds me a lot of me when I was his age."

When Hope's cell phone lit up next to her, he could see her sitting on the porch with half a glass of wine next to her. She picked up the phone to read the text. "Oh damn."

"What's wrong?"

"It's from Katie Lawry. Lisa has taken a turn for the worse. They don't expect her to make it through the night."

"Oh God." Lisa Chandler, a single mother, was in the final stages of lung cancer, and Hope had been helping Katie and Mallory Vaughn, both nurses, with Lisa's hospice care. "That was fast."

"I know," she said with a deep sigh. "I hate to say it's merciful."

"Her poor kids."

"Thank God for Seamus and Carolina. They've really stepped up for the boys. Dan Torrington was there the other day to set up a custody agreement for them to live with Seamus and Carolina afterward that Lisa signed."

"Such a tragedy." Paul took a drink from his beer as the silence stretched between them. "Do you want to go over there?"

"I can't with Ethan asleep."

"We could bring him over here. I'd be happy to have him if you want to go."

After another long pause, Hope said, "Are you sure? I'd like to be there for Lisa, as well as Katie and Mallory."

"Of course. It's totally fine."

"If you're sure…"

Paul got up and crossed the yard to Hope's front porch. "I'll carry him for you."

"Oh. Okay. Thanks."

"No problem." Paul followed her inside the cozy cabin.

Hope turned on a lamp in the living room and then led him to Ethan's bedroom.

He resisted the temptation to try to see into her room across the hall. By the glow of a Spider-Man night-light, Paul lifted Ethan from his bed and headed for the door.

When they reached the living room in his house, Hope produced Ethan's pillow, blanket and well-loved teddy bear. They worked together to make Ethan comfortable on the sofa.

"Are you sure about this, Paul?"

"Totally fine. Go be with your friends. I'll be here with Ethan."

"Thank you. I really appreciate it."

"I'm sorry about Lisa. She's a good person." Lisa had worked for them in the retail store for two summers years ago. He'd been profoundly saddened to hear about her illness.

"Yes, she is. You have my number if you need me."

"We'll be fine. Go do what you need to."

She nodded. "Thank you again."

"No problem."

After she left, Paul went into his room to change into pajama pants and a T-shirt. He brushed his teeth and then went to the living room to stretch out on the other sofa. If Ethan woke up, he wanted to be there so he wouldn't be afraid.

Paul turned off the light and tried to make himself comfortable on the sofa. He was on his way to sleep when Alex and Jenny came in giggling and whispering. She let out a squeak of laughter when Alex wrapped his arms around her and lifted her, carrying her the rest of the way to their room.

Long after the door closed behind them, Paul was awake, staring into the darkness, wondering how his life had been reduced to nothing more than work and endless responsibility.

The next thing he knew, he was awakened by a sound that had him sitting up and wiping the sleep from his eyes to see Hope in the pre-dawn darkness. "Hey."

"Sorry to bother you," she whispered. "I was going to try to take Ethan home."

"Are you okay?"

"I... Lisa died at four a.m."

Before he took a second to think about what he was doing, Paul stood to hold her while she cried. He guided her to the sofa where he'd been sleeping.

She cried silently, sobs shaking her shoulders.

Paul rubbed her back in small circles while trying not to notice how amazing she smelled or how perfectly she fit in his arms.

"I'm so sorry to lose it," she whispered.

"Don't be."

"It's just… What happened to her… It's my worst nightmare as a single mom." She shuddered as another sob echoed through her. "My heart breaks for those poor little boys. Their lives will never be the same."

"It's so sad. She was lucky to have had you and Katie and Mallory at the end."

"We did what we could to make her comfortable." She wiped the tears from her face. "I shouldn't be crying all over you. You're my boss."

"Come on. I thought we were friends by now."

To his dismay, she started crying again. "Hope…" He hugged her to him as she continued to sob.

"God, this is mortifying."

"No need to be mortified."

She raised her head from his chest and stared at him. In the pearly light, he watched her zero in on his lips.

His heart stopped while he waited to see what she would do. He had no idea whether he should pull her closer or push her away.

She solved the problem for him when she laid her lips on his.

For a second, Paul was too shocked to react, but then instinct kicked in and the long dry spell was forgotten. He cupped her face and tipped his head, wanting to delve deeper.

Hope moaned and then her hand was in his hair, pulling him closer.

A thousand reasons why this was a bad idea flashed through his mind with machine-gun speed, but that didn't stop him from lying back on the sofa and taking her with him. Their bodies came together in the ideal position for much more than kissing. Her tongue rubbed against his, hungry and needy.

Then she was pushing him away, struggling to break free.

Paul released her immediately while his reawakened libido tried to catch up with the change in plans.

"That… That shouldn't have happened." Her hand trembled as she covered her mouth.

"Hope—"

"No, don't say anything. Please, don't say anything." She got up and slid her arms under Ethan before Paul could offer to do it.

He got up to open the door for her.

She breezed past him without another word.

Paul stood in the door, watching until he saw lights go on in the cabin. Then he closed and locked the door, leaning against it, trying to find some composure. His lips were still tingling as he grabbed his pillow from the sofa and went into his room, where the sheets on his bed were cold and unwelcoming.

"What the hell just happened?" he whispered. Was she attracted to him, or had she been using him to ease the ache of her loss? Had that kiss been the start of something, or would it only lead to awkwardness between them? God, that would suck. He saw her every day. She worked for him, for Christ's sake, and for that reason, his father would have been appalled by his behavior.

Paul couldn't remember the last time he'd been this confused about a woman. It reminded him of high school, when everything having to do with girls had been a mystery to him. They'd all seemed to like him—and his brother—but he'd felt awkward around them until he'd grown into adulthood and finally figured out the secret to getting laid regularly.

Except for lately, that is. Lately, he'd been so overwhelmed by running his family's business and taking care of his mother that he'd forgotten everything he once knew about how to handle himself around women.

Ugh, what if she quit over this? His worries kept him awake for the remaining time he had to sleep. At six, he dragged himself out of bed and into the shower, standing under the hot water to wash away the cobwebs. He took the time to shave and was standing in the kitchen drinking coffee when Hope came in with Ethan, who was scowling and dragging his backpack behind him.

"There it is." Hope pointed to a book on the counter. She looked tired and frazzled and seemed to be going out of her way to avoid looking at Paul.

Ethan retrieved the book, stuffed it into his backpack and headed for the front door with his mother following behind him. She walked him out to the bus stop every morning, even though her son had told her she didn't have to. He was almost eight after all.

Paul remembered having the same conversation with his parents around that age with the same results. One of their parents had put him and Alex on the bus until the middle school kids started making fun of them and they'd begged them to stay home. He hadn't thought about that in years, and the memory made him smile.

Since Alex and Jenny would be getting up any minute, Paul decided to meet Hope on the way back from the bus stop. There was no way he was letting that middle-of-the-night kiss fester all day. He had to make sure they were okay, that she wasn't planning to quit or anything else equally unimaginable.

This was exactly why his father had told them to keep their hands off the employees. Alex had once asked their dad what he would've done if he'd met their mother when she came to work at the store for a summer. George had famously said, "I would've waited until the day the summer ended and then chased after her until she agreed to be my girl."

That's what he should do, too. He hated to think of the day when Hope would no longer be in their employ, because that would mean his mother had passed away or required more care than they could provide at home. They weren't just talking about a summer in this case. His mother could live for years yet, and Paul wanted that. So if he was interested in Hope, was he supposed to wait until his mother died or moved out and Hope no longer worked for them?

He couldn't help but think that even his late father would find that a foolish waste of valuable time, especially when Paul wasn't getting any younger and felt like his life was slipping away while he was held captive to his many responsibilities.

On her way down the long lane from the main road, Hope stopped when she saw him coming.

Paul held up his hands. "I come in peace."

That drew a small smile from her. She folded her arms into that protective pose she preferred and dropped her gaze. "I'm so sorry, Paul. I don't know what came over me."

"You aren't going to quit, are you?"

Gasping, she looked up at him. "Do you *want* me to?"

"Hell no, I don't want you to quit. We'd be lost without you."

"It was very unprofessional of me to kiss my boss like that."

"Your boss kinda liked it."

"Oh. Um…" She seemed to force herself to look at him. "You did?"

Paul nodded.

"Still, it was extremely unprofessional."

"No, it wasn't. You were upset, and it just happened. We're in an intense situation here dealing with my mom's illness and the isolation of the island and everything that goes with it. I'd like to think this isn't your typical job."

"It's not. It's the best job I've ever had, and I'd hate to do anything to mess it up."

"Then let's not allow it to mess things up for either of us."

"Thank you for being so nice about it."

He smiled, hoping to reassure her. "It was no hardship to kiss you, Hope."

"It's been a really long time since I've kissed anyone. I probably suck at it."

"Ahhh, no, you definitely don't suck at it." Something compelled him to take a step closer to her, closing the small distance that remained. "Hasn't anyone ever told you that kissing is just like riding a bike? You never forget the fundamentals, no matter how much time passes?"

"I, um… Your mom. I should get her up and ready for her appointment this morning."

Startled to realize he'd been on the verge of kissing her again, Paul took a step back. "Leave at eight forty-five?"

Hope nodded.

"I'll be ready."

She started toward the house, and Paul fell into step with her. The early morning sunshine beat down upon them as another crystal-clear September day began.

"Is this going to make everything weird between us now?" he asked.

"No," she said quickly—almost too quickly. "At least I hope not."

"I won't let it if you won't."

"Deal."

*

Oh my God, oh my God, oh my God... Those three little words had been on the tip of Hope's tongue since the early morning hours when she'd *lost her mind* and *kissed her boss*! After crying all over him. Oh. My. God. The crying was understandable in light of Lisa's sad death, but the kissing? In no way was that understandable or acceptable or justifiable or any other *–able* word that she could think of.

After everything she'd been through to start a new life for herself and Ethan. To risk it all so foolishly... It made her feel queasy as she went through the morning routine of getting Marion up and showered and dressed, all while answering a million questions about why she was there and who did she think she was helping her into the shower.

Different day, same questions. Such was the sad routine of working with dementia patients. In her old life, she'd worked at a memory care facility that specialized in dementia in all its many forms. She was used to the questions, the outrage, the indignity and the despair of the relentless disease that stole people from themselves and their families.

In a few months of working with Marion, Hope had become fond of her and her sons, both of whom were endearingly devoted to their mother. As the mother of a son, she could only hope that Ethan would care as much about her if such a fate should befall her someday.

God forbid.

She helped Marion with her breakfast, served her coffee exactly the way she liked it and navigated the morning battle of getting her meds into her, while Marion accused Hope of trying to poison her. She was used to it, as they had the same conversation three times a day.

"Mom, be nice to Hope," Paul said when he emerged from the shower wearing a button-down shirt and jeans and looking far too handsome for her own good. "She's trying to help."

"I don't need help from a stranger, George. I've told you that."

Every time Marion mistook one of her sons for her late husband, Hope watched the light in their eyes go dim. It chipped away at both of them.

Hope poured a cup of coffee for Paul and pushed it across the counter to him.

His grateful smile for the small gesture tugged at her. He had so much on his shoulders, so many people counting on him, and at times Hope wondered who *he* counted on. Who did he turn to when it all became too much?

Not that she was paid to psychoanalyze her boss or his family. *It's not your problem, Hope. You aren't being paid to worry about him. He's a grown man who can take care of himself. Except—*

"Are you ladies ready to go?" Paul asked.

With her thoughts interrupted by reality, Hope glanced at Marion, who muttered to herself as she perused the *Gansett Gazette*, her cereal gone soggy from inattention.

"Ready when you are," Hope said.

"Hey, Mom," Paul said. "We need to go see Doctor David this morning, okay?"

"Whatever for?"

"He wanted you to come in for your physical. I told him I'd drive you."

"Why didn't he call me? It's none of your concern."

"I know, but I promised him I'd bring you, so help me out, okay?"

Poor Paul had to repeat the entire conversation six times before he had Marion strapped into the front seat of his truck.

Hope climbed into the back, carrying the bag she brought with her everywhere she went with Marion. It contained a change of clothes, an adult diaper, wipes, snacks and a bottle of water. She tried to be ready for any possible catastrophe.

Since Paul was driving and the sun was shining, Hope took advantage of the rare opportunity to gaze out at the bright blue sky, to let the cool September air wash over her face.

The battle began anew when they reached the clinic where Paul had to bribe and cajole his mother inside against her will. By the time they were seated in one of the exam rooms, Paul looked as exhausted as he did after a hard day of work.

"Where am I?" Marion asked in a small voice. Her gaze skipped right over Hope to focus on Paul. "George? Why are we here?"

"Doctor David wanted you to come by, remember?"

"Why? Am I sick?"

"No, Mom, you're fine. Just a checkup."

The conversation continued in circles until David knocked and entered the room. "Good morning. Hi there, Marion."

She shrank from a man she saw almost every day, except for the last week when he'd been off island on vacation.

David was wonderful with her, answering Marion's indignant questions over and over while somehow managing to examine her. His brows knitted as he assessed her.

Hope wondered if he saw what she did—Marion was declining rapidly. Despite the years of experience she had with dementia patients, it was no less heartbreaking to witness the relentless march of the awful disease.

"Anything new or different since I last saw you all?" he asked, encompassing both Paul and Hope in his kind gaze.

"There's more of a shuffle to her walk in the last week or two," Paul said.

"What time is Daddy coming to get me?" Marion asked Paul.

"Not until he's done working," Paul replied.

David asked if he could speak to Paul and Hope in private. His colleague, Victoria Stevens, came into the exam room to stay with Marion. As Hope left the room, she heard Marion asking Victoria to call her husband to come pick her up.

They followed David into his office. David, who'd grown up with Paul and Alex, shut the door and went around to sit behind his desk. He seemed to choose his words carefully. "I thought about your mother a lot when I was on vacation," he said to Paul. "We've talked before about the seven stages of dementia. I believe your mother is well into the sixth stage. I'm actually surprised by the amount of decline in her physical condition since the last time I saw her."

"I've noticed the contractures in her wrists and fingers," Hope said. "I was going to mention it to you today."

"What does that mean?" Paul asked. "Contractures?"

"It's when rigidity sets in and causes the hands to curl in on themselves." David demonstrated by bending his fingers. "I fear that your mother's condition has reached the point where I don't feel comfortable being the only doctor involved. I'd like to have her evaluated by someone who specializes in dementia and memory disorders, just to make sure we're doing everything we can to keep her comfortable and safe."

Paul glanced at Hope. "What do you think?"

"I agree with David. It certainly won't make anything worse."

"It would take a lot out of her to travel," Paul said.

"I'd be there to make sure she was comfortable," Hope said. She could ask Jenny to keep Ethan for a couple of days while they were away. Ethan was familiar enough with her and Alex by now that he'd be okay staying with them.

"That's a lot to ask. You have Ethan…"

Paul looked so sad that Hope's heart went out to him. If she could somehow make this easier on him, she'd do it in a minute. "He'd be fine with Jenny and Alex for a couple of days, if they'd be willing."

"They would," Paul said.

She could almost see him trying to figure out how he could be off the island and away from the business for even a few days.

"How soon are we talking?"

"I think it should be done as soon as possible," David said.

"Okay," Paul said, resigned. "You can set it up?"

"I'll take care of everything."

"We would've been so lost without your help, David."

"I only wish I could do more to slow the progression."

"Nothing short of a miracle could do that," Paul said.

"One thing I'm sure of," David said, "is the care you and Alex have given her and keeping her at home all this time has given her a much better quality of life than she would've had otherwise. You should be very proud of yourselves."

Paul nodded in acknowledgment of the compliment, but he didn't look proud. He looked defeated.

CHAPTER 3

By the time he got his mother and Hope home and settled, Paul was ready to give up on the day. But that wasn't an option when there was work to be done. There was always work to be done. He changed into work clothes and then sat on his bed to put on socks. A wave of despair overtook him, threatening to suck him under.

"We've tried so hard, Pop," he whispered. "We tried to do what you would've done and kept Mom home with us. But it's so hard."

Before he got sick with cancer, George Martinez had been a strong, capable man who never let anything get him down. He worked hard, loved hard, played hard and had very high expectations for both of his sons. Disappointing their father had never been high on their to-do list.

His father's voice was always in Paul's head, guiding every decision he made in business and in life. George Martinez was the yardstick by which Paul measured himself as a man, and today he found himself sorely lacking. They were going to the mainland to have his mother evaluated by a dementia expert who would—again—recommend she be placed in an in-patient residential home for her own good—and theirs.

Except how could it be "good" for any of them to have her living a ferry or plane ride away from the two people who loved her most? They were tied to the island thanks to the business their father had founded more than forty years ago. It wasn't like they could suddenly abandon what they'd all worked so hard to build. When they hired Hope, they'd bought themselves some time. But what if that time was up now? What would that mean for her and Ethan when they'd recently uprooted their lives to move to Gansett?

Paul's stomach was tied up in knots, and he still had to talk to Alex about the appointment with David, not to mention what he'd learned about Ethan's father. Steeling himself to face today and whatever lay ahead with his mother, Paul stood and tried to shake off the gloomy mood. He had to believe his father would be proud of the herculean effort he and Alex had put forth to keep their mother at home for as long as they had. He had to believe that because the alternative didn't bear entertaining.

He left his room to encounter angry shouts coming from the living room, where he'd left his mother and Hope.

"I don't know who you think you are, young lady," Marion said, "but I have no time to take naps during the day. I have a husband and two sons to care for. Who will do the washing if I'm napping? Who will cook their dinner?"

"You'll have plenty of time to do all that when you get up," Hope said calmly.

No matter how much crap Marion shoveled on Hope, she never lost her temper, never lost her composure or her patience. It was admirable, because at times, Paul wanted to scream his head off when his mother went off on him. Thank God for Hope. He and Alex had said that so many times since she arrived over the summer and literally saved their lives.

"Can I help?" he asked.

"Nope," she said. "Go on ahead to work. We'll be fine."

"There's my George now! Tell this woman, whoever she is, that I have things to do, will you please?"

It was a source of never-ending black humor to him and Alex that their mother couldn't remember what happened a minute ago, except in the middle of an argument in which her memory became crystal clear. They had morbidly joked that they should fight with her constantly.

"Marion, Hope is just trying to help," Paul said, channeling his father, who'd adored his wife to the point of distraction. "Will you please let her help?"

He watched as some of the starch went out of Marion's rigid shoulders. "If that's what you'd like me to do, George."

"It is. It's what I'd like you to do."

"All right, then." She glanced at Hope tentatively. "What did you want me to do again?"

Hope nodded for the door, encouraging Paul to get while the getting was good. He and Alex had made her promise from the outset to call them if anything ever happened that she couldn't handle—even if they were working. They'd promised to come running. She'd yet to call.

As he walked out of the house and crossed the yard to the building where they kept their equipment, Paul texted his brother. *Where are you?*

Alex replied immediately. *Chesterfield.*

Stay put. I'm going to stop by.

I'm here for the day.

Paul loaded the truck with the tools he'd need for the abbreviated workday mapped out for him by Jenny, who now managed their workload as well as the store, and headed to the Chesterfield property, which was now owned by Jared and Lizzie James. They'd turned Mrs. Chesterfield's estate into a first-class wedding venue, which would host Alex and Jenny's wedding next month.

Alex had made the secret garden inside the elaborate hedges his own pet project, which Paul supported and encouraged. His brother had given up a fantastic job working at the US Botanic Garden in Washington, DC, to come home to help Paul when their mother's condition took a turn for the worse.

If cultivating the gardens at the Chesterfield gave Alex an outlet for his considerable horticultural talents, Paul refused to begrudge him that. He'd never begrudge either of them anything that brought them even the slightest bit of joy in the midst of the never-ending sorrow of their mother's illness.

Jenny brought Alex joy, too. His brother had been a different person since she came into his life, and no one was happier for both of them than Paul.

He parked in the circular driveway in front of the huge stone house and headed directly for the garden. Inside the tall hedges, Paul found his brother clipping and pruning and tending to the blooms, whistling while he worked. Paul supposed if he got laid three times a day without fail, he'd whistle while he worked, too.

The thought made him feel petty, so he squelched it as fast as he had it.

"Hey."

"Hey, what's up? How was the appointment with David?"

"That's what I wanted to talk to you about."

"Uh-oh. That doesn't sound good."

"It's not bad, but there was a development." He explained David's concerns and the plan to take Marion to the mainland to be evaluated by a dementia specialist.

Alex sighed, wiped the sweat from his brow and took a long gulp of the ice-cold water he guzzled all day long. "We've known we were living on borrowed time for a while now."

"I guess. What're we going to do if they tell us—again—that she needs in-patient care?"

"We'll have to cross that bridge when we get to it. No sense speculating about what-ifs."

After two years of living with his mother's rapidly declining health, Paul had become an expert in speculating about what-ifs and worst-case scenarios. "I'll go with her. Hope will come, too, if you and Jenny wouldn't mind having Ethan for a couple of days. He can stay in my room."

"Of course we will. He's no trouble. Are you sure you're up to going? I could do it."

"You've got a lot going on with the wedding and the house. You need to be here right now."

"I can take a couple of days away."

"It's fine. I'll do it."

"What else is bugging you?"

"Other than our mother's increasingly depressing illness?"

"Yeah, other than that."

"I keep thinking about Dad. You ever think about him?"

"Every day. Hard not to when Mom mistakes us for him all the time."

"I just hope he knows we've done everything we could."

"He knows, bro. People tell us all the time how proud he'd be of the way we've taken care of Mom and kept the business afloat, too. What else could we do that we haven't done?"

"I don't know." Paul kicked at the dirt, frustration beating through him like an extra heartbeat. "I just feel like if he was here, it wouldn't feel so chaotic and out of control. He'd know what to do."

"No, he wouldn't. He'd be so heartbroken to see her this way. He wouldn't have the first clue how to cope with it. Maybe this is why he died first. You ever think of that?"

It had never crossed Paul's mind that his supremely competent father would've been unable to cope. "No."

"We've elevated him to god status in our minds," Alex said. "But in fact, he was just a man who loved his wife, and this would've killed him. It would kill me to see Jenny this way someday. I hope to God that never happens, because it would wreck me."

Alex had certainly given him something to think about other than the fact that his father would be disappointed in them.

"You know what you need?" Alex asked.

"I can hardly wait to hear this."

"A few days away from it all. Take Mom to the mainland and then go somewhere while she's in the hospital. Do something fun. Hell, take Hope with you. She could use a break, too."

Paul was immediately hit with the unreasonable fear that Alex knew he'd kissed Hope. But how could he possibly know that? He'd been asleep when it happened. And it wasn't like it was going to happen again, so what did it matter?

Except... the idea of a few days away from it all with Hope as his companion had his mind racing with all sort of inappropriate images. That, right there, was dangerous thinking, so he shook it off.

"I gotta get to it. See you at home later."

"Hey, Paul?"

"Yeah?"

"Don't be too hard on yourself. We're both doing the best we can in an awful situation. No one is judging us, least of all Dad. If anything, he's watching over us and making sure we don't lose our own minds."

"Probably." It was a far better scenario than some he'd entertained recently.

"Let me ask you something else…" He'd debated whether he should say anything about what Ethan had told him. On the one hand, he felt disloyal to Hope for telling anyone, but he was more loyal to his brother and mother.

"Sure."

"Yesterday, Ethan told me his dad is in jail."

"What? *Seriously?* What for?"

"He didn't say, and I didn't ask. I didn't want to make a big thing of it with him, but it's got me wondering."

"There was nothing about a spouse in jail on the background check we had done."

"Which leads me to more wondering."

"Wow." Alex leaned against the handle of the rake he'd been using, seeming to need the support. "So what does this mean?"

"It means that we have a fantastic nurse helping us with our mom who has a past that she doesn't want anyone to know about."

"Maybe he went to jail after they split up."

"Maybe."

"Should we ask her about it?" Alex asked.

"I really don't want to do that."

"Neither do I. Are we taking chances with Mom's safety by not looking into this further?"

"I don't think so. I trust Hope, and the guy's in jail so it's not like he's about to come after her or anything."

"We need to keep a close eye on things."

"Agree."

"Let me know what you hear from David."

"I will."

"Could I ask *you* something?" Alex asked, seeming weary all of a sudden.

"Of course," Paul said, becoming resigned to getting nothing done that day.

"Have you noticed anything…different…about Jenny lately?"

"Different how?"

"She's quiet and withdrawn, which isn't like her."

"I know it's hard to sneak in conversation when you're having constant sex, but have you asked her?"

Alex grunted out a laugh. "That's not *all* we do, and yes, I've asked her. Several times."

"And?"

"She says everything's fine, and that's all she says. I don't know what to do. I'm starting to wonder if she's having second thoughts about the wedding and everything."

Incredulous, Paul shook his head. "No... No way. For some strange reason, she's crazy about you. That much I know for sure."

"I thought I knew that for sure, too. But now... I don't know anymore."

"For what it's worth, I live with you two, and I haven't sensed any sign of discontent in her. I'm not paying the same level of attention that you are, so I could've missed it, but all I see is happy and crazy in love. Is it possible you're seeing trouble where there isn't any?"

"I've asked myself that same question, but I keep coming back to how glum she is every time we have to deal with the wedding."

"Try to find a way to get her to tell you why. It would suck to get to the big day thinking she has doubts about something."

"Yeah, I know. She's due here soon. We're meeting with Lizzie to go over final details."

"Sounds like a good opportunity to figure things out."

"Hope so."

"Try not to worry too much. Could just be wedding jitters."

Alex nodded. "I'll see you at home."

"See you then." Worried now about Alex, too, Paul returned to his truck and headed to the other side of the island to do a fall cleanup for a regular client. The mindless work gave him far too much time to think. He could only hope the situation with Jenny didn't turn into a big disappointment for his brother. They had enough on their plates without more turmoil.

Though he'd never wish his mother's illness on anyone, least of all himself, sometimes he wondered what it would be like to be free from the routine worries of everyday life. He'd like to have a switch he could flip when he didn't want to think about dementia or taxes or all the paperwork he'd let pile up in the office or the new equipment he needed to purchase before the spring.

He'd like to be able to flip the switch and not think about how long it had been since he'd had sex or how much he'd liked kissing the lovely nurse who worked for them. He'd like to stop thinking about that, and he really wished he didn't want to know so badly why Ethan's father was in jail.

*

After Paul left, Alex continued to work in the garden while trying not to slip into total panic mode over what was going on with Jenny. Other than the short time they spent apart at the start of their relationship, things between them had been remarkably easy. The connection they'd shared from the first minute they met had carried them through some rough times.

He was well aware that theirs was her first significant relationship since she lost her fiancé in the 9/11 attacks on New York City. He'd tried to be respectful of her memories and to give her space to grieve on Toby's birthday, their anniversary and the date of his death. At the same time, she'd stood by his side as his mother's condition worsened, her support never wavering no matter how awful it got.

And at the end of every long, trying day, he had her in his bed, and nothing in his life could compare to the sublime pleasure he found in her arms. He couldn't get enough of her, and until recently, he'd thought the feeling was entirely mutual. Now he wasn't so sure—and that scared him more than anything ever had.

The crunch of tires on the driveway drew him out of the secret garden in the hedges that had been Mrs. Chesterfield's pride and joy and was now his special project. Jenny brought her car to a stop in the circular driveway.

Alex put down his rake, wiped his hands on his pants and went to meet her. She wore jeans that did great things for her ass and a denim shirt with the Martinez Lawn & Garden logo embroidered over the breast pocket. She'd turned their retail store into a profitable business and simplified his life and Paul's with her organizational skills and management abilities.

He'd be lost without her in every corner of his life, which was why he felt such an urgent need to know what was troubling her. More than anything, it frightened him that she was clearly keeping something from him, which was also unlike her. When he reached her car, he opened the door to help her out.

"Hi there," he said.

"Hey. How's your day going?"

"It just got a whole lot better."

She smiled at him, but her eyes were sad.

His heart ached at the thought of her being sad about something and not being able or willing to talk to him about it for whatever reason. "Ready for this?"

"Ready as I'll ever be."

"Everything all right, hon?"

"Sure." She hooked her hand into the crook of his elbow and let him lead her inside, where Lizzie James waited for them in the foyer. She looked glamorous in a navy suit and three-inch heels.

Lizzie greeted them both with hugs and kisses.

"Don't get too close," Alex said. "I'm dirty."

"You're fine," she said. "I'm so glad you're here. I have so many new things to show you. Come in. Come in. Champagne?"

"Not for me," Alex said. He'd be asleep by two if he drank at noon.

"I'll have some," Jenny said.

They followed Lizzie into the room she used as an office, where a conference table was laden with flowers, mini cakes, place settings and other things he couldn't easily identify. *Chick stuff,* he thought, keeping the sexist commentary to himself.

Jenny took a close look at all of it, and he was relieved to see her taking an interest in the wedding they'd been anticipating for more than a year now. Hell, Lizzie's husband, Jared, had bought this place and turned it into a wedding venue primarily because he and Jenny couldn't find a place on the island to hold their wedding. Jared had taken their distress and turned it into yet another gold mine.

Lizzie led them through every detail, from the ceremony that would be held on the back veranda overlooking the water to the pictures that would be taken in various locations around the estate, including their secret garden, to the reception that would be held in the downstairs rooms and on the back porch. It was a beautiful spot, and as Lizzie ran through the particulars, Alex could almost see it in his mind as it would unfold in three short weeks.

That didn't give him much time to figure out what was troubling his bride-to-be, a thought that filled him with an urgent need for answers. Once they'd dealt with all of Lizzie's questions and taken a taste of the cake they'd chosen to make sure they still loved it, Lizzie declared them finished.

"We're in great shape with plenty of time for last-minute tweaks if you think of anything you'd like to change," Lizzie said as she walked them out.

"Thanks for everything," Alex said.

"Yes," Jenny added, "thanks, Lizzie. You've made this so much easier than it would've been otherwise."

"Happy to help and can't wait for your big day. Jared and I are looking forward to it."

"We're still getting together this weekend, right?" Jenny asked her.

"Wouldn't miss it. We'll see you then."

CHAPTER 4

Jenny and Alex walked outside, and the bright sunshine had Alex reaching for the shades he'd pushed to the top of his head while they were inside. "Let's go home for lunch."

She looked up at him. "How come?"

"Because I want some time alone with my fiancée."

"We're both working today."

"So? Are we too busy for lunch?"

"Your mom and Hope are there and—"

"I want to go to *our* home."

"Oh. Okay."

"Go on ahead. I'll grab some food and meet you there." He bent to kiss her and once again noted the slight hesitation before she returned his kiss. By the time this afternoon was over, he was going to get to the bottom of what was going on with her. If she told him she didn't want to get married anymore—

No, he thought, as he got into his truck and followed her out of the Chesterfield driveway. She couldn't have changed her mind. If she told him she didn't want to get married, he wasn't sure how he would cope. After the incredible year they'd spent together, he'd never be able to face a future without her. Alex was fully prepared to fight for her, no matter what it took.

He stopped at the grocery store and picked up sandwiches as well as a bottle of the iced tea she loved and headed for home. As he passed the retail store, he slowed to take a look at the activity, more out of habit than actual interest. The only thing he was interested in at the moment was Jenny.

Behind the retail store, he hung a left onto a new dirt lane that had been created by the construction vehicles that had traversed the property while their house was being built. It was down to finish work now, and he was doing most of that himself. They were on schedule to move in before the wedding, and until recently, he'd been under the impression that she was looking forward to the next month as much as he was. Now he wasn't so sure.

Jenny was sitting on the front stairs waiting for him when he pulled up and shut off the truck. The two-story shingled colonial had four bedrooms, plenty of space for the family they hoped to have. He grabbed the bag from the store and got out to walk over to her. "Inside or out here?"

"It's so pretty outside today."

"Outside it is."

"Is it me or is the air different this month?"

"It's not you. Happens every September. The humidity disappears, the days are clear, and the nights are chilly. I love it."

"I do, too." She accepted the turkey wrap he'd gotten for her and smiled at him when he produced the iced tea. "Thank you."

"You're welcome."

They ate in silence, which had Alex's roast beef sandwich landing like a brick in his stomach. His Jenny wasn't quiet or withdrawn, especially not with him. He couldn't take it anymore. He had to know what was bothering her. "We need to talk, babe."

She glanced at him, the trepidation in her expression tugging at his heart. "What's wrong?"

"That's what I'd like to know."

"I'm not sure what you mean."

He had to force himself to say the words, to ask the question that had to be asked, even if the answer had the power to devastate him. "Do you still want to get married?"

She gasped. "Why would you ask me that? Do *you* not want to?"

"Jenny, God, all I want is to be married to you, but lately, you seem so…so sad and like you're forcing yourself through the motions with the wedding."

To his dismay, she began to cry.

Alex put his arm around her and gathered her in close to him, fortified by her reaction to his initial question. "Baby, whatever is wrong, we can fix it, but I can't help if I don't know what's bothering you. Is it me? Did I do something?"

She shook her head vigorously but was crying too hard to speak.

"Jenny, sweetheart, I love you so much. There's nothing I wouldn't do to make you happy. If you'd rather wait a while longer before we get married—"

"No, that's n-not what I want."

"Then what is it? Please tell me so I can help."

She buried her face in her hands as he continued to caress her back.

"Talk to me. Whatever it is, I want to know."

Lifting her head and looking at him, she said, "I'm so sorry you thought I didn't want to marry you. That's not it. I swear. I love you, and I can't wait to marry you."

Relieved to hear her say that so forcefully, he said, "Then why do you seem so unhappy? Is it the wedding itself?"

Shaking her head, she sighed. "I know what you're going to say. It seems ridiculous to me, but I can't seem to help it."

"What can't you help?"

She wiped the tears from her face and looked at him. "I've been right here before, right where we are now. Less than a month until my wedding…"

And then he knew exactly what was bothering her and felt terrible that he hadn't realized it sooner. "Nothing's going to happen, sweetheart." He took hold of her hand. "I promise you. Nothing will happen. Not this time."

"You don't know that. Every time you leave me, I'm afraid, and I hate myself for feeling that way."

"Then I won't leave you again until after we say 'I do.'"

Smiling even as tears rolled down her cheeks, she shook her head. "That's very sweet of you, but we both have work to do, and we can't spend every minute together for the next three weeks."

"Yes, we can. If it means you'll relax and stop worrying that something bad is going to happen, we can absolutely do that."

"It's not necessary. You're busy. I'm busy. I'm just being foolish."

"No, you're not. I can't bear the thought of you being afraid every minute that we're apart for weeks. But you know what was even worse than that?"

"What?"

"Thinking you'd changed your mind about us. About me."

"Not for one second. I'm so sorry I made you worry about that." She leaned her head on his shoulder. "I'm also thinking a lot about seeing Toby's parents at the wedding and how that'll feel for me—and for them. It's been a while since I've seen them."

"You know they're happy for you. They said so when you called to tell them we were engaged."

"Still… For them to see me marry someone else…" She raised her head to meet his gaze. "I want that day to be about you and me and no one else, but it's not just about us."

"It's never been just about us. Toby is part of us. Remember what I said when I proposed about how I wanted to honor him and his memory and what he meant to you?"

"I could never forget that."

"We need to find a way to do that on our wedding day."

"We don't have to—"

"I know we don't have to, but I want to. We should."

She blinked rapidly, trying to contain more tears. "What do you have in mind?"

"You know how we're doing the unity candle thing during the ceremony?" She nodded.

"How about we light a third candle in his memory? No one needs to know why we're doing that, but we'll know. What do you think?"

"That would be very special, and you're very sweet for thinking of it."

"I understand and respect what he meant to you, Jenny, and I know that the only reason I get to have forever with you is because he didn't. I'll never forget that."

"I hate that you thought, for even one second, that I didn't want to marry you."

"I didn't know what to think when you got really quiet and withdrawn."

"I'm sorry. I should've talked to you about it, but it seemed so silly."

"It's not silly, and I get it. But this time… This time you're going to have that magical day and every day after, because I'm not going anywhere."

She smiled at him, but the sadness lingered in her big brown eyes. What they both knew but didn't say was that Toby hadn't planned to be anywhere but with her either. This time she was going to get her happily ever after, no matter what.

He stood and gave her hand a gentle tug. "Come inside with me."

"We have to get back to work."

"I own the company, and as your boss, I'm telling you to come inside with me."

"Paul's my boss," she said with a playfully defiant look in her eyes that he much preferred to the tears.

"Get your sexy ass in the house before I spank it."

"Do you want me to start throwing tomatoes at you again?"

"You can throw anything you want at me."

They were halfway up the stairs when Jenny turned to him, meeting him at eye level from the stair above his. "Thanks for making me talk about it."

"I always want to know what you're thinking. If you're unhappy, so am I."

She put her arms on his shoulders, encircling his neck. "I'm not unhappy. I'm happier than I've been in a very long time, all because of you."

Reaching around her, he cupped her bottom and lifted her off her feet as he continued up the stairs, carrying her into the master bedroom where he'd surprised her with an air mattress a couple of weeks ago to hold them over until their new furniture arrived.

"We can't be doing this in the middle of a workday. It sets a terrible example for the employees."

"I love when you're stern with me. It's so hot."

Jenny rolled her eyes the way she always did when he said something outrageous, which he did frequently because he loved pushing her buttons. "Everything makes you hot."

"*You* make me hot," he said, molding his lips to hers as he lowered them to the mattress without missing a beat in the kiss. "Tomatoes make me hot."

Jenny started laughing and couldn't seem to stop. "Am I ever going to hear the end of the tomatoes?"

"Never." Hearing her laugh hard made him realize how long it had been since she'd done that. Her belly laugh was another thing that made him hot. He helped her out of her clothes and then pulled off his own, ignoring the fact that he probably needed a shower after the morning spent working. But that would take time he didn't want to waste with her naked and eager beneath him.

He kissed her all over, starting at her neck and working his way down to her breasts, her belly and between her legs. She came twice, one right after the other, and was still in the throes of the second one when he drove into her, triggering another wave. There was nothing in this entire world that felt better than being with her this way, and he couldn't wait to be married to her.

And as he made love to her, he promised himself to spend as much time with her as he possibly could over the next few weeks, to reassure her that nothing was going to go wrong this time.

*

The house was full of people who'd come to pay their respects to Lisa, to deliver food, to check on the boys, to offer to help in any way they could. Seamus appreciated the outpouring. Hell, he'd expected it of the Gansett Island community. But his entire focus was on the two little boys who were now his responsibility. His and Caro's.

Lisa had signed over custody to them days before she died, but the boys had felt like theirs for much longer than that. He and Caro had been caring for them, as well as the mixed-breed puppy they'd named Burpy, for weeks now as their mum slowly faded away from the ravages of lung cancer.

He held the younger boy, Jackson, who was five, on his lap. The poor kid had been inconsolable all day, even though they'd done what they could to prepare him and his brother Kyle, age six, for the inevitable. But what did little guys their age know about death and dying? He'd been much older than they were now when he lost first one brother and then the other, and he hadn't been able to make sense of it then. How were they to make sense of losing their young mum so tragically?

Having to tell them that Lisa had died overnight was one of the hardest things he'd ever had to do. Though they'd known it was coming, the reality had been heartbreaking for them.

The boys lit up at the sight of Shane and Mac McCarthy, who'd been building them a house when their mother got sick. Now the house, like their mother, was lost to them, but Seamus was determined to fill the void in every possible way that he could.

Jackson showed the first sign of interest in something other than Seamus when Shane held out his arms to him and his brother. Both boys went to him and then Mac, allowing the two men to provide what comfort they could.

Mac had tears in his eyes when he released the boys.

Caro came into the room, and her tired eyes met his.

Seamus smiled at her and held out his hand.

She took his hand, gave it a squeeze and sat next to him. "Hey, guys," she said to the boys. "I made some of the lasagna you love, and Grace brought brownies. Do you think you might feel like eating something?"

As he always did, Jackson looked to Kyle to decide for both of them.

"Yeah, sure, thanks," Kyle said.

Caro gave Seamus's hand another squeeze before she got up to lead the boys into the kitchen with Burpy hot on their heels.

Jackson looked back over his shoulder.

"I'll be right here, buddy," Seamus said, hoping to reassure the boy. They were so darned cute with their white-blond hair and big brown eyes that were sadder today than any child's eyes should ever be.

"How do they seem to be doing?" Shane asked.

"It's minute by minute," Seamus said, relaxing into the sofa while he could.

"What can we do for them?" Mac asked. "I feel so helpless."

"We need to add on to this place, and we need to do it fast. They're all jammed into our tiny guest room. They need some space—a bedroom, bathroom, playroom."

"We're on it," Mac said, glancing at his cousin, who nodded in agreement. "Our cousins Finn and Riley are sticking around for the off-season, too. We'll make it our top priority."

"I can't thank you enough, and I know Lisa would, too. She thought the world of you both. In fact, she asked that you be pallbearers at her service, if you're willing."

"We'd be honored," Shane said gruffly. "And we'll do whatever we can to support those boys. Not just now, but always."

Mac nodded in agreement.

"Appreciate that. Caro and I will take all the help we can get. To say we're in well over our heads here is putting it mildly, but we wouldn't want them anywhere else if they can't be with their mom. We're crazy about them."

"And vice versa," Mac said. "They're lucky to have you both, and they know it."

Grace Ryan came into the room, looking for him.

Seamus got up to hug his friend.

"I'm so sorry about Lisa," she said. "How're you doing?"

"Hanging in there and trying to help the boys, but it's a tough thing, sweet Grace."

"It sure is. How can I help?"

"I heard you brought brownies. That helps."

She smiled and kissed his cheek. "That's the easy stuff. I'm here to help with the hard stuff, too."

"We could use some help picking songs and readings for the service. Lisa never got around to doing that."

"I'll take care of it. I'll get Maddie, Katie, Hope and Mallory to help me. We'll make it lovely for her."

"I have no doubt it'll be lovely in your hands."

"Stephanie wants to have everyone to the Bistro after," Mac said. "She asked me to let you know to count on that."

Seamus had held it together for the boys' sake all morning, but the generosity and support from their friends had him wrestling with his emotions. It had been a long time—he'd left his home in Ireland more than twenty years ago—since he'd felt so at home anywhere else. "Thank you. Thank you all so much."

*

Mac and Maddie spent a couple of hours with Seamus, Carolina and the boys. Mac and Shane even got the boys to go outside to toss a football around for a while, their puppy darting between their feet, making both boys laugh at his antics. But laughter had turned to tears when Kyle fell, skinned his knee and wailed for his mother.

His heartbroken sobs would remain with Mac long after today.

Maddie reached across the center console for his hand, and Mac took comfort in the gesture.

"Sort of puts some things into perspective, doesn't it?" she asked after a long period of quiet.

"Yeah. Not that our grief isn't real and valid." It had only been a few weeks since they'd lost their unborn child, and they were both still coming to terms with the loss.

"At least we're adults and know how to deal with it," she said. "For the most part. Those poor babies will never understand this."

"Seamus and Carolina will help them through it."

"They won't remember much about her." Maddie wiped away a tear. "They're too young. It kills me to know that if something happened to me today, Thomas and Hailey wouldn't remember me."

"Don't even say that." The very thought of something happening to her was enough to send Mac into a full-on panic. "Please don't even think it."

"This is a big reminder that we need to talk about these things, Mac. We were just recently off the island for a couple of days. What if something had happened to us? We need guardians for the kids. Hell, we need a will."

"I have a will. I leave everything to you."

"That's nice to know, but what if we both die at the same time? What happens to our kids?"

"Do we have to talk about this today when we've just come from the saddest thing I've seen in a really long time?"

"No, but we do need to talk about it. I want to make an appointment with Dan to go over this stuff."

"Okay."

"We have to decide who'd get the kids if something happens to us."

"That's easy. They'd go to my parents."

"What about my parents?"

Mac glanced across at her, and the challenging expression on her face indicated this might not be as easy as he thought.

"You see? We need to have this conversation. What if your parents don't want to raise their grandchildren?"

"Of course they would. If they couldn't, Janey and Joe could."

"Or Tiffany and Blaine."

"Are we going to fight about this?"

"There's a very good chance we will if you automatically assume they're going to your family, as if mine doesn't exist."

"Point taken. And you're right. We do need to talk about it. Just not today, okay?"

"Okay. I know you cared a lot about Lisa, and you love those boys."

"I really do, and Shane and I were so happy to be building that house for someone who truly deserved the break. This whole thing is so unfair."

"It's made me extra thankful that I have you, because if anything happened to me, you'd be there for our kids."

"I'd be a disaster without you, so please don't let anything happen to you. For the sake of your children, you have to stick around."

"I'm not going anywhere. Don't worry."

They arrived home to an empty house. The kids were with Ned and Francine for the afternoon. Mac trudged up the stairs to the deck behind Maddie, feeling exhausted and drained after seeing the boys. He ought to go back to work at the marina, and he needed to start getting his shit together on the addition he'd promised to oversee for Seamus. But right now, he couldn't seem to summon the desire to do anything other than be with his wife.

She made sandwiches that they took out to the deck to eat.

"It's such a beautiful day for something this sad to happen," Maddie said.

The day was so clear, they could see all the way to Newport from the deck, a view that was often obstructed in the summer by fog and the humidity that hung like a drape over the island. "Sure is."

"I've been thinking…"

"About?"

"Trying again."

Mac sat up a little straighter in his chair. He'd avoided the subject of trying for another baby in the weeks since they'd lost a child in utero. To hear her say she'd been thinking about trying again had his full attention. "Really?"

She bit her lip, which made her look madly vulnerable as she nodded.

"Not because you think I want to, right? Because you do?"

"Hopefully because we both do. Do we?"

"Hell, yes, I want to. I want as many kids as you'd like to have. But I'm also perfectly satisfied with the two perfect babies we already have."

"You've certainly changed your tune by saying as many babies as I want. Have you forgotten your moratorium after Hailey was born?"

Mac shrugged. "Everything is different after losing one. Now the only thing that matters is that they—and their mother—are healthy. But…" He hesitated, unsure of how to say the one thing he felt he had to say before this went any further.

"What?"

"You scared me with the way you checked out after we lost Cameron," he said of the baby they had decided to name out of respect to his memory. "You scared me bad."

"It took me a while to bounce back, but I did."

"It wasn't that so much as the way you punched out of this." He moved his hand between them. "*Us.* That scared me more than anything. If that happened again… I don't know, Maddie, it kinda made me crazy to feel like you'd left me even though you were right next to me. I never want to feel like that again."

She got up from her chair and came over to his, making herself at home on his lap.

He put his arms around her and held her close.

"I'm sorry I made you feel that way. I didn't mean to. I was just a mess after losing him."

"I know. I was, too, but you turned away from me rather than toward me. That was almost worse than losing the baby, because I lost you, too."

"I won't let that happen again. I promise."

"Even if the worst possible thing happens with this new baby we're talking about having?"

"Even then."

"You gotta promise me."

"I do. I promise." She sealed her sweet words with an even sweeter kiss.

"In that case, it'll be my extreme pleasure to try to knock you up again."

Her laughter filled him with unreasonable joy and hope on a day that had been filled thus far with sorrow.

"And this time," he said, nuzzling her neck, "it'll be entirely on purpose with no booze involved and no little eyes catching us in the act."

"I never want to forget about the night Cameron was conceived."

"Neither do I, honey. That was one for the ages."

"Yes, it was. Maybe someday we'll be able to think of it and laugh at how funny it was without our hearts breaking over what was lost."

"We'll get there. And in the meantime, we get to make new memories and a new baby to love."

"Could we maybe start on this project of ours now?"

"They said you had to wait."

"Until I'd had a regular period. I've had one." She ran her finger down the front of him, over his chest and stomach. "So what're you doing this afternoon?"

"I thought I was going to work, but apparently I have to help my wife with something at home."

Her caramel-colored eyes sparkled with delight as he kissed her. "Yes, you do," she said, "and no one else will do."

"No one else had better do anything to you, Mrs. McCarthy."

"I don't want anyone but you, Mac. Take me to bed."

CHAPTER 5

As they did most evenings after work, David Lawrence and his girlfriend, Daisy Babson, stopped by so Daisy could spend some time with Marion. Tonight, David came with information about the in-patient evaluation he was arranging for Marion.

Hope paid close attention to the paperwork the hospital had sent, outlining the various tests that would be performed and the timing of everything.

"You can expect her to be there for at least one night, possibly two," David said. "They'll let you know after the first day how it's going."

Hope tried to remain professionally engaged in what David was saying, but in the back of her mind was the thought of at least one night—possibly two—alone with Paul. After what'd happened between them the other night, that might make for an awkward couple of days.

"If you have any questions at all, don't hesitate to call me," David said. "Even when you're on the mainland. I can listen in to the meeting with the doctors, too, if that would help."

"I'm sure Paul and Alex would appreciate that."

As she said his name, Paul came in from work, looking the same as he did every day—tired, dirty and sexy. Before she moved to Gansett, Hope would've said her "type" was white-collar career men. That was then. This was now. Dirty and sexy did it for her big-time. But then she reminded herself, as she often had to, that he was her boss and thus off-limits to her.

She couldn't think of their middle-of-the-night kiss without feeling mortified by her behavior. The way she'd all but attacked him when he'd been offering comfort after Lisa died. Ugh.

"Hope?" Paul said, making her realize he'd been speaking to her while she'd been daydreaming about kissing him.

"Yes?"

He smiled, and oh, what that smile did to his already-gorgeous face. "Where'd you go?" he asked, although judging by the way he looked at her, he knew exactly where her mind had wandered. Had he been thinking about it, too?

"I was just going over what I'll need to do to get Ethan ready for me to be gone for a couple of days."

"If it's too much, I can take my mom by myself."

"It's not. Not at all. Unless you'd rather—"

"Not even kinda," he said, smiling again.

"I made the appointment for next week because I knew you'd want to be here for Lisa Chandler's funeral," David said to Hope.

"Yes, thank you for thinking of that. Have you seen the boys today?"

"I was there earlier, and they seem to be doing okay. Seamus and Carolina are taking good care of them."

"Poor babies," Hope said. "It's so sad."

"It really is. I guess I should go collect Daisy and take her to dinner."

"Thank you again for everything, David," Paul said.

David shook hands with him. "I wish there was more I could do. I'll see you all tomorrow." He walked out to join Daisy and Marion on the front porch. They wouldn't leave without letting someone know, so Hope took advantage of the rare opportunity to relax for a minute.

The minute was short-lived when Ethan came running in through the back door, letting the screen slam behind him. "You're home!" He nearly crashed into Paul, who moved quickly to scoop up the boy and flip him over his shoulder, making Ethan scream with laughter.

"What's the rush, little man?"

"I wanna check the pumpkins, but Mom said I had to do my homework and wait for you. Can we go? Can we?"

Hope wanted to tell Paul he didn't have to take him if he was too tired, but before she could get the words out, they were headed to the front door with Ethan still over Paul's shoulder like a sack of potatoes and laughing all the way. It did funny things to her insides to see Paul with her son, to know that Ethan was completely infatuated with him. But that also scared her. Was it safe to allow Ethan to become attached to Paul, Alex, Jenny and Marion?

If the doctors on the mainland recommended in-patient care for Marion, where would that leave her? Out of a job and out of a home, too. Her stomach ached at the thought of starting over—again. They were so happy here on Gansett, which felt like home after only a couple of months. Ethan was happily settled in his new school and making friends who didn't know about their painful past.

It would be awful to have to leave this island that had begun to feel like home, not to mention the family that she, too, had become attached to. Paul, Alex and Jenny were more than just her employers. They were new friends, too, the first new friends she'd made in years, as were David, Daisy, Erin, Jared and Lizzie, among others.

David stuck his head in the front door. "We need to run, Hope."

She shook off the melancholy and got up to see to Marion. On the porch, Daisy was hugging Marion. Thank goodness for Daisy, who brightened Marion's days with her sunny disposition and ability to roll with whatever Marion tossed her way. They all looked forward to Daisy's daily visits as a respite in the storm of Marion's illness.

"Thanks again for coming by, Daisy—and David," Hope said.

"We enjoy our time with Marion," Daisy said.

"I'll see you tomorrow, right?" Marion asked.

"Yes, you will." Except for their recent week off island, Daisy never missed a day with Marion, not since the day Marion turned up, barefoot and confused, on Daisy's front porch in town. The incident had led to Hope's hiring, and she was careful to keep a close eye on Marion, knowing her penchant for wandering.

Hope and Marion waved to David and Daisy as they drove off.

"Such a nice girl," Marion said with a sigh. Then she looked over at Hope, her smile fading. "Who are you?"

"I'm Hope, and I'm here to help you."

Marion sniffed with indignation. "I don't need your help, so you can just go back to wherever you came from." She got up and went inside, letting the screen door slam the same way Ethan had. Hope was about to get up to go after her when Paul came around the corner from the fields with Ethan on his shoulders. Her little boy was laughing hysterically.

Paul was smiling, too, and the sight of the two of them laughing together filled her with giddy feelings of gratitude and hope. She liked him. She'd liked kissing him. And despite all the reasons why she shouldn't, she was looking forward to two days alone with him on the mainland.

*

On Saturday night, Jared, Lizzie, David, Daisy and Erin came to the Martinez home for a cookout. Marion's friends had taken her to a spaghetti dinner at the church hall, and Ethan was spending the night with one of his new school friends, so Hope was officially off duty and could enjoy a relaxing evening with her own new friends.

Jenny had the blender going at full speed and produced a frothy salted margarita that she handed to Hope. "You've earned this times ten today," Jenny said.

Marion had been in a foul mood all day, until her friends showed up and her disposition sweetened considerably. Hope certainly understood that the moods were part of the illness, but it wasn't easy to be on the receiving end of hours' worth of frustrated rage.

Hope took a big sip of the delicious drink and let the heat of the tequila warm her from the inside.

"Good?" Jenny asked.

"Perfection."

"Excellent! Erin, Daisy, Lizzie! Come get your margaritas."

The guys had opted for beers and were on the front porch messing with the grill, as men did.

"Really good, Jenny," Lizzie said.

"So how're the wedding plans coming?" Erin asked.

"Excellent, thanks to Lizzie," Jenny said. "She's got everything under control."

"Or at least I hope I do. This is our first really big wedding at the Chesterfield, so Jenny and Alex know they are our test subjects."

"Since you guys bought the place for us, the least we can do is be your guinea pigs."

Lizzie wrinkled her nose. "I never said anything about pigs, so don't tell anyone that. It wouldn't be good for business."

The others laughed.

"You know what else this island needs?" Hope said.

"What's that?" Lizzie asked.

"A home for the sick and aged. Where are people supposed to go when their families can't care for them at home anymore? They have to go to the mainland, which separates them from their families."

"That's so true," Jenny said. "Alex and Paul wrestle with that every day. They know Marion probably needs to be in a place devoted to the kind of care she needs, but to do that, they'd have to put her somewhere far away from them." She raised her glass in toast to Hope. "Thank God for Hope. We say that every day, but she works nonstop because dementia never takes a day off."

"This is very interesting," Lizzie said. "I'll talk to Jared about it."

"I didn't say that expecting you guys to do something about it," Hope said, slightly horrified that Lizzie had taken her so literally when she'd been venting.

"I'm not sure we can do anything, but it's worth a conversation. Besides," Lizzie added with a saucy grin, "you all know my favorite thing to do is spend Jared's money on worthwhile causes."

"She's very good at that," Daisy said. "The way you guys mobilized help for Lisa Chandler made her final days so much better than they would've been otherwise."

"Jared and I both believe there's a responsibility that goes with having the kind of resources he has," Lizzie said. "It made us happy to help Lisa and her boys. If you don't use your money to do good for others, you're just another rich billionaire asshat, and I won't let him become an asshat."

"You're too funny," Erin said.

"Well, it's true," Lizzie said. "I'm all about keeping it real, and I will look into the possibility of starting a place on the island for people like Marion."

"Wow," Hope said. "You don't fool around."

"No, she doesn't," Jenny said. "And I'll always be thankful to her and Jared for buying the Chesterfield for me."

"Me, too." Alex came into the kitchen and put an arm around Jenny from behind. "We're going to have the most beautiful wedding that Gansett Island has ever seen."

Jenny smiled back at him, and the powerful connection they shared was so obvious that Hope experienced a twinge of envy. As much as she'd once loved her ex-husband, they hadn't had what Jenny and Alex did. Or what David and Daisy had or Jared and Lizzie. After spending time with them, Hope was determined to never again settle for less than what they had.

*

Paul grilled steaks and potatoes for their guests, who'd brought salads and dessert to add to the party. It was nice to take a break from their many responsibilities and to spend some time with good friends.

Over dinner, the conversation went from Alex and Jenny's wedding and their plans to move into their new house, to the vacation David and Daisy had recently taken in Bermuda, to Erin's adventures at the lighthouse.

"Hope mentioned something earlier that I want to look into further," Lizzie said to her husband during dessert.

"Is this going to cost me money?" Jared asked with a good-natured grin.

The look Lizzie gave him had them all laughing. "Of course it is."

Jared groaned. "What now?"

"We need a senior care facility on this island so elderly patients can get the help they need and remain close to their families, too."

Paul glanced at his brother, who was listening intently to Lizzie.

"Hmm," Jared said to Hope. "Speak to me."

She glanced at Paul, seeming tentative. "It was just a thought I had that I said out loud in front of the wrong person," she said with a smile.

"Or the *right* person," Lizzie said. "Depending on how you look at it."

"She's like a dog with a bone when she hears about someone in need," Jared said.

"Awww, isn't he sweet calling his new wife a dog?" Lizzie said, setting off a new round of laughter. "Woof woof."

"It's a brilliant idea, Hope," David said. "I can think of ten people right off the top of my head who would benefit from such a place, including Marion."

"And we know the perfect person to oversee it," Lizzie said to her husband, who frowned.

"I don't know…"

"What don't you know? Your brother is between jobs and looking for something new. What would be better for him than this?" To the others, she said, "Jared's brother Quinn was an army medic and recently returned to civilian life. He was a GP before the army, so he could easily take on something like this, couldn't he, David?"

"I'm sure he's probably overqualified," David said.

"See?" Lizzie said, her eyes flashing with excitement.

"Do you guys see what I live with?" Jared asked, his smile conveying his obvious affection for his wife.

"I know, I'm such a hardship," Lizzie said, winking at him.

"If you're serious about this," Paul said, "the town is about to put the old school building on the market now that the new one is open."

"Can we look at it tomorrow?" Lizzie asked.

Jared groaned again. "There go my plans to chill by the pool all day."

"Can we?" Lizzie asked again.

"I'll see if I can set it up," Paul said, amused by her enthusiasm.

"Dog meet bone," Jared said.

Lizzie let out a bark that had them all howling with laughter.

Much later, after the others had left, Hope helped Alex, Jenny and Paul clean up.

"Can you imagine if this idea of yours actually comes to fruition?" Alex asked.

"I didn't mean to set Lizzie off on such a tangent," Hope said. "I was just saying how nice it would be to have something like that here. Of course, I probably put myself out of a job with my big idea."

"No way," Jenny said. "If it happens, and that's a big if at this point, they'll need tons of people to staff the place."

"True," Hope said. "I just hope you guys don't think I was overstepping by bringing it up."

"Why would we?" Paul asked. "We value your opinions and ideas, and if this one comes to pass, we'll owe you a huge debt of gratitude for finding a way to get Mom the care she needs right here on the island. That'd be a miracle to us."

Alex pointed at Paul. "What he said."

Hope smiled at their effusive praise. "Well, thanks. You guys are too kind. This was a really fun time tonight. Thanks for including me."

"You and Ethan are part of the family now," Jenny said. "Whether you like it or not."

Hope laughed. "We like it very much."

Paul was thrilled to hear her say that. At times he wondered if they asked too much of her, especially on days like today when their mother was verbally abusive. Speaking of Marion… Headlights lit up the front of the house. The festive mood the four of them had been in immediately shifted to something far more serious.

"I'll get your mom to bed," Hope said.

"I'll help," Paul said. "You've already put in a full day."

"I don't mind."

He couldn't deny the attraction he felt for her when she looked at him with those kind eyes and that warm smile. It had been nearly a week since she kissed him, and he'd thought about it at least a thousand times since then. They were leaving on Tuesday to take Marion to the mainland, and he couldn't wait to have some time alone with Hope to get to know her better.

Despite the guilt Paul felt over being interested in an employee, he had to think his dad would approve of his affection for Hope, especially because of the way she took care of Marion.

"Since you guys have got bedtime covered, we're going over to our house to do a few things," Alex said.

"We'll take bedtime tomorrow," Jenny said.

"See you in the morning," Paul said.

Between the two of them, Paul and Hope got Marion changed and ready for bed. Hope cajoled her to take her medicine, and by the time they got her tucked in, Paul was completely worn out. The relaxing night with friends might never have happened.

"I don't know about you, but I could use another drink," he said when they returned to the kitchen.

"I wouldn't say no to that."

"Beer, wine or more tequila?"

"I've consumed my yearly limit of tequila tonight. I'll have a beer."

He opened two of them. "Let's go outside," he said, gesturing for her to go out ahead of him to the back deck, where the stargazing was at its best.

CHAPTER 6

Hope and Paul sat on the stairs to enjoy their beers.

"I'm sorry she's so awful to you," Paul said. "Alex and I feel terrible about that."

"Don't. It goes with the territory. It doesn't bother me."

"*How* does it not bother you? We love her, and it makes us nuts."

"I guess I'm just used to it. I've worked with dementia patients for years, and I've learned not to take their abuse personally. Most of them are lovely people who, in their right minds, would be appalled by their behavior. I try to stay focused on who they were rather than who they are now."

"I feel guilty because sometimes I forget who she used to be."

"Tell me what you remember."

"She loved to cook and fuss over Alex and me and our dad. They were crazy in love, constantly dancing and kissing and whispering to each other. It used to gross us out when we were teenagers."

Hope laughed. "I'm sure it did."

"Alex used to tell them to get a room."

"And isn't he one to talk these days?"

"I know, right?" Paul laughed. "Such a hypocrite."

"I think he and Jenny are adorable together."

"I do, too, even if I could do with a little less PDA."

"They're moving out soon."

"None too soon, if you ask me. I've had to learn to sleep with headphones on or hear things that can't be unheard."

Hope lost it laughing. "Aww, poor Paul. How do you stand it?"

"I can't stand it. I'll be first in line to move them the hell out of here."

"Anyway, about your mom…"

"Right," he said, wondering how he'd gotten off on a tangent, with her of all people, about sex. "She ran the business after my dad died. Did all the paperwork, managed the retail store, dealt with the customers. We had a good groove going for a long time, and then she started forgetting stuff, confusing one customer with another, arguing with the college kids in the store. I couldn't figure out what the hell was up with her until one of the kids took me aside and told me the same thing had happened with her grandmother. She was the first to use the word dementia with me. I felt like I'd been electrocuted or something."

Overcome by the painful memories, Paul took a drink from his bottle and stared out at the darkness. "I asked David to meet me for a beer. He wasn't the official Gansett Island doctor yet. He was home recovering from chemo."

"Wait, what? David had *chemo?*"

"He had lymphoma. He's in remission now and doing great, but he was pretty sick for a while there."

"Wow, I had no idea. So what did he say when you told him about your mom?"

"That what she was displaying were classic signs of dementia. He recommended I take her to a doctor on the mainland for an official diagnosis. You should've heard that battle. She accused me of all sorts of things, including conspiring to get rid of her so I could have the house and business to myself."

"Aw, jeez," she said with a sigh. "That had to hurt."

"It was awful. But I managed to drag her kicking and screaming to the doctor on the mainland who confirmed the diagnosis and put her on medication that slowed the progression, for a while anyway. We lived in a perpetual state of battle for about a year before I called Alex and begged him to come home to help me. I hated making that call. He had a good life in DC, a job he loved and a girlfriend who dumped him when he told her he was moving home."

"It worked out pretty well for him here."

"Eventually, but at first he was freaking miserable, and even though he knew he needed to be here, it was tough to see him so unhappy. He hated living here when we were kids. Couldn't wait to get the hell off this island. So to ask him to come back…"

"You did the only thing you could at the time. He knows that."

"Yeah, he does, but it still sucked until he met Jenny and then became the happiest SOB you ever met."

"That he is," Hope said with a laugh.

"I'm glad for him. No one deserves it more than he does."

"You do, too."

Paul had no idea how to respond to that statement. Was she referring to the kiss or was he reading far too much into an innocuous statement? Probably the latter.

"Sorry," she said. "Didn't mean to make things more awkward."

"You didn't."

"Yes, I really did. I keep thinking about what happened the other night, and how ridiculously out of line I was. It's so embarrassing!"

Maybe it was the four beers he'd had that gave him the liquid courage to put his arm around her.

Her body went rigid next to him.

"No need to be embarrassed. You're not the only one who's thought about that kiss a few thousand times."

"Oh," she said, exhaling and relaxing ever so slightly. "I'm not?"

"Definitely not."

"A few thousand times?"

"At least. Might be even more than that."

"Oh. Well…" After a long pause, she said, "Is it possible that we're only thinking about it because we're convenient to each other?"

Paul laughed at her use of the word convenient. "This, whatever it is, is hardly convenient. All I can think about is that my father would skin me alive for kissing one of our employees, let alone wanting to do it again. In that way, it's incredibly *inconvenient*."

"You… You want to do it again?"

"Yeah, and not at all because you're *convenient*. It's because you're you, and you're gorgeous and amazing and a great mom and…"

"And what?" she asked, sounding breathless.

He wished he could see her face more clearly, but it was too dark. "Sexy. Really, really sexy."

"Paul…"

"Tell me no if you don't want me to kiss you again."

"I kissed you the last time."

"This one will be all on me, unless you say no."

"I'm not saying no, but—"

He didn't wait to hear the second half of her sentence. Before she could change her mind—or he could change his—he pulled her closer and relied upon instinct to find her lips in the dark. Until he was one hundred percent certain she was on board with this kiss, he only rubbed his lips against hers.

Then her lips parted and her hand curled around his neck, which was all the encouragement he needed. Paul ran his tongue over her bottom lip, making her gasp. For a second, he wondered if he'd been too forward, but then her tongue touched his, and he forgot about all the reasons why this was a bad idea and lost himself in her. Other than her, he hadn't kissed anyone in longer than he could remember, and he'd never kissed anyone with quite so much pent-up need.

Hope's need seemed to match his, and she met every thrust of his tongue with her own, driving him slowly crazy. They got so caught up in the kiss that they nearly fell off the back steps, laughing at the near miss. When they broke the kiss, the sound of heavy breathing filled the night air.

Paul found her hand in the darkness. "Come inside for a little while."

"What about Jenny and Alex?"

"When they said they had stuff to do at the house, they meant each other."

Hope sputtered with laughter. "How do you know that?"

"Because it's gotten a lot 'quieter' around here since the carpet went in over there."

"That's too funny."

"They're not coming back here tonight. The coast is clear…"

"Are you sure this is a good idea?"

"No," he said, laughing, "I'm not sure of that at all, but I'm sure that it feels great to kiss you, and I don't want to stop. Not yet."

"I'm afraid…"

"Of what? Not me…"

"No, not you, but if this, whatever this is between us… If it goes bad, my job…"

"I promise you that no matter what happens or doesn't happen between us, it will never, *ever* impact your job. You have my word on that."

"What is happening between us?"

"I don't know, but I'm looking forward to finding out. Are you?"

"Yeah," she said softly.

He stood and gave her hand a gentle tug. "Come inside."

She stood and let him lead her indoors, where he faced a decision—the sofa or his room? Because he couldn't be entirely sure that Jenny and Alex were gone for the night, he took a left down the hallway to his room, where the rising moon provided a faint hint of light through the open windows.

"Paul," she whispered, hesitating. "We shouldn't…"

He closed the door and put his arm around her waist, bringing her in close to him. "Just this," he said as he kissed her. "Nothing more."

Her arms encircled his neck and her body pressed tightly to his, making him want much more than her enthusiastic kisses. They stood there like that, in the dark room, for a long time, kissing like two people who'd been starving until they found each other.

Paul walked her backward to his bed and came down on top of her, making her gasp from the press of his erection against her center.

Her fingers tightened in his hair as she dragged him into another kiss.

He wanted to touch her everywhere, to explore the curves that had captured his attention from the first time he met her. However, he kept his hands flat against her back, because he'd promised they wouldn't go any further. That promise wasn't easy to keep, however. Now that he'd had another taste of her, he wanted so much more. He broke the kiss and moved to her neck, where he kissed and licked the sensitive skin there, making her arch into him in silent demand.

Her hands moved down his back, finding the hem of his shirt and then sliding underneath.

Paul trembled from her touch, his desire for her exploding the instant her skin brushed against his. As much as it pained him to stop, he pulled back from her, mindful of his promise not to take advantage of the opportunity she'd given him. But God, he wanted to.

"What's wrong?" she asked.

"Nothing."

"Why did you stop?"

"Because if I don't, I won't be able to."

She slid her hand from his back to his stomach and then up to touch his chest.

Paul forced himself to stay perfectly still, afraid that if he so much as uttered a sound, she might remember all the reasons this wasn't such a great idea.

"Touch me, Paul."

He closed his eyes and summoned the control he needed to go slow, to give her tenderness rather than the desperate need that every stroke of her hand was building in him. Beginning with her bare arm, he ran his fingertips over her soft skin, causing an outbreak of goose bumps that made him smile. Returning to her shoulder, he eased the strap of her tank down, kissing the length of her collarbone.

She squirmed under him, pushing against his erection and nearly making him forget all about going slow. He wanted to strip her naked and lose himself in her warm sweetness right now.

"I'm having highly indecent thoughts, and all of them involve you," he said.

"Right there with you."

He tugged on her top. "Could we maybe take this off?"

"Only if we take this off, too." She smoothed her hands up his back and took his shirt with her.

"Deal." He lifted her tank up and over her head and was shocked to discover she was bare beneath it. "Hope… You're so beautiful."

She pulled on his shirt, and he helped her remove it, then rolled to his side, bringing her with him.

He could think of no way to adequately describe the thrill that traveled through him when her breasts pressed against his chest. Recapturing her lips, he kissed her again, more intently this time around, his tongue exploring every sweet corner of her mouth.

Hope squirmed in his arms, trying to get closer, or so it seemed to him. "This is crazy," she whispered between kisses. "We shouldn't be doing this."

"Why not?" He cupped her breast and teased her nipple with his thumb until it was hard and tight.

"I, um… There's a reason we shouldn't, but I can't think of it when you're doing that."

"How about when I do this?" He eased her onto her back and took the same nipple into his mouth, running his tongue back and forth over the tip before sucking on it.

She grabbed a handful of his hair and held on so tightly that he winced from the pleasurable pain. Her legs shifted restlessly, so he grasped her thighs and pulled them up around his hips without letting up on her nipple. The heat of her arousal pressed against his cock, making him want so much more.

He switched his attention to the other side, teasing her nipple with his tongue, lips and teeth as she arched rhythmically against him.

"Don't stop," she whispered in a tone he'd never heard from her before. It was needy and desperate and incredibly sexy.

Paul pushed harder against her, torturing himself as he gave her what she wanted and needed.

And then she released a keening moan and tightened her legs around his hips.

He wanted so badly to go with her, but he held back, giving her his full focus and attention, until she relaxed into the mattress, breathing hard.

"That," she said, "has never happened before."

Inordinately pleased to know he'd given her a new experience, he teased her parted lips and fell into another passionate kiss.

Her hands moved from his chest to his stomach and down to his shorts, which she unbuttoned and unzipped before his brain could catch up with what was happening.

"Hope..." His brain shut down completely when she wrapped her hand around his erection and began to stroke him.

"Definitely shouldn't be doing this."

"No, you should. You really should."

Her laughter made him smile, even as he tried to hold back the orgasm that had wanted out from the second her bare breasts touched his chest.

He closed his eyes and gave himself over to the incredible high of being with her this way. The heat of her hand and the pleasure of her gentle yet firm touch made for the perfect combination. Paul groaned as he came, his fingers digging into her hips to keep her close to him.

She kissed him softly and sweetly.

He opened his eyes to find her watching him. "I made a mess of you."

"I don't mind."

"Let me get a towel. I'll be right back." He kissed her again and disentangled their limbs so he could get up, tugging his shorts back up as he went. The bathroom was across the hall, so he opened the door and looked both ways before leaving the bedroom. He returned with a towel that he used to wipe up her belly and chest.

"I should go and let you sleep," she said, looking shy all of a sudden despite what they'd done.

Paul dropped the towel on the floor and snuggled up to her, unwilling to let her go just yet. "Or you could stay awhile longer. It's only midnight."

"It's weird to not have Ethan at home for a night, but I'm glad he's made such good new friends so quickly."

"I'm glad for him and for you, because you deserve a break every now and then."

"I guess, but it still feels weird to have him sleeping somewhere else."

This would be a great time to ask about the boy's father, but Paul couldn't bring himself to bring her past into their very lovely present. He dragged his fingertips over her flat belly, which quivered under his touch.

"Please tell me we aren't making a huge mistake here, Paul."

"Doesn't feel like a mistake to me," he said, though his conscience was still troubled because his father would disapprove of what he was doing with her.

"I'm too busy feeling great to think about all the reasons why it might not be a good idea."

"I don't do things like this."

"Like what?"

"Fool around with my boss, for one thing."

"I'd like to think this situation is a little different than your typical work environment. I'd like to think we've become friends over the last few intense weeks with my mom. I'd like to think we're both adults who can handle whatever complication something like this is sure to cause at some point."

"You say that as if you're certain it will."

"It will," he said, sighing. "But that doesn't mean I don't want to see where it goes. As long as you do, too."

"I've had a crush on you from the first time I saw you with your mom and how amazingly patient you are with her."

"Is that right?" he asked, amused and touched by her confession.

"Uh-huh."

"Well, I suppose it's only fair that I confess to having had a crush myself after watching you in action with Mom and Ethan. You're so good with both of them, not to mention sexy as all hell."

"I am not."

He cupped her breast and kissed her. "Yes, you are. That skirt you wear?"

"What skirt?"

"The denim one."

"That skirt is a thousand years old!"

"Maybe so, but it does amazing things for your sexy ass." He ran his hand down her back to give her bottom a squeeze. "I might've once had a highly inappropriate thought about my mother's nurse wearing that skirt, without underwear, while I take her from behind."

"I never knew you had such a vivid imagination."

"Are you appalled?"

"Quite the opposite, in fact. You've got my imagination running wild now, too."

Paul laughed at her frank reply and pulled her in closer, keeping her tucked up against him.

"I really ought to go home."

"Stay."

"I shouldn't."

"Yes, you should." As he drifted off to sleep, he tightened his hold on her so she couldn't get away.

CHAPTER 7

A sniffling whimper woke Seamus from a light sleep. He'd been on alert since the boys went to bed hours earlier, but now he sat up in bed, listening intently. Hearing it again, he disentangled himself from Caro without waking her and went into the room across the hall, where the boys were sleeping.

Another sniffle led him to Kyle's bed. "Hey, pal," he whispered.

Kyle turned his face into the pillow, as if he didn't want to be caught crying.

Seamus rubbed the little boy's back. "I'm sad, too, you know?" He spoke softly, hoping he wouldn't wake Jackson. "Maybe you could come and sit with me for a while and we can be sad together. What do you think?"

He continued to rub Kyle's back, giving the child a minute to decide if he wanted comfort or if he preferred to be left alone.

Slowly, Kyle turned over and held out his arms to Seamus.

His heart ached as he scooped up Kyle and carried him out of the room, closing the door behind him. He went into the living room and sat in Caro's rocking chair with Kyle's head resting on his shoulder. For a long time, they were quiet, with only the gentle sway of the rocker breaking the silence.

"Why are you sad?" Kyle asked. "Did your mommy die, too?"

Seamus released a deep breath. "No, but I'm sad that yours did. I'm sad for her and you and Jackson."

"It's not fair."

"No, it isn't."

"Is she really not going to come back?"

Aw, God, Seamus thought. *Give me strength and wisdom to get these poor kids through this.* "No, honey, she's not."

A sob shook the boy's small body, and his tears soaked through Seamus's T-shirt. After a while, the sobs morphed into hiccups, but Seamus never stopped rubbing the little back. Eventually, Kyle's breathing settled, and Seamus wondered if he'd fallen back to sleep. He kept the rocking chair moving until he was certain the boy was back to sleep.

Then he stood carefully and walked back to the bedroom, where he deposited Kyle in his bed, pulled the covers up and over him and kissed his sweaty forehead. He sat on the edge of the bed for a long time, waiting to make sure Kyle had settled into sleep. When he got up to leave the room, he fixed Jackson's covers and smoothed the hair off his forehead before leaving them to sleep.

Though he was now wide awake and overwhelmed by the weight of the responsibility he and Caro had assumed for these precious children, Seamus got back in bed.

"What's wrong?" Caro asked as she curled up to him.

Seamus put his arms around her. "Kyle was awake and crying, so we spent some time in the rocker. The poor guy asked me if his mom is really not coming back."

"Oh Lord. What did you say?"

"I told him the truth. What else could I say?"

"That was the right thing to do. I remember when Joe asked me that after his dad died. I was always honest with him. It took a while for him to understand how long forever really is."

"I forget that you've already been through this with one heartbroken little boy, and now I've got you back in the same boat again."

"I wouldn't want to be anywhere but in that boat with you and Kyle and Jackson. We're going to get them through this, Seamus. It won't happen overnight, but one day they'll find a way to accept what's happened, and when they do, they'll go back to being the happy little guys they once were."

"You promise, love?"

"Yes, I do."

"I sure hope so, because I already love them an awful lot, and I find myself wishing for a magic wand that could make everything right in their world again."

"Since we don't have a magic wand handy, we'll just have to love them through it."

"We did the right thing taking them in, didn't we?"

"Are you having second thoughts?"

"Not about wanting them or anything like that."

"Then what?"

"I guess I worry that I'm not up to the job of being their dad. We know you've got this mother gig mastered. You've already raised one fantastic son, so you're an expert. But they're getting a rookie with me, and I'm feeling out of my league already."

Her shoulder shook under his hand.

"Are you *laughing* at me, Carolina O'Grady?"

"I might be." She cupped his face in her hand and kissed him. "Seamus, my love, every new parent feels the way you do. Outmatched, overwhelmed, certain that disaster is looming around the next corner. Those boys have suffered a terrible tragedy. There's no way around that. But you're their silver lining."

"*We* are."

"*You* are. I'll give them everything I have to give, but you... You'll teach them how to be men, and if they're even half the man you are, you will have done an amazing job."

"Awww, Caro, that's a sweet thing for you to say."

"It's the truth. What happened to their mom is a terrible stroke of bad luck, but they got lucky the day you decided we needed to be there for them. They may not know it yet, but someday they will."

"I hope you're right."

"When have you ever known me not to be right?"

"Um, how about the months you spent pushing me away when you *knew* we were meant to be?"

"Other than that."

"That's a pretty big other than."

"Shut up and kiss your wife."

"My sassy wife, you mean." Since there was truly nothing else he'd rather do than kiss his wife, he did as he was told like the good husband he was. And as he did every day, he gave thanks to whatever higher power had brought her and her good sense into his life.

They were in for one hell of a challenging ride with their boys, but Seamus was confident that with her by his side to make sure he didn't screw it up, they'd do right by Kyle and Jackson.

*

Lizzie James was up before the sun on Sunday morning. She'd been awake for hours thinking about the idea that had taken root the night before and how they might make it happen. It was such a brilliant idea—a place on the island for seniors and others in need of health care so they could remain close to their loved ones. She and Jared certainly had the resources to make it happen, and it might turn out to be an ideal situation for her brother-in-law Quinn, who'd returned from his service as a medic in Afghanistan badly injured and in need of a new direction.

The more she thought about the idea, the more brilliant it became. She made it until seven o'clock before she brought a mug of coffee into the bedroom with her, hoping to butter up Jared.

She kissed him awake.

"Hey," he said when his eyes finally opened. "What time is it?"

"Seven."

"It's Sunday, right?"

"Uh-huh."

"What the heck are you doing up so early on the one day we get to sleep in?" He made himself get up and be productive the other days of the week, lest he become a slovenly "retiree." Sundays were his day "off."

"I couldn't sleep anymore. And I've been thinking."

"Ugh," he said with a dramatic groan. "Any time you get to thinking, it costs me money."

Lizzie responded with a big giddy smile.

Grinning, he shook his head. "It's a good thing you're so damned cute, or I might be tempted to be annoyed with you for waking me up at the butt crack of dawn."

"You love me too much to be annoyed with me, and you have to admit I have good ideas."

He sat up and took the mug from her. "They're not *all* bad."

Lizzie waited until he'd had three big sips of coffee. "So about this home for the aged that everyone was talking about last night..."

"What about it?"

"I want to go see the old school that Paul mentioned. He said the town is about to list it for sale."

"When do you want to do this?"

"Um, now?"

"Lizzie! It's seven o'clock in the morning on the one day we take to chill out and do nothing. Does it have to be right now?"

She smiled again, knowing that was all it took to get him to see things her way. He loved to see her smiling and happy, so she played her best card.

"I never knew you were so devious when I married you."

"You did, too. Now get your lazy butt out of bed and drive me to see this school." She started to get up, but he took hold of her hand, stopping her from getting away.

"On one condition."

"What?"

"When we get back, we spend the rest of the morning in bed."

She raised a saucy brow. "Sleeping?"

"You've got me wide awake after a good night's sleep. I doubt I'll need more sleep for many, *many* hours."

He was so damned sexy, especially first thing in the morning with his blond hair standing on end and his jaw covered in whiskers.

Lizzie pretended to think about his very tempting offer for a moment or two. "Okay, we have a deal. Now get up." She'd showered an hour ago and was already dressed. She tugged on his hand to "help" him up.

He groaned as he let her pull him out of bed.

Lizzie took a good long look at her gorgeous husband, who stood before her fully nude and fully erect. She licked her lips.

"Don't do that and then tell me we've got to go somewhere."

"What did I do?"

"You looked and you licked."

Lizzie laughed at the foul expression that marred his handsome face. "You're so grumpy in the morning."

He hooked an arm around her waist. "I'm only grumpy when I get blasted out of bed far too early by my beautiful but exasperating wife who's like a little kid at Christmas every time she gets one of her big ideas."

"But you love me, right?"

"Yeah, baby, I love you so much that I let you drag me out of bed when all I want to do is drag you *into* bed." He kissed her neck and nearly had her forgetting why she wanted him up so early.

"No way, buster," she said, wise to him as she pushed him back. "No nookie until we take a lookie."

He walked into the bathroom laughing, giving her a great view of his most excellent ass as he went. A few minutes later, he reemerged wearing shorts, a T-shirt and flip-flops. His hair had been combed into submission, and he looked nothing at all like the ex-Wall Street billionaire that he was. She loved him this way—casual, relaxed, removed from the rat race that had once been his life.

Jared grabbed his wallet and keys from the dresser. "You're so cute when you're excited about something, Lizzie."

"I must be *really* cute right now, then."

He kissed the tip of her nose and then her lips. "You're positively adorable. Let's go see what's got you all wound up."

They drove to the north end of the island in Jared's Porsche. Lizzie opened the window and took deep breaths of the cool, crisp September air. "This might be my favorite month here."

"You say that every month."

"I haven't seen a month yet that I haven't liked."

"Wait until December."

"When I'm marooned with you and a cozy fireplace while it snows outside? I'm not seeing the downside."

He took hold of her hand and used their joined hands to shift the car. "I'm so glad you're happy here."

"I love everything about it, especially the part where I get to be married to you."

"Sometimes, when I think about how close we came to missing out on what we have now…"

"Don't think about that."

"Hard not to when it was such a close call."

"We got lucky, and the planets aligned in our favor."

"I'll never, ever take this for granted, Lizzie, even on days when you blast me out of bed way too early to tend to one of your big ideas."

"That's good to know," she said, smiling over at him. "I worry about the day when I push you one step too far and you tell me, 'That's *it*, Elisabeth with an S. No more big ideas for you.'"

"I'm not seeing that day ever coming, as you well know, which is why you play me like a well-used fiddle to get what you want."

"You are kind of easy," she said with a giggle.

"Easy," he said with an indignant huff. "I'll show you easy when I get you back home."

"Oh boy. I can't wait."

They pulled up to the building that had served as Gansett Island's K-12 school since the seventies, and Lizzie saw right away that the abandoned school looked tired, worn and dated. But that was nothing a little TLC couldn't fix. The second Jared brought the car to a stop, she got out to go peek into dirty windows.

"Be careful," Jared said. "There might be broken glass in those weeds."

Lizzie didn't see the dirt or the weeds or the broken glass. She only saw the big rooms that had once housed students and might one day be rooms for elderly patients. "This is perfect," she declared.

"You can't tell that just by looking in a few windows."

"It's got good bones, and check out the size of the rooms. Come over here and look."

Jared joined her at the window, peering inside with his hands around his eyes blocking the sunlight. "The rooms are big."

"They're *perfect*. Who can we talk to about seeing the inside?"

"You can ask your buddy Paul about that, but before you do, are you really sure you want to take this on, babe? This would be a really, really big deal, and we've already got a pretty big deal going on at the Chesterfield. I thought the goal when we moved out here was to simplify our lives. This is not going to be simple."

"No, it isn't," she said, her heart racing with excitement as plans came together in her mind. "It's going to be a huge pain in the ass, but think of the good we could do here. Look at what Alex and Paul are going through with their mother, and David said he knows of ten other families on the island in similar straits. We'd have the place sold out before we begin construction. And then there's Quinn. This could be ideal for him."

"That's a whole other kettle of fish—smelly, complicated fish."

She glanced at him. "Did you just refer to your brother as smelly fish?"

"His situation is dicey, Lizzie, as you well know."

"This might be the sort of thing that'll give him a new purpose in life. It wouldn't hurt anything to ask him, would it?"

"You're so far down the road on this, and you only had the idea last night."

"What's wrong with trying to make things happen?"

"Nothing. Absolutely nothing is wrong with it as long as you know what you're getting into from the outset."

"I'm well aware that this won't be easy, but I want to do it anyway." She withdrew her cell phone from her pocket and scrolled through her contacts.

"Who're you calling, babe? It's seven thirty on a Sunday."

"Paul will be up," she said as she placed the call, smiling at her husband, who just shook his head once again.

*

The ringing phone pulled Paul out of a deep, satisfying sleep. For a second, he couldn't figure out who was in bed with him, but then the memories of the night before came back to remind him that Hope had stayed with him. He moved carefully so he wouldn't disturb her and reached for his phone on the bedside table to see that Lizzie was calling him awfully early.

"Hello," he said, taking the phone with him as he left the room, closing the door behind him.

"Hey, Paul, it's Lizzie. I hope I'm not waking you."

"It's okay. What's up?"

"Jared and I are out at the old school, and I think it'll be perfect for what we have in mind."

Paul was so groggy that he had to think about what they had in mind. "You're out there already?"

"Uh-huh. Jared and I got up early to come check it out."

"She dragged me out of bed early," Jared said into the phone. "I told her not to call you at this hour."

Paul laughed even as he rubbed the sleep from his eyes.

"How can we get inside?" Lizzie asked. "And I want first dibs on buying it."

"You're serious," Paul said. The sort of facility Lizzie envisioned on Gansett Island would be an answer to a prayer for him and Alex.

"I'm dead serious."

"She's dead serious," Jared said.

"Hush," Lizzie said to her husband. "I'm conducting business here."

"I'll make a few phone calls and see if I can get someone out there to let you inside. Can you wait for a bit?"

"Sure, we've got nothing planned for today."

Jared's groan in the background carried through the phone.

"Something tells me you don't speak for your husband," Paul said, amused by her doggedness.

"He can wait on the plans for later. It'll keep."

"No, it won't!" Jared said.

"I'll call you back," Paul said, laughing at their banter. He ended that call and placed another to the police station. When the dispatcher answered, he asked for the officer in charge.

"Taylor," a gruff voice replied.

"Hey, it's Paul Martinez. They've got you working Sundays, huh?"

"I've got two guys out sick, so I'm holding the short straw. What's up?"

"I have someone interested in buying the old school building and wondered if you have keys, since Town Hall is closed today."

"Yep, I've got keys."

"Any chance one of your guys could run them out there? Lizzie and Jared James are there now, and she's eager to see the inside."

"What's she got in mind for the place?"

"An elderly-care facility, of all things."

"Wow, that's a cool idea."

"My brother and I couldn't agree more. We're getting to the point with our mom that we're going to need more involved care than we can provide at home. If this materializes, it would solve a huge problem for us."

"I imagine it would. I'll take the keys out there myself."

"Are you sure? I could come get them if you're busy."

"No problem. I've got to do my rounds anyway."

"Thanks a lot, Blaine. Appreciate it."

"You got it. So I'll see you next weekend, huh?"

"Yes, you will." Paul was hosting Alex's bachelor party next Saturday night. "Looking forward to it."

"Me, too. Talk to you then."

As Paul ended the call, Alex and Jenny came in through the front door.

"Hey, you're up early," Jenny said with a cheerful smile.

Paul was frozen in place as it dawned on him that he'd missed his opportunity to get Hope out of the house before they were caught together. Crap. "I, um…"

"Everything okay?" Alex asked as he peeled a banana while Jenny made coffee.

"Um, yeah. I'm going back to bed for a while. I'll just… I'll see you later."

"Okay," Jenny said.

Out of the corner of his eye, Paul saw Alex shrug at Jenny's inquiring look. Yes, he knew he was acting strangely, but he had a good reason. Lately, Jenny had been dragging Alex to church on Sunday mornings. He could only hope today would be a church day.

He went back into his room, where Hope was still asleep. Paul got back in bed, moving carefully so he wouldn't wake her. Listening intently to what

Alex and Jenny were doing, he hoped to hear the shower go on or the car start or something to indicate the coast was clear. But all he heard was the low hum of conversation.

Hope stirred, her legs moving before she turned, her eyes opening and widening at the sight of him. "Oh, um, wow. I didn't mean to stay here all night."

When she started to get up, he stopped her with an arm around her waist. "Wait. Alex and Jenny are out there."

She fell back against the pillow, groaning. "I'm thinking of a four-letter word that I shouldn't say, but it fits the situation."

"I'm thinking of the same word."

"And of course I really need to pee."

"She's been dragging him to church lately, so we may get lucky."

"What time is church?"

"They've been going to the eight-thirty mass."

She glanced at the clock and groaned again. "That's in forty-five minutes, and what if they don't go?"

"Let's pray that they do."

"Very funny. In the meantime, my bladder is going to explode, which is way more information than you need on our first morning together."

"What can we do to take your mind off of it?"

"Find me a bathroom?"

"Next best thing?" He held out his arm and brought her into his embrace.

She rested her head on his chest. "Does this feel weird to you in the bright light of day?"

"It actually feels really good. Does it feel weird to you?"

"Just the part about being half-naked in a bed with my boss."

"Do you think you'll ever think of me as anything other than your boss?"

"I already do, Paul. That's the scary part."

"It doesn't have to be scary."

"Things like this never end well for me."

Paul filed away that information to chew on later.

"And there's a lot at stake. Your mom and her care, Ethan and how attached he's getting to you, my job." She shrugged. "This was fun, but I don't think it should happen again. You know?"

"No, I don't know. There's nothing wrong with two consenting adults spending time together if they enjoy each other's company."

"If people could get hurt, there's something very wrong with it."

"I don't want to hurt you or Ethan. I've come to care for both of you. All I'm asking for is a chance, Hope."

The shower went on across the hallway, and the voices of Jenny and Alex disappeared when the bathroom door closed.

Hope sat up, reached for her top and pulled it on over her head. "They're in the shower. I'm going to run home and change clothes, and then I'll be over to get your mom up."

"I can do that. Today is your day off."

"I don't mind."

"Can we please talk about this before you run away?"

"Later. We'll talk later." She opened the door, apparently saw the coast was clear and darted out the door, closing it behind her.

Paul had to laugh at the irony. The first time he spends the night with a woman in longer than he can remember and she runs away like her ass is on fire the next morning. Great way to start the day.

CHAPTER 8

The words "walk of shame" went through her mind as Hope rushed into her cozy cabin and went straight for the bathroom. After taking care of urgent business, she dropped her head into her hands. "God, what the *hell* was I thinking, letting that happen?"

She took a shower and stood under the hot water for a long time, wishing it could wash away the shame. Paul was such a nice guy, as well as handsome, sexy and wonderful with Ethan, not to mention how great he was to his mother. He was everything any woman could ever want in a man. But she couldn't have him.

She and Ethan had too much at stake in this new life of theirs to be taking the kind of chances she'd taken with Paul last night. It had to stop, and it had to stop now, before emotions were engaged and someone got hurt. If things went bad between them, and things always went bad, it would be a disaster for everyone involved.

As much as she liked him and enjoyed being with him, not to mention the powerful attraction they shared, it couldn't continue. They had to go back to being just friends and cordial colleagues. She emerged from the shower with new resolve. It wasn't just about her and what she wanted. Ethan had been through too much to subject him to another potentially messy situation. If she remained friendly with Paul but not romantically involved, there was no chance of Ethan being hurt when the whole thing went south.

He was the most important person in her life, and this was the right decision for him, even if it sucked for her.

While she got dressed and ate some cold cereal, Hope tried not to think about how amazing it had felt to be held and kissed and touched by Paul. She tried not to think about the best orgasm she'd had in years or the way he'd felt hard and hot and thick in her hand. Her mouth watered as she imagined how he would feel inside her—

"No! Stop. It's not going to happen, so stop thinking about it." She gathered her damp hair into a ponytail, her movements jerky. Thinking about what might've been didn't do a thing to quell her desire for more of him. It'd been so long—years—since she'd done anything like what'd happened last night with Paul that she'd forgotten how much she had enjoyed sex before her life blew up in her face like a nuclear bomb.

Now sex was the least of her concerns. Keeping a roof over her head and Ethan's was what mattered most, and if that meant having to ignore her own needs, well, so be it. She'd been doing that for years, and would continue to do whatever it took to ensure her son's safety and security. Never again did she want to be in the boat she'd been in after her marriage imploded, when she'd been left in debt up to her eyeballs and mired in the kind of scandal that stuck to people forever.

If Paul had any idea who he'd been rolling around in bed with last night, he'd never come near her again, a thought that profoundly depressed her because she hadn't done anything other than marry the wrong man. Unfortunately, she hadn't known he was the wrong man until permanent damage had been done to her and Ethan.

Protecting Ethan from any further hurt was at the top of her list of priorities. The next time she was tempted to get busy with her boss, it would do her good to remember that. Armed with resolve and determination to get things back to normal, she called the mother of Ethan's friend to check on him, heard he was having a great time and was told to enjoy a day "off" while the other woman took the boys to the beach. Hope was delighted to hear Ethan was having fun with his new friend, but her day stretched out before her, long and lonely without him around to entertain her.

Reminding herself once again about what was not going to happen with her sexy boss, she crossed the yard to the family's back porch and stepped inside to fulfill her promise to get Marion up and dressed for the day.

Paul was standing in the kitchen, shirtless, eating a bowl of cereal.

One look at his muscular chest and well-defined abs and Hope's resolve evaporated. She wanted to touch him and kiss him and do so many other things with him that she hadn't done in far too long. She averted her gaze and headed for Marion's room, knocking softly before she stepped inside.

"Good morning, Marion."

As she did every day, Marion eyed Hope warily. "Who are you? Where's George?"

"George has gone off to work, but he asked me to help you get up and showered."

"I don't need help showering. How dare you be so impertinent?"

Impertinent was one of Marion's favorite words, and Hope had grown used to hearing about her impertinence daily. "Let's get you up and about."

"Who are you? What're you doing here? Where's George?"

Marion's confusion was far worse at the beginning and end of each day. As she did every day, Hope replied to the same question a hundred times without ever losing her patience. Dementia patients didn't mean it when they were insulting or demeaning or just downright nasty. That was the disease talking, not the perfectly nice people they'd been before dementia struck.

From all accounts, Marion had once been an absolute doll, devoted to her husband and sons and the business they all ran together. Every so often, Hope caught a glimpse of that woman, never more so than when she interacted with Ethan. For whatever reason, the two of them had bonded, and Marion was never nasty to him.

After her marriage ended, Hope had begun keeping a gratitude journal. Marion's kindness to Ethan had made the list many a time.

"Can I help?" Paul asked from the doorway.

Hope turned to him, relieved that he'd put on a shirt. Speaking of gratitude… "I got it."

"Are you sure? You're supposed to have a day free of us today."

"I'm sure, and I don't mind. We'll be out in a few minutes."

"George, tell this woman I don't want her in my bedroom. This is my private space, and she's not welcome here."

"It's okay, Mom. Hope is just trying to help. Be nice to her."

Hope sent him a grateful smile before returning her attention to Marion, despondent to realize that the sound of his voice and his offer of support had her entire body tingling once again with awareness of him. Ugh!

*

The day that had begun with bright sunshine turned cloudy and stormy around noon. With his mother out for the afternoon with her devoted friends from church, Paul found himself with an unusual break in the manic action that made up his life. So naturally, he wandered out to the retail store, which closed at noon on Sundays, to do some much-needed paperwork and updating of the accounting software.

He was halfway across the yard when the heavens opened, leaving him completely drenched by the time he reached the wooden building that housed the store. Rain in September was a cold rain that had him shivering. Inside the store, he pulled off his shirt, hung it up to dry and found an old towel in the office that he used to wipe his face.

Paul was waiting for the computer to boot up when he heard a clattering noise from the store. With the towel slung around his neck, he got up to investigate and found Hope, soaking wet and shivering, inside the door he'd left unlocked.

She startled when he appeared out of the office. "Oh. Sorry. I was out for a walk, and it started to rain. I didn't know you were here. I'll just head up to the house."

"It's monsooning out there." He handed her the towel. "You can wait it out here."

Hope took the towel from him. "Thanks." She wiped her face, but her teeth continued to chatter since her shirt was soaked through.

"I might have an extra shirt here somewhere," he said. "I can go look."

"That's okay." She unbuttoned the wet denim shirt and took it off, revealing a form-fitting tank.

He knew he shouldn't take a long greedy look at the wet T-shirt that did nothing to hide her nipples, but he couldn't seem to get that message to his eyes. "How did you manage to keep your hair from getting wet?"

She put her arms up over her head, giving him a spectacular view of her breasts.

Paul took three steps toward her, closing the distance between them.

Hope dropped her arms to her sides, bit her lip and shook her head. "Don't."

He put his hands on her shoulders and slid them down over the soft skin of her arms, noting her shiver and wondering if it was from the cold or his touch. "Why not?"

"I can't. We can't do this."

"We're already doing it. It's happening. Tell me I'm not the only one who feels it."

"You're not, but—"

Because he didn't want to know how that sentence was going to end, he kissed her. For the first second or two, he waited for her to push him away. If she did that, he would respect her wishes. But she didn't push him away. No, she pulled him closer and opened her mouth to his tongue. If possible, this kiss was even hotter than the ones they'd shared last night, and those had been pretty damned hot.

He'd thought about little else since she ran away this morning, leaving him with so many unanswered questions. Paul wasn't thinking about the questions now or all the reasons this could be the worst thing for both of them. When she was in his arms, kissing him back with enthusiastic strokes of her tongue, it felt like the best thing that'd ever happened to him.

His hands slid down her back to cup her bottom. He lifted her up and into his arms. She gasped in surprise, but then recovered, wrapping her arms and legs around him. Good God... He loved the way she responded to him and couldn't get enough of her sweet mouth or the sexy strokes of her tongue. They needed a wall or a flat surface, something that would allow him to get as close to her as he could.

Paul started walking them toward the office, knocking a glass vase off a shelf that shattered on the floor. He kept moving, ignoring the crash, the broken glass and everything that wasn't about Hope, warm and soft and pliant in his arms.

Then she broke the kiss. "I can't, Paul. I can't. I *can't*."

"Why?" he asked, kissing her neck. "*Why?*"

She arched her neck to give him better access and tightened her arms around his neck. "I… I just… Paul."

"Hmm?"

"I can't."

The finality of her statement had him drawing back from her, reluctantly and painfully. She slid down the front of him, rubbing against his erection on the way. It was all he could do not to whimper from the desire that beat through him like a live wire.

"You tell me you can't, but you kiss me like you want to."

"I'm sorry." Her hand trembled ever so slightly as she smoothed the hair off her face. "I don't mean to send you mixed messages."

"Which message do you mean to send?"

"I like you. You're a really great guy."

"But?"

"I can't do this."

"You haven't said why."

"You *know* why."

"I told you this, between us, will never impact your job. I gave you my word, and that means something."

She bent her head and leaned it against his chest. "I know it does, and it's not because I don't *want* to pursue this with you. It's just… I can't."

Though he could see and feel her inner torment, he dropped his hands from her shoulders and took a step back, which was the last thing he wanted to do. What he really wanted was to wrap his arms around her and hold her until she conceded that what was happening between them was a good thing. But until he understood more about her inner torment, he didn't know where to start with convincing her.

"I'm sorry, Paul."

"Me, too. I didn't mean to push you."

"You didn't. Everything that happened was because we both wanted it."

"I wish..." Paul thought better of what he was going to say and shook his head. "Never mind."

She didn't ask him what he wished for, probably because she already knew. Hope turned away from him and walked around the broken glass on the floor to get the shirt she'd taken off. The rain continued to come down hard outside, beating against the tin roof on the building in a steady rhythm.

"You can wait out the storm here if you want to."

"That's okay. I have stuff to do at my place. I'll see you later." She was out the door before he could say anything.

Paul blew out an unsteady deep breath. He reached for a broom and dustpan and cleaned up the broken glass. The shards of glass were a fitting metaphor for how he felt at the moment. Shattered. To have had something so amazing yanked away when they hadn't had the chance to see what might be possible was nothing less than devastating.

He wasn't a man who couldn't take no for an answer. She'd left him with no choice but to accept her wishes. As he dumped the broken glass into a trashcan, he decided he wasn't going to let himself descend into self-pity. Before the flirtation, or whatever it had been with her, he'd been determined to start dating again, so that was what he would do.

Withdrawing his cell phone from his pocket, he went through his list of contacts, determined to make this call before he lost his nerve or gave in to the urge to descend into misery over what he couldn't have. Hope was an amazing woman, and he wished that things could be different. But with reality staring him in the face, he pressed send to make his call.

"Hello?"

"Oh, hey, Chloe, it's Paul Martinez."

"Hi, Paul, how're you?"

"Doing good. You?"

"Better now that the summer is over and things are back to normal around here."

"I hear that." *Do it, Paul. Ask her.* "Listen, I was wondering if you might want to meet for a drink later. If you're not busy."

In the long pause that followed, he tried to remember the last time he'd asked out a woman.

"Um, sure. That would be fun. Where do you want to meet?"

"The Beachcomber at eight?"

"Great. I'll see you then."

"See you then." Relieved, he put the phone back in his pocket and went into the office to get back to the work he'd been about to do when Hope showed up. He'd been fine before her, and he'd be fine after. He wasn't about to beg her or talk her into spending time with him. He'd tried and failed to get past whatever was stopping her from pursuing a relationship with him.

It was time to move on.

CHAPTER 9

Hope ran through the rain, past the house to her cabin, where she shed her clothes inside the door and headed for the shower. Her teeth were chattering and her heart was breaking. The warm shower would fix at least one of those things. The other one would take a while.

Standing under the warm water, she finally released the deep breath she'd been holding since she'd bolted from the store, leaving Paul bewildered by her behavior.

A sob escaped through her clenched jaw, and she slid down the shower wall to sit on the floor. This kind of pain reminded her far too much of how she'd felt after everything happened with Carl. At the time, she'd promised herself that she'd never again risk so much for any man. And here she was, on the verge of risking it all once more.

The stakes were too high. She couldn't afford to gamble her sanity and Ethan's well-being, no matter how great Paul was or how wonderful she'd felt in his arms. It didn't matter that his kisses set her on fire or that she wanted so much more than the little bit they'd had. None of that mattered as much as Ethan did. Under no circumstances could she put him through another ordeal like the one they'd both suffered through at the hands of his father.

She wouldn't survive another situation like that, and what would happen to Ethan if she fell apart? Hope liked to think of herself as a fairly pragmatic person. Life had taught her to put away girlish dreams of happily ever after and true love to focus on reality. And her reality right now was Ethan and providing a stable home for him. To do that, she had to keep her life free of drama. She had to avoid what one of her friends from home had referred to as "self-inflicted" wounds.

So what if it felt great to be held and kissed and caressed by a sexy, desirable, *nice* man. Carl had been all of those things at first, too. Until he wasn't any of them anymore, and she'd been the last to know. All men were lovely until they got what they wanted, and then their true colors came through.

Except, a tiny voice inside her said, *Paul is always amazing with his mom*. She'd never seen him be anything other than patient and kind and tolerant of the many inconveniences Marion's illness brought to his life. Didn't that say something about who he really was?

When the water began to grow cold, Hope stood to shut it off. She dried herself and put on her warmest robe. Then she went into the kitchen to put a kettle on to boil, hoping a cup of tea would have its usual calming effect. Her nerves were stretched to their limit, the way they'd been for one awful, devastating summer two years ago when her whole life fell apart in spectacular, embarrassing fashion.

Ethan had been old enough to know something awful was happening, but too young to understand the nuances, for which she was grateful. That she was even revisiting that horror was a sign that she'd done the right thing backing off with Paul. But if that were true, why did she ache so badly inside?

Was she doomed to be alone forever because she was too scared to take a chance with someone new? Wow, talk about depressing thoughts. The slam of the screen door jarred her out of those thoughts as Ethan came bounding in, dropping his overnight bag on the floor and kicking off his sneakers.

"What's for dinner, Mom?"

"Hello to you, too. Don't I even get a hug?"

He gave her the fastest hug in the history of fast hugs and pulled back. "Why are you wearing a robe in the afternoon?"

"I got stuck in the rain, so I took a shower to warm up."

"We got stuck, too! We had to run off the beach, but it was so fun. Can Jonah sleep over here next weekend? Can he?"

"Sure."

"He's my best friend in the whole world. Well, other than Paul. He's my bestest friend ever. I wanna go see him and Mrs. Marion."

Hearing him refer to Paul as his bestest friend ever brought tears to Hope's eyes.

Thankfully, Ethan was jamming his feet back into his sneakers and didn't notice her emotional reaction to his innocent, yet heartfelt, statement.

Hope grabbed him by the shoulders to stop him from shooting out the door. "Mrs. Marion is out with her friends, and Paul is at work."

"It's a Sunday! He doesn't work on *Sundays*, Mom." The disdainful tone was a sign of things to come in the teenage years.

"He's doing stuff in the office. Computer stuff."

"That's boring." The sneakers came flying off again, spilling sand he'd brought home from the beach onto the wood floor. "I'm going to watch *Star Wars*. What's for dinner? Can we have ziti?"

"Yeah, we can have ziti."

His smile lit up his face, reminding her what was most important in her life. Yes, it would be nice to pursue a relationship with Paul, but that wasn't where her attention needed to be right now. The squiggling boy who tried to resist her hugs and kisses was her whole world. She'd do whatever it took to protect him from any further hurt, even if it meant she had to hurt instead.

The rain cast a damper on Mac's plans for a Sunday afternoon cookout with his siblings, cousins, uncles and closest friends, forcing him to improvise with a makeshift tent over the grill on the deck. As he cooked chicken and ribs and hot dogs for the kids, he thought about the plan he wanted to run by his siblings, in particular.

Their parents would be married forty years in December, and he wanted to do something to commemorate the occasion, but he wasn't sure what exactly. He was hoping they would have some ideas. With his parents off-island for a weekend getaway in Boston, this had been the perfect time to bring the gang together to talk about them when there was no chance of getting caught.

He carried the meat in on a platter Maddie had given him and placed it on the counter, where she'd set out a buffet that the others had contributed to. "Come and get it!"

Mac loved having his siblings living nearby as well as their cousins Laura and Shane, who now lived on the island, and Finn and Riley, who had spent the summer and were sticking around for the fall. They hadn't made any promises about the winter, but Mac was hoping they'd stay. He could really use their help on the addition to Seamus and Carolina's home, for one thing. And he'd gotten the strangest call from Lizzie James earlier, who'd wanted to gauge his availability to convert the former island school into a nursing home of all things.

When everyone had a plate, Mac stood and cleared his throat. "The reason I invited you all here today—"

"Oh God, Mac," Janey said with a groan. "What now?"

"Hush up, brat, and I'll tell you. Mom and Dad's fortieth anniversary is coming up in December, and I think we ought to do something."

"That's a great idea," Grace said, earning a warm smile from Mac. "What did you have in mind?"

"I was hoping you all would have some ideas. I have no clue what we should do."

"We need a party," Grant said. "A big bash."

"We could do it at the restaurant," Grant's new wife, Stephanie, said. "We're open on weekends in the winter, but we could shut down on a Saturday night for a private party. I'll look at the calendar and give you some dates."

"That would be perfect," Mac said. "What does everyone else think?"

"I can't believe they've been married forty years," Frank said. "That makes me feel older than dirt."

"You are older than dirt, Dad," Laura said with a teasing smile.

"Gee, thanks a lot, hon."

"We know better, don't we?" Frank's girlfriend, Betsy, said to groans from Laura and Frank's son, Shane.

"So gross," Shane said.

Frank grinned at Betsy. "See why I love her?"

Mac's Uncle Kevin got up and walked over to the big windows that looked over the meadow behind the house. Normally, the view stretched all the way to the ocean in the distance, but today the low clouds hampered the visibility.

While the others hashed out ideas for the party, Mac went over to check on his uncle. "How you doing, Kev?"

"I'm good."

"Are you really?"

Kevin shrugged. "Just getting used to the fact that I'll never have a fortieth anniversary. Hell, I won't have a thirtieth either. Just missed."

"I'm sorry about you and Aunt Deb."

"Thanks. It's a bummer, but it is what it is."

"There's really no hope for reconciliation?"

"Nope. She's off enjoying her new romance with a younger guy of all things."

"Is it a mid-life crisis?"

"Could be. But what does it matter? She's gone."

Mac squeezed his uncle's shoulder. "I'm really sorry, Kev. And I'm sorry if I threw salt in the wound by bringing up my parents' anniversary in front of you."

"Don't be silly. Of course we need to celebrate them. They're the best couple we all know." He smiled at Mac. "Go on over there and figure out a plan. I'll be okay. It's just going to take some time to figure out what's next."

"Have you told Riley and Finn?"

"Yeah, we have, and they're taking it hard. They're angry with her, but I've tried to tell them this is between her and me, and there's no need to get pissed. But they don't see it that way."

"Hopefully, they'll work things out with her in time."

"We'll see."

"We're glad to have you here with us in the meantime."

"It's good to be here. It's been years since I took any real time off, so I was due, and where else would I rather be than here with all of you?"

"Mac," Evan said. "Get over here."

"Duty calls," Mac said. "They can't function without my leadership." He left Kevin laughing and returned to the dining room table, where the others were hashing out ideas.

"You ought to do a video of photos from all their years together," Mac's recently discovered half-sister, Mallory, suggested.

"That's a great idea," Janey said, "and that can be Adam's job."

"Sure, brat, sign me up," Adam said.

Janey stuck out her tongue at him. "Who else could do that?"

"No one," he said, grinning. "I'm all over it."

"The girls will handle decorations and the cake," Maddie said as the others nodded.

"Owen and I have got the music covered, in case you wondered," Evan said.

Sitting beside him, Owen smiled in agreement.

"Me and Francine will take care of gittin' 'em there," Big Mac's best friend, Ned Saunders, said. "We'll invite 'em out fer dinner."

"Perfect." Mac rubbed his hands together. "I love when my master plans come together so smoothly."

"So what exactly is *your* job in all of this?" his cousin Laura asked.

"It was my idea. What else do you want from me?"

The entire group howled and threw balled-up napkins at him.

Laughing, Mac batted them away. "I'm so underappreciated in this family."

"You're perfectly appreciated," Maddie said, tossing another napkin at him.

"I nominate Mac to pay for the whole thing," Janey said. "All in favor, say aye."

A loud chorus of aye votes had Mac groaning.

Mac's son, Thomas, ran over to him. "Dada, why they throwing stuff at you?"

Mac picked up the blond-haired toddler. "Because they're being silly."

Thomas wrapped his arms around Mac's neck. "I take care of you, Dada."

Sighing, Mac closed his eyes and squeezed the little boy. When he opened his eyes, he caught Maddie watching them with tears in hers.

"I can always count on you, buddy."

Thomas squirmed out of his embrace and scampered off to play with his cousin Ashleigh and his baby sister, Hailey.

Maddie reached for Mac's hand, and he curled his fingers around hers.

"So everyone is going to AM's bachelor party next weekend, right?" Evan asked, referring to Alex Martinez's high school nickname. Paul had been known as PM back then.

"Can't wait," Grant said to murmured agreement from the other guys.

"However shall we entertain Jenny while the guys are off partying?" Sydney asked with a mysterious grin.

"Gee, I have no idea what we should do," Maddie replied.

"They're up to something," Mac said.

"Do ya think?" Adam asked.

"You hired the male strippers, right?" Maddie asked Adam's fiancée, Abby.

"All set," Abby said. "They'll be on the five o'clock boat, and we'll bring them right to Syd's place."

"Wait just a second," Luke said. "Syd's place is *my* place, too, and I never signed off on strippers."

"It's okay, babe," Sydney said, patting Luke's arm. "I don't need your approval to have some friends over."

"They're not friends! They're strippers!"

"Who will be *very good* friends by the end of the evening," Stephanie said with a dirty grin.

"You're not partying with strippers," Grant said.

"Oh yes, I am, honey," Stephanie said, laughing at her husband's outrage as the other women egged her on.

"Maddie won't be there," Mac said.

"Grace won't be there either," Evan said.

"No Abby," Adam said.

"Laura is pregnant," Owen said.

"What the hell does that have to do with anything?" Laura asked him.

"It's indecent for pregnant women to party with strippers."

"Color me indecent, then," Sydney said. "Pregnant and partying with the boys."

"You are not," Luke said, glaring at his wife.

"Janey can't make it that night," Joe said.

"In your dreams," Janey shot back. "I wouldn't miss it for anything."

Mac noticed that Ned was laughing his ass off. "What the hell is so funny over there?"

"All ya fools thinkin' ya can tell yer ladies what to do." He dabbed at laughter tears. "Funniest thing I ever heard."

"What do you know about it?" Mac asked. "You're a newlywed. Us crusty veterans know how to manage our women."

More napkins and other items flew in Mac's direction.

"You're such a freaking blowhard," Janey said.

"No kidding," Maddie said. "I have a few ideas of how I can show him who's really in charge around here. I believe I'll begin his retraining program at bedtime tonight."

"Oh damn, dude," Adam said. "You're getting the deep freeze."

"I know a few ways to defrost her," Mac said.

"Better bring your blowtorch," Maddie said.

"I carry it with me everywhere I go."

"I'm going to puke," Janey said.

"So about the strippers," Evan said. "We're clear on how we feel about that, right?"

"Crystal clear, honey," Grace said with a smile for the other women. "We heard you loud and clear."

"They're going to do it anyway, aren't they?" Evan asked no one in particular.

"I believe they are," Grant said.

"Wait till you ladies see the guys Abby and I hired," Tiffany said with a wink. "They make the Chippendales look ugly."

"Wait till your husband hears you're hiring strippers while he's off protecting our fair island," Mac said to his sister-in-law.

"What can I say? The ladies consulted the expert, and I came through for them."

"Blaine will hit the roof when he hears about this," Mac said.

"I can't wait," Tiffany said. "I love when he gets stern with me." She shivered dramatically, making the others laugh.

"I was living such a nice quiet life in Nashville," Evan said, shaking his head. "What was I thinking moving home to be treated this way?"

"Awww, baby," Grace said. "No one has ever treated you better than I do."

"Most of the time, that's very true. Today? Not so much."

Grace covered her mouth but couldn't hide her laughter.

"It's very inappropriate of you to laugh in my face, my love."

"I'm so sorry."

"You are not!"

The laughter and joking continued until everyone began to leave when the kids started getting cranky. As they did every night, Mac and Maddie worked together to get their kids bathed and into bed. Stories were told, night-lights illuminated and kisses were given to sweet-smelling cheeks.

They left Thomas's room and propped the door open so they could hear him if he got up in the night.

Mac put the gate across the top of the stairs just in case Thomas went wandering. Exhausted after the long day and a little buzzed from the beer he'd consumed, Mac went into the bedroom, where Maddie was applying lotion to her arms as she sat up in bed. She wore one of the sexy silk nightgowns he bought her for every occasion. They were more for him than her because he loved how she looked in them.

He took a quick shower, shaved the stubble off his face and emerged from the bathroom to a dark bedroom, which was unusual. Maddie usually waited for him to come to bed before turning off the light. The sheets were cool against his naked skin, but he found the heat when he curled up to her.

"Nice time tonight, hon. Thanks for letting the family invade."

"Mmm, it was fun."

He slid his hand from her flat belly to the valley between her spectacular breasts. The rest of his body reacted predictably to her closeness, her scent, her sexy curves. Mac pressed his erection against her ass and kissed the back of her shoulder.

A soft snore from his wife was like a bucket of cold water on his plans. "Maddie," he said softly. Cupping her breast, he ran his thumb over her nipple until it stood up.

Her breathing changed before she turned over, dislodging his hand and nearly unmanning him with her knee.

"Oh, sorry," she murmured sleepily. "Did I hurt your blowtorch?"

"Oh my God! You were *faking*?"

She began to laugh and couldn't stop. "You've got some defrosting to do, Mr. McCarthy. I can't make it too easy on you."

With his hand on her ass, he tugged her in tight against him. "I know how to defrost you, Mrs. McCarthy."

"You really are an awful blowhard, Mac."

"You can blow me hard any time you want."

She slapped his shoulder but rocked with silent laughter. "It's a good thing I love you so much, or I'd have to do something about your out-of-control ego."

"My ego is very healthy, thank you very much. And you're not going anywhere near male strippers, you hear me?"

"What was that you said? I can't hear from all the noise your blowtorch is making as it tries to thaw me out."

Growling, he turned her onto her back and settled into the V of her legs, one of his favorite places to be. The nightgown was now hitched up around her hips, and he was delighted to realize his lovely wife hadn't worn panties to bed. How convenient for the kind of defrosting he had in mind. "You're very sassy these days, my love."

"You like me that way."

He kissed her sweet lips. "I like you every way, but I don't want you going near those strippers."

"Mac?"

"What?"

"Shut up and make love to me before I change my mind about forgiving you."

Never one to have to be told twice, Mac did as directed, entering her in one smooth stroke that took his breath away. God, he loved her. He loved being inside her. He loved laughing with her and raising their beautiful kids with her. He loved every minute he spent with her, even when she was pushing his buttons, which was most of the time.

"No strippers near my gorgeous wife," he whispered.

She responded by tightening her internal muscles and nearly finishing him off.

"That was dirty."

"I can fight dirty when need be."

"As long as you're only fighting dirty with me, that's fine."

Running her hands down his back, she grasped his ass and squeezed.

He captured her mouth in a ravenous kiss. She made him crazy every time she touched him. Hell, she made him crazy every time she walked into a room and looked at him with those golden eyes. The thought of her looking at—or, God forbid, *touching*—any other guy made him positively feral.

When he was fully seated inside her, he said, "I'm not letting you come until you promise me you won't even look at those strippers."

She shocked the shit out of him when she ran her hand down the front of her body to tease her clit, brushing up against his cock in the process.

He could feel her smile against his lips.

"Damn it, Madeline. You're making me mad."

"Seems to me I'm making you harder."

"That, too."

She laughed, and he couldn't help but smile at how cute she could be—even when pushing buttons.

"Your sister is right about you."

"What does that mean?" he asked indignantly.

"You're a bossy pain in the ass."

He slid his hands under her and pinched her butt. "This family would fall apart without my steadfast leadership."

"You've really sold yourself a bill of goods, haven't you?"

"I only speak the truth, babe." Because he did, in fact, know just what it took to push *her* buttons, he picked up the pace, thrusting into her repeatedly until her body was quivering beneath him and her legs were wrapped around his waist. Then he went for broke and felt her orgasm hit. Bending his head, he bit down on her nipple, making her cry out as she continued to come. Satisfied that she was satisfied, Mac let himself go, too, giving in to the pounding need that she inspired in him every damned time he touched her.

Spent, he collapsed on top of her and loved the way her arms came around him, how her fingers slid through his still-damp hair.

"We didn't use anything," she said softly.

"I know."

"Are we really doing this?"

He pressed his hips against hers. "I believe we already did."

"You know what I mean, Mac."

"Yeah, baby," he said, kissing her. "I know what you mean, and I hope we made another little person who looks just like you."

"Because God forbid he's anything like you."

Chuckling softly, he kissed her again before withdrawing from her.

She took hold of his hand to keep him from getting out of bed. "You know I'm joking, don't you? I want Thomas and any other son we might have to be just like you."

"Even if I'm a pompous blowhard?"

"You're both of those things, but you're also loyal and faithful and strong and loving and sexy. Very, *very* sexy."

Touched by her kind words, he leaned in to kiss her one more time. "Don't forget funny."

Laughing, she said, "That, too, although I hesitate to laugh at your outrageousness because that might encourage you."

"I'm easily encouraged by you." He cleaned up in the bathroom and brought a towel to the bed to clean her up, too. Then he crawled back into bed with her, wrapping his arms around her. "I might be a pompous blowhard, but I'd be lost without you. You're the one who makes it all happen."

"We make it happen together."

"You think we'll be celebrating our fortieth anniversary someday?" he asked.

"I know we will. I have no doubt whatsoever."

With her warm and snug in his arms and her promises of forever together to lull him, Mac closed his eyes and let sleep take him.

CHAPTER 10

Though he was exhausted from pushing himself to get things done all day, Paul couldn't sleep. All he could think about was kissing Hope in the store and how it had felt to hold her and kiss her and touch her. He wanted so much more than the little taste he'd had of her.

His body vibrated with tension and arousal as the erotic memories refused to leave him in peace. Groaning, he turned over onto his belly, his throbbing erection wedged between his body and the mattress. He hadn't suffered like this over a woman since he'd been a horny teenager lusting after Leslie Donald, who'd never given him the time of day.

Chloe had called to cancel their plans because her mother wasn't feeling well and needed her help. It had sounded like an excuse to Paul, but he'd been gracious about it. She'd promised to call him, and he didn't plan to hold his breath to see if it happened. His indifference led to the realization that he had no business going out with another woman when he was totally hung up on Hope.

A thump from the room next door caught his attention. It was closely followed by a low giggle and another pronounced thump.

"Fucking hell," Paul muttered, pulling a spare pillow over his head so he didn't have to listen to his brother having sex while he was dying a slow miserable lust-infused death alone in the next room. The pillow nearly suffocated him, so he came out for air to more thumping and giggling. Oddly enough, Jenny wasn't a giggler in the rest of her life. Apparently, his brother's sexual prowess brought out her inner giggler, which was information Paul wished he didn't have about the woman who would soon be his sister-in-law.

Pissed off, frustrated and exhausted, he got out of bed and headed for the kitchen to get a beer. Anything was better than listening to the happy lovebirds go at it. He took the beer out on the back deck to get some air, hoping maybe they'd be done by the time he went back inside. Although, knowing them far better than he'd ever wanted to, they'd probably be on to round two by then.

Paul sat on the back stairs and looked up at the stars. Wearing only a pair of boxer briefs, he let the cool air wash over his heated skin. His thoughts wandered back to his plans to get back to dating.

If it wasn't going to happen with Hope and if Chloe was giving him the polite brush-off, there were plenty of other women on Gansett Island who might be into having some fun with a reasonably good-looking guy who made a decent living and took good care of his mother. That was an attractive quality, wasn't it?

Jesus, was he really so desperate that he was preparing to use his mother's dementia to get laid? He ran his fingers through his hair, the frustration pounding through him like a drumbeat. Sadly, he didn't want any of those many other women. He wanted Hope, but he couldn't have her.

A sound from across the yard had him going still, hoping he might hear it again. There it was again, and it sounded like a sniffle. Paul put down his beer bottle and was walking across the small strip of yard between the main house and Hope's cabin before he could think of all the reasons why he shouldn't.

"Hope."

"Go home, Paul."

"You're upset."

"It's not your problem," she said, her voice catching on a sob that brought him closer to her.

"I thought we said we were friends, if nothing else."

"We are, but—"

"No buts. Friends are there for each other when they're needed." He took the steps to her porch and followed the sound of her sobs to the small wicker sofa, then sat next to her. "What's wrong? It's not Ethan, is it?"

"No, he's fine."

"Then what?" He put his arm around her.

"Dear God, what're you wearing?"

"Not much of anything."

"You shouldn't be here, especially when you're mostly naked."

"I can't stand that you're upset. Is it because of me?"

She wiped her face but didn't reply.

"I'm sorry. I'll go."

"Don't," she said softly—so softly he almost didn't hear her.

Emboldened by her invitation to stay, he drew her in closer until her head rested against his bare chest and her hand lay flat against his stomach, inches above the proof of how badly he wanted her. And it was *her* he wanted. Not just any woman, but *this* woman who'd tied him up in knots for weeks now, if he were being honest with himself.

"What's wrong, honey?"

"Everything is wrong."

"That can't possibly be true."

"If I told you what's wrong, you'd want nothing to do with me or Ethan."

"I can't imagine wanting nothing to do with you or Ethan. I care about both of you. We all do. You're part of the Martinez family now."

That only made her cry harder.

Her despair made Paul feel helpless. He ran his hand over her back, wishing there was something he could do to comfort her. She was always so strong and capable, even when his mother was being mean to her. To see her reduced to tears was painful for him.

"Talk to me. Tell me what has you so upset. I want to help if I can."

"There's nothing you can do. There's nothing anyone can do."

Paul recalled what Ethan had told him about his father and tried to decide whether he should tell Hope what he knew. Would that make things worse or would it make it easier for her to talk about what had upset her? Since it didn't seem possible to make things worse, he decided to put it out there before he lost his nerve.

"Ethan told me about his dad."

She gasped and raised her head off his chest. "What did he tell you?"

"That he's in jail."

"How long have you known that?"

"A couple of days."

"And you didn't say anything?"

"It's none of my business."

She covered her mouth with her hand, and in the faint light of the moon, he could see her shaking her head. Her hand dropped to her lap. "How can you say that? I kept it from you and Alex when you hired me—"

"You have no criminal record, Hope. We checked. Whatever he did, I assume it had nothing to do with you."

"Oh, it had everything to do with me."

Paul's stomach knotted with tension. "Are you going to tell me what you mean by that?"

"Could we go inside? It's getting cold out here."

Paul was practically naked, but he wasn't cold at all. However, he noticed she was trembling. He doubted that had anything to do with the temperature. As he got up to go inside, he was thankful she hadn't sent him away.

He followed her inside to the sofa, sat next to her and pulled a throw blanket over her. It took all the fortitude he could muster not to press her to talk about things that obviously caused her pain. If she wanted to tell him, he would happily hear her out, but he was not about to push her.

"Carl and I met when we were in college," she said with a deep sigh that told him how hard it was for her to talk about this. "I was studying nursing, and he majored in sports medicine. He was so different from the other guys I'd dated. He was serious and focused and determined to make something of himself. We got married right out of college and had Ethan a year later. We tried to have other kids, but it never happened. I guess that turned out to be a blessing in the end."

Paul had so many questions that he didn't ask, hoping she would keep talking.

"He got a great job working for a college outside of Boston, and he coached girls' lacrosse at our local high school. I worked for a memory care facility at night, so I was home with Ethan during the day."

Paul wanted to ask when she slept, but he didn't want to interrupt her.

"It was a busy life, but a nice one. We had a lovely home south of Boston. We had good friends and family close by. We weren't rich, by any means, but we had enough left over to take a couple of vacations every year. And I was happy with him. A lot of my friends were bitter toward their husbands, always complaining about this or that, but not me. I was in love with my husband."

New tears slid down her cheeks, and Paul brushed them away.

"I was at work when the police came. They said something about Carl, and I immediately thought he was dead. Why else would they come to find me at work? But he wasn't dead. He'd been arrested for having sex with one of the girls on the lacrosse team."

Paul sucked in a sharp deep breath.

"She was fifteen, and when her parents found out, they called the police. They came to me to find out what I knew, which was nothing. I was so shocked, I couldn't speak or breathe or function. I ended up in the hospital for a night because I apparently had a panic attack. I couldn't believe it. I thought there had to be some mistake. *My* Carl would never do something like that."

Paul's mind raced with thoughts and questions and rage for what the man she'd loved had put her through.

"Then we found out that girl wasn't the only one. There were four of them in total. During his trial, I found out he'd had a vasectomy so he wouldn't get them pregnant. That's why we never had more kids."

"Dear God," Paul whispered.

"I can only imagine what you must be thinking."

"I'm only thinking about you and Ethan and what you must've endured. I'm thinking how sorry I am that you had to go through something so horrible and how terribly hurt you must've been by someone you trusted and loved."

A sob hiccupped through her as she took hold of his hand. "People were vicious. It didn't matter that Ethan and I had nothing to do with what Carl did. We were lumped into the same boat with him. I was asked to resign from my job because my situation was a 'distraction.' We lost our house when I couldn't make the mortgage payments, and Ethan's friends weren't allowed to play with him anymore."

"I'm so sorry, Hope."

She shrugged off his sympathy.

"I have to be honest with you. After we had some trouble with the former manager of the retail store, we investigate everyone we hire. None of this came up when we looked into you before we hired you."

"Russell is my maiden name. I legally changed my name and Ethan's after Carl was convicted."

"I can't say I blame you."

"I should've disclosed this—"

He squeezed her hand. "No. There was no need for you to do that. Your professional references were impeccable, and your background check was clean. You didn't owe us anything more than that."

"Really?"

"Really. Your business is your business, and it has no impact on the amazing way you take care of my mother."

"Alex might not agree."

"Yes, he will. He thinks you're amazing, too."

When her chin quivered, Paul cupped her cheek and ran his thumb over her chin. "Why were you crying earlier? What happened?"

She glanced up at him with a tremulous smile. "You happened."

"Me? I thought you said this wasn't going to work."

"I did, and I meant it because I'm still so messed up over everything with Carl. It wouldn't be fair to get involved with you—"

"Do you still love him?"

"No. God, no."

Paul didn't think. He acted, laying his lips over hers. For the longest time, he did nothing more than rub his lips against hers, hoping she was getting the message that even knowing what he now did, he still wanted her. In fact, if possible, he wanted her more after hearing what she'd survived.

Tears tumbled down her cheeks, but her hand wrapped around his wrist, holding him close rather than pushing him away.

"I'm scared," she said.

"Of what? You're not afraid of me, are you?"

She nodded.

"Hope… Why? I would never hurt you or Ethan. If I had you both in my life, I'd consider myself the luckiest guy in the world. Tell me why you're scared."

"I had no idea about Carl. I never even suspected. If I let myself go there again…"

"Carl was a bad guy. I'm not a bad guy. I'm not the best guy who ever lived, but I do the right thing most of the time. In fact, most of the men I know do, too."

"I want so badly to believe you."

"You *can* believe me. You can believe *in* me. I can't promise you that whatever this is between us will last forever, but I can guarantee that I'll never intentionally do anything to cause you or Ethan any more pain than you've already endured."

Closing her eyes, she leaned into the hand he still had on her face. "I love the way you make me feel, Paul. I never thought I'd ever feel that way again."

Paul kissed her, this time more insistently, sliding his tongue back and forth over her lips until they parted to allow him in. God, she was sweet and responsive and sexy. He was thankful that she'd told him about her past so he knew what he was dealing with.

Her arms encircled his neck as her tongue rubbed his, setting him on fire with desire. Instinct took over, leading him to arrange her under him without breaking the increasingly desperate kiss. The alignment of their bodies had his erection pressed against the heat of her core. He wanted to touch her there. He wanted to touch her everywhere. But more than anything, he wanted her to trust him, and that wasn't going to happen overnight.

So he softened the kiss and kept his hands firmly planted on the sofa on either side of her head.

The scrape of her fingernails over his scalp made him tremble.

"Why'd you stop?" she asked in a small voice.

"Same reason as last night. Because if I don't stop, I won't be able to."

She squirmed under him, and he had to bite his lip to keep from moaning.

"Paul…"

"We're going to the mainland on Tuesday. We'll have a day or two alone together. Between now and then, think about whether this is what you really want. And if you're in, you have to be all-in. Okay?"

"All or nothing?"

"We can't do this halfway, Hope. It wouldn't be fair to any of us, particularly Ethan."

"You're right. I know you are, but if we're going all-in, you need to talk to Alex about it."

"I will." Though it was literally painful to tear himself away from her, he pushed up and withdrew. He offered her a hand and helped her sit up, tucking her hair behind her ear. "Are you okay?"

"I'm better. Thank you for listening."

"I'm sorry for everything you went through, but that has nothing at all to do with us. Okay?"

"Okay," she said tentatively, letting him know it would take a while before she truly believed him.

That was fine. He had nothing but time that he was willing to give her until she realized he was nothing like the man who'd hurt her so badly. Paul kissed her one more time. "I'll go to the funeral with you in the morning. I don't want you to go through that alone"

"That's really nice of you. Thanks."

"You're going to figure out that you can count on me, Hope. I'll see you in the morning." He kissed her forehead and got up, forcing himself to walk away, to give her the time to decide if this was what she really wanted. And if she decided it wasn't? What then? Well, he'd have to accept it and move on, but at least he'd know why.

He took the steps to the back porch and went in through the screen door, stopping short at the sight of Alex, nude, standing in front of the open refrigerator, guzzling a bottle of seltzer water.

"What the hell?" Paul muttered, averting his gaze from his brother's naked rear end.

Alex closed the fridge, killing the light. "Sorry. Where you been?" When the light over the stove came on, Alex was, thankfully, leaning against the counter.

"Outside."

"In your underwear?"

"At least I'm wearing underwear."

"I thought you were asleep."

"It was a little too noisy around here to sleep."

"Oh, um…" Alex flashed a big dopey grin. "Sorry again?"

"Hate to say I'm getting used to it, but…"

"We're moving out next week."

"Thank God," Paul muttered.

"So you're just walking around the backyard in your underwear?"

Paul debated for a second before he said, "Not exactly. I was over at Hope's."

"Again I say in your underwear?"

"We… She and I…"

"Oh my God, Paul. *Seriously?* Since when?"

"I don't know yet if it's serious. It's new."

"You have to know I'd never begrudge you the chance to be happy, but if she quits, we'll be screwed."

"Why would she quit?"

"If it goes bad between you guys? Hello?"

"I've already told her that whatever happens between us will never affect her job."

"Paul… Dad would flip out."

"Dad's not here! You said that yourself just the other day. Or is the gospel according to Dad selectively applied?"

"I shouldn't have said that. I'm sorry. I'm just surprised by this news. I hadn't noticed…"

"You've been a little preoccupied lately."

"I don't want you to think I don't approve, because that's not the case. I like Hope and Ethan. They're great, and she's incredible with Mom. I'm only concerned about somehow messing that up when we need her so badly."

"I'm not going to mess it up. I won't let that happen." As he said the words, he hoped they were true.

"Good enough, then."

"That's it? That's all you're going to say?"

"If you were thinking I was going to be a dick about it, you'll be disappointed. You know what you're doing, and you know what's at stake for everyone. What else do you want me to say?"

"Nothing, I guess."

"I hope it works out. You deserve to be happy, Paul. I'd never stand in the way of that."

"You're right about one thing. Dad would flip out."

"Like you said, Dad's not here, and I can't believe he'd feel any differently than I do, especially after all you've sacrificed for this family over the last few years."

Alex's kind words left a lump in Paul's throat. "Thanks," he said gruffly. "I'm going to take a couple of hours in the morning to go to Lisa's funeral with Hope. Daisy is off tomorrow and coming to stay with Mom while Hope is gone."

"And you guys are still heading for the mainland on Tuesday?"

"That's the plan, but don't worry, I'll be back in plenty of time for the festivities on Saturday."

"*Great*," Alex said with a laugh. "Just remember—what goes around comes around, little brother. Someday it'll be your turn, and revenge is a bitch."

"I'll take my chances. I'm covering my eyes to give you a chance to get out of here without leaving me with images that can't be unseen."

"I'm gone. See you in the morning."

Paul kept his eyes covered until he heard Alex's bedroom door close. Then he dropped his hands, shut off the light and headed for bed, hoping the progress he'd made with Hope tonight wouldn't disappear in the morning.

CHAPTER 11

Still reeling from what he'd learned in the kitchen, Alex got back into bed with Jenny.

She slid into his arms. "What took so long?"

"Paul came in from the yard wearing only underwear. I had to get the scoop."

"Is there scoop?"

"Oh yeah. He was at Hope's."

"Wearing only underwear?"

"Yep."

"So does that mean... *Paul and Hope?*"

"Apparently."

"Wow, how did we miss that?"

Alex squeezed her sexy ass. "We've been a little busy."

She crawled on top of him and used his chest as a pillow.

Alex loved the way she fit so perfectly in his arms, as if she'd been made just for him.

"How do you feel about that? With her being an employee and all?"

"You're an employee," he said with a chuckle.

"I was your girlfriend before I was an employee."

"My dad had a thing about us dating employees."

"I remember you saying that before."

"I made the mistake of reminding Paul of that just now. I shouldn't have done that. I could tell he's already been wrestling with it himself."

"Your dad would be so proud of both of you. I feel like I've gotten to know him through you and Paul and your mom, so I can say that fairly confidently."

"God, I hope so. We loved him so much. We were scared of him, too, which I now know was part of his master plan to raise decent men."

"He did a great job at that."

"I'm glad you think so."

"*Everyone* thinks so. What you guys have done for your mom while keeping the business afloat is nothing short of heroic."

"I don't know about that. We did what anyone would do for their mother."

"That's not true, Alex. Lots of people would've put her in a home on the mainland and gone on with their lives. That would've been the easy thing to do."

"We never considered that."

"Which makes you two extraordinary, especially with a booming business to run, too."

"I've never felt it was extraordinary. It's what family does for family."

Jenny sighed and kissed his chest. "I can't wait to officially join the Martinez family."

"Are you starting to believe it's actually going to happen?"

"I'm getting there."

"I want you to relax and enjoy the next couple of weeks. There's nothing to worry about."

"Intellectually, I know that. Emotionally, however…"

"I know, baby. I can't wait to see you coming toward me on the arm of your dad so I can say, 'Told ya so. It's all good.'"

"I can't wait for you to say that."

"I want you to talk to me whenever you're worried or upset about anything. I never want you to struggle with something by yourself. You're not alone anymore. You'll never be alone again."

Jenny pushed herself up so she could reach his lips and kissed him. "That's the sweetest thing you've ever said."

He scowled at her. "I am *not* sweet."

"Yes, you are."

"You're turning me into a regular pussy."

She slapped his chest. "Don't say that word! I hate it."

"What word? Regular?"

"You know what word."

He knew exactly what word and said it and others she hated regularly because she was so damned cute when she got pissed with him. "You're going to have to tell me, because I'm not sure which word you're talking about."

"Knock it off. Quit trying to get me to say things I never say."

"You can do it. Come on… Just say it."

"I won't."

"I can make you."

"I'd like to see you try."

He shuddered dramatically. "I get so hot when you go all Southern belle on me."

Rolling her eyes, she said, "Whatever. As far as I can tell, you're hot all the time."

"I'm hot for *you* all the time."

"Even now?" she asked, moving on top of him with deliberate purpose.

"Mmm, especially now." His hands moved from her hips to her breasts. After so many months together, he knew just what it took to turn her on, and he loved knowing her secrets.

She had a few tricks of her own, however, and when she took him inside her, he forgot all about his tricks to focus on hers. And hers were something to behold as her hips swiveled and her breasts bounced. He freaking loved the way she looked on top of him, uninhibited, focused on her pleasure, which always led to his, too. At times like this, when he had her all to himself, he wondered how he'd managed to get so lucky. Alex sat up and drew her nipple into his mouth, making her gasp as her back arched in response to him.

At the same time, he reached between them, pressing his fingers to her clit and then immediately removing them, which made her moan. "Say the word I want to hear, and I'll make you come."

"I'm not saying it."

He continued to tease her with light touches of his fingers over her clit, backing off each time.

"That's so mean."

"Talk dirty to me, baby. You can do it. Tell me what word you hate."

She put her lips against his ear and in a husky whisper, she said, "Pussy."

"Ahh, fuck, that's so hot." He returned his fingers to her clit, bit down on her nipple and felt her detonate, which finished him off, too. "Jenny, God…"

She mumbled something, and if he heard her correctly, she'd said he was the devil. He liked that.

Keeping his arms around her, he reclined against the pillows, still embedded deep within her as she pulsed with aftershocks. This, right here, was the closest thing to heaven he'd ever experienced, and he couldn't wait to be married to her.

"Love you so much, Alex, even when you're making me say terrible words I've never said in my life. I wish you knew how much I love you."

"I do know, and I love you just as much, especially when you talk dirty to me. I bet I love you more than you love me."

"No way."

"Mmm, yes way." He smiled in the darkness, content and looking forward to everything they had ahead of them. Every time they made love, he hoped she would conceive. Fatherhood was another thing he couldn't wait for. When he'd been forced by circumstances to come home to Gansett Island, he'd never expected to find the love of his life here. Now that he had her, warm and soft in his arms, he planned to spend every day of the rest of his life making sure she knew how much she meant to him.

*

A light knock on the door had Seamus rushing from the living room where he'd been watching late-night TV. He threw open the door to his friend Slim Jackson, who held up a bag.

"I've got the goods, my friend."

"Come in." Seamus stepped aside to admit Slim and then went to the fridge to grab a beer for the pilot. "How'd you make out?"

"It was easy enough."

"Caro and I really appreciate this."

"I'm happy to help. No way you're going to find suits for little boys on this island."

Seamus opened the bag to find two identical tiny navy blue suits, white dress shirts, clip-on ties and shoes. He was appalled when tears filled his eyes. The clothes were a reminder of what those little boys would have to endure in the morning.

"You okay, bud?" Slim asked, clasping his shoulder.

"It's just..." Seamus blew out a deep breath. "You even got belts for them. I can't thank you enough."

"A man can't wear a suit without a belt."

Seamus appreciated his friend's efforts to bring some levity to the grim situation. "It's tough, you know? I hope I'm doing the right things, but I've got no fecking clue what the right things are in this situation."

"You're providing them with love and support and comfort. That's what they need right now."

Seamus ran a hand over the stubble on his jaw. "I suppose. But what if they need other things that I don't know about? What if I miss something important?"

"You remind me of my brother when his first kid was born. The poor guy was beside himself. He was afraid to hold the little princess out of fear he might break her or something."

"I felt that way the first time I held PJ."

"You're going through what all new dads experience. It's perfectly normal. And the plus side is if the little guys need something, they're old enough to tell you."

"That's true."

"I know it seems overwhelming right now, but it's going to be fine. They're damned lucky to have you and Carolina to look out for them."

"We're the lucky ones, mate," Seamus said softly. "My heart breaks for what they've endured, losing their mum the way they did, but on the other side, I'm so damned thankful to have them in my life. Makes me feel selfish to even say that."

"You're not selfish, Seamus. You're the opposite of selfish. Look at what you're doing for those kids. I heard you're even adding on to the house for them."

"That has to be done. They're squeezed into that little room."

"That's about as self*less* as it gets, my friend."

"Thanks for the pep talk. I've been all over the place today."

"Today was a tough day. Tomorrow will be a tough day. The next couple of weeks are apt to be rough. But one day, not too far off from now, they'll begin to act like little boys again, and you and Carolina will be there to show them the way through it."

"Yes, we will."

Slim downed the last of his beer and put the bottle on the counter. "I'm going to let you get some sleep. I'll see you in the morning."

Seamus withdrew two one-hundred-dollar bills from his pocket and handed them to Slim. "You don't have to go to the funeral. I know how busy you are."

"I'll be there." He hugged Seamus and then put the money back in his hand. "The suits are on me because I want to do something to help them—and you. Hang in there."

Once again, Seamus found himself swallowing a lump in his throat. He was a disaster today. "Thanks, man." He saw his friend out the door, and after Slim drove off in his pickup truck, Seamus locked up for the night.

Carolina came into the kitchen, tying her robe around her waist. "Did I hear voices?"

"Slim was here to drop off the suits he bought on the mainland for the boys." Seamus pointed to the bag on the table.

Caro peered into the bag. "He even got belts."

"I said that, too, and he insisted on paying for everything because he wants to do something for them. We're lucky to have such great friends."

"Indeed we are. The boys are also lucky to have you to think of things such as suits at such a difficult time."

"They needed the right clothes to say good-bye to their mum."

Caro crossed the room and put her arms around him, laying her head on his chest. "I can tell you're all wound up."

"Can't help it."

"Come to bed. There's nothing more you can do for them tonight, and they're going to need us both tomorrow."

He let her lead him from the kitchen, shutting lights off as they went. In the bedroom, she pulled his T-shirt over his head and helped him out of his shorts. Despite the emotional day, her tender care had a predictable effect on him, and by the time he crawled into bed next to her, he was hard as concrete. Upon encountering the evidence of his arousal, his lovely wife giggled like a girl.

"Honestly," she said, "you are too much."

"I'm just enough. You say so all the time."

"Here I think I'm offering comfort because you're upset, and this is the thanks I get?" she asked, wrapping her soft hand around his hard cock.

"Can't help it, love. Even in the worst of times, if you strip me naked, that's going to happen." He stopped her hand from moving. "Doesn't mean we have to do anything about it."

"Who are you and what've you done with my husband who says a good boner is a terrible thing to waste?"

He snorted out a laugh. "I've corrupted you terribly, haven't I?"

"No, you've loved me perfectly. Now get over here and do some more of that."

Never one to say no to his gorgeous wife, Seamus happily obliged, settling on top of her.

She ran her fingers through his hair, which soothed and comforted him. "It's all going to be okay. I promise."

"Since you're always right, love, I suppose I need to listen to you."

She hooted with laughter. "Can I have that first part in writing?"

"Aye, you can," he said, kissing her softly. "You can have any damned thing you want from me, as you well know."

"All I want is for you to be happy."

"I'm so happy, love. That I get to sleep with you every night..." As he spoke, he slid into her, loving that she was always so ready for him. "I want to get the boys through this so they can be happy again, too."

"You will. *We* will."

Because she was, in fact, usually right, Seamus took comfort in her assurances, pushing away his worries to focus entirely on her. And there was nothing better than losing himself in her. He pushed her leg to her chest, opening her to his fierce possession. For a while, he'd worried about hurting her when he took her this way, but she loved it as much as he did. The bed creaked and the headboard struck the wall, but he paid no mind to anything other than the sweet relief that overtook him when he let himself go, surging into her as they climaxed, her fingernails scoring his back.

"We're going to have to be more quiet," he whispered, releasing her leg, which she curled around his hip.

"That'll be a challenge."

"Mmm, indeed." He nibbled on her earlobe.

"You have to stop trying to make me scream."

"Or I'll have to ask Mac about soundproof walls for the boys' new room. I like that idea better."

"Those poor boys have no idea what they're in for living with us."

"We'll show them how much we love each other."

"I'm fine with that, but I don't think they should *hear* how much we love each other."

Seamus chuckled softly. "You may be right about that, love."

"I thought we'd already established that I'm always right."

"Aye, I walked right into that trap." He withdrew from her and moved to lie next to her, reaching for her.

She curled up to him, her hand on his belly, her leg intertwined with his. "Try to get some sleep. It's going to be a long couple of days, and we need to be ready."

Seamus knew she was right about that, too, but he had no idea how to get ready to see the boys through this difficult time in their lives. He could only hope for the best.

CHAPTER 12

Slim left Seamus's house and took the long way around the island on the way to his home on the west side. He'd flown four round trips to the mainland that day, and on the last run had borrowed a car from a buddy at the airport in Westerly to do an errand for Seamus.

All day he'd thought of those poor little boys and the difficult road they had ahead of them as they came to terms with their unbearable loss. Seamus and Carolina had done an amazing thing by offering to take them, and Slim had no doubt that the boys were in good hands with them. But it wasn't going to be easy for any of them to make this transition to being a family.

A year ago, Seamus had been a happy single guy. In fact, they'd bonded over beers at the Beachcomber, toasting to their freedom. And now he was married and an instant father to two boys. Life was funny that way. *Better him than me*, Slim thought as he took a hairpin curve and slammed on his brakes when he saw a woman in the road.

What the hell? He shifted the truck into park, turned on his hazard lights, released his seat belt and got out to investigate.

"Who's there?" she asked warily, standing outside the glow of his headlights.

"Slim Jackson."

"Oh, Slim, thank goodness it's you. It's me, Erin, from the lighthouse."

They'd met over the summer at a gathering at the Tiki Bar. Her shoulder-length light brown hair framed her pretty face as she looked at him with sparkling brown eyes. "What the devil are you doing out here in the dark of night?"

"I was riding my bike home from town when I got a flat tire. I was walking the bike home when I stepped into a hole and sprained my ankle. At least I hope it's only sprained. I can't tell."

"How long have you been out here?"

"More than an hour now, and you're the first one to come along."

"You could've called for help."

"My phone died about five minutes after my tire went flat. It's been a series of unfortunate events."

"I guess so. How can I help?"

"Would you mind giving me and my bike a ride to the lighthouse?"

"Of course. No problem. Are you okay to stand without the bike to lean on?"

"I can hop."

"Stay right there. I'll grab the bike and then come back for you." He waited for her to get her balance and then stashed the bike in the back of his truck before returning quickly to her side. "Hang on to me."

She put an arm around his waist, and he put one around her shoulders. Working together, they shuffled over to his truck. Placing his hands on her hips, he easily lifted her into the passenger side of his truck.

"This is way above and beyond the call of duty," she said with a wry smile when he had her settled. "You're going to throw your back out hauling me around."

"Nah, you're light as air."

She snorted with laughter. "Sure, I am."

He took a closer look at her ankle, which was hugely swollen and beginning to bruise. "How's the pain?"

"It doesn't feel great, but I'm very thankful that I don't have to hobble home."

The lighthouse was only a mile away, but that would've been a long mile on a badly sprained ankle. It took a few minutes to drive there, and when they arrived, he noticed the gate was locked. "Do you have the key?"

"It's a combination," she said, giving him the numbers.

"Got it. Be right back." Slim opened the gate, returned to the truck to drive through and then went to close it again, leaving the lock propped open so he could get out. "It's awful dark out here at night."

"The floodlights by the door will come on when we get closer."

"You ever get scared out here all by yourself?"

"The first week, I slept with the lights on," she confessed. "But you get used to it."

"I don't know if I would."

"Are you scared of the dark, Slim?"

"You'll never get me to admit that." Opening the door to get out, he discovered he quite enjoyed the sound of her laughter. With her hair up in a ponytail and her face devoid of makeup, she was refreshingly pretty. Slim appreciated women who didn't feel the need to fall into a vat of makeup. He'd always preferred the natural look, which he'd liked about Erin the first time he met her. At the time, he'd meant to ask Alex about her, but he'd never gotten around to it. He was glad to have been given a second chance to get to know her.

Slim opened the passenger door. "How about a lift inside?"

"I think I can walk."

"You probably shouldn't put any weight on it until you're sure it's not broken. You don't want to make a bad situation worse."

"I suppose you're right."

"It's certainly no hardship for me to give you a lift," he said with a smile and a wink that brought a flush of color to her cheeks. Oh, he liked that. He liked it a lot. "Shall we?"

"Sure, thanks."

He slid his arms under her legs and behind her shoulders, lifting her effortlessly from the cab.

Her arms came around his shoulders. "This is mortifying."

"How come?"

"You barely know me and you're carrying me around."

"I'm helping a damsel in distress and hoping that maybe she'll reward me for my troubles by letting me take her to dinner when she's feeling better."

"Is 'she' in this damsel-in-distress scenario of yours supposed to be me?"

"Pretty *and* smart. That's a very attractive combination. So what do you say? Will you thank me for carrying you around by having dinner with me sometime soon?"

"I'll have to see how you manage the spiral staircase before I decide anything. I mean, if my head is bouncing off the wall or my injured ankle smacks against the railing, you won't seem quite so heroic to me."

"Oh wow, you have so little faith. I'll have you know that I'm an expert at carrying damsels in distress."

"Where did you get all this expertise?"

Slim started up the winding staircase and discovered it was rather narrow. He was careful to navigate the twisting turns so no part of her smacked anything. "I come from a long line of circus performers. We're known for our agility and ability to transport damsels of all kinds, whether they're in distress or not."

She shook with laughter. "Circus performers, huh?"

"Uh-huh. Wow, this is so cool," he said when they arrived in a combined kitchen and living room, which was circular and had a three-hundred-sixty-degree view of the island. He set her carefully on the sofa. "Where do you keep your first aid kit?"

"Under the sink."

He went to retrieve it and grabbed a bag of frozen corn from the freezer.

"What's that for?" she asked about the corn.

"It makes for an excellent ice pack." Slim untied her running shoe and removed it and then the ankle-high sock, revealing her injured ankle, which was even more swollen and purple than it had been a few minutes ago. "Ouch. That's gotta hurt."

"It does. I feel so stupid. I went to the movies and figured I'd have plenty of time to get home before it got dark, but the projector was acting up, so the movie started half an hour late and then the movie ran long. It was dumb to be out there by myself in the dark."

He opened the first aid kit, found an Ace bandage and began wrapping it around her ankle.

"I can do that," she said. "You were on your way somewhere."

"I was on my way home. It's no problem."

"You seem to know what you're doing. Did you learn that in the circus, too?"

"Nope," he said with a laugh. "That's EMT training from a previous lifetime."

"You've had a lot of lifetimes."

"Indeed I have." He finished wrapping her ankle and then placed the bag of corn on top of it. "Painkillers?"

"In the cabinet by the sink."

He went to get them and returned with a glass of water and two pills. "Now, what're we going to do about the bathroom?"

Her brown eyes went wide. "Excuse me?"

"I don't see one on this level, so what're you going to do when you gotta go?"

"Um, I suppose I'll hobble to the stairs and get myself up there."

"I'll stay." He plopped into the chair next to the sofa and put his feet up on the coffee table.

"Wait a minute…"

"What's the problem? You need help. I've got nowhere to be. Seems like a perfect solution to me."

"Are you always so…" She rolled her hand, giving him the opportunity to fill in the blank.

Raising an eyebrow, he said, "Pushy?"

"Yes. That's a good word for it."

"I can be when the situation warrants it. It's rather simple, in my opinion. You're injured and in pain and can't do anything about it until the clinic opens in the morning. You've got a wicked set of winding stairs between you and the bathroom. We hardly know each other, so naturally you're going to want to be rid of me as soon as possible. You're a nice girl, so you'd never ask me to stay even though you know you need my help." He shrugged. "By being *pushy*, I save us both a lot of time that we could spend on more important topics, such as whether or not you're going to have dinner with me."

She stared at him, seemingly flabbergasted.

"It's a rather simple question that requires a rather simple answer. Dinner. Yes or no?"

"What suddenly made you decide you want to have dinner with me? Were you bored on the way home and I was the first woman you encountered along the way?"

"A, it's not 'suddenly.' And B, I haven't been bored in longer than I can remember. Too busy to be bored."

She eyed him shrewdly, which was a major turn-on. He loved a woman who was not only gorgeous but intelligent and funny and challenging, too. "Going back to answer A, what's that supposed to mean?"

"After Alex introduced us, I wanted to get to know you better, but things have been crazy, and I haven't had a chance to pursue it further. So imagine my surprise—and pleasure—when I encounter you on a dark road and you're in need of my assistance."

"So you're pleased I sprained my ankle?"

"Not at all. That's a huge bummer. But I'm glad it was me who found you out there and that I was able to kill two birds with one stone. And before you can give me that look again, I'll say that bird one was getting you home safely and bird two is having the chance to ask you out."

"You're smooth. I'll give you that."

He sent her his most rakish smile. "Why, thank you, honey."

She rolled her eyes.

"Is that a yes or a no?"

"I'll think about it."

"I'll take you up in my plane."

"Does that line work for you?"

"Almost all the time."

"You're probably long overdue for someone to make you work for it."

"I'm your faithful servant. Work me over."

"Oh my God, you're too much." She sounded annoyed, but her eyes sparkled with delight that told him she was enjoying this conversation every bit as much as he was.

"You got any booze around here?"

"There's beer in the fridge and whisky over the stove."

"Oh, my two favorites. How about a shot of whisky to take the edge off the pain?"

"That actually sounds good."

"Coming right up." He went to the kitchen and returned with a glass of whisky for her and a beer for himself. "Here's to new friends and damsels in distress."

She touched her glass to his bottle. "To new friends."

CHAPTER 13

Paul dressed in khaki pants, a light-blue dress shirt, a striped tie and the navy-blue blazer he hadn't worn since his dad's funeral. Inside one of the pockets, he found a mass card from the funeral, with a photo of George Martinez's smiling face and the Bible verse they'd chosen from St. Timothy: "I have fought the good fight, I have finished the race, I have kept the faith."

He stared at the photo for a long moment, seeing himself and Alex in his father's face. It was no surprise to either of them that their mother mistook them for him so frequently. They both looked like he had as a young man.

"I hope you'd understand, Dad," he said, speaking to the photo on the laminated card. "I really care about Hope and Ethan. I'd never want to do anything to disappoint you, but I can't seem to help the way I feel about her."

Sighing, he returned the photo to the pocket where he'd found it, taking comfort in knowing it was there. On a whim, he put on a little cologne while reminding himself that a funeral didn't count as a date, even if he'd be going with Hope. As much as he dreaded what promised to be a terribly sad event, he was glad to lend his support to her.

He went out to the kitchen, where he found her supervising breakfast for Ethan and Marion. The sight of her in a formfitting black dress that wrapped at her waist with a small elegant bow on her hip made his mouth go dry. Her hair fell in soft waves around her pretty face, and all he could think about was kissing her last night. Before his body could react predictably, he forced those thoughts from his mind so he could focus on whatever she needed today.

"Morning, everyone," Paul said, giving his mother a kiss on the cheek.

"Morning, honey," Marion said. "You look very handsome."

Paul took note of the unusually sharp look in his mother's eyes and experienced a pang of longing for the loving mother she used to be.

"You look funny," Ethan said with a goofy smile for Paul.

"He looks *nice*," Hope told her son. "Go brush your teeth. Time to go."

"I wanna go with you guys," Ethan said.

"Nice try, but you're going to school. Move it, mister."

Ethan clomped off to the cabin to brush his teeth.

"Get your backpack, too," Hope called after him. When she came around the counter into the kitchen, he got the full view of what three-inch heels did for her sexy legs.

"Wow," he whispered.

"Same to you."

They shared a small, intimate smile that let him know nothing had changed overnight. Relief flooded through him at that realization.

"How about I walk Ethan to the bus today?" he offered.

"I wouldn't say no to that. These shoes are far more about style than they are about function."

He took hold of her hand and gave it a gentle squeeze. "I'm digging your style."

As her face heated with an appealing blush, she gazed into his eyes.

Paul had to remind himself that he was not allowed to kiss her right there in the kitchen with his mother at the table and her son coming back any second. But, damn, he wanted to.

The moment was lost when Ethan came barreling through the door, the screen slamming behind him.

Paul released her hand and turned his attention to Ethan. "Ready to go?"

"Uh-huh."

"Paul is going to walk you to the bus today, E."

"Okay."

"Come give me a kiss."

Ethan's face wrinkled with displeasure.

"Give your mom a kiss," Paul said.

He did as he was told while Paul picked up the backpack from where Ethan had dropped it on the floor.

Ethan went over to Marion and kissed her cheek. "Bye, Mrs. Marion."

"Have a good day at school, honey," Marion said.

Paul marveled at his mother's lucidity whenever the little boy was around. He followed Ethan out the front door and down the driveway. They went past the retail store on their way up to the main road where the bus would pick him up.

"Can we check the pumpkins later?" Ethan asked.

"Sure."

"Do you like my mom?"

Paul felt like he'd been hit in the gut by a full-grown pumpkin. "Um, well, yeah. I do. Is that okay?"

"It's okay. She's a nice mom."

"Yes, she is. You're very lucky to have her, and you shouldn't make faces when she asks for a kiss."

"I didn't do that."

"Yes, you did. You always do. I think it hurts her feelings when you do that."

"Oh. I didn't know."

"Well, now you do, so you can try harder."

"I will." After a brief pause, Ethan said, "She used to be sad a lot, but she's better now. You won't make her sad, will you?"

Once again, Paul felt sucker-punched by the earnest expression on the boy's adorable little face. "I'll try really hard not to."

Ethan seemed to think about that for a minute before he nodded. "Do you like to watch football on TV?"

Paul's head spun from the rapidly shifting conversation. "I do. I'm a big Patriots fan."

"Me, too. Maybe we can watch football sometime."

"Any time you want. Alex likes to watch, too."

"Cool. Here comes the bus. See you later." He took off like a shot, covering the last twenty feet of driveway.

Paul jogged after him to make sure he didn't get too close to the road or the bus as it came to a stop.

When Ethan was safely on the bus, Paul watched him take a seat.

Ethan smiled and waved.

Paul returned the smile and the wave. What a cute kid he was. When he thought about what Ethan and Hope had been through with Ethan's father, Paul felt enraged for both of them. As he walked back to the house, he replayed the conversation with Ethan. It touched him to know how concerned Ethan was about his mother.

Despite everything he'd been through, he was a good kid who didn't seem damaged by the trauma of losing his father from his life so suddenly and dramatically. Most of the credit for that went to Hope, who'd probably sacrificed her own well-being to see to his. Knowing that made Paul want to make it up to her, to give her everything she'd been living without for so long now.

She was loading the dishwasher when he came back into the house. He took note of his mother's occupation with the morning edition of the *Gansett Gazette* and went over to Hope.

"Everything okay with Ethan?"

"Yep, he's on his way." Before they could be interrupted, he said, "Where do you want to go this week?"

"Oh, I, um… I don't know."

"Anywhere you want as long as it's drivable from Providence."

She bit her lip as she thought about it. "There was this place we used to go with my grandparents on the Cape."

"What's the name of it?"

"It was called the Seaside Inn in Yarmouth. There was nothing fancy about it, but it's right on the beach. My grandparents used to take my sister and me every year. I haven't been there in ages. I don't even know if it's still there."

"Sounds great. I'll look into it."

"You don't have to… We don't have to…"

"I know I don't have to. I want to." Paul squeezed her shoulder and went to sit with his mother for a few minutes before they had to leave.

Jenny and Alex appeared a few minutes later, looking sleepy and dopey and sex drunk.

"Coffee," Jenny said, making a beeline for the coffeepot.

"I just made a fresh pot," Hope said.

"God bless you, woman. I need all the fortification I can get today. It's seating chart day."

"Better you than me," Hope said, shuddering. "I'll never get married again." The words were no sooner out of her mouth when she was wincing. "Sorry, that wasn't very nice of me to say when you're so excited about your wedding."

"No worries," Jenny said, stirring cream into her coffee. "I get it. I've planned two weddings now, so I know what you mean. It's a lot."

Paul felt like he'd been gut-punched yet again. She'd never get married again? Like *ever*? And Jenny didn't know what Hope meant. She thought Hope was talking about the logistics of planning a wedding when Paul knew that Hope's real opposition was to marriage itself. Great…

Just when he was beginning to feel optimistic that they were on the brink of starting something that could go the distance, she pulled the rug out from under him. He wanted to be married someday. He wanted a family and a white picket fence and a minivan and all the trappings. But apparently the woman he wanted didn't share those dreams.

Before he could begin to process the fact that they had very different ideas about what the future might entail, Jenny's phone rang, and she took a call from her friend Erin.

"Wait," Jenny said, "what happened?" Pausing to listen, she said, "Oh my God! I'll be right over to take you to the clinic. No, I'll get someone to cover. Of course I'll take you. I'll be right there."

"What happened?" Alex asked when she ended the call.

"Erin sprained her ankle last night, or at least she thinks it's a sprain. She needs to get it looked at, so I'm going to take her to the clinic. I'll figure out coverage at the store."

"I hope she's okay," Alex said.

"Me, too."

With a knock on the front door, Daisy arrived to stay with Marion while Hope went to the funeral.

As usual, Paul's mother was thrilled to see her friend Daisy, whom she unfailingly called by name even as she confused her own sons. When Hope had fully briefed Daisy on everything she needed to know to care for Marion for a few hours, Paul followed her out of the house. He held the passenger-side door for her and waited for her to get settled before he closed the door and went around to the driver's side.

He wanted to ask her if she'd meant what she'd said to Jenny, but what right did he have to dig into such issues when everything between them was so new? What had probably been a throwaway comment to her had rocked him profoundly. If she honestly felt that way, he'd be a fool to go all-in with her and Ethan, and he hated that they would have to have that conversation before things went any further.

"Everything okay?" she asked when they were on their way.

"Yeah, sure," he said, deciding on the spot that today wasn't the day for that conversation. Tomorrow would be soon enough, but today... Today he would keep his distance a little until he knew for sure that he wasn't risking too much by allowing his feelings for her to flourish.

"I really appreciate you coming with me to this."

"You shouldn't have to go alone."

"Still... It's above and beyond. And very nice of you."

He glanced over at her and found her watching him intently. "What's the matter? Did I cut myself shaving or something?"

"Nothing's the matter. You just look really good. Handsome, I mean." She laughed. "I've clearly forgotten how to give a compliment."

"No, you haven't. And thank you. You're rather stunning yourself."

She surprised him when she reached across the center console and took hold of the hand that had been resting on his leg. "I couldn't sleep after you left last night. I just kept thinking about how great you were when I told you about Carl. It's not easy for me to talk about that, and you made it easy. Thanks for that."

"I'm sorry you went through what you did, but I'm glad it brought you to us." And he was glad of that, no matter what might happen—or not happen—between them.

"I'm glad, too." She held his hand all the way to the church. When he helped her out of the car, she again took hold of his hand as they joined the stream of people heading into the island's Catholic church. It seemed as if the entire island had come out to honor the young mother who'd died far too soon.

Every pew in the church was filled to capacity when the pallbearers, including Mac and Shane McCarthy, led the casket into the church, followed by Seamus and Carolina, each of them holding the hand of one of Lisa's sons. The sight of those solemn little boys, dressed in tiny suits and ties, brought tears to Paul's eyes.

By the time the four of them were seated in the front row of the church, there wasn't a dry eye to be found. Lisa's longtime friends spoke of her big heart, her love for her sons, her affection for her friends and the island they called home. They talked about how hard she worked to support her family. Everything that was said about Lisa came down to her two boys, who'd been the center of her world.

Hope held his hand through the entire service, even when tears ran down her cheeks unchecked.

Lisa was buried in the island's cemetery, which boasted a spectacular view of the ocean. Her little sons sprinkled dirt over her casket in yet another heartbreaking moment.

Paul slid an arm around Hope's waist, and she leaned her head against his shoulder. He was grateful that she felt comfortable enough to lean on him, because he wanted to be there for her. But in the back of his mind, her words from earlier echoed loudly, reminding him to proceed with caution.

Everyone was invited to Stephanie's Bistro, where Lisa had been a waitress, for refreshments after the service concluded.

"We don't have to go to the reception," Hope said when they were in his truck. "I should relieve Daisy."

"She said she had no plans for the day and to take all the time you needed."

"You have to work."

Though he had a million things he needed to do before he left the island for a few days, he'd never say so to her. "It's fine. Let's go for a little while anyway."

They arrived to a crowd outside the Sand & Surf Hotel. The hotel's owners, Owen and Laura Lawry, stood by the front doors, welcoming everyone who came in.

Paul shook hands with Owen. "Hell of a turnout."

"Lisa was well loved around here."

"Are we all set for Saturday night?" Paul asked.

"Yep. Evan and I are looking forward to it."

Paul had tried to hire them to play at Alex's party, but his friends had insisted on doing it for free. "It'll be a good time. I'll see you then." With his hand on Hope's lower back, he guided her through the lobby to Stephanie's Bistro, which was located inside the charming old hotel that had been lovingly restored by Owen and Laura.

Mac and his wife, Maddie, were standing right inside the door when Paul and Hope entered the restaurant. Paul shook hands with Mac and kissed Maddie's cheek. "You guys have met Hope Russell, right?"

"Yes, of course," Maddie said, shaking hands with Hope. "Mallory tells us you and Katie were a great help to everyone who cared for Lisa."

"We did what we could," Hope said. "It's such a sad thing."

"How're the boys holding up?" Paul asked Mac.

"They're a bit shell-shocked, of course, but Seamus and Carolina are doing everything they can to get them through it."

"If there's anything I can do," Paul said, "I hope you'll let me know."

"There is one thing," Mac said. "We're going to be doing an addition to Seamus and Caro's house and could use all the help we can get to finish it as quickly as possible. I know you've got a lot on your plate, but we'll take whatever you can give."

"I'm in, and Alex will want to help, too."

"Appreciate it," Mac said.

Though the restaurant was packed to the gills with people, Stephanie's staff circulated with trays of Bloody Marys and mimosas as well as delicious hot hors d'oeuvres.

Paul reached for a Bloody Mary and then took a second one for Hope.

"I shouldn't drink when I'm working later," she said.

"One won't hurt anything. Boss's orders." As soon as he referred to himself as her boss, he regretted it. But she only smiled and accepted the drink from him. They circulated around the room, stopping to talk to a variety of people Paul had known most of his life.

While Hope talked with Mallory and Katie, Paul took a moment to chat with Big Mac McCarthy, who'd been his Boy Scout leader growing up and was now a fellow town councilman. Paul had always looked up to Mr. McCarthy, and respected him even more after serving on the council with him over the last couple of years.

"Heard you were off-island," Paul said after he shook hands with Big Mac.

"I was. Took Linda to Boston for the weekend, but we both wanted to be back for the funeral. Terrible thing this is." He glanced at the two boys, who were seated at a nearby table, eating mac 'n' cheese and chicken tenders. Seamus and Carolina were seated on either side of them, watching over them.

"It's awful."

"Thank goodness for Seamus and Caro," Big Mac said. "Those boys have no idea how lucky they are to have such amazing people stepping up for them."

"They'll figure it out in time."

"Yes, they will." Big Mac glanced at Paul. "Couldn't help but notice you're awfully cozy with that lovely nurse."

Paul's gaze landed on her as she talked with her friends. "She is lovely," Paul said with a sigh. He'd woken up with high hopes for them that had been effectively dashed with one offhand comment.

"You sound troubled, son. Is everything all right?"

Paul looked up to find Mr. McCarthy's wise blue eyes trained intently upon him. "Could I ask you something?"

"Of course. What's on your mind?"

"You knew my dad."

"Knew him well and thought the world of him. Everyone did."

"That's really nice to hear. I miss him." His gaze found Hope once again. He was helplessly drawn to her despite all the many reasons why he shouldn't be. "He had a real thing about Alex and me getting involved with the employees. When we were in high school and college, the place was always crawling with summer help, many of them women—"

"I think I know where you're going with this, and I had a similar rule with my boys. Last thing I needed was messy entanglements during the busiest months of the year. Not to mention, I was always a little afraid of getting sued by a disgruntled employee who failed to land one of the McCarthy boys. Sounds sort of silly, but you can never be too careful."

"Yeah, true."

"That said, your dad and I were dealing with boys and young men who hadn't figured themselves out yet. You're a full-grown man now, Paul, and everything is different. You know how to handle yourself in any situation, and I have faith you'll do the right thing no matter what. Your dad would certainly feel the same, especially in light of what you and Alex have done for your mom in recent years. He'd be very proud of both of you."

Overwhelmed by his kind words, Paul had to gather himself before he could speak. "Thank you. That means so much coming from you."

"At the risk of being presumptuous, I hope you know you can come to me any time you need a little paternal advice or wisdom. I'm always here for you, Paul."

"I hope your kids know how lucky they are to have you."

"Of course they do," Big Mac said with a guffaw. "I tell them every day."

Paul laughed at the big smile that accompanied the hilarious comment.

Mrs. McCarthy joined them, winding her hands around her husband's arm. "What've you said to poor Paul, my dear?"

Paul wiped the tears from his eyes. "He's just being his usual charming self."

"That's right," Big Mac said.

"You about ready to go?" Linda asked her husband. "I'm babysitting PJ this afternoon."

"Oh, hey, I want to go, too."

She smiled indulgently at her husband. "As long as you don't rile him up at naptime."

"Now when have you ever known me to rile up anyone at naptime?"

She glanced at Paul. "Do you believe this baloney?"

"Um, no comment?" Paul asked with a grin.

"He's a born politician," Big Mac said, winking at Paul. "Let's go see our grandson. Paul, I'll see you this weekend at the party."

"Looking forward to it."

After they left, Paul went looking for Hope and found her at a table with Katie Lawry, Shane McCarthy, Abby Callahan and Adam McCarthy. Paul shook hands with Shane and Adam.

"Are you ready to go?" she asked.

"Whenever you are."

They said their good-byes, ending at the table where Seamus and Carolina sat with Lisa's boys. Hope ran her hands over their heads fondly and leaned down to kiss their cheeks. "Ethan and I would love to have you for a sleepover sometime soon," Hope said. "Any time you'd like to come."

"Thank you," Kyle said for both of them. "That would be fun."

"I'll call Carolina to set it up." She squatted so she'd be at their eye level. "I can only imagine how sad you must be feeling today, but I hope you know you have a lot of friends on this island."

"Everyone has been so nice," Kyle said.

"I'll see you soon, okay?" Hope asked, kissing them both again.

"Okay," Jackson said.

As they left the hotel, Paul noticed she was contending with tears. "That was sweet of you."

"They're great kids. I got to know them well when I was helping out with their mom. Ethan likes them, too. I'm glad to pitch in any way I can."

They were quiet the rest of the way home and quickly absorbed into their usual routines when they got there. Paul took off to get in half a day at work, while Hope sent Daisy on her way and took over with Marion. Hope and Ethan weren't at dinner, and he didn't see her until nine o'clock that night when he took a beer out to the back porch and saw her coming out of the cabin.

"I was just coming to find you." She came down the stairs from the cabin and crossed the yard, stopping just in front of where he was seated on the top step. "We're still on the nine o'clock boat in the morning?"

"Yep. I talked to Joe earlier, and it's all set."

"Okay. I've got Ethan packed up to spend a few nights at your house with Jenny and Alex. It's good of them to have him."

"They don't mind." He looked up at her. "I called the place in Yarmouth. They only had one room available for the next two nights. I told them to hold it for us and I'd check with you about whether that's okay."

She crossed her arms into her favorite defensive pose. "It's okay with me if it is with you."

The words were strong and confident, but the waver in her voice gave away her true feelings.

Paul held out a hand to her. "Come sit for a minute."

She took his hand and sat next to him on the step.

"We can go somewhere else if you'd be more comfortable with separate rooms."

"I-I'm looking forward to the time alone with you," she said. "It would be foolish to have separate rooms."

"Before we go, there's one thing we need to talk about." Paul hated that he had to bring this up, but he had to know before he spent more time with her, before he fell deeper into whatever this was between them.

"What's that?"

"What you said this morning to Jenny..."

"What did I say?" she asked, seeming genuinely baffled.

"About how you'd never get married again."

"What about it?"

How to say this in a way that would make sense to both of them... "I'm thirty-four years old, Hope. At some point, I'd like to be married and have a family. I've done all the casual dating I want to do. If there's absolutely no hope of ever getting there with you, I'd prefer to know that now rather than when it's too late to turn back."

"Oh."

"Did you mean it?"

"Sort of."

He wanted to ask her what that meant, but he waited, hoping she'd say more.

"After everything happened with Carl, I said I'd never get married again, and I meant it. I never wanted to be in such a vulnerable position again. Extricating my life from his was ugly and messy and costly. But that was then."

"And now?" Paul held his breath in anticipation of her reply.

"I don't know, Paul. I just don't know. I wish I could tell you I've totally changed my mind, but I can't say that for sure."

"What happens if this thing between us gets serious and feelings are involved on both sides? What then?"

"I can't speak for you, but I already have feelings for you. I want to see where they lead."

He brought her hand to his lips. "I have feelings, too. But I'm not looking to get hurt any more than you are. Would you be willing to keep an open mind to all the many possibilities?"

"I suppose I could do that."

"I don't mean to put a ridiculous amount of pressure on you, but I just want to know going in that a future together isn't outside the realm of possibility."

"That's fair enough."

Paul dropped her hand and put his arm around her, bringing her in closer to him. "I'm really looking forward to the next few days."

"So am I, but I feel guilty, too."

"How come?"

"I've never spent a night away from Ethan, and I feel guilty for looking forward to it as much as I am."

Her confession made him laugh. "He'll be totally fine with Jenny and Alex."

"I know, but still… What kind of mother looks forward to time away from her baby?"

"The best kind of mom. No need to feel guilty for taking a little time for yourself when you do so much for others."

"If you say so."

"I say so." He kissed the top of her head and dropped his arm from around her shoulders. "I'm going to let you get to bed, and I'll see you in the morning."

"Sleep well."

"I doubt I'll sleep at all."

"Why not?"

"I'll be too busy thinking about two days alone with you."

She surprised him for the second time that day when she turned toward him and kissed him.

Paul cupped her face and lost himself to the sweetness of her lips and the innocent seduction of her tongue. She had no idea what she did to him when she kissed him so tenderly. He wanted to devour her and had to remind himself that tonight was not the time for that.

Though it was the last thing he wanted to do, he backed off the kiss in slow increments. He leaned his forehead against hers while continuing to stroke her cheek with his thumb. "Is it tomorrow yet?"

She laughed softly. "I wish."

"I'm going to get up and go inside before I give in to the urge to walk you home and tuck you in."

"Would that be so bad?"

Paul groaned. "I'm trying to do the right thing here."

Her fingers slid down his arm to grasp his hand. "I really want you to tuck me in."

Paul looked at her for a long moment, giving her time to change her mind. "Let me make sure Alex will be here with Mom."

CHAPTER 14

Paul got up and went inside to see what Alex was doing, though part of him didn't want to know. He encountered his brother in the hallway, wearing only a towel, which was a huge improvement over the night before.

"Hey, bro, what's up?" Alex said.

"That's what I was going to ask you."

"Nothing much. Jenny is over at Erin's, checking on her after she sprained her ankle. I was going to watch the Sox. You wanna join me?"

"Maybe later. I was going to go to Hope's for a little while if you're going to be here with Mom."

"I'm here and not going anywhere."

"All right, then. If I don't see you tonight, I'll see you in the morning before we leave."

"Sounds good. You're practicing safe sex, right?"

"Oh my God. Fuck off, will you?"

Alex bent in half laughing at his own joke.

"You're such an asshole."

"Paul Michael Martinez," Marion yelled from her bedroom. "Watch your language."

That set Alex off all over again.

This time Paul laughed, too. How could he not laugh at the incredible irony of how his mother's dementia disappeared whenever one of them swore? "I'm outta here."

"Mind your manners, Paul Michael."

Paul flipped his brother the bird on the way to the back door, where Hope waited for him. "Let's go," he said.

She got up and went with him across the yard to her cabin. "What's wrong?"

"Nothing. Alex was busting my balls."

"Are you mad?"

"Nah, it was funny. And then Mom yelled at me for swearing at him. I got the full Paul Michael Martinez."

"Paul Michael, huh?"

"Yep, and that's when I know I'm really in trouble. I have to say I love that the dementia goes away at the strangest of times, and then she becomes Mom again."

"And then Mom disappears into the dementia, and your heart breaks."

"Yeah."

She closed the door behind them and turned to him, sliding her hands from his chest up to encircle his neck. "I'm sorry you have to go through that so many times each day."

"I'm sorry she does. She's sixty-two years old and could live like this for decades. It's so unfair."

"It really is."

He put his arms around her. "But you didn't lure me over here to talk about sad and depressing things, did you?"

"I didn't *lure* you over here, and we can talk about whatever you want to talk about."

"You did so lure me with promises that involved beds and hopefully lingerie."

"I don't recall mentioning lingerie."

He kissed her neck, dragging his tongue over her soft skin. "Does that mean you sleep naked?"

"No! I have a child."

Paul laughed at her outrage. "Go do what you do before bed. Call me when you're ready for tuck-in." He kissed her. "Don't make me wait too long."

She walked away from him, tossing a look over her shoulder. "I'll be quick."

While he waited, Paul sat on the sofa and took advantage of the opportunity to take a closer look at what she'd done to make the cabin a cozy home for her and Ethan. He leaned in to inspect the photos of Ethan on a side table and his framed artwork on the wall. In the corner were buckets of Legos in every shape and color. Paul appreciated that her home was reflective of the most important person in her life.

"Paul," she called. "Come on in."

He got up and followed the sound of her voice to her room.

Propped up on one elbow, her hair falling over her shoulder, she dazzled him with how beautiful she looked in the glow of the candle she'd lit on the bedside table.

"Are you coming in, or are you just going to stand there and stare at me?"

"I might stare for another minute or two. I don't ever want to forget the way you look right now."

"How do I look?"

"Stunning. Sexy. Gorgeous."

She held out her hand to him.

He went into the room and took her hand, letting her draw him down onto the bed with her. "Ethan…"

"Has been asleep for an hour, and he rarely wakes up during the night." She brushed the hair back from his forehead. "You know what the best part of the tuck-in is?"

"What's that?"

"The good-night kiss."

"That's my favorite part, too."

She fell back against a pile of pillows, bringing him with her.

Paul wrapped his arms around her, discovering she wore formfitting silk to bed, or at least tonight she did. Her leg slid between his, and her arm encircled his waist.

"You give good tuck-in."

"This is only my introductory package," he said. "Tomorrow, I'll show you my deluxe offerings."

"I can't wait to see what comes with the deluxe package."

He was smiling when he brought his lips down on hers.

"Best tuck-in ever," she whispered against his lips.

Their bodies moved together as if they'd been lovers for years, and Paul couldn't wait to have two days completely alone with her.

*

Erin was settled on the sofa, her injured ankle propped on a pillow, when she heard a rapping on the door downstairs. She groaned at the thought of having to answer the door.

"Don't get up," a voice from downstairs called. "It's me, Slim. Is it okay if I come up?"

"Sure," Erin said, giddy that he'd come back.

His footsteps pounded up the metal stairs, echoing through the lighthouse. He burst into her living room, grinning from ear to ear, looking ridiculously handsome, carrying something behind his back and a bike tire hooked over his shoulder. "What'd the doctor say?"

"I saw Victoria, the nurse practitioner, because David was at the funeral. They did an X-ray and determined nothing is broken, thankfully. Just a bad sprain."

"Glad nothing is broken, but sprains can hurt worse than breaks sometimes." From behind his back, he produced a bouquet of flowers. "Oh damn, I forgot to get a vase. You don't have an extra one lying around, do you?"

"Under the sink. And thank you. The flowers are gorgeous. Sunflowers are my favorite."

"You're welcome." He found the vase, filled it with water and stashed the flowers, still bound, in the water in typical guy fashion.

She'd tend to them herself in the morning. "What's up with the tire?"

"I grabbed it for you on the mainland today so we can fix your bike."

"That's really nice of you."

He brought the flowers to her coffee table and plopped down in the chair across from her, resting his long legs on the table. His dark hair was tousled from the wind or his fingers, and his brown eyes took a measuring look at her that made her skin tingle with awareness. "How long are you going to be laid up?"

"I have to take it easy for a week and wear this glamorous brace, but at least I should be off those evil things in time for the wedding." She gestured to the crutches on the floor beside the sofa.

"Ahh, a week on crutches. That sucks. Have you ever needed them before?"

"Nope."

"You'll hate them after two days."

"I already hate them. They hurt my hands and my armpits."

"Poor baby."

"I know I'm pathetic, so don't pile on."

"I'll try not to," he said with a grin.

"What're you doing here anyway?"

"You're here."

"I'm not quite sure how to take that."

"I guess I could be more clear. You're here. You're lovely. I want to get to know you better, and you never said whether you'll go out with me."

Erin swallowed hard at the "you're lovely" comment. "No, I didn't, did I?"

Slim stuck out his lip and shook his head. "I had to fly all day not knowing whether I was going to see you again after we spent the whole night together."

"Don't say that like it was something it wasn't."

"You can't blame a guy for trying, can you?"

"I can blame a guy for trying too hard."

"Touché. I meant what I said about wanting to get to know you. Tell me who you are, Erin."

"I'm a lighthouse keeper at the moment."

"What were you before that?"

"Let's see. I've been a hotel concierge, a waitress in five-star restaurants, a nanny, an office manager and, for a very brief time, a student at a hairdressing academy. That was an unfortunate segue, especially for the people I practiced on."

"You've had a very eclectic life."

"That wasn't always my plan."

"What was your plan?"

"Law school."

"What happened?"

Erin hesitated, but only for a moment. This was her story, and she'd learned to own it. "9/11 happened at the start of my third year of law school. My twin brother, Toby, who was Jenny's fiancé, was killed in the World Trade Center. I left school, and I never went back."

"God, Erin, I'm so sorry."

"Thank you. Over the years, I've learned to say that as if it happened to someone else. Toby. His name was Toby. He was my twin, my closest friend. After he died, I couldn't seem to figure out what I was supposed to do without him. I've spent a lot of years spinning my wheels, trying to find the answer to that question."

"And have you?"

"Not yet, but I'm still looking, so I suppose that's something, right?"

"That's more than something. That's everything."

It was the absolute perfect thing for him to say.

"I'll have dinner with you."

"Yeah?"

"Yeah."

His smile lit up his face.

"Don't go getting cocky just because I said yes."

"I wouldn't dream of it," he said, but his cocky grin told the true story. "When am I allowed to take you out for this dinner?"

"As soon as I'm off the crutches."

"That's a whole week from now!"

She shrugged, enjoying the game more than she had in longer than she could remember. "Cocky and impatient. Not very attractive qualities."

"I'm also persistent. If you're going to make me wait until the crutches are gone, I guess I'll have to come by to visit every day and make a pest of myself so you don't forget about me."

"You're going to drive me crazy, aren't you?"

"Baby, that's the very least of what I want to do with you."

Erin had absolutely nothing at all to say to that.

*

Paul's alarm went off at seven, dragging him out of a deep sleep. He'd gotten four hours of sleep after sneaking back into the house at three. His lips were sore from kissing Hope until they were both crazy from the need for more. Later, he told himself. They'd have the time and the privacy to take the next step.

The thought of that next step had him hard and needy in a matter of seconds. "Christ," he muttered as he ran his hands through his hair and then got up to face the first half of the day, which promised to be challenging. His mother hated leaving the house, let alone the island, and he expected her to be contentious when she realized what was happening.

He took a cold shower that woke him up and cooled what was left of his ardor. There'd be time for that later. But first they faced the monumental task of getting his mother to the hospital on the mainland.

Paul dressed in shorts and a polo shirt and then packed a bag for two nights away. From his bedside table, he withdrew the box of condoms he'd bought earlier in the week and tossed them into his duffle bag. Just in case. *Ha*, he thought. *Who am I kidding?*

After that make-out session last night, there was no *just in case* about it. He wanted her. She wanted him. They were going to be alone in a hotel room for at least one night and maybe two. He planned to make the most of the time they had alone together. He zipped the bag closed and brought it with him to the kitchen, where Hope was once again overseeing breakfast for Ethan and Marion.

If she ever got tired of the endless sameness of each day, she never let on, and she never showed a moment of frustration with either of her charges. She was all about patience and serenity, which was just another thing to admire about her.

Ethan was cranky this morning, fussing at Hope about the crust on his toast, the fact that she was leaving and why he couldn't come.

Paul glanced at her, offered a smile and tipped his head toward Ethan, asking her permission to intervene.

She nodded tentatively, as if she wasn't sure she should let him help her out. He wanted her to be able to count on him, even when it came to Ethan.

"Hey, pal," Paul said, "Alex told me they're going to start harvesting some of the pumpkins while we're gone. I thought you might be able to help out after school if you're up for that."

Ethan's big eyes got even bigger. "Really? Like I could actually get the pumpkins out of the pumpkin patch?"

"Yep, but only if you want to."

"I want to! Can I, Mom?"

"Sure, as long as you do exactly what Mr. Alex tells you to do and don't get in the way."

"He won't be in the way," Alex said as he came into the kitchen, dressed for work. "Will you, Ethan?"

"No way. I'll be such a big help."

"I have no doubt," Alex said, smiling.

"Run over and brush your teeth and grab your backpack," Paul said. "I'll walk you up to the bus if it's okay with your mom."

"It's fine with her," Ethan said as he tore out the door at top speed.

"Wow, nice save," Hope said with a warm smile for Paul. "He was winding up to a full-blown meltdown over me leaving."

"Pumpkins to the rescue," Paul said. To Alex, he added, "And thanks for letting him help. He's been watching them for weeks now."

"Happy to have him," Alex said as he downed his first cup of coffee standing up, like he did every day. "Don't worry about a thing while you're gone. Jenny and I will take good care of him."

"Yes, we will," Jenny said when she joined them, her hair wet from the shower. "We're looking forward to it."

"You guys are so nice to do this when you have so much else going on," Hope said.

"You do us a huge favor every day just by showing up," Alex said.

"Well, you do pay me to show up," Hope said, making them all laugh.

"Still," Alex said, "it's no small thing you do around here, and we appreciate it. I hope you enjoy the break from the routine and relax."

"I will, thank you."

Ethan came barreling back into the house at full speed as usual. He took his lunch from his mother and paused to endure the hug and kiss she bestowed upon him before going to kiss Marion.

"Be a good boy," Marion said, fixing his hair the way she used to do for her own boys.

"I'm always a good boy."

Amused by his witty reply, Paul followed him out the door and up the lane to the bus stop.

They were halfway to the road when Ethan looked up at him. "Could I ask you something?"

"Sure you can."

"You'll take good care of my mom while you're gone, right?"

Stunned by the heartfelt question, Paul nodded. "You can count on it."

"My friends Kyle and Jackson… Their mom died."

"I know, buddy."

"I don't want that to happen to my mom."

They arrived at the bus stop, and Paul squatted to bring himself to Ethan's eye level. "Nothing is going to happen to her," Paul said, his hand on Ethan's shoulder. "I'll take very good care of her. You have my word on that. And a man's word is a solemn promise."

"Okay." Ethan surprised him by hurling himself into Paul's arms and hugging him tightly, making sure to let go well ahead of the bus's arrival. God forbid such things be seen by his friends on the bus.

"We'll call you," Paul said as the bus came to a stop.

"'Kay." Ethan bounded up the stairs and waved from his seat the way he did every day.

Looking at that little face framed by the bus window, Paul realized he was falling for the son as much as the mother.

CHAPTER 15

Marion fought them every step of the way. From refusing to shower to battling over the clothes that Hope laid out for her, they were already drained by the time they got her into Paul's truck for the ride to the ferry landing. When she saw where they were going, she began to rage all over again.

"Turn this car right around and go home," she said. "I'm not leaving the island."

"You have a doctor's appointment in Providence, Mom."

"Whatever for? There are perfectly good doctors right here. Now take me home."

"We're not going home right now, Mom."

"Paul Michael Martinez, I'm going to tan your hide if you don't mind me. I don't know where you get off talking back to your mother, but Daddy will certainly have something to say about that."

"Okay, Mom."

"Now you're just patronizing me, and I won't have that either."

And so it went as he backed the truck onto the ferry, helped her out of the passenger door and walked her up the stairs to a table for the hour-long ride to the mainland. He smiled weakly at Hope, who sat across from him and his mother.

"Who is she?" Marion asked, glaring at Hope.

"That's Hope, Mom. She's a friend."

"She's no friend of mine."

"She's my friend. My good friend." Paul winked at Hope. "So be nice to her."

"Don't tell me what to do."

The ferry's horn sounded, indicating their imminent departure.

"Where are we going?" Marion asked. "Where's George? I never leave the island without George."

"He's meeting us there," Paul told her, feeling guilty, as he always did, for lying to her.

"He won't be happy to hear how fresh you've been with me this morning, young man."

"I know, Mom."

Thankfully, the crossing was smooth and Marion didn't fight them when it was time to return to the truck to drive off the boat. They got stuck in some beach traffic on the way to Providence, but still arrived well ahead of their eleven o'clock appointment.

As Paul was parking the truck, he received a call from work that he had to take. So Hope went to help Marion out of the truck.

"Get your hands off me, young lady. I have no idea who you think you are, but I don't want you touching me."

"It's okay, Marion. I'm a friend here to help you."

Paul watched as Hope tried to put the shoes Marion had taken off back on her feet. "I've got to go," he told the man who'd called him. "Alex is in charge this week. Check in with him." He stashed the phone in his pocket and walked around the truck to help Hope. Just as he reached her, Marion hauled off and slapped Hope in the face.

She fell back, and Paul caught her. "Oh my God. Are you okay?"

"I, um, yeah, I'm fine." A bright red welt appeared on her flawless cheek, and Paul wanted to rage against his mother and the hideous illness that had turned her into someone he didn't recognize.

"Mom! Apologize to Hope."

"I will not apologize. I told her not to touch me."

"She was trying to *help* you."

"I don't need her help. I don't need anyone's help."

Paul wanted to scream from the frustration and anguish that overtook him. More than anything, he wanted to stop everything so he could comfort Hope and ensure she was really okay, but he couldn't do that until they had his mother safely delivered.

"Let's go, Mom," he said firmly, leaving no room for argument.

She seemed to sense he was at the end of his patience, so she got out of the car and let him escort her inside. Two nurses from the memory care clinic that would be overseeing the testing met them. All the pre-admission paperwork had been done in advance, so there was nothing left for them to do but say their good-byes.

"Wait," Marion said when Paul kissed her. "Where're you going?"

"The doctors are going to help you, Mom. I'll be right here to pick you up when you're ready."

"It's okay, Mrs. Martinez," one of the nurses said kindly. "We'll take very good care of you."

"I want George. Where's my husband? He'd never leave me with strangers. Where's George?"

She screamed for her husband until she was out of earshot, leaving Paul emotionally spent by the ordeal.

Hope's hand on his back jarred him out of his troubled thoughts.

He looked over at her and noticed the mark on her face was still red and beginning to swell. "Excuse me," he said to one of the nurses. "My mother hit my friend. Is it possible to get her an ice pack?"

"I'm fine, Paul," Hope said.

"Of course," the nurse said. "I'll grab one for you."

"You're not fine," he said, touching his fingertip to the angry red mark on her face. "I'm so sorry. She's never done anything like that before, even when Alex and I gave her reason to."

"Believe it or not, that wasn't the first time a patient has hit me. The frustration and anger are part of the illness. I don't take it personally."

"Well, I do. I take it pretty fucking personally when she hits you, of all people."

She smiled at his outburst. "You're very sweet when you're protective."

The nurse returned with a disposable ice pack.

"Thank you so much."

"No problem. Don't worry about your mom. We'll take very good care of her, and we have your number if we need you for anything."

"I appreciate it. Thanks again." With his hand on Hope's lower back, he guided her out of the building and into the warm sunny day outside. His body was rigid with tension and frustration and rage he didn't know what to do with. How could he justify being angry with his mother when she couldn't help what she did? No, he was furious with the illness that had snatched her away from them in the prime of her life. She'd worked by his father's side for decades, and just when she should be heading into her relaxing retirement years, the dementia struck. It was so unfair to her, to all of them.

He opened the passenger door for Hope, and when she was seated, he took the ice pack from her and held it against her face.

She closed her eyes and leaned into his hand. "Feels good."

"I'm so sorry, sweetheart. I hate that she did this to you."

"And I hate that you're so upset about it. I mean it when I say I'm fine and that stuff like this goes with the territory when you work with dementia patients. It's not the first time, and it probably won't be the last time."

"How do you do it? How do you stay so patient and calm when you must want to scream sometimes from the aggravation of it all?"

"Screaming isn't going to change anything for her or for me. It's just going to make everything worse. I tell myself over and over it's the disease. It's the disease. As a medical professional, you can't take it personally, or you'd go crazy. That's one of the first things we're taught when we work with this population."

"I just want you to know... I admire you so much for the way you handle her—and Ethan. You're so great with both of them."

"Aww, thanks. That's nice to hear."

"I mean it. I watch you with them, and I'm floored every day by how calm you are. Where does that come from?"

"Lots of yoga and meditation. I'm in tune with my inner Zen."

"I need to find my Zen, because I'm feeling anything but calm or rational right now."

"Let's go to the Cape, and I'll help you find it."

"Why, Ms. Russell, are you coming on to me by any chance?"

She flashed a saucy grin. "You know it."

Paul laughed and felt some of the tension leave his body. He leaned in to kiss her before he closed the door and walked around to the driver's side, eager to get on the road to the Cape.

*

Lizzie handed Jared his cell phone, which she had taken from the charger in the kitchen. "Are you going to call him?"

Jared was sitting by the pool reading the morning edition of *The Wall Street Journal* on his tablet. You could take the man out of Wall Street... "Has anyone ever told you that you can be a bit like a dog with a bone when you get one of your big ideas?"

"You tell me that all the time." She stuck his phone under his nose. "Woof."

Laughing, he took the phone from her, shaking his head at her tenacity. "I see that you've already got his number cued up for me."

"I like to make things easy for you."

"You like to make things *expensive* for me."

"At least I'm not spending all your money on diamonds and furs."

He glanced up at her, looking absolutely gorgeous with his blond hair still wet from his morning swim and aviator sunglass perched on his nose. "You know you could do that, right?"

"What the heck do I want with diamonds or furs when there're so many people in need?"

"You're the only wife of a billionaire who's ever uttered those words."

"I doubt that."

"You're the only wife of mine who ever uttered those words."

"Make the call, Jared."

"Yes, dear." He pressed the green button to initiate the call. "Hey, Q, what's up?"

Lizzie stood by and forced herself to be patient while they talked about the Yankees' playoff chances and Quinn's new puppy, which was apparently chewing everything in sight.

"Are the ladies going mad over your new baby?" Jared asked.

Lizzie rolled her hand, encouraging him to get to the point of the call.

"Apologies in advance, but my wife is breathing down my neck because she's got a big idea that seems to involve you." Jared explained Lizzie's plan for a senior care facility on Gansett Island. "She's even got the location already scouted and a builder on board to do the renovations. The one thing we need to make this happen is a staff doctor, and Lizzie's got her heart set on you."

She couldn't hear what Quinn said in reply, and Jared's expression didn't give anything away.

"Maybe you could come out, take a look and see what you think? You've been promising me a visit since you got out of the hospital." After another pause, Jared said, "Sure. Think about it. Hit me up with a text. Will do."

He ended the call and put the phone on the table. "He said he'd think about it."

"Did he show any interest at all?"

"You know how he's been since he got home. He doesn't show much interest in anything. Let him sit on it for a day or two, and then we'll see what's what."

Lizzie didn't like having to sit on anything when she had a plan. She had calls to architects she could make in the meantime, but she'd like to know for sure that she had a doctor on board.

"There's smoke coming out of your ears from gerbils working overtime on the treadmill."

"There are no gerbils on treadmills inside my head."

"Something is fueling that crazy brain of yours, my love."

"I'm sorry," she said with a sigh. "I don't mean to drive you nuts all the time."

He gave her hand a gentle tug that brought her tumbling onto his lap. "You don't drive me nuts. I just have to act like you do, or I'll totally lose control of things around here."

She raised a brow in amusement. "So you still think you've got the control?"

His bark of laughter made her smile. "We both know you've got *all* the control. You're the boss, baby. I'm just along for the ride, and it's a beautiful ride. I love your energy and your passion and your desire to make things better for others. You heard about Paul and Alex's predicament the other night and you've already got a plan in place to fix it for them."

"That's nice of you to say, but it's no fun if you're not as into it as I am."

"I'm into whatever you're into. Whatever you want, whenever you want it. Don't you know that by now?"

He touched her heart when he said such sweet things. And the best part was he meant every word he said. "So there's never going to come a day when you say, '*Enough*, Lizzie!'?"

"As long as we have an occasional day off to be lazy together—preferably naked and lazy—then I'm good."

"What're you doing today?"

He peeked at her over the top of his sunglasses. "As in *today* today?"

"As in one and the same. I'm on hold until we hear from Quinn, and the Chesterfield is closed today. I find myself with a rare bit of free time—" The air whooshed from her lungs when he stood and slung her over his shoulder, handling her as if she were weightless when she was anything but. "*Jared!*"

"I can't talk right now. I'm having a naked lazy day with my very busy wife. Hold all my calls."

Lizzie laughed all the way inside, where she spent the rest of the day being naked and lazy with her husband while hoping and praying that his brother would take them up on their offer.

*

"Are you still meeting me in town at lunchtime?" Alex asked Jenny before they parted ways for the day.

"That's the plan. Marriage license day." She rolled her lip between her teeth before seeming to remember he was watching. "Noon at Town Hall?"

"I'll be there." He hooked his arm around her waist. "What's with the lip?"

"The lip?"

"You bite your lip when you're worried about something."

She looked up at him with bottomless eyes that saw all the way through him the way no one else ever had. Sometimes it was hard to remember that she'd had that connection once before with someone else. Not that it mattered, but still…

"Toby died the day after we applied for our license."

"I'm not going to die tomorrow."

"I know."

"Do you? Do you really?"

Tears filled her eyes. "I'm a hot mess, and I'm so sorry to do this to you when we should be worry-free and looking ahead not back."

An idea occurred to him right then and there, leaving him breathless with the desire to see it through immediately.

"Do me a favor," he said, running with it.

"Sure."

"Wear something really pretty to Town Hall, and I'll take you to Stephanie's for lunch after."

"I can do that."

Alex leaned in to kiss her. "Everything is going to be just fine, babe. I promise you."

"Keep telling me that."

"Any time you need to hear it." He went into their room to retrieve what he needed to make his plan a reality and dropped her at the retail store on his way to work. "Kiss me."

She reached for him over the center console and obliged him, wiping away the lipstick she left on his lips. "Love you. Be careful today."

"I'm always careful. See you at noon. Don't be late."

"I'll be there."

The second the door shut behind her, he was on the phone with Evan McCarthy. "I need a favor, buddy."

"Sure. What's up?"

Alex outlined his plan to Evan and told him the reason for it.

"Dude, that's seriously awesome. I'm in. I'll meet you there at two."

"Great, see you then." Next, Alex called Sydney and Erin to get them on board.

Erin sniffled when he told her what he wanted to do and why. "Poor Jenny," she said. "And you... You're brilliant, Alex Martinez. I'm so happy you came into her life and made everything better."

"That means a lot to me coming from you, Erin."

"Toby would approve of you. And he would like you."

"Christ, you're going to make me bawl like a baby over here."

"I'll see you at two."

"Thanks, Erin." It totally sucked that Paul was off-island today, but Alex hoped his brother would understand. He made a call to Town Hall, spoke to the clerk about what he wanted to do and received her full support. His final call was to the mother of Ethan's friend to ask if he could go to their house after school for a couple of hours. Hope had given him the number in case he needed it, and Jonah's mom was happy to have Ethan and promised to pick him up from the bus stop. Another hurdle cleared. This was coming together almost too easily.

The hours at work were largely a waste as he was incredibly preoccupied with his plans. The clock inched slowly forward until it was finally eleven thirty. Feeling like a little kid on Christmas morning, Alex changed into shorts and a clean polo shirt in his truck before heading for town. He would've worn something nicer, but he didn't want to tip his hand before he was ready to.

Looking gorgeous in a pretty summer dress, Jenny waited for him on the front steps at Town Hall. As they were going in, Blaine Taylor was coming out.

"Hey, guys," Blaine said. "What's up?"

"Marriage license time," Jenny said.

"Wow, it's getting close. Looking forward to the party this weekend."

"I am, too," Alex said. "See you there."

"Wouldn't miss it." He shook hands with Alex and kissed Jenny's cheek before continuing on his way.

"I love living here and seeing friends everywhere we go," Jenny said.

He patted her on the ass as they walked through the main doors. "I love living here a whole lot more since I met you."

She giggled at his words and the ass grab.

They filled out the paperwork and emerged from Town Hall twenty minutes later, marriage license inside a sealed envelope, just the way Alex had requested. After a leisurely lunch at Stephanie's, Alex made his move. "Take a ride with me."

"Where? Don't you have to get back to work? Paul's off-island—"

"It'll only take a few minutes. I want to show you something."

"All right, but you can explain to my boss why I was late getting back from lunch."

"Your boss can suck my dick."

"Ugh, that's so gross."

"You love to suck my—"

Jenny's hand over his mouth ended the sentence prematurely. "Shut up, or it'll never happen again."

"Shutting up now," he said, his words muffled by her hand, which he nibbled. After she dropped her hand, he said, "Love you, Jenny Wilks-soon-to-be-Martinez."

"Love you, too, Alex Martinez, even when you're being nasty."

"You love when I'm nasty." He loved riling her up and every other damned thing about her. As they drove through the gates to the lighthouse where they'd met more than a year ago, his heart beat with excitement and anticipation and a tiny bit of fear that his big idea might not go over well with her.

"What're we doing here? I saw Erin last night."

"I have a little surprise for you."

"What kind of surprise?"

"The kind you're going to have to wait and see."

She sat up straighter in her seat, but there was nothing to see—yet.

Alex pulled up to the spot he used to take when he was coming here to visit her and cut the engine. Then he turned to her, reaching for her hand.

"What's going on?"

"You're worried about something happening before our big day, right?"

She bit her lip and nodded.

"Today's our big day. Right here where we first met, we're going to get married. We'll still have our wedding as planned, but that'll be for everyone else.

This, today, is for us. There'll be nothing left to worry about once we're legally and officially married."

Tears filled her eyes, and she covered her mouth as a sob escaped from her lips.

One by one, the people he'd called earlier filed out of the lighthouse: Evan, his uncle Frank, Sydney and Erin, moving slowly on crutches.

Jenny saw them and began to cry harder.

"If you don't want to do this, we don't have to. I just thought—"

She launched herself across the truck and into his arms, kissing him repeatedly. "You are the best guy in the whole world to think of this."

"So you like the idea?"

"I *love* the idea, except Paul isn't here."

"He'll understand completely, and he'll still be my best man at our official wedding."

"When did you think of this?"

"This morning."

"And you made it happen for today?"

"I can't bear to see you worrying when there was something I could do to fix it short of enclosing myself in bubble wrap for the next two weeks."

"I'm sorry to have been worried—"

Alex placed his finger over her lips. "You have every good reason to feel the way you do. Do you care that your parents aren't here for this?"

"No. They'd understand, too. The only one I truly need is you."

"And the only one I truly need is you. So what do you say we go out there and get married?"

"What about the rings?"

"I've got them with me."

She seemed stunned that he'd thought of that. "And the license?" Her smile faded. "It's dated for two weeks from now."

"I took care of that, too." He handed her the envelope from the town clerk. "It's got today's date."

"Ethan!"

"Is all set." He explained the arrangements he'd made with Jonah's mom.

"Alex…" She wiped away more tears. "God, you're amazing. Any time I'm annoyed with you for the rest of our lives, please remind me of what you did for me today, and all will be forgiven."

Touched by her excitement, he said, "You got it, baby. Let's go get married." With her still in his arms, he got out of the truck to applause from their friends. Erin and Sydney hugged Jenny, and Sydney handed her the bouquet Alex had asked her to get. "Where do you want us, Frank?"

"Right here," Frank said, gesturing to a spot to the left of the lighthouse with a breathtaking view of the water.

"I see that someone has mowed the lawn," Jenny said sarcastically, making Alex laugh.

"And I see that Erin hasn't planted any tomatoes this season. Bummer."

"Such a bummer."

He reached for her hand, put his ring into her palm and then rolled her hand over the ring, kissing the back of it.

"Jenny and Alex," Frank said, "I'm honored to have been asked to preside over this incredible moment in your lives, and I love a good surprise. Well done, Alex."

"Thanks, Your Honor."

"This, right here," Frank said, gesturing to the two of them. "This is the epitome of love. What you've done for Jenny today, Alex, is something she'll remember for the rest of her life. And Jenny, you'll someday have the opportunity to return the favor for your husband by easing his worries and his sorrows. As long as the two of you can do that for each other, everything else you face will seem easy in comparison."

Jenny wiped tears from her eyes, while Alex was forced to do the same. The import of the moment swept down on him all of a sudden, leaving him humbled by the knowledge that from this day forward, Jenny would be his wife, his partner, his lover, the mother of his children, the center of his world.

What had begun right here in this yard with flying tomatoes and angry shouts had become the best thing to ever happen to him. Alex couldn't wait to have the rest of his life with her.

Frank led them through the recitation of vows and the exchange of rings.

Alex noticed how Jenny's hand trembled as she put the ring they'd bought months ago on his finger.

"It is my great honor to now pronounce you husband and wife. Alex, you may kiss your bride."

He swept her up in his arms and kissed her with all the love and desire he felt for her. And she returned his kiss with equal ardor.

Only the sound of Frank clearing his throat and Evan laughing had them breaking apart.

Alex let her slide down the front of him until she was once again standing, but he suspected it would be quite some time before their feet touched the ground.

CHAPTER 16

The Seaside Inn in Yarmouth sat directly across the street from Seagull Beach. After lunch on the waterfront in Hyannis, Paul and Hope checked into their room. She was hit immediately by a bout of nerves that had her hands shaking as she unpacked. It had been years since she'd shared a hotel room—or a bed—with a man, and she hoped she remembered how to behave.

"What do you feel like doing?" he asked.

Hope knew a moment of pure relief that, despite the days of buildup, he wasn't expecting to fall into bed the second they were alone. "Do you want to take a walk on the beach?"

"Sounds good to me."

They left the room for the short walk to the beach, where they kicked off their shoes and left them by the stairs.

Paul reached for her hand, which was all it took to get her heart beating faster. It had been so long since she'd known the affection of a man, and before Paul, she'd been certain that this kind of excitement and anticipation was all in the past for her. Carl hadn't liked to hold hands. He'd thought it was foolish. Only now did Hope realize how much she loved to hold hands—with the right man.

"It's beautiful here," Paul said. "Almost as beautiful as Gansett."

"I've always loved this beach. We came every summer for a week with our grandparents, and we had the same room every year. It became almost a joke that we ate at the same place the first night, the same place the second night... We looked forward to that all year."

"Where's your sister now?"

"She lives in Oregon with her husband and kids."

"Are you guys close?"

"We talk every week and text back and forth about the kids. I haven't seen her in a couple of years, though. Ethan and I stayed with them for a short time after Carl was arrested. I had to get out of town, and she offered. The other side of the country looked really good to me right then."

"I imagine it did. What's her name?"

"Camille."

"How many kids does she have?"

"Three boys—Sam, Michael and Josh. They're a little older than Ethan."

"Is she older than you?"

"Younger, actually. By a year."

"How about your folks? Are they still alive?"

"Yeah. They live in New Hampshire where we grew up."

"I had no idea you were from New Hampshire. What part?"

"North Conway."

"I love it there. I've spent a lot of weekends skiing at Cranmore."

"Me, too. I wonder if we were ever there at the same time?"

He smiled down at her and then dropped her hand so he could put his arm around her.

She liked that even better than the handholding.

"Were your parents supportive when everything happened with Carl?"

"They tried to be, but they were so disgusted with him, and it was hard for me to have to listen to my dad's tirades when I had my own tirades going on inside. The sad part was that he and my dad were close until then. He used to call Carl the son he never had. He was so, *so* disappointed. Naturally, he aired that out with me."

"Which made a bad situation worse for you."

"It really did. I felt like I'd disappointed him by marrying the wrong guy or something."

"But you know it was no reflection on you, right?"

"For the most part. I still sometimes think that maybe if I'd done something differently or been a better wife—"

"No." Paul stopped walking and turned to face her, keeping his hand on her shoulder. "It had nothing at all to do with you. There was something wrong with him if he thought it was okay to have sex with children."

"Maybe if I'd had more sex with him, he wouldn't have done what he did with children."

"Hope, come on. You don't really believe that. This was all on him."

"In my heart of hearts, I know that. But sometimes I wonder if I could've prevented it somehow."

"You couldn't have. It's not the same, but I had a similar thing happen when I was in college. One of my best friends raped a girl at a fraternity party. I remember being so shocked that he'd been accused of such a thing. I felt like I knew him as well as I knew myself. I defended him—even to the police. I said, 'No way, no way. That's not how he rolls.' And then the DNA confirmed that it *was* him. I can vividly recall how incredibly shocking it was to realize I didn't know him at all."

"I know that feeling."

With his arm back around her shoulders, they started walking again. "The worst part is that I was at that party and never saw anything amiss. I liked to party with the best of them, but I never blacked out or passed out or anything like that. I paid attention, kept an eye out for my friends. In a way, I felt responsible for what'd happened right under my nose. Took a long time for me to understand there was nothing I could've done to prevent or stop something I didn't know was happening."

"I still wrestle with that one. You feel clueless and naïve and stupid. *Everyone* assumed I'd known, even my own family, when no one was more shocked than I was to find out what he'd been doing."

"Your family thought you knew about it and didn't say anything? Your friends thought that?"

"They never came right out and said as much, but I got the 'how could you not know?' vibe from a lot of people, including my parents and sister. Carl and I were like a lot of busy parents—we went to work, we took care of Ethan, we tried to squeeze in some family time and occasionally some couple time. Where, in the midst of that busy schedule, did he have time for sex with minors? That's the part I still can't reconcile."

"He must've told a lot of lies."

"Lies that I believed because I had no reason not to."

"You trusted him. You loved him. Why would you ever think he was capable of something like this if there was never anything to indicate he had such a thing in him?"

"I wouldn't, I guess. After it all went down, I spent many a sleepless night going over every detail—every text message, every phone call, every night together. He never slipped up. Or if he did, I missed it. I wasn't the kind of wife who felt the need to look at his text messages when he was in the shower. I had friends who did stuff like that, but I never did."

"You respected his privacy—and you trusted him. That's the way it should be."

"I've had a hard time talking about this stuff with my closest friends, but for some reason, it's easy with you."

"I'm glad you told me about it, and I'm sorry it happened to you. You deserve way better than you got from him."

"Yes, I do."

"How much longer will he be in jail?"

"Another couple of years, but it could be less. Naturally, he's been an exemplary prisoner, so he's apt to get out early for good behavior."

"Oh the irony."

They reached the end of the beach and turned to head back.

"And then there're the lawsuits," she said.

"What lawsuits?"

"The ones filed by the families of the girls he slept with."

"Are you tied up in that, too?"

"Thankfully, no, but I had to start from scratch financially after we divorced because our assets were frozen and our house was taken by the bank. They even came after my ten-year-old car because we owned it outright. Lucky Carl was in jail when phase two of the nightmare kicked in."

"Jesus, Hope. I hope someone kicks the shit out of him in jail. That'll be the least of what he deserves."

"That's not likely to happen. He's in a minimum-security facility with a lot of white-collar criminals."

"How in the hell did that happen?"

"He used most of our savings to get himself a really, *really* good lawyer."

"Is it okay to say I hate him?"

She laughed. "It's absolutely fine."

"How much does Ethan know?"

"Very high-level stuff. Daddy got in trouble and had to go to jail. He asks sometimes if he'll get to see him after, but I dodge those questions. I have sole custody, and if I have my way, he'll never see Carl again."

"What if he wants to see him?"

"I'm hoping by the time it actually happens, Ethan will have moved on and won't ask. I don't know. I guess I'll deal with that when it happens, but I hope it's a long way off."

"I hope so, too." He squeezed her shoulder in a show of support that she greatly appreciated. "I have to tell you what Ethan and I talked about on the way to the bus the last couple of days."

"What did you talk about?"

"Yesterday he asked if I like his mom, and I said yes, I like her very much. Today he was concerned about something happening to you, the way it did to Jackson and Kyle's mom. I assured him that you're perfectly healthy and he didn't need to worry. He asked me to promise him that I'd take good care of you while we are away."

"Oh God, the poor kid. I hate to think of him worrying about stuff like that."

"It's natural that what happened to Jackson and Kyle's mom would worry him. I remember meeting Joe Cantrell when he first moved to the island after his dad died and asking my mom if that was going to happen to my dad, too."

"Thank you for reassuring him."

"I care for him just as much as I care for you, which is a whole lot."

She leaned her head against his shoulder. "I keep thinking I'm going to wake up and none of this will have happened. It'll turn out to be nothing more than a lovely dream."

"I feel the same way. I'm almost ashamed to admit that I've been envious of Alex because he found someone who made him so happy, not that he doesn't deserve it. But I kept wondering if I was ever going to get my turn. And then you kissed me."

"Ugh," she said, sputtering with laughter. "Don't remind me of that. I'm still mortified."

Once again, he stopped walking, but this time, he drew her in close to him, gazing down at her with a tender, amused expression on his face. "Why are you mortified?"

"Because I *kissed my boss*! My nursing school professors would freak out if they knew that."

"You kissed *me*. I wasn't your boss in that moment. And I'm not your boss now." Caressing the faint bruise on her cheek, he said, "Does it hurt?"

She shook her head. "Not so much."

He captured her mouth in a sweet, sexy kiss that had her clinging to him, trying to get as close as she could to the amazing way he made her feel. As he kissed her, he walked them backward toward the stairs where they'd left their shoes, only breaking the kiss when they ran out of sand.

Keeping a firm grip on her hand, he scooped up their shoes with his free hand and headed for their hotel.

This is going to happen, Hope thought. *It's going to happen right now, and I want it. I want him. If only I weren't so nervous. I hope he can't tell I'm having a meltdown on the inside.*

They rinsed the sand off their feet at an outdoor shower and were back in their room a few minutes later. He immediately reached for her to continue what they'd started on the beach.

"Paul," she said as he kissed her neck. His erection was hard and thick between them, and it was all she could do not to rub shamelessly against him.

"Hmm?"

"I-I haven't done this in a long time. And I've only ever done it with him. I have no idea if I'm any good at it."

"Sweetheart, you're beautiful and sweet and kind and so sexy. And the best part is you have no idea how sexy you are. Whatever we do is going to be amazing. I know it."

No one had ever said such things to her, and for the first time in her life, she felt sexy because of him. She caressed the handsome face that had overtaken her thoughts and many of her dreams, too.

"We don't have to do anything that you're not ready to do," he said. "I'm not going anywhere."

Once again he'd said exactly what she needed to hear. "Maybe we could just see what happens?"

"We can do whatever you want."

She went up on tiptoes to kiss him, running her tongue over his full bottom lip.

His arm encircled her waist, bringing her in close to the evidence of how badly he wanted her.

Hope tugged on his T-shirt and helped him out of it, her eyes boggling once again at how ripped he was. He had muscles on top of muscles from years of hard physical work, and just the right amount of dark chest hair. She ran her hands over each hill and valley, dragging her fingertips over the bumps of his six-pack. Or was that a twelve-pack?

Releasing a low growl, he swept his hands under the hem of her shirt, laying them flat against her back. "Could we take yours off, too?"

She nodded, and he eased the shirt up and over her head, leaving her in only the lacy bra she'd worn with this moment in mind.

His jaw pulsed with tension, and his eyes flared with desire as he took a good long look at her. "So, so beautiful, Hope." He lowered her to the bed and came down on top of her. For a long moment, he gazed into her eyes, seeming to gauge if she wanted this as much as he did.

He'd shown her that there were still good men in this world, and all she had to do was have some faith. He made her want to put her faith in him.

She reached for him, loving the way he looked at her before his lips met hers. This kiss was unlike all the others that came before. There was a hint of desperation to it that drove all her worries and fears right out of the room. For the first time in longer than she could remember, she had no responsibilities, and she was free to fully enjoy this escape from reality with a hot, sexy man who treated her like a queen.

He broke the kiss to turn his attention to her neck, making her shiver from the sensations that zinged through her body. Her nipples tightened and chafed against the confines of her bra, and the throb between her legs intensified with every brush of his lips over her sensitive skin. He set her on fire for him.

The rough scrape of his late-day whiskers over the tops of her breasts made her moan.

"Tell me to stop if it's too much," he said.

"*Don't* stop." For a second, she feared that she sounded too desperate, but her words encouraged him to move things along. Her bra fell away, baring her breasts to his ravenous gaze.

"Goddamn, you're gorgeous," he whispered as he took her nipple into his mouth, sucking and licking and tugging on it until she was nearly delirious from wanting more of him.

She wanted to tell him to hurry, but he wouldn't be rushed.

He moved with deliberate slowness, or so it seemed to her. If his goal was to bring her to the verge of begging, he was about to succeed. Everything he did, every touch, every kiss, every breath on her fevered skin ramped up the desire for more.

After kissing his way from her breasts to her belly, he tugged on the button to her shorts and watched her closely as he removed them, perhaps looking for signs of reluctance that didn't exist. She helped him along by removing her panties and flinging them to the floor.

Paul's eyes went wide with surprise when she did that, nearly making her laugh. He hadn't seen that coming.

Hope sat up and unbuttoned his shorts, pushing them down over his hips, revealing the boxer briefs he wore under them. His long, thick erection reached nearly to his belly button and was peeking out over the waistband. She ran her finger over the tip, making him gasp and then hiss.

Tucking her hands into the back of his briefs, she pushed them down as she cupped his tight, muscular ass. The second his cock sprang free, she drew him into her mouth, sucking and licking and teasing him the way he'd done to her breasts. Judging by his sharp inhale, he hadn't seen that coming either.

His hands fisted her hair, and his hips began to move to her rhythm. "Fuck," he muttered. "Stop. Hope… *Stop*."

She released him from her mouth and looked up at him. "What's wrong?"

"Absolutely nothing, but you're going to finish me off if you keep that up."

"Are you only good for once?" she asked and then wondered where this sexy, vixen side of her was coming from. She'd never been like this with Carl.

His mouth fell open and then snapped closed. "Hardly, but the first time, I want to be with you." Cupping her breasts in big callused hands, he ran his thumbs over her nipples, making her tremble.

"Paul…"

"What, sweetheart? Tell me what you want."

"I want you. Now."

"Do we need protection?"

She shook her head. "I'm on the pill, and I'm clean. I was tested after…" In his dark gaze, she saw that he understood what *after* meant.

"I'm clean, too, and I haven't done this in a while, but I don't mind using a condom."

"No," she said, sinking her fingers into the dense muscles of his back to pull him closer. "Just you."

He tested her readiness with his fingers, sliding them through the dampness between her legs and sending her to the point of madness before driving them into her.

Hope cried out and arched into him. God, it felt so good to be touched this way, to feel like a woman again, to know he wanted her as much as she wanted him. It had been such a long, lonely time since the last time she'd felt desired. Tears filled her eyes, and she closed them tight against the burn. This was no time to get emotional. He removed his fingers and replaced them with his cock, pushing gently against her before retreating, over and over again, gaining greater depth each time.

She was swept away by him, so much so that even the slight bite of pain she experienced as he entered her barely registered.

"Look at me, Hope," he whispered as he kissed her. "Look at me."

She opened her eyes, blinked away the tears that had gathered and met his intense gaze.

"There you are," he said with a small, sexy smile that she returned. "Are y ou okay?"

"Mmm, so okay."

"Does it hurt?"

"A little. Been a while."

"We'll go slow." He bent to nuzzle her neck. "You're so hot and so tight. I've never felt anything better than this."

His words were as much of a turn-on as the insistent press of his cock into her. He was much bigger than Carl had been, and the extra-tight fit triggered sensations she'd never experienced before. And then he hit a spot deep inside, prompting an orgasm that seemed to come from her very soul. *That* had certainly never happened before.

"Paul," she said, gasping and clinging to him as he picked up the pace, hammering into her and riding the waves of her release until he found his own.

"God," he muttered when he came down on top of her, breathing hard and sweating from exertion.

She loved that she'd made him sweat. She loved the way he smelled and how his whiskers felt against her skin. And she suspected she was well on her way to loving all of him. *So much for proceeding with caution*, she thought. A deep breath shuddered through her at the possible implications that came with giving her heart to another man.

"Am I too heavy?"

"No." She tightened her arms around him, wanting to keep him there for a while longer, to enjoy this never-to-be-repeated moment of sheer perfection. Perfection had been hard to come by for her—and for him, too, she suspected. And they would never again experience this first time together.

CHAPTER 17

Paul's world had been tipped upside down in the course of a couple of hours. From the instant his mother's hand had connected with Hope's face and he'd known a second of pure, unmitigated rage that anyone, even his own mother, would dare to strike the woman he thought of as his, to their talk on the beach to making love to her, his life had been altered. It now included her—and Ethan—and he wouldn't have it any other way.

"I'd like to say for the record that I told you it would be amazing."

"Yes, you did," she said with a low chuckle that made him smile.

He raised his head so he could see her gorgeous face. "Was it amazing for you, too?"

"You have to ask?"

"Just making sure."

"It was beyond amazing. It's never been like that for me."

He planted his elbows on either side of her head and used his thumbs to brush the hair off her face, mindful of the bruised area on her cheek that served as a painful reminder of what'd happened earlier. "How was it different?"

"You want, like, specifics?"

"Specifics would be good." The heated blush that infused her face made him laugh. "Oh, this is going to be *really* good."

"I can't say it."

"We're naked in bed together. I'm still inside you. What can't you say?"

Her face got even redder, and she looked away.

Her shyness turned him on, and he felt himself hardening inside her. "Come on," he said, kissing her lightly. "Tell me."

"You…you're… You're bigger."

"Mmm, was that so *hard*?" he asked, pressing against her and making her gasp when she realized he was hard again. "What else?"

"You hit something inside me. I've never felt that before."

He began to move, pressing deep into her, hoping to find that elusive spot again. "Your G-spot. It's the magic."

She looked up at him, her eyes liquid with emotion and desire. "You're the magic."

Could she be any sweeter? He was falling so hard and so fast for her. He'd never felt anything as good as this. Not even close. Wrapping his arms around her, he turned them so she was on top of him, the move surprising her. She faltered for a second before she recovered and found her groove.

Ahh, fuck, her groove is incredible, he thought as she moved on top of him. "That's it, sweetheart. Take all of me."

She moaned from the effort to accommodate him, her body shuddering and her breasts jiggling.

Paul reached up to cup them and pinched her nipples.

Her head fell back, and her lips parted.

He slid his right hand down to where they were joined to caress her clit as he pushed hard into her.

Her fingernails dug into his arm as she came with a loud shout that echoed through the room.

"Yes," he whispered roughly. "Come for me, baby. I want to feel your tight heat all around me." She was gorgeous as she let loose, and he vowed in that moment to do whatever it took to keep her right here with him, where she belonged, forever.

They collapsed into a sweaty pile on the bed, and the next thing Paul knew, he was awaking in a dark room to his ringing cell phone. What the hell time was it and how long had they been asleep? Disentangling himself from Hope, he reached for the phone on the bedside table.

"Hello?"

"Hey, it's me," Alex said.

Paul ran a hand over his face and held back a yawn. "What's up? Everything okay there?"

"Yeah, we're all good. Ethan just finished his homework and went to the cabin to take a shower. Jenny is over there supervising."

"Is he doing all right?"

"He's been fine. He had a fun time with his friend Jonah this afternoon, and we made burgers for dinner, so he's happy."

"Thanks again for that, Al. Hope is enjoying the break." As he said the words, she turned over and reached for him in her sleep. He put his arm around her and settled her into the crook of his neck.

"I have a little news that I didn't want you to hear through the grapevine."

"What's that?" Paul asked, wondering what could've happened that counted as news in the one day he'd been away.

"Jenny and I got married this afternoon."

"You-you *what*?"

"Remember the other day when I asked you if she seemed off?"

"Yeah. What about it?"

"I figured out why. She and Toby were right about where we are now when he was killed. She's been stressing out about something happening to me before our wedding, so I got the big idea this morning to surprise her by moving up the date. I'm so sorry it happened when you and Mom weren't here, but the minute I had the idea, I knew I needed to do this for her right away. I hoped you'd understand."

"I do. Of course I do. I can't believe you're actually married."

"I know," he said with a laugh. "It's awesome."

"What about the wedding?"

"It's going on as planned. Today was a formality to ease her mind."

"You did a really nice thing for her. She must've loved it."

"Cried her eyes out. It was quite a day."

"And you've got a seven-year-old underfoot on your wedding night."

"He's no trouble, and he goes to bed early. We'll have plenty of time to celebrate later."

"I'm so sorry I'm not home for that," Paul said dryly.

Alex laughed. "We'll miss you."

"Don't do anything to traumatize the kid for life, you hear?"

"We'll see if we can control ourselves. Have you heard anything from the hospital about Mom?"

"Not yet."

"How'd the drop-off go?"

"Not so great." He told her about Marion slapping Hope.

"Jesus, Paul. She actually *hit* her?"

"Yep. And she hit her hard. Hope's face is bruised, but she says she's fine and it doesn't hurt anymore."

"But still…"

"Yeah, I was a fucking wreck over it earlier, not to mention fucking furious."

"I can imagine. I never told you why Jenny and I split for that short time when we were first together, did I?"

"No, you didn't want to talk about it. What happened?"

"Mom basically implied—in front of Jenny's parents the first time I met them—that Jenny was a whore for seducing me."

"Oh my God. She did not."

"Yes, she did, and that broke me, man. That she would say such a thing about the woman I love… I know it's the disease, but you couldn't tell me that then. I decided it would be easier to push Jenny away than it would be to subject her to that kind of shit."

"And we all know how that went."

Alex's bark of laughter made Paul laugh, too. His brother had been a miserable son of a bitch until he reconciled with Jenny a couple of weeks later. "I'm only saying that I know how it feels to have Mom strike out at the woman I care about."

"It was awful, Al. For the first time ever, I sort of hated her. And then I immediately felt like shit for thinking that, because God knows she can't help it."

"I get it. Believe me, I do. Are you guys having fun?"

Paul slid his hand from Hope's shoulder down her arm. "Yeah, we are."

"What're you doing?"

"None of your business."

"Must be something good, then. Oh, here comes Ethan barreling through the door. Does Hope want to say good night to him?"

"I'm sure she does. Let me get her. Hang on." Paul put the phone down and kissed her awake. "Hey, sweetheart, Ethan is on the phone to say good night to you." He could tell by her dazed expression as she came awake that she too had lost all track of time.

Pushing the hair back from her face, she took the phone from him. "Hi, honey."

Paul could hear Ethan's excited voice coming through the phone as he relayed every detail of his day to his mother, who couldn't get a word in. "And Alex took me to see the pumpkins, and he said just another couple of days until we start to harvest."

It had been good of Alex to keep that promise to Ethan in light of what else had happened that day, Paul thought.

"Make sure you brush your teeth before bed," Hope said.

"Duh, Mom. I already did. Jenny reminded me."

"That's good. You sleep tight, and I'll talk to you tomorrow, okay?"

"Okay."

"Love you," she said, but he was gone, handing the phone back to Alex with a clatter that Paul could hear, too. "I think he missed the part where I told him I love him."

Alex relayed the message to Ethan. "He loves you, too."

"Thanks again for watching him, Alex."

"It's been fun. He cracks us up."

"That's good to hear. I'll give you back to Paul." She handed him the phone.

"I'll call the hospital," Alex said, "and shoot you a text with any updates."

"Sounds good. Talk to you tomorrow, and congrats again."

"Thanks."

Paul stashed the phone on the table and turned to put his arm around Hope. The feel of her soft skin against his made him forget all about the fact that he'd already had her twice. He already wanted her again.

"What's with the congrats?"

"He and Jenny got married today."

"They did *what*?"

Paul relayed the story Alex had told him.

"Oh my God," she said, sniffling. "Poor Jenny, to be so worried. She sure hid it well. And Alex... That's the sweetest thing I've ever heard."

"Apparently, it went over well with her, too."

"Of course it did. It was so thoughtful and romantic."

"Two things Alex was never known for until she came along."

"With the right inspiration, any guy can find his A game."

"Is that right?"

"Uh-huh."

He pressed his erection against her hip. "My A game is back."

She dissolved into laughter. "Your A game is going to need to feed me before round three." Her laughter died on her lips all of a sudden.

"What?" he asked.

"I just realized they're taking care of Ethan on their wedding night!"

"They don't mind. Alex said they'll have plenty of time to celebrate after he goes to bed, and I made him promise they won't traumatize him for life—and trust me, they're capable."

"Thank you for thinking of that," she said with a giggle that warmed his heart. He loved to hear her laugh. "So, about dinner..."

"You want to go out or order in?"

"Is ordering in an option?"

"Let me check." He reached for his phone and did a search for delivery places in Yarmouth. "We're in luck. There's a pizza place that delivers. But I can do better if you want to go out."

"That would require showering and blow-drying and makeup and getting out of bed." Her belly let out a loud growl that made them both laugh. "And pizza sounds great."

"What do you like on it?"

"Veggie?"

"Got it." He called in the order for a large half-veggie, half-meat-lover and once again stashed his phone on the bedside table.

"Meat-lover, huh?"

"Oh yeah." He beat his chest dramatically. "Me man. Me need meat. *Lots* of meat so I have lots of stamina for my woman."

"Easy, Tarzan. You might hurt yourself."

He glanced a fingertip over the bruise on her face. "Speaking of hurting, you're sure this doesn't hurt?"

"Positive."

His phone chimed with a text from Alex. *Nothing yet from the hospital. They gave her something to help her sleep. They'll call tomorrow with more.*

Okay, thanks for checking.

No prob.

Paul showed Hope the texts so she'd be up to speed, too.

"I'm glad she's getting some rest," she said. "She's got to be worn out from the stress of the day."

"You keep saying you're fine and that your face doesn't hurt, but I can't stop thinking about her hitting you." He sighed deeply. "I'm so sorry that happened. I wish you could've known her before. You'd never believe she's the same person."

"I feel like I do know her from what you and Alex have told me. And there's no need to be sorry. I know what happened today had nothing to do with Marion Martinez and everything to do with an awful illness."

"How do you separate it like that?"

"Unfortunately, I've had a lot more experience with this disease than you have, and as much as I care about Marion, she's not my mother, so I'm not as emotionally invested as you are." She ran her hand over his chest. "Although I'm becoming more invested all the time."

He raised a brow. "Is that so?"

She bit her lip and nodded. "I've gone from kissing my boss to sleeping with him. I'd say that counts as invested."

"You forgot about having sex with him."

"Um, no, I didn't. That falls under sleeping."

"Sex is very different from sleeping. Whole other category, in fact."

"Who says?"

"I say." He kissed her, lingering over the sweet taste of her lips. "Hold that thought." Paul got up and put on his T-shirt and shorts, leaving the button undone so he could get them off again faster when he returned. He grabbed his wallet and went to the lobby to get the pizza, thinking about Hope and what'd transpired between them during this mostly magnificent day.

If only he could stop thinking about his mother hitting her. At the lobby bar, he inquired about purchasing a bottle of wine and was tucking his credit card back in his wallet when the pizza delivery guy came in. He returned to their room with the wine and pizza.

"Food for my hungry lady."

"It's about time," she said with a teasing grin.

He loved this playful, relaxed side of her. He wondered if he would see more of that when they got home. They ate the pizza in bed right out of the box and drank the wine from plastic cups the hotel had provided.

"This is better than anything we could've gotten in a restaurant."

"I doubt that, but there's something to be said for the view." He focused intently on the tops of her breasts, which were peeking out over the sheet.

"My view could be a little better." She tugged at his T-shirt. "I'm just saying…"

After removing his shirt, he refilled their glasses. "I love you like this." He realized what he'd said about one second after the words left his mouth. But he didn't regret saying it.

She swallowed her bite of pizza and a sip of wine. "Like what?"

"Happy, relaxed, funny." His fingertip made a path from the base of her throat over her collarbone and down to the valley between her breasts.

"I haven't been any of those things in a long time. Don't get me wrong—I'm happy every minute I get to spend with Ethan. He's the best thing to ever happen to me. But I've missed having someone special in my life. I didn't realize how much I'd missed it until very recently."

"What happened very recently?" he asked.

She flattened her hand over his chest. "You happened."

He covered her hand and linked their fingers. "Is this a good thing?"

"I think so."

"You're not sure?"

"I want to be sure, but I'm wired differently than I used to be. I'm skeptical and overly cautious. I haven't been as cautious with you as I usually am."

Paul rested their joined hands over his heart, hoping to quell the ache that settled there on her behalf. "I wish I'd met you first, before you were skeptical."

"I do, too. But I believe I was meant to be with Carl so I could have Ethan. That was the whole point of everything I went through."

"That's a great way to look at it."

"That's the only way I can bear to think about it." She looked up at him. "I'm going to try my best not to ruin a very nice thing by being skeptical and jaded."

He took her cup and put it next to his on the table. Then he snuggled in close to her, cupping her cheek to kiss her. "And I'll do my best not to let you."

CHAPTER 18

"Is he asleep?" Jenny asked Alex when he came into their bedroom and started removing his clothes. If she lived forever, she'd never grow tired of the sight of his sexy, muscular body. And after what he'd done for her today, she loved him even more than she had this morning, which she wouldn't have thought possible.

"Out like a light," Alex said. "He was so excited to be sleeping in Paul's room. I didn't think he'd ever go to sleep." He took a closer look at her, his eyes bugging adorably. "What in the name of hell are you wearing?"

"Oh, this old thing?" She toyed with the bodice of the sexy silk gown she'd intended to save for their honeymoon. She'd broken it out early to reward him for being the most amazing husband in the history of the world. After what he'd done for her today, he deserved nothing less. She loved watching him harden before her eyes as he wrestled his way out of his clothes.

Then he was upon her, pulling the covers back for a closer look at the gown she'd bought at Tiffany's shop.

"Someone's been keeping secrets," he said, running his hand over the silky baby-doll nightgown that ended at mid-thigh.

"More like making plans." She reached for him, and he came down on top of her, his lips hovering just above hers. "I will never have the words to adequately thank you for what you did today."

"Neither will I."

"Wait, what did I do?"

"You married me. You made me the happiest guy to ever walk this earth just by saying 'I do.'"

"That was all it took?"

"Yep."

"That was nothing compared to what you did."

"I couldn't stand to see you so worried. It was killing me."

She touched the ring on his finger, loving the way it looked there. "We're going to have to take these off, or we'll give ourselves away." They'd asked the people who were there today to keep their secret so as not to take anything away from the big day they had planned for next Saturday. Other than Paul, they planned to tell no one else about their first wedding.

"I know, but we can leave them on tonight."

"Yes, we can," she said, smiling up at him. "Can you believe we're actually *married*?"

"No, I can't. This whole thing has been like a dream. From the first moment your tomato hit my back, I've been living the sweetest dream I've ever had."

She blinked back tears. "You saved me."

He shook his head. "We saved each other."

Trailing a finger down his chest, she looked up at him. "I had a surprise for you today, too, but yours totally trumped mine."

"I love surprises, especially your kind. Do tell."

"You know that other project we've been working on for a while now?"

"The house?"

She shook her head. "The *other* one," she said, waggling her brows. Taking his hand, she laid it flat upon her abdomen. "Success." Just as she would never forget what he'd done for her, neither would she forget the look of stunned amazement that overtook his face when he realized what she was telling him.

"Yeah?" he asked in a gruff tone as tears filled his eyes.

"Uh-huh. I think that's part of the reason why I've been such an emotional basket case lately."

"When did you find out?"

"This morning. I had planned to tell you at bedtime."

He gathered her up into a tight hug. "Jenny... God, could this day get any better?"

"I can think of one way it could be better." Jenny drew him into a deep, sexy kiss, expecting that to set him off the way it usually did, but everything was different tonight. He went slowly, kissed her softy, touched her reverently, worshiping her and making her burn for him, especially when he dropped his forehead to her abdomen, clearly overcome by the news she'd shared. Alex worked around the gown, easing it down to reveal her nipple, pushing it up to kiss between her legs and leaving it on when he finally entered her, after what felt like an eternity spent waiting for this very moment.

She'd expected to be married for years now, but her plans had been thwarted on another clear September day so long ago. All the pain and suffering she'd withstood in the ensuing years had led her to Alex and a second chance she'd never expected to have. He'd shown her what was still possible and had mended her broken heart with his unwavering love and devotion.

At times, he could be gruff and crude, but she loved those qualities as much as she loved his sweet, tender side. She loved everything about him.

"Jenny," he whispered as he pushed into her and withdrew almost completely before going deep again. "I love you so much. So goddamned much."

"I thought I knew how much I love you, but today..."

"I'd do anything for you—and our baby."

And he'd shown her as much with what he'd done today. "I'll never, ever forget this day."

"Neither will I. This is the anniversary we'll celebrate. Just us."

"Yes." She arched her hips into him, the now-familiar climb making her legs quiver.

"Come for me. I want to feel you tight and hot around me."

He never held back, especially when they were in bed, and tonight was no exception. His words were as powerful as the deep thrusts of his body into hers, taking her right to the edge of madness the way he always did. She held on tight to him, her rock, her love, and let him take her away in a storm of desire and need and love so deep it could never be described in mere words.

And then he was right there with her, surging into her and taking his own pleasure.

After a long quiet interlude, he said, "What do you think of marriage so far?"

"I think it's the best thing that's ever happened to me."

"Me, too, baby." Kissing her, he said, "Me, too."

*

The night sky was littered with stars that stood out in the complete darkness that covered Erin's little corner of Gansett Island. Like she'd told Slim, when she'd first lived here, she'd been scared of the dark. But now, after more than a month of dark nights, she'd gotten used to it and had learned to embrace the peace and quiet.

She had her sore foot propped up on a cooler and a glass of wine in hand as she stared up at the heavens with tears streaming down her face—tears she deeply resented. How could she be anything other than thrilled for Jenny, the woman who would've been her sister-in-law but had instead become one of her closest friends?

They were bound by the tragedy that had marked their lives by taking the most important person to both of them away forever. It had taken years for them to recover their equilibrium after they lost Toby, and Erin was truly happy for Jenny that she'd found her second chance with Alex.

But... Seeing the love of her late brother's life marry someone else had hurt worse than anything had in a very long time. It had hurt much more than she'd expected it to. As one of Jenny's bridesmaids, Erin had been mentally preparing herself for Jenny's wedding for months now. She wasn't quite there yet, which was why today's surprise wedding had left her reeling.

She brushed away the stupid goddamned tears that should've stopped a long time ago but still came despite her relentless desire to stop crying about things that couldn't be changed. Toby would be so pissed with her if he knew she was still crying over him all these years later. Though she thought of him every day, it had been a long time since she'd cried over him. Hopefully that would count for something with him.

Erin was jostled out of her pity party by the roar of an engine coming up the long dirt driveway to the lighthouse. The motorcycle headlight found her in the darkness, giving her a whole new appreciation for how it felt to be a deer.

The engine died. "Just me," a now-familiar male voice said.

She frantically wiped her cheeks so he wouldn't know that she'd been sitting alone in the dark, crying for her dead brother. "You sort of scared the crap out of me."

"Sorry about that. What're you doing out here alone in the dark? Thought you were scared of it."

"I *was* scared. I'm not anymore."

He took a seat on the grass next to her. "What changed?"

"I got used to it, I guess."

"How's the hoof?"

"Better today. The crutches are worse than the ankle."

"I remember that from when I was on them once after I messed up my knee. Couldn't wait to be rid of them."

"Did you fly today?"

"Uh-huh. Five round trips. I'm spent."

Something about the way he said that made her laugh. "Sure you are. You love every second of it."

"I really do. Nothing I'd rather be doing. Well, almost nothing."

Thanks to the low sultry tone of his voice, there was no way she could misunderstand what "almost nothing" entailed.

"How was your day?"

She started to say quiet and uneventful, but there was something about the blanket of darkness, the burgeoning friendship and how easy he was to talk to that had her telling him the truth. "I went to a wedding."

"On a Tuesday?"

"It was a special sort of wedding. Can you keep a secret?"

"Pilots are like bartenders. We keep everyone's secrets."

"This is kind of a big one."

"I won't tell anyone, Erin. You have my word."

She couldn't say how she knew, but instinctively she understood that he was the kind of guy who stood by his word. After all, he'd come back to check on her, hadn't he? "Jenny and Alex got married today."

"Wait, I thought their wedding was next weekend. I'm flying her folks over for it."

"It's still on. You know how I told you she was supposed to marry my brother, Toby? Well, apparently she's been really stressed as the wedding gets closer. Even though she knows the likelihood is infinitesimal, she's been afraid of something happening to Alex the way it did to Toby. Alex couldn't stand to see her so wound up and worried, so he put together a wedding for today so they could get it done and she could relax and enjoy their actual wedding."

"Wow, that's pretty cool."

"I thought so, too."

"Is that why you've been crying?"

Erin closed her eyes against the rush of grief and pain and emotion that she hadn't wanted anyone else to see.

Before she could formulate a reply, he said, "She was supposed to marry your brother, and today was hard for you."

"Yeah," she said softly. "As happy as I am for her..."

"I get it. I'm sure she would, too."

"She'll never know I was anything other than thrilled for her and Alex. They're great together, and she's certainly earned the right to be happy."

"You're a good friend to feel that way. She's lucky to have you."

"We're lucky to have each other. We've been through the fire of hell together and come out on the other side, stunned and altered, but we survived." She wiped her face and laughed. "How do you get me to tell you these things? I don't even know you."

"Pilots and bartenders," he said, making her laugh again. "What do you want to know about me?"

"Did your mother name you Slim?"

"No, my grandfather did, actually."

"I don't mean to be insulting, but you aren't exactly super skinny or anything." He had the muscular build of a man who took good care of himself.

"Is that a fat joke?"

"Hardly! And you know it."

"Yeah," he said, chuckling, "I know. I was a skinny kid who had the same name as my dad, so my gramps started calling me Slim, and it just sort of stuck long after I wasn't a skinny kid anymore."

"What's your real name?"

"Was your brother's real name Toby?"

Surprised by the question, she said, "No, it was Tobias, after our grandfather, but he hated that name and always went by Toby. Why?"

"My real name is Tobias Fitzgerald Jackson Junior."

"It is not."

"It is, too."

A sob hiccupped from her chest as disbelief warred with hope. Was it possible that her beloved Toby had sent a new Toby to her? Did things like that even happen? Who was to say they didn't?

"I almost said something the other night when you told me his name had been Toby, but I wasn't sure if I should." In a cajoling tone, he said, "I can show you my license if you don't believe me."

"I believe you," she said softly.

He reached up and took hold of her hand. "It's kind of cool, right?"

"It's way cool. I'm glad you told me."

"In light of this incredible coincidence, you're going to have to have dinner with me soon."

Laughing despite the tears that continued to cascade down her cheeks, she said, "You don't give up, do you?"

"Not on something worth fighting for."

And here she'd thought Alex's surprise wedding had been the romantic grand gesture of the day. Slim was giving him a run for his money.

"Does anyone call you Toby?"

"Nope. I've never gone by that. I was Tobias to my mother a few times during my reckless youth. Otherwise, I've always been Slim. But you could call me Toby if you wanted to."

"Would you answer to it?"

"Probably not the first few times. I'd come around eventually if it meant getting your attention. So about this dinner you promised me. Still a yes?"

"I believe it is."

"Really?"

His reaction made her giggle like the girl she used to be. "Really."

"When?"

"I'll let you know."

He groaned. "You're going to make me work for it, aren't you?"

"A wise man once told me that anything worth having is worth fighting for."

"That man needs to be stoned."

Erin dissolved into a fit of laughter that morphed into a gasp when he ran his lips over the back of her hand. A jolt of awareness traveled up her arm that sucked the breath from her lungs. She'd never reacted to any man that way—ever.

"I'll do the work if you promise it'll be worth it in the end."

"Define 'worth it.'"

"Dinner, of course. What's your dirty mind thinking?"

"Dessert. Does this dinner of yours include dessert?"

"It comes with whatever you want."

"In that case, do your worst."

"Game on."

CHAPTER 19

Big Mac McCarthy entered the bar at the Beachcomber and took a look around, locating his younger brother at the far end of the long bar.

Chelsea, the bartender, caught his eye. "Thanks for coming, Mr. McCarthy."

"I'm glad you called, sweetheart. How long has he been here?"

"Couple hours now."

"Is he talking?"

"Not much. Just drinking. I told him no more after the last one."

"I'll take care of it." Big Mac moved to the far end of the bar and slid onto the stool next to Kevin's, nudging his brother. "What's up?"

"What're you doing here?"

"Same thing as you." He accepted an icy bottle of light beer from Chelsea with a smile and a wink for her.

"Did she call you?"

"Nope." He'd never toss Chelsea under the bus for doing the right thing.

"So you just happened to turn up out of the fog? Total coincidence?"

"No fog tonight. Beautiful clear night out there. You want to get out of here and take a look?"

"Nah, I'm happy here." He noticed his glass was getting low and scowled. "Or I was until she shut me off."

Despite having consumed a lot of alcohol, Kevin sounded remarkably sober. "You must've been here awhile for that to happen."

Kevin's shoulder lifted into a shrug. "Nothing else to do."

"You coulda come to my house. I wouldn't have shut you off. Lots of empty bedrooms upstairs if you ever need one."

"You and Linda don't need your miserable little brother underfoot."

"Hate to see you this way, Kev."

"Hate to feel this way. All these years I've spent counseling other people on how to save their marriages, and mine went up in flames right before my eyes. And the best part? I didn't even see it coming. How's that possible?"

"You didn't think you had anything to worry about."

"So I slacked off. I didn't pay attention. Look at where that got me."

"Have you talked to her at all?"

"Here and there. Mostly logistics about the house and the bank accounts and filing papers."

"No talk of reconciliation?"

"Nope. She's done, and with hindsight, I guess I don't blame her. She got a better offer with a younger guy, of all things."

"Is that what bugs you most? That he's younger?"

"The whole thing bugs me."

"Do you know the guy?"

Kevin shook his head. "Someone she met through work, I guess. She swears nothing happened between them until she left me, but she's talking physically. She's been having an emotional affair with him for a while now."

Big Mac signaled to Chelsea to bring Kevin one more drink, pointing to himself to let her know that he'd take responsibility for him.

A short glass of bourbon landed on the bar in front of Kevin.

He looked up, seeming surprised. "How'd that happen?"

"It's all in who you know around here, my friend."

"Another one of your groupies?" Kevin asked with the first hint of amusement Mac had seen in him.

"I like to call them *friends*."

Snorting, Kevin said, "You always were popular with the ladies."

"We're not talking about me here. We're talking about you and how we're going to get you out of this funk you're in. Your sons are worried about you."

That got his attention. "They are? How do you know?"

"They've told me so. You haven't been yourself since things went south with Deb. They've noticed it. We all have. I told them you're grieving the end of something that meant a lot to you, and in time you'll be back to your old self. I suggested they give you a little space to work things out."

"Is that what you're doing? Giving me some space?"

"I'm making sure you don't do something stupid like get behind the wheel of a car after you've been here for hours."

"I wouldn't do that."

"Good to know."

"Always the big brother."

"I take my responsibilities seriously," Mac said with a grin. "What can I do, Kev? How can I help you through this?"

"Damned if I know."

"It's going to take some time, but you'll get past it. We'll make sure of it."

"What would you do if Linda suddenly up and left you for a younger guy?"

The very thought of it was like an arrow filled with fear landing in the vicinity of Big Mac's heart. "I, um…"

"Sorry," Kevin said. "That was unfair. She's not going anywhere. She's as crazy about you today as she was the day you married her a long-ass time ago."

"Gonna be forty years this Christmas."

"I remember. I was twelve. Had my first beer at your wedding. Did you know that?"

"How'd you get that by Dad?"

"I waited until he'd had at least six and wasn't paying attention anymore."

Big Mac laughed at the memory of their late father. "He did love a good party."

"And that was a great party. I remember it vividly. My first time in a monkey suit, too." He ventured a sideways glance at Mac. "Mom and Dad thought you were too young to get married. Did you know that?"

"No, I never knew. Really?"

"Yep. They had fights about it. Dad thought twenty was way too young to tie yourself down for the rest of your life, but Mom said you always knew what you wanted and how to go after it. She told him it was your life and he should butt out."

Big Mac grunted out a laugh. "I can picture it."

"You're just like him with your kids, you know."

"And you're not with yours?"

"True."

"Let me give you a ride home, Kev."

"Okay." He pulled a twenty from his wallet and left it on the bar for Chelsea.

Big Mac did the same, in part to thank her for looking out for a member of his tribe.

"Despite her ratting me out to you, she's really cool," Kevin said of Chelsea.

"Yes, she is. She's the best. I keep trying to hire her away from the Beachcomber for the Tiki Bar, but she's been here forever and doesn't want to leave."

"Loyalty is a nice trait to have."

The double meaning wasn't lost on Big Mac, who steered Kevin in the direction of where he'd parked his truck. "Deb was loyal to you for a long time, Kevin, and she handled this the best way she could from all reports. People change. Shit happens. The most important thing for you to remember is she's the mother of your sons. That'll never change. No matter how bitter you may feel, keeping it cordial with her is in their best interest."

"I know. And I'm not really bitter. I'm just sort of wrecked that it happened in the first place. How could I *not know* she was that unhappy?"

"You can go over and over it a thousand times and never find the answers you're looking for. Or you can accept that she's made her decision and try to find the way forward. You can also try to learn from it so if you're ever in a serious relationship again, you remember to pay attention."

"The thought of starting all over with someone new makes me nauseous."

"Frankie would tell you there's a lot to be said for starting over."

"He's happier than a pig in shit."

"I'm sure he'd love that description."

"It's true."

"Yeah, it is, and he's waited a long time for it."

"Don't get me wrong," Kevin said. "I'm happy for him and Betsy. She's great."

"She really is. You'll find your Betsy, too. When you're ready."

"You sure about that?"

"Absolutely. And my family would tell you I'm always right about these things."

Kevin groaned. "And you wonder where Mac gets his blowhard tendencies."

"I don't wonder at all."

Kevin laughed harder than Mac had heard him laugh in a long time.

Big Mac pulled into the driveway of the house Kevin had rented from Ned Saunders for himself and his sons. The light was on over the back door.

"Check it out," Kevin said. "They left a light on for me for a change."

"They do grow up, even when we think it's never going to happen."

"They've been great through all of this," Kevin said of Riley and Finn.

"Have they talked to Deb?"

"Here and there. I've told them there's no point in holding a grudge, because I'm not going to. And if I'm not going to, they don't need to hold one on my behalf. Like you said, shit happens. People change."

"Like you, they need some time to absorb it. They'll be fine, and so will you."

"Thanks for coming tonight when Chelsea called you."

"She didn't call me."

"Whatever. You always were a terrible liar." Kevin opened the passenger door to get out.

"Hey, Kev?"

"Yeah?"

"Come to me the next time you think it's a good idea to tie one on, okay?"

"Will do. Maybe you can actually get me drunk enough to forget why I wanted to get drunk in the first place."

"I'll do my best."

Laughing, Kevin shut the door and headed for the house, turning to wave before he went inside.

Poor guy, Big Mac thought as he drove home. He'd never seen Kevin so low. As the baby of the family, Kevin had been the joker growing up, the one who always made them laugh. He'd grown into a serious, well-respected doctor who still made his brothers laugh when they were together. Until recently, anyway. Big Mac decided to keep a closer eye on his "little" brother over the next few weeks to ensure he was coping with the ringer life had thrown his way.

He also couldn't stop thinking about the question Kevin had asked him. *What would you do if Linda suddenly up and left you for a younger guy?* The very thought of it gave him chills.

Big Mac pulled into the driveway at home, killed the engine and went inside, eager to see her, to make sure she was still there and had no plans to be anywhere else. Ever. Bounding up the stairs, he pulled off his jacket and went into the bedroom, where she was in bed with her e-reader.

Breathing a sigh of relief at the sight of her, he started unbuttoning his shirt.

"Hey," she said. "How's Kevin?"

"Not great, but we had a good talk."

"Am I allowed to say that I'm so mad at Deb for doing this to him?"

He sat on the bed to kick off the boat shoes he wore year-round. "Yeah, you are, because I am, too. But he's not. More than anything, he's upset that he never saw it coming."

She held out a hand to him, and he took it, bending to kiss the back of it. "Be right there, love."

He went into the bathroom to use the facilities and brush his teeth, leaving his jeans in a pile on the floor near the hamper, which would give Linda something to talk to him about in the morning. He crawled into bed with her, putting his arm around her waist.

She covered his hand with hers but didn't stop reading.

Sometimes he hated the attention she paid to that e-reader, but other times the books she read put her in an "interesting" mood that benefited him. "What're you reading?"

"The usual."

That meant romance. His wife was a sucker for a good romance. "Is it one of those hot and sexy ones?"

"Maybe."

"Hey, Lin?"

"Yeah?" she asked, but her eyes continued to dart over the screen.

"Do I pay enough attention? To you and to us?"

The e-reader fell to her lap, and her head turned toward him. "What?"

"You heard me. Do I pay enough attention to you?"

"Mac… What is this really about?"

"Answer the question."

"Yes, of course you do." She glanced at him. "Do I? Pay enough attention to you?"

"Except for when one of those romance novels gets you by the throat," he said in a teasing tone.

"You like when my romance novels get me hot and bothered."

"Yes, I do. I like that very much."

"Where are these questions coming from?"

"Something Kevin said had me thinking about it. That's all."

"What did he say?"

"It'll make you mad."

"Tell me anyway."

"He asked how I'd feel if you suddenly left me for a younger guy."

"What did you say?"

"I was so shell-shocked by the thought of it that I didn't say anything. And then he apologized for even suggesting it."

"Good," she said. "He should apologize, because that's never going to happen. Ever. Where would I ever find a younger guy with your stamina?"

He stared at her, momentarily shocked that she would say such a thing.

Then she smiled, her eyes dancing with glee at having shocked him. "What in the world could I ever want that I don't have right here with you?"

"I don't know," he said gruffly. "And that's what scares me. That maybe there's something you want that I don't know about."

She laid her hand on his cheek. "There's nothing I want that I don't have, Mac. I have everything as long as I have you."

"So there's no younger guy lurking around the hotel trying to lure you away from me?"

"I couldn't be lured. What about you with your girlfriends you call 'sweetheart' all over the island?"

"You're my only girlfriend and my only true sweetheart. The others are my *friends*. Big difference." He pushed himself up onto his elbow so he was looking down at her. "In more than forty years, I've never wanted anyone else. I swear."

"I know. I haven't either."

"Not even kinda?"

"Not even kinda."

He smiled then, relieved by the affirmation of what he already knew. "That makes us pretty damned lucky."

"It certainly does."

"We ought to do something big for our fortieth this winter. Have a blowout or something."

"The kids will do it, and we'll act surprised."

"How do you know that?"

"I'm Voodoo Mama. I know everything."

"I thought you hated that nickname?"

"I only let them *think* I hate it. I love that they know they can't get away with anything with me."

Amused by her, he said, "You know what else I heard tonight?"

"What's that?"

"My dad was worried about us getting married so young. Mom had to tell him to leave me alone and let me live my own life."

"Sounds familiar."

"Whatever. You're the one always butting into the kids' lives."

That earned him a raised eyebrow that called him out on his bullshit. "All right. Maybe I do my share of butting in, too."

She busted up laughing, and the only way he could think of to make it stop was to kiss her. When she reached for him, her e-reader slid off her belly and onto the bed between them.

Without breaking the kiss, he put it behind him and then wrapped his arms around her. He kissed her with deep sweeps of his tongue before easing back. "You'd tell me, wouldn't you?" he asked as he kissed her face and neck.

"Tell you what?"

"If you were unhappy or wanted something."

"I'd tell you."

"Promise?"

"Mmm." She arched her neck, giving him full access. "I promise. Do you promise to do the same?"

"Uh-huh." He cupped her breast. "But I've got everything I want right here. If you're happy, I'm happy."

Linda slid a smooth leg up and around his hip. "I could be happier."

"Do tell."

"Why tell when I can show?" She freed his erection from his boxers and began to stroke him, just the way he liked it.

He ran his hand up her inner thigh to discover she wasn't wearing panties under her nightgown. "Sexiest granny ever."

"It was a good book," she said, making him chuckle.

Placing his hand over hers, he stopped her from finishing him off. He shifted so he was on top of her, moving carefully so he wouldn't hurt her because he was so much bigger than she was. As he began to enter her, he said, "Remember the first time we did this and you were afraid that I'd break you?"

"I still worry about that sometimes."

"Nothing to worry about, my love. I'd never break you. Where would I be without you?"

"Mac," she said on a whisper when he was fully embedded in her.

"What, honey?"

Her fingers combed through his hair as her hips lifted to meet his every stroke. "I love you too much to ever leave you. Don't worry about that, okay?"

"Okay. Don't you either."

"I won't. I never have. Not for one second."

With her assurances soothing him, he gave himself to her completely, thankful for the life they had together and that he'd had the good sense to marry her before someone else beat him to it.

CHAPTER 20

"Are you sure it's not too soon?" Seamus asked Carolina, long before the alarm they'd set was due to go off.

"It's what they want, Seamus. Their teachers know what happened, and they'll call us if it's not working."

"It feels too soon."

"To them it feels like normalcy."

"How long was Joe out of school when his father died?"

"That was a slightly different situation because we moved here about a month later, so that year was a bit of a mess for him at school. Thank God for Mac McCarthy. The two of them bonded almost immediately and were inseparable all the way through school. Sometimes I think Mac is the one who saved Joe. Mac and his incredible family that took us both in and made us feel loved in our new home. My parents were instrumental, too. "

"I'm sure you had a lot to do with saving Joe."

"I did what I could, but I was a wreck for a long time after Pete died. I tried to hide that from Joe, but he knew. He was always a smart, insightful kid, as are Jackson and Kyle. We have to follow their lead and do this their way, not our way."

"As always, you're right, love."

"I'm glad you've figured that out so early in our marriage," she said with the dry humor he loved so much.

He turned on his side to face her. "You'll keep me from making a mess of this, won't you?"

"Of course I will. I'm much older and wiser, so just do everything I tell you to do, and we'll be fine."

He snorted with laughter. "That'll be the day."

She flashed the sly, sexy smile that had been the first thing he loved about her. "It was worth a shot."

Seamus put his arm around her and dragged her across the bed to him.

"Such a caveman."

"You love that about me."

"I love everything about you, but you know what I love best?"

"What's that?" he asked, slayed by her sweet words and the power of her love.

"I love how badly you want to do right by those boys."

"I want that so much. I don't want to screw it up. I want to make everything better for them."

"You already have, Seamus. It was your idea for us to take them in. What would've become of them otherwise?"

"Someone would've stepped up."

"We have no way to know that for sure. They could've ended up wards of the state or in foster care or God knows where. Who know if they would've been allowed to stay together?"

Seamus shuddered at the thought of any of those scenarios.

"You saved them from an uncertain future. The reason they're ready to go back to school so soon is because they know you'll be here and I'll be here, waiting for them to get home. We're going to make this work."

"It means so much to me that you fully embraced my desire to have them, love. At this point in your life, you probably want to be relaxing and sleeping in and doting on your grandbaby, and I've made you a mum to two small boys."

"I had plenty of years to relax and sleep in before you stormed your way into my life and ruined my sleep. I'm as thrilled as you are to be able to make a difference for those little guys. Don't think for a minute I'm not."

He pushed himself up onto an elbow and leaned over to kiss her. "Let's go get our boys up for school."

*

Hope came awake suddenly at six o'clock, the time Ethan usually got up. For a moment, she couldn't remember where she was, but the heavy weight of Paul's arm around her waist and the hairy leg wedged between hers was a reminder of what'd transpired between them.

They'd been up most of the night and had ended up making love in the shower at three a.m. She'd never had shower sex before and had to say there was something to be said for the way he'd pressed her against the wall and surged into her while the water came down upon them.

Sexiest night of her life, hands down. It pained her to think of what she'd missed out on when she'd thought she was happy with Carl. But in all those years, he'd never paid the kind of attention to her that Paul had in one night.

Her eyes blurred with tears that frustrated her. What in the world did she have to be teary-eyed over when she was having such a marvelous time with a hot, sexy guy who cared about her son as much as he cared about her? Her belly tightened around the grinding sense of dread she'd carried with her since Carl was arrested, while she waited for the next disaster to strike.

Surely nothing that felt as good as she did with Paul could possibly last. With tears sliding down her cheeks, she eased herself out of Paul's embrace and got up to go to the bathroom. Every muscle in her body protested against the movement, and the soreness between her legs was indicative of an overly indulgent night. She hadn't ached like this since her first time with Carl.

She'd been just a kid then. What did she know about what truly mattered in life? She brushed her teeth and caught sight of the rat's nest her hair had dried into after going to bed with it wet from the shower and ran a brush through it. Her jaw was covered in red spots from where Paul's whiskers had rubbed against her skin. She brought her fingers up to touch them, amazed by the passion that had resulted in her skin being rubbed raw.

How could she have lived for so many years without knowing it was possible to do and feel the things she'd experienced last night?

She startled when his arm slid around her waist from behind.

"I woke up, and you were gone." He kissed the back of her shoulder. "Scared me."

"I woke up at my usual time after almost eight years of six a.m. wake-ups."

"That's brutal."

"That's my life."

"Not today it isn't. Come back to bed for a little while."

She let him lead her back to bed and tuck her in.

He leaned over to kiss her. "Be right back." He went into the bathroom, closing the door and returning with the fresh taste of toothpaste on his lips when he kissed her again. "You going to tell me what's wrong?"

"Nothing is wrong."

"Why do you look so lost, then? Was last night too much? I kept telling myself to let you sleep, but you kept looking so sweet and sexy."

"It wasn't too much."

He slid his hand up her thigh to cup her intimately, making her gasp. "Are you sore? Here?"

"Yeah."

"It was too much, then."

"It was perfect. I loved everything we did. I'm sore because it's been such a long time since I did anything like that. Forever, if I'm being honest."

"What do you mean?"

"I've never had sex like that, Paul. I didn't even know it was supposed to be like that."

His brows narrowed with displeasure. "He didn't take care of you?"

"Not the way you did."

"Well, that's a goddamned crime. They should've put him away for that, too."

His vehemence made her laugh, and then the tears were back, once again pissing her off with the way they appeared out of nowhere to remind her that her heart had once been shattered. It had healed, but she was different now than she'd been then, less trusting, more cynical.

With gentle strokes of his fingers, he brushed them away. "Why the tears?"

"I don't know exactly. Emotional overload maybe?"

"If this is happening too fast for you, we can dial it back a notch."

"What would that entail?"

"Whatever you want it to. The last thing I want to do is overload you—physically or emotionally."

"I kind of liked the way you overloaded me last night."

"Only kinda?" He pushed his erection against her leg. "I gotta work harder."

"Please don't," she said with a laugh. "You'll kill me."

"Since I have no desire to kill you, how about we go find some breakfast and then hit the beach?"

"You want to get up this early on a rare day off?"

"I'm already up." He pressed against her again, making her laugh. "May as well seize the day. We can nap later."

"Mmm, a nap. What's that like?"

"You haven't lived until you've had the Paul Martinez nap special."

"I'll look forward to that all day."

"Hey, Hope?"

"Hmm?"

"It's okay to relax and enjoy yourself a little. Nothing bad is going to happen."

There was nothing he could've said that would've meant more to her in that place and time. After they checked in at home and called the hospital to learn Marion had spent a quiet night, they set out to take full advantage of their scenic location. Hope did as directed and threw herself into enjoying a blissful day with Paul. He was funny, charming, solicitous and affectionate—the same way he'd been before they had sex.

It was a relief to realize he wasn't going to turn into someone different because he'd gotten what he wanted.

By the time they returned to their room later that afternoon, she was drunk off the sun and the thrill of being the subject of his undivided attention. He made her feel important by listening carefully to everything she had to say. His unwavering focus made her feel *seen* in a way she never had been before.

She wanted to dive into bed with him and pick up where they'd left off in the early morning hours, but her body wasn't having it.

"I know what you need," he said.

"I told you. I don't think I can."

"Such a dirty mind! That's not what I was suggesting at all."

Hope eyed him skeptically.

"Take off your bathing suit and get on the bed, facedown."

"And I have a dirty mind?"

"Trust me?"

Oh God, what a loaded question! "I want to."

He kissed her forehead and tugged at the tie to her bikini top. "I promise you won't be sorry."

"Okay then…" She removed her top and then her bottoms, feeling her skin tingle as he took a long, leisurely look at her. Averting her gaze, she went to lie on the bed as directed, telling herself that everything that'd happened so far had been awesome. Surely this would be, too, right?

*

Paul had sensed her underlying tension all day. It was a huge step for her to become intimate with him, and it was almost as if she expected him to turn into a dick today or something. After everything she'd been through, that was understandable. But he was determined to prove that she could trust him and that he was nothing like the man who'd hurt her so badly.

He went into the bathroom to get the bottle of bath oil he'd noticed there earlier. It wasn't exactly what he wanted, but it was close enough in a pinch. Filling a sink full of steaming hot water, he put the plastic bottle in the water to heat up and took a moment to settle himself.

Here she finally was—the woman he'd hoped to someday find, the one who challenged and intrigued him and turned him on like no one else ever had. It wasn't lost on him that he faced an uphill battle in convincing her that she could let go of past hurts and allow herself to love and be loved by someone new.

He was well on his way to falling in love with her and had been for quite some time, if he were being entirely honest. Thinking back to the recent day when he'd contemplated jumpstarting his dating life, he'd initially considered everyone but her because she was technically an employee. That was the only reason she hadn't been at the very top of his list.

And then she'd kissed him and changed everything. One taste of her sweet lips had left him hungry for so much more of her. Add in the adorable, precocious son who came with her, and they made for one very attractive package deal. She'd said she would never get married again, and he hoped he could change her mind about that.

But he had to go slow, or she'd run as far away from him as she could within the tight confines of their living arrangement. The small space of yard that separated their homes could become an impenetrable distance if he wasn't careful.

With the oil heated, he took it with him to the bedroom, where she was right where he'd left her—facedown on the bed with her smooth back and supple ass on full display. He went immediately hard at the sight of all that gorgeous skin, but kept his bathing suit on when he climbed on the bed next to her.

"What took so long?" she asked.

"You can't rush quality." He tested the temperature of the oil before dribbling it over her back.

She took a deep inhale that evolved into a sigh when he began kneading her tight muscles. "Oh God, Paul. That feels so good."

"Relax. Let me take care of you." Starting at her shoulders, he worked his way down slowly, giving careful attention to every inch of her back and then her legs, saving her sexy ass for last. As he ran his hands over her cheeks, squeezing and massaging, he noticed the subtle lift of her hips, the slight squirm of her body, and realized she was fully aroused. "Everything okay down there?"

"Mmm, so okay. Never been better."

That was exactly what he wanted to hear. He let his fingers slide into the deep valley between her cheeks, drawing a gasp of surprise followed by a moan of pleasure from her when he encountered the abundant proof of her arousal. Hooking his arm around her waist, he drew her up to her knees and put two pillows under her hips.

"P-Paul, what're you doing?"

"Relax, sweetheart. I'm taking care of you. Just let go and enjoy." Mindful of her soreness, he gently ran his fingers over her clit, retreating to slide them into her and then repeating it again and again. Then he added his tongue, pressing it to her clit as he pushed his fingers into her.

She exploded, crying out as the orgasm hit her hard and fast.

He stayed with her until the contractions eased and he retreated slowly as the aftershocks made her tremble. "Ready to do the front now?"

Hope released a tremulous laugh. "I'm ready to sleep for about twelve hours after that."

He removed the pillows and helped her turn over.

Looking up at him with eyes gone liquid with satisfaction, she offered a tentative smile. "You give a great massage."

"It's my happy endings special."

When she laughed, her whole body got in on it, and a deep sense of longing overtook him. He wanted to make her laugh every day for the rest of their lives, if only she would let him.

"What are you thinking right now?" she asked. "You look so serious." With her hair spread out on the pillow and her face flushed from her orgasm, she was more beautiful than she'd ever been before.

"That I like to hear you laugh."

"It's nice to have something to laugh about again. Something other than the antics of a seven-year-old boy, which can be quite funny."

"I want to keep making you laugh after we get home."

"That would be nice."

He started at her feet this time, massaging her legs and giving extra attention to her inner thighs, which she'd mentioned earlier were sore from what they'd done yesterday. With her legs spread before him, it took every bit of self-control he could summon to stay focused on the massage and not the throbbing need that pulsed through him with almost painful intensity.

Skipping her core, he slid his oiled hands over her belly, drawing a sharp inhale from her when his thumbs caressed her hipbones. She was writhing again by the time he got to her breasts.

"Paul…"

"What, sweetheart?"

"I want you."

"You have me. I'm right here with you, and I'm not going anywhere."

She held out her arms to him, and he went willingly to her. "I want you inside me."

"You're too sore."

"You'd go slow, right?"

"We could go slow." What did it say about him that he was so desperate for her that he let her talk him into making love when he'd planned to let her rest and recover from what they'd already done? Despite his reservations, he found himself removing his bathing suit and coming down on top of her.

She wrapped her arms around him and released a sigh that sounded like relief to him.

Her oil-slick skin heated on contact with his body, which was the hottest fucking thing he'd ever experienced until he began to enter her. That was hotter. She was so wet but also so tight, and he was forced to go so slowly, lest he hurt her. It was pure torture of the best kind, and it didn't help that she moved beneath him like a sexy siren determined to have her wicked way with him.

"Does it hurt?"

"Not too bad."

"That's not no."

"It burns a little, but that's because of you, not me."

He stopped moving and looked down at her. "Because of me?"

"You're big, Paul. Like you didn't know that already."

Unfortunately, her words only made him bigger, which drew a groan from her. "Note to self, never mention he's big when he's trying to get inside you." Her eyes widened, and her mouth fell open. "Stop! I can't take any more!"

He grinned at the face she made at him. "Then you need to stop talking dirty to me, baby."

Her fingers dug into the muscles of his back as he entered and retreated over and over again until she finally relaxed and allowed him in.

"Ahhh, God, that feels so good," he whispered into her neck, making her shiver. Her muscles pulsed and rippled around his cock, which nearly finished him off before he'd even gotten started. "Can I talk dirty to you?"

"If you must..."

"How dirty am I allowed to get?"

"As dirty as you want."

She had no idea what she was asking for. With his lips nearly touching her ear, he said, "You have the tightest, hottest, wettest pussy. I love the way you grab hold of my cock and squeeze me so hard."

Her inner muscles contracted around him.

"Christ," he said through gritted teeth. "Do that again." She did it again and again, and the sensations triggered his inner beast, making him forget all about his plans to go easy on her. He started to move, giving her the deep thrusts that she'd loved so much last night.

"*Yes*," she whispered. "Don't stop."

"I'll never stop." He slid his hands under her, gripping her ass in both hands as he let loose. "Feels so fucking good."

Her thighs tightened around his hips, and the spasm of her inner muscles let him know she was close, so he went for broke, drawing another keening cry of completion from her. That was quickly becoming his most favorite sound in the world, he thought, as he went deep one more time and lost himself in her as she clung to him.

"Hope… God…" He wanted to tell her he was falling in love with her. He wanted to tell her he wanted a life with her and Ethan. He wanted to tell her everything, but he held back. More than anything, he was afraid to scare her away, so he bit his tongue for now. But eventually, when she was ready, he would tell her everything.

The ringing of his cell phone interrupted his thoughts. He took the call from the hospital.

"Mr. Martinez, the doctor would like to meet with you tomorrow at eleven if that's convenient."

"I'll be there."

With those three words, reality returned to remind him that this time away with Hope had been a mere interlude. The real challenge would begin when they returned home.

CHAPTER 21

Mac and Maddie had breakfast at the South Harbor Diner and then took the stairs behind the diner to Dan Torrington's new office. Wearing a pink polo shirt with plaid shorts and loafers, Dan met them in the reception area.

Mac cringed at his friend's flashy outfit. "*The Preppy Handbook* called. They want their cover model back."

"Ha-ha, very funny. A man has a bit of style, and this is the abuse he takes."

"If you want to call that style…"

"Be nice, Mac," Maddie said. "We're here because we need his help."

"Come on in." Dan led them into his office in which a desk sat amid boxes in various stages of unpacking. "Sorry for the mess. My stuff from LA arrived on Friday, and I haven't had a chance to do much with it."

"So this is an official move, huh?" Mac asked as he took one of the visitor chairs and Maddie took the other.

"Looks that way. I'm keeping my office in LA, but this is where Kara wants to be, so it's where I want to be, too." He offered a sheepish grin and a shrug. "Plus, I seem to have a practice here since Jim Sturgil was charged with a felony." He held up the hand that bore a healing pink scar across the palm where Jim had sliced him with a carving knife during Dan and Kara's engagement party.

"I still can't believe he did that," Maddie said. "He's lost his mind."

"He stands to lose a lot more than that," Dan said. "My contact in the attorney general's office tells me they're going for prison time for the assault with a deadly weapon charge."

"Wow," Maddie said on a long exhale. "Poor Ashleigh. How could he do this to his daughter?"

Mac took hold of her hand and gave it a squeeze. Jim Sturgil had done a lot of things to his wife and daughter that Mac couldn't believe, beginning with leaving them in an empty house after he moved out and took most of what they'd owned with him. The assault on Dan, whom he'd accused of ruining his law practice, was the latest in a long string of bad moves by his former brother-in-law. Thank goodness Tiffany was happily remarried to Blaine Taylor now, and Ashleigh would have Blaine's influence in her life growing up.

"So you're here for estate planning." Dan shuffled some papers on his desk. "I'll confess that I haven't done much of that since my first years out of law school, but I'm hoping it'll be like riding a bike. I printed out some worksheets to get you started. You'll have to list assets and other tangible property."

"We're mostly concerned about making sure our kids are taken care of," Maddie said.

"After what happened to Lisa Chandler, it's on our minds," Mac added.

"You're not alone in that," Dan said. "I've gotten quite a few calls from other parents with the same concerns. Looks like I'm about to get back up to speed on estate planning right quick." He reviewed the worksheets in depth with them, highlighting the areas he needed them to complete before their next meeting. "It's all pretty straightforward."

"Except for the part about who we want to get our kids if the worst should happen," Maddie said. "That's not straightforward at all."

"What's the issue?" Dan asked.

"We have too many candidates," Mac said.

"That's not a *bad* problem to have," Dan said.

"No, but we're concerned about causing divisiveness in our family by choosing one sibling over another," Maddie said. "How do people handle that?"

"One thing I'd suggest is to decide on who you want and speak to that person and only that person about what you're asking of them," Dan said. "Make sure they fully understand what they'd be taking on and that they're willing. After we make it legal, you don't need to ever speak of it again. There's a very good chance no one else will ever know who you chose. Or at least we hope that's the case."

"I like that," Mac said. "Why would anyone else need to know as long as the person or couple we choose knows?" Speaking directly to Dan, he said, "You have a way of making sure that everyone involved understands that whatever we decide is what we wanted for them, right?"

"Yep. We'll sew it up nice and tight so there's no room for interpretation."

Maddie glanced at him, her golden-brown eyes seeing right through him as usual. God, he loved that face, those eyes, those lips, the way she looked at him with love—except for when he was exasperating her, which was often. He could tell the conversation was distressing her, so he decided to wrap it up.

"This is a great start, Dan," Mac said. "We'll get going on this and make an appointment for next week."

"Let's do that now while you're here."

After they set up their next meeting, Dan walked them out. "See you Saturday night at Paul's party?"

"I'll be there," Mac said. "Did you hear what the girls are up to for Jenny's bachelorette party?"

"No, what?"

"Strippers," Mac said. "Male strippers."

Dan's mouth fell open. "No way."

"Yes, way. They were all abuzz over it at my house the other night."

Dan glanced at Maddie, who smiled and shrugged. "I know nothing."

"She lies," Mac said. "Right to my face."

"Well," Maddie said, "gotta go get the kids from my mom. Come on, Mac." She took him by the hand and dragged him down the stairs while Dan laughed at them. They met up with his fiancée, Kara, as they emerged onto the sidewalk.

"Hey, guys," she said. "Is he up there?"

"Yep," Maddie said. "He's all yours. See you Saturday night?"

Kara grinned widely. "Wouldn't miss it." She went inside, leaving them on the sidewalk.

Mac had a million things he needed to do, beginning with the job he had pending at Seamus and Carolina's, but his top priority was looking up at him with amusement dancing in those beautiful eyes. "You're not going to Jenny's party if there's going to be strippers there."

"You can't tell me what to do."

"Wanna bet?"

"Yep."

When he glared at her, she laughed right in his face!

"You're so cute when you're trying to boss me around, Mac." She went up on tiptoes and bit down on his earlobe, making him instantly hard.

He yanked her in close to him, not caring in the least that they were standing on a sidewalk where anyone might see them. "No strippers for my wife."

"You're really being ridiculous about this."

"No, I'm not. How would you feel if I was cavorting with strippers?"

She raised a brow. "Male strippers?"

"No," he said emphatically. "The female variety."

Shrugging, she said, "Boys will be boys."

"Are you freaking kidding me right now?"

"Do you honestly think I'm going to leave you for a male stripper, Mac?" She kissed him and disentangled from his embrace. "Now go to work and let me go get the kids from Mom. She has a hair appointment to get to."

"We're not done talking about this."

Walking backward, she flashed a sexy smile and waggled her fingers at him. "Bye, Mac. Love you."

"We're not done!" he yelled after her.

The last thing he heard before she rounded the corner and disappeared out of view was her ringing laughter. They were definitely going to talk more about this later—and she was *not* going to that party.

*

Kara entered Dan's office and found him sitting with his feet on his desk, pen in his mouth, papers in hand, brows knitted in concentration. He was so damned sexy, not that she could ever tell him that, because it would go straight to his already overinflated ego. But she loved that overinflated ego, just like she loved everything else about him.

Leaning against the doorframe, arms crossed, she cleared her throat.

When he saw her there, his smile lit up his whole face. She loved that, too, the way he was always so damned glad to see her, even when he'd just woken her with slow, sultry morning lovemaking two short hours ago.

"Why, hello there, young lady. Are you in need of legal counsel?"

"Not at this time, but it appears you're in need of some unpacking help. This place is a disaster."

"You're not spending your one day off unpacking my office."

"Why not? I don't have anything else to do, and this way I get to spend my one day off with my fiancé. It's a win-win."

Dan held out his hand to her. "Come over here and see me."

She went to him, took hold of his hand and let him guide her onto his lap.

He nuzzled her neck, his whiskers abrading her skin. "I have a bone to pick with you, my love."

Shifting on his lap, she felt his erection settle between her cheeks. "I thought we already picked that bone this morning."

"Ha-ha, very funny. I'm talking about the male-stripper bone."

"Oh. You heard about that, huh?"

"You're goddamned right I did, and I'm none too pleased that I didn't hear about it from you."

"I was going to tell you."

"When?"

"Sunday?" she asked with a grin.

"So we're going to keep secrets in this marriage of ours? Is that how it's going to be?"

"We're not technically married yet." She loved to wind him up, and judging by the stormy look he gave her, the comment was a direct hit.

"You're actually going to get me on a technicality?"

"I've learned about such things from the best lawyer I've ever known."

"No strippers."

"Yes, dear."

"I mean it, Kara. No one touches this sweet body except for me." To make his point, he cupped her breast and teased her nipple.

"Do you really think I'd let anyone else touch me the way you do? Especially knowing what happened to you the last time you were engaged?"

He sighed deeply. "No, I don't think you would, but the thought of it... It makes me crazy, Kara. I don't want to be like that, but I can't help it."

She brought her lips down on his and ran her tongue over his bottom lip. "You have nothing to worry about where I'm concerned. I'm all yours. Forever and always yours."

Cupping the back of her head, he dove into the kiss like a man who'd been starving until she came along. Another thing she loved about him was how much he wanted her. She kept expecting their ardor to wane, to burn itself out, but it only burned brighter the longer they were together.

"I don't know how I'll survive until next June when I can put a second ring on your finger," he said when they came up for air.

"That's a formality, Dan. As far as I'm concerned, we're already married in all the ways that matter most."

"I thought you said—"

"Forget I said that. I'd never, ever want you to feel insecure about me or us."

"I don't. Not really."

Those two little words he added on at the end exposed the truth.

She took him by the face and stared into his glorious eyes. "I will never, ever, *ever* do to you what she did."

"And I will never, ever hook up with one of your sisters the way he did."

"Please don't have those worries until June. I'd hate to think of you feeling like that between now and then."

"I'll try not to."

"I know I've said this before, but it bears repeating—I'm sort of glad now that Kelly hooked up with Matt, and that your ex did your best man before the wedding. Both of those awful things led us to exactly where we belong—with each other. And nothing has ever been like this for me."

"Me either, baby." Burying his face in her hair, he held her tight, seeming to breathe her in.

"Now that we have that resolved, can we please do something about this office of yours?"

"If you insist."

"I do." Kara got up from his lap and tugged at his hand to bring him with her. Dropping to her knees in front of one of the open boxes, she started taking things out.

"Thanks for the help, babe."

"Happy to do it."

"Now, about those strippers…"

"Shut up, Dan, and get to work."

Chief of Police Blaine Taylor paced from one end of Naughty & Nice to the other, full of barely contained rage as he waited for his wife to finish a customer transaction that she seemed to be dragging out. Or so it seemed to him. He could not believe what he'd just heard over coffee at the South Harbor Diner with Adam McCarthy and Joe Cantrell.

Strippers? Male strippers? Were they out of their *goddamned minds?*

The customer finally left the store, and Blaine pounced on Tiffany. "You want to tell me what the hell you're thinking hiring *male strippers* to perform at Jenny's party?"

"Hi, honey." Wearing a cheerful smile, she came around the counter to hug and kiss him.

When she would've pulled back, he anchored her to him with an arm around her waist. He wanted to rage and scream and protest, but she was pregnant with his baby, and he'd never do anything to hurt or upset her. "Don't try to use your considerable charms on me, Mrs. Taylor," he growled. "Answer the question."

"A, I did not hire strippers. Sydney is Jenny's matron of honor, so you'll need to take this up with her." She batted her eyes at him. "I'm just an invited guest."

"What's B?"

She thought about that for a second. "No B. Just an A. I had nothing to do with it."

"I don't believe that for one second. In fact, I happen to believe this whole thing was *your* idea."

"Why, Blaine, whatever are you inferring about your wife?"

"That she's an operator of the highest order, and if anyone knows where to get male strippers, it's the island's sex-toy queen."

"I'm offended by the implication."

"But you're not denying it, are you?"

She tightened her lips as she looked up at him, seeming to be deciding how much she should say. "Out of fear of self-incrimination, I'd like to plead the Fifth."

Though he was seriously concerned about this harebrained plan of theirs, he couldn't help but laugh at that. She was so damned cute and so damned sexy—never more so than she'd been since conceiving his baby.

"Listen to me," he said sternly when he was done laughing. "You need to let me run background checks on these guys. I'm dead serious, Tiff. You have no idea who they are or where they're coming from. What if they have criminal records?"

As she patted his chest, he sensed condescension coming his way. "Don't worry about that. Sydney and Abby went through a reputable agency to hire them."

He put his hand on top of his head, fearing it was going to blow off at any second. "This is *not* happening."

"Blaine, honey, take a deep breath. It's all in good fun. Who deserves a big blowout of a sendoff more than Jenny does? After all she's been through… Come on. You wouldn't do anything to ruin that for her, would you?"

"You're doing that thing you do…"

"What thing?"

"With your eyes. You think if you look at me that way, I'll melt into putty at your feet."

"I don't know what you're talking about."

"Sure you don't," he said with a laugh.

"Promise me you won't mess with Jenny's surprise."

"I don't know if I can make that promise."

She leaned in so her lips were brushing against his ear. "If you do," she said in a husky whisper, "I'll suck your dick until you explode down my throat later."

"Motherfucker," he muttered. He was no match for her. He never had been, but damn, he loved her anyway.

To make her point completely, she cupped his suddenly rock-hard erection and dragged her fingernail over the full length of him, making him shudder from the effort it took not to come in his pants like a horny teenager.

"Promise?"

"I promise not to do anything to screw with Jenny's party. You, on the other hand…"

"You may screw with me to your heart's content."

"Oh, I will. You'd better be ready when I get home tonight to pay up on that promise you made."

"I'd never renege on a promise to you."

He tightened the arm he had around her. "I want one other promise from you."

"What's that?"

"You will not touch those strippers or let them touch you, or I won't be responsible for my actions. You got me?"

"Yes, dear."

"Are you pacifying me?"

"Would I do that?"

"You absolutely would."

She smiled up at him, her eyes twinkling with mirth. "I love you."

"I love you, too, even when you're manipulating me."

"I'll make it well worth your while tonight." She gave his hard cock an extra squeeze for good measure.

"You're really going to make me walk around in this condition all day?"

"What would you have me do about it?"

Though he was on duty and absolutely shouldn't do this, he released her, strode to the door, locked it and put the Closed for Fifteen Minutes sign in the window. Then he took hold of her hand and half-walked, half-dragged her to the back of the store.

"Blaine," she said on a nervous laugh. "I'm working here. You can't just—"

Pressing her against the same wall that had hosted one of their very first encounters, he kissed the words right off her lips. His hand worked its way under her skirt, where he encountered a tiny string thong, the kind that never failed to turn him into a stark raving lunatic whenever he saw it wedged between her sweet cheeks. He pushed it out of his way and sank two fingers into her.

She turned her face to break the kiss and drew in a sharp breath.

He froze. "That didn't hurt, did it?"

"God, no. Don't stop."

Keeping her anchored to the wall with the tight press of his body, he used his free hand to open his uniform pants. This was madness. He was on duty. He was the goddamned chief of police about to fuck his smoking-hot pregnant wife against a wall in her store in the middle of his shift.

"What?" she asked, tuning in to his reluctance.

"I shouldn't be doing this."

"Yes, you should. You absolutely should." She finished freeing him from his pants and stroked him until his eyes crossed with lust. "Don't leave me like this."

What could he say to that? Nothing, so he forgot he was on duty and that she was working. He forgot about everything other than her and how much he loved her. The one thing he couldn't forget was that she was pregnant, which was the only reason he didn't hammer into her the way he wanted to. Rather, he took it slow and easy, cupping her ass cheeks as he worked his way into her tight channel.

"You take my breath away every goddamned time," he whispered harshly.

"Same. Same, same, *same*." She clung to him. "Don't hold back, Blaine. It feels so good."

"Afraid," he said, faltering. "The baby…"

"It's fine. We're fine."

"Hold on to me."

She tightened her arms and legs around him. "Love me. Just love me."

"I love you so fucking much. I want you all the time, even when I'm on duty and shouldn't."

"You should. You really, *really* should."

As he laughed, he faltered, losing his rhythm for a second before he recovered. "This is going to be fast."

"I like fast."

Blaine groaned as he gave her what she said she wanted, more gently than he normally would have, so he wouldn't hurt her or the baby. The very thought of that made his knees go weak, and with her pressed against the wall, he couldn't afford weak knees.

His radio crackled to life with a call from dispatch that he had no choice but to ignore—something else he never did.

And then she was coming with loud cries that shattered his control. He surged into her, gasping from the wave after wave of exquisite pleasure that seized his body as her release sparked his.

The dispatcher called again.

Blaine could barely breathe, let alone speak.

"Blaine, babe… The radio."

"I hear it." He focused on dragging air into his lungs, and when his head stopped spinning, he keyed the mic on his shoulder to respond to the dispatcher and listened to her report of a multiple-car accident on the island's north end.

"I'm on my way." Blaine leaned his forehead against Tiffany's. "How'd you get me to do this while I'm on duty?"

"As I recall, you didn't give me much choice."

"Aww, baby, you always have a choice."

She smoothed the sweaty hair off his forehead. "And I choose you every time."

"You make me so incredibly happy, Tiffany. I keep thinking it's not possible to feel this good all the time, but it just gets better and better."

With her arms still tight around his neck, she kissed him. "Yes, it does, but you'd better get going before you get in trouble with Mayor Upton again."

"I'm not entirely sure I can still walk."

Her giggle filled his heart to overflowing. He loved making her laugh and smile. She'd been so grim when he first met her, and her lighthearted joy was a reminder of how far they'd come since then. Reluctantly, he withdrew from her and held her until she regained her footing.

As expected, his legs wobbled under him.

Tiffany leaned back against the wall while he went into the tiny bathroom in the back of the store to clean up. She was still there when he returned, her lips swollen from their kisses and her cheeks flushed from exertion.

"You look like you've been thoroughly ravished, my love."

"This insanely sexy cop came in and had his wicked way with me."

Blaine raised a brow. "I dare any man to lay a hand on my woman. I'll kill him."

She smiled and reached for him.

He took her hand and let her draw him back in for one last tongue-twisting kiss. "I'll never survive until tonight."

"Yes, you will, and I'll make good on my promises."

Even though he'd been fully satisfied not even five minutes ago, Blaine whimpered like a little girl at the thought of what she'd promised him. "I'll think of nothing else all day."

"Go," she said, giving him a little push. "The sooner you get done with work, the sooner you get your reward for not messing with Jenny's party."

He literally tore himself away from her. "We're going on a vacation. Just you and me by ourselves. Very, *very* soon. You hear me?" Their busy season was coming to an end, and they'd earned some time alone.

"Ohhh, yes, please."

"Very, very soon." He kissed her again, taking a close look at her gorgeous face. "You okay?"

"Never been better in my life."

"All right. I'm going, then." One more kiss. "We'll get over this craziness someday, won't we?"

"God, I hope not," she said with a happy sigh.

One last kiss. "This time I'm really going."

"This time I'm really letting you."

The chatter on the radio indicated the accident was a bad one, which propelled him out of the store and into bright sunshine that nearly blinded him. Pulling his aviators down from the top of his head, he walked toward his department-issued SUV to head to the accident scene. But all he could think about was going home to her later to collect on that promise she'd made him. This was going to be a very long day.

CHAPTER 22

Sitting in the doctor's office, Paul heard what was being said, but he couldn't seem to process it. Late-stage dementia, difficulty swallowing, bedridden, vulnerable to infections, risk of pneumonia, unable to speak or communicate…

This was a whole new ballgame.

"I know it's a lot of information to take in all at once, but we feel it's imperative for you to prepare for what's ahead sooner rather than later."

Hope's hand covered Paul's, and her warmth made him realize he was freezing in the air-conditioned office.

"Mr. Martinez, I'm sure you must have questions." The doctor's deep voice permeated Paul's frozen state. The man looked at him with piercing blue eyes, but the only thing Paul could seem to focus on was his paisley bow tie. Who wore paisley these days?

Paul couldn't think of a single thing to say. There would be questions. Hundreds of them. But right now, there was only despair.

"What are your thoughts about continuing to care for Mrs. Martinez at home on Gansett Island?" Hope asked.

Paul would have to thank her for that later. It was a good question and one that needed to be asked.

"I believe it's going to become increasingly more difficult to care for her at home. That's not to say it can't be done, but it won't be easy."

Over the next thirty minutes, Hope quizzed the doctor on every aspect of his mother's care. While Paul sat like a useless zombie, reeling from the shock, they covered practicalities such as medication and equipment and how to handle the inevitable agitation that Marion would experience as her symptoms worsened.

Paul's tongue felt too big for his mouth, like if he tried to speak, nothing would come out. It had been years now since his mother was first diagnosed, but this was the first time his own brain seemed to shut down at one of her appointments. He simply couldn't get his head around it.

Thank God Hope was here to do it for him. When she stood, Paul realized they were wrapping up the meeting, and he'd yet to say a word.

"Is he okay?" the doctor asked Hope.

"Paul." He blinked her into focus. "Are you all right?"

"I'm… Yeah, I'm sorry. It's just a lot to take in."

The doctor handed each of them his card. "I'm here to help in any way I can. You and your brother have some big decisions to make, and if I can be of assistance, please let me know."

"Thank you," Paul said, humbled by the kindness of a stranger.

"I've signed the discharge paperwork." The doctor handed a sheaf of papers to Hope. "The nurses will have your mother ready to go home."

Still feeling dazed, Paul shook his hand, thanked him again and followed Hope out of the office, through a maze of hallways that led to the room where his mother waited to go home.

"There you are, George," she said when they walked in. "I've been waiting so long to see you. Where have you been?"

The tears in her eyes finally snapped Paul out of the stupor he'd been in during the meeting. He went to her and bent to hug her. "Sorry I made you wait, Marion. It couldn't be helped."

"It's okay," she said, stroking his hair like a lover rather than a mother. "You work so hard. I understand."

"What do you say we go home?"

"I want to go home. I've been telling them that." Her arms were covered in bruises from the many needle sticks, and her hair was in need of Chloe's special touch.

"We'll get you home," Paul said.

"Who's she?" Marion asked, casting a suspicious glare at Hope.

"That's Hope. She's our friend. I'd like you to be nice to her, okay?"

"Of course, George. Whatever you want."

The nurse came to push Marion's wheelchair, but Paul told her he'd do it.

"Why am I in the hospital, George? Who's staying with the boys? Are they all right?"

"They're fine," Paul said.

"What about work? You can't be away from work, especially this time of year."

"I left Louis in charge," Paul said of the man who'd once been his father's right hand. "And Hilda is with the boys." Louis and Hilda had been gone longer than his father had, but the information pacified his mother.

Hope squeezed his arm in a show of support that he appreciated.

By the time they arrived home three hours later, Paul was spent. The break from reality he and Hope had enjoyed was but a distant memory, obliterated by the more pressing reality of his mother's deteriorating condition. Naturally, Alex and Jenny wanted to hear everything the doctor had had to say, and after Marion was tucked into bed for a nap, Hope did most of the talking for him.

"Fuck," Alex said on a long exhale, summing up the situation rather succinctly.

"So what does this mean?" Jenny asked.

"I don't know," Paul said. "Maybe it's time to look into a permanent solution on the mainland."

The comment was met with resounding silence.

"We knew it would get to this point eventually," Paul said.

"Yeah, but we didn't think it would be this soon," Alex replied.

Jenny took hold of his hand, cradling it between both of hers.

"If I may…" Hope said.

"Please," Alex said. "Speak freely. You have to know by now how much we value your opinion."

"While the doctor painted a rather dismal picture, none of it is going to happen tonight or tomorrow or even next week. We can keep doing what we've been doing for the time being while you explore your options."

"That's true," Jenny said. "It took two years for her to get to this point. The next stage isn't going to happen all at once."

Their comments brought a small measure of comfort to Paul because they were right.

"Let's get through the wedding, and then we'll start to look for places on the mainland," Paul said. "We can take turns going over to visit her. We'll figure it out like we always have since this began."

Ethan, who'd been watching a movie in Paul's room, came bounding into the room, looking for his mother. He'd been clingy since she returned, which Paul could tell she loved. She scooped him up onto her lap and put her arms around him, kissing every part of his face that she could reach. He squealed with pretend outrage, but he loved the attention.

"I'd better get him home to start his homework," Hope said. "We can talk more about all this after the wedding."

"Thanks so much for everything today," Paul said with the warmest smile he owned. "You saved me in there with the doctor."

She returned his smile, but he noticed it didn't quite reach her eyes the way it normally did. "I'm happy to do anything I can to help."

Paul wanted to ask if he could see her later, but there was no way to do that in front of everyone. So he let her go. For now. As soon as the coast was clear, he'd seek her out to continue what they'd begun at the Cape. The thought of being with her later was the only bright spot in this otherwise dismal day.

*

Hope went through the motions with Ethan—homework, dinner, bath, bedtime stories, tickling, snuggling. After two nights apart, he wanted the full program, and she was happy to give it to him. His joyful giggles were a balm on the wound of this day.

Inside, however, she was dying from the realization that their idyllic time on the island would come to an end as soon as Marion was moved to a permanent care facility on the mainland. Just when they'd found their groove and settled into a new routine, it would all be upended again.

And Paul... She couldn't allow herself to even think about the incredible interlude they'd had at the Cape. Other than every minute she'd ever spent with Ethan, it had been the most perfect time of her life.

"Are you sad, Mama?" Ethan asked, stroking her face.

He called her Mama only when he was sad or tired. Otherwise, she was Mom in the loudest voice he possessed.

"I'm just tired, honey, and so are you." She kissed his forehead. "Time for lights out."

"One more story."

"No more stories. It's a school night."

"All right," he grumbled, but his heavy eyes told the true story of how tired he was.

Leaving him with one last kiss, she turned on the night-light and left the door propped open so she could hear him if he needed her. She went into the kitchen to tend to the dishes and was halfway through them when the tears reappeared. The last thing she wanted to do was leave this wonderful place or the Martinez family, who'd begun to feel like family to her and to Ethan. He'd be heartbroken. But the fact was, she needed a job. After a costly divorce, she no longer had a cushion to tide her over between jobs. She'd managed to save some money since this job came with a free place for her and Ethan to live, but her small nest egg wouldn't last for long if she was out of work.

Sighing, she reached for a bottle of wine on the counter and poured herself a healthy glass, feeling guilty for letting her own worries get the better of her when Paul and Alex had much bigger ones weighing them down tonight. She wouldn't soon forget the utter devastation that had overtaken Paul in the doctor's office. He was always so strong and capable. To see him in such a state of shock had been upsetting.

She hated that this was happening to him and Alex, but she especially hated it for Marion, who'd never really know her grandchildren or the women her sons married. It was so unfair.

Hope had just had that thought when a soft knock sounded at her door. She went to answer it, knowing it would be Paul. He stood with his hands propped on either side of her door.

"Can we talk?" he asked.

"Come in." When he stepped inside, she said, "Wine?"

"I wouldn't say no to that."

While he took a seat on the sofa, she went into the kitchen to pour him a glass and to gather her resolve. If Marion were leaving soon, she and Ethan would be, too. It would be better, in that case, to end this before it really began. To let it continue would be to invite in heartache for herself and Ethan as well as Paul. Even as everything inside her cried out for him, she knew it was what she had to do.

She just couldn't go through it again, even if the circumstances were vastly different this time. She couldn't do it—and she couldn't do it to Ethan either. He was already bonded to Paul, Alex, Jenny and Marion. It would be hard enough to leave as it was. To get even more involved would be a fool's errand.

And then Paul was behind her, his arms encircling her waist and his forehead leaning on her shoulder. "Whatever you're thinking, knock it off."

"How do you know what I'm thinking?"

"I can see it in the tension you carry in your shoulders." He gently massaged her neck and shoulders, sending a sigh shuddering through her. "Talk to me."

"Is Alex with your mom?"

"Yeah, I asked them to stay so I could come talk to you. Tell me what's on your mind, Hope."

"This. Us."

"That's on my mind, too."

"We need to stop this, Paul." As she said the words, a sharp pain registered in the area of her heart, which was exactly when she realized that at some point over the last few weeks, she'd fallen in love with him.

He turned her to face him, his hands on her hips. "Please don't say that. I can't take any more bad news today."

"And I can't take any more heartache in this lifetime. We're setting up ourselves—and Ethan—for disaster by pursuing this when we both know it can't last."

He tucked her hair behind her ear, and the simple gesture made her heart flutter. "Why can't it last?"

"Because! When your mom goes, I have to go, too. I need a job, Paul, and it's not like there're tons of nursing opportunities here."

"If Lizzie succeeds in getting the rest home opened, they'll need qualified nurses."

"Who knows how long that'll take? It could be a year or more before they get the renovations done, permits filed and the many other details seen to. Something like that doesn't happen overnight. I can't sit around and wait for something that may or may not happen. I don't have that luxury."

"Hope…"

"This isn't what I want to do, Paul, but it's what I *have* to do. I just can't—"

He kissed her, and she forgot everything she'd been about to say, as well as the many reasons this was a bad idea. She could only remember the exquisite pleasure she'd found in his arms. Hungry for more of it, she returned his kiss with an ardor that equaled his.

"Please don't take this away from me, Hope," he whispered many passionate minutes later. "I need you."

"I need you, too, but I can't do this. I just can't."

He once again dropped his head to her shoulder.

She rested her hand on his neck, wishing with every beat of her heart that things could be different for them. But their reality was that once his mother was moved from their home, Hope's job on Gansett Island would be done. Paul's life and his business were on the island. So there was no point to continuing a romantic entanglement that would lead straight to heartache when it ended.

"I'm so sorry," she said as tears slid down her cheeks. "You have no idea how sorry I am."

"I think I have a pretty good idea."

"It's not what I want. If things were different…"

"I know." He kissed her so softly, so tenderly that she wanted to whimper from the bolt of desire that zinged through her body and settled into a sharp throb between her legs. Drawing back from her, he looked at her for a long moment before he turned and went out the door.

The glass of wine he hadn't gotten to enjoy stood beside hers on the counter as a metaphor for the many things they'd never get to enjoy together. Leaving the glasses on the counter, she shut off the lights and went to bed alone. She'd done the right thing sending him away. But knowing that didn't lessen the ache of loss that had her crying herself to sleep for the first time in a long time.

*

Over the next few days, Paul forced himself through the motions. He got up, went to work, helped take care of his mother, attended an emergency town council meeting that turned out to be about nothing, made himself eat and sleep. He finalized the plans for Alex's bachelor party, took Ethan with him to help harvest the pumpkins and worked with Jenny on the plan for closing the retail store for the month of November before reopening to sell Christmas trees in December.

He did what was expected of him. And every time he laid eyes on Hope, which was several times each day, he died a little more on the inside. They'd had a taste of heaven that had been yanked away before he'd begun to satisfy his appetite for her. Of course he understood where she was coming from. When his mother left home, her job would be done, and she and Ethan would have to go elsewhere.

It was the wise thing for both of them to take a step back, but knowing that didn't make it any easier. Staring into the mirror as he got ready for Alex's party, Paul tried to summon the cheerfulness he'd need to see his brother through the party and the wedding. He was determined not to let his own problems—and the larger, more pressing issue of what to do about their mother's care—take anything away from the joy of Alex and Jenny's big day.

A long, lonely winter stretched ahead of him. He could tend to his own wounds then. It occurred to him that if they moved Marion to the mainland and Hope and Ethan left, Paul would be alone in the house that now teemed with activity. Alex and Jenny would move into their own home, and with Marion gone, there'd be no reason for David and Daisy to come by every day or the women from the church, who had been so generous about providing regular meals for them during Marion's illness.

The house would be awfully empty and lonely without the endless activity, a thought that only added to his profound depression.

"You gotta snap out of it, man," he whispered to his reflection. "Alex has waited a long time for this. It wouldn't be fair to bring him down." He gave himself a couple of minutes to summon the celebratory mood the night demanded of him before he left the bathroom.

Dressed in a gorgeous black dress, Hope came into the house as he stepped into the kitchen.

Paul stared at her. "You look amazing," he said after a long, charged moment of silence.

"You look great, too."

His mother's friends had taken Marion to bridge night so Hope could attend Jenny's bachelorette party. The ladies were fully briefed on what to expect from Marion. Paul and Alex had agreed that they should let her spend as much time with her friends as she could, while she could. Ethan was spending the night with his friend Jonah. Paul couldn't help but wish that he could look forward to spending the night with Hope after the parties, but he couldn't let his mind go there.

"Have a good time tonight," Hope said. "Be careful."

"I'll be fine. My job is to stay sober so he can go nuts."

She smiled, and he had to fight the overpowering urge to cross the room, haul her into his arms and kiss her senseless. It took everything he had not to give in to the need that drew him to her. "I'm sure it'll be a great time."

Alex and Jenny came into the house through the front door, holding hands and laughing about something.

Paul experienced yet another profound feeling of envy that his brother had his life worked out to his obvious satisfaction. Why was it that he couldn't seem to do the same? The brief brush with happiness he'd experienced with Hope had only served to make him want it more than he had before.

"You ready to roll?" he asked Paul.

"Whenever you are."

Alex wrapped his arms around Jenny and laid a deep, sensual kiss on her that had Paul squirming with discomfort as he tried to look anywhere but at Hope.

"Behave tonight, you hear me?" he said when they finally resurfaced.

"You do the same."

Alex whispered something in Jenny's ear that had her giggling like a schoolgirl before she pushed him back. "Go away and leave me alone to party with my ladies." To Paul and Hope, she said, "My old man is such a ball and chain."

Alex patted her bottom. "You'll pay for that later."

"And that's our cue to get the hell out of here," Paul said, grabbing his brother's arm to lead him from the house. "Have fun, ladies."

"Oh, we will," Jenny said, making Alex growl at her.

Paul steered Alex toward his truck, pushing him toward the passenger side.

As they drove out of the driveway, Alex looked back, possibly hoping for a last glimpse of Jenny, who was riding to her party with Hope.

"You'll see her again in a couple of hours, Romeo," Paul said. "You'll survive until then."

Alex responded with a stupid grin and a deep sigh. "Not sure I'll make it." He turned to take a closer look at Paul. "What gives with you the last couple of days, man? Other than the obvious, of course."

"Nothing gives. Business as usual."

"Try telling that to someone who doesn't see you every day and doesn't know you as well as I do. Something is wrong, and you may as well tell me what it is so I don't have to beat it out of you."

"I'd like to see you try."

"We both know I could, so let's save ourselves the bother."

"Whatever."

"Come on, Paul. You know there's nothing you can't tell me."

"It's not the time. Tonight is about you. We'll talk after the wedding."

"We'll talk now."

Paul recognized that bullish tone and knew it was pointless to argue with him. Growing up with Alex, he would've at least tried. Today he couldn't be bothered. "The thing with Hope isn't going to happen."

"Oh. Wow. I sort of thought it was already happening."

"It was."

"So what happened?"

"The meeting with the doctor happened."

"Umm, you want to fill in the blanks for me?"

"She realized that if Mom leaves Gansett, her job here will be done and she'll have to go elsewhere to find work. Her ex-husband wiped out their savings, so she has no cushion of any kind, apparently."

"So she called it off with you because of that?"

"She said she couldn't get further involved with me knowing she'd be leaving."

Alex scratched at the stubble he left on his jaw these days because Jenny had told him she liked it—and he'd told Paul that when Paul asked why he never shaved anymore. "That is a tough one. On the one hand, I can see where she's coming from. I don't know the details, but I assume the ex put her through the wringer."

"It was bad business."

"I figured it had to be if the guy's locked up."

Paul didn't feel it was his place to tell Alex her story, at least not without her permission.

"Have you considered asking her to stay with you?"

"Not really."

"Why not? I assume you want her to."

"Hell, yes, I want her to."

"Then tell her that."

"Am I just supposed to ask her to stay, knowing she has no way to make a living here?"

"I hate to point out the obvious, but she doesn't need to work if she's with you. She could focus on Ethan and make more babies with you and maybe get a job at this place Lizzie is determined to open on the island."

Paul's mouth watered at the thought of such an easy solution. "I don't think she'd go for that. She would say she's perfectly capable of taking care of herself, and no way is she putting all her eggs in some man's basket again. Not after what happened to her before. He totally screwed her over."

"And you'd never do that. Make the grand gesture."

"What grand gesture?"

"The *grandest* of grand gestures."

"Are you seriously suggesting I propose to her? We just started actually seeing each other a week ago."

"Oh please. You two have been eye-fucking each other since the day she arrived. And it's not just me who thinks so. Jenny said the same thing."

Though he was flabbergasted to hear they thought that, he said, "No way did Jenny say *that*. Those are your words."

"Maybe so, but she agrees anyway. We were thrilled that you guys took some time away together while Mom was in the hospital."

"I'm glad you approve," Paul said sincerely. "But it's too soon for the kind of grand gestures you're suggesting."

"Is it? You're thirty-four, and I've never seen you like this over a woman before. She's wise enough to know that you're a catch. I assume the sex was hot, because you looked like a new man when you came home. So what's the hang-up? What's another six months going to tell you that you don't already know?"

Paul didn't have a good answer for that, so he stayed quiet.

"The sex was hot, wasn't it?"

"Shut up. I'm not talking to you about that."

"Which means it was. If it hadn't been, you wouldn't have been moping the last couple of days like a little boy who lost his puppy."

"I have not been doing that."

"If you say so."

"Happy, married Alex is a huge pain in my ass."

He grunted with laughter. "Single Alex was a pain in your ass, too."

"That he was, but I like happy Alex better."

"So do I, and I want the same for you. Go for what you want, Paul. Worst thing, she says no, but at least you'll know you tried. Think about it."

As Paul drove them to the party at McCarthy's Marina, he wondered how he would think about anything else.

CHAPTER 23

The party that Sydney and the girls threw for Jenny was fabulous and over the top. It seemed as if every woman on Gansett was there, and everyone was thrilled that Jenny was finally getting her long-delayed happily ever after. Hope wondered what they would think if they knew Alex and Jenny were already married. She loved being in on the secret that only Sydney and Erin knew, too.

She loved being a part of this group of women. They'd made her feel so welcome from the first time she met Jenny, who'd assured her there'd be no lack of fun things to do if she and her son moved to Gansett Island.

That had proven very true, and this group was a big part of the reason why. Unlike the women she'd known back at home, these women didn't thrive on gossip. They built each other up rather than tearing each other down. They thrived on being happy and productive. They were also some of the funniest women Hope had ever met.

Take Tiffany, for example, who was relaying the fact that her husband, the police chief, had wanted to do background checks on the male strippers the women had hired for Jenny's party.

"Wait," Jenny said. "You guys got *strippers?*"

Hope wasn't sure if Jenny was intrigued or appalled. Probably some of both.

"No!" Tiffany screamed with laughter that drew the others in, too. "We've been *telling* them that all week. They're out of their minds over it."

"Oh. My. God." Jenny laughed right along with them, and Hope couldn't help but join in, even though she hadn't felt like laughing in days.

Each of the women chimed in, sharing their significant others' reaction to hearing there would be strippers.

"Mac said he's going to dust me for prints when I get home," Maddie said to more hysterical laughter.

"You guys are *so* bad," Jenny said, though she was obviously and thoroughly amused.

Sydney came into the room holding a piece of paper and a bag of money. "Has everyone placed their bets?"

"What bets?" Jenny asked.

"On how long it'll take them to crash tonight," Sydney said. "We've still got a few spots open, but most of the earlier guesses are taken."

"You people are diabolical," Hope said, making sure to smile so they knew she was joking.

"You have no idea what we've been through with them," Janey Cantrell said.

"They crash *everything* we do," Abby Callahan added. "Everything."

"We'll never, ever admit that we actually like that they crash," Grace Ryan said. "Because then they'd be totally out of control."

"Unlike now?" Stephanie McCarthy asked.

"Worse than now," Maddie said.

"We can't have that," Laura Lawry said. "They're already totally full of themselves."

"Who had the stripper idea?" Jenny asked. "It's brilliant."

All eyes went to Maddie, spurring more laughter.

"What?" Maddie asked. "It's always Mac's idea to crash, so I figured it was time to take back girls' night out. I never expected they'd freak out to the level that they did."

"Really?" Laura asked, her brow lifted in amusement. "You thought they'd be fine with it?"

"I knew Mac would have something to say, but I didn't think he'd flip his lid."

"Blaine lost his mind," Tiffany said, "but it led to some of the hottest sex we've ever had."

"And that's saying something," Maddie added, raising her glass in a toast to her sister.

"Yes, it is," Tiffany said.

"Jenny needs a drink!" Janey said. "What kind of bachelorette party is this?"

"Sad to say none for me," Jenny said. "I'm on new stuff for my allergies, and it doesn't mix well with alcohol."

"Oh damn," Abby said. "That's a bummer."

"Double or nothing, ladies," Sydney said. "If your guy is the first one through the door, you have to double the pot."

Jenny reached for the paper Sydney still held. "Well, I want to place my own bet on how long it'll take Alex to get here once he hears y'all are having strippers." She filled in a square and tossed a five into the bag of money.

"You aren't disappointed we didn't really get strippers, are you?" Sydney asked.

To her amazement and mortification, Jenny's eyes flooded with tears. "How could I be disappointed in anything when this is my life now?" She used her hand to include the women who'd come to help her celebrate tonight.

"Awww," Sydney said, gathering Jenny into a hug. "We love you."

"Love you, too," Jenny whispered.

Hope wiped subtly at her own eyes, moved by the love in the room and a yearning to be part of this group of women, rather than a peripheral member of their clan.

They ate, they drank, they laughed—a lot—they showered Jenny with an array of inappropriate gifts, most of which had been procured from Tiffany's store. The more Jenny burned with embarrassment, the harder they laughed.

Shortly after nine, the front door burst open, and Mac McCarthy was the first man through the door.

A roar of laughter went through the group of women.

"Pay up, Maddie!" Stephanie said.

"Get out of here, Mac." Maddie got up to push her husband back toward the door. "This is a private party! No men allowed."

"Where're the strippers?" Evan asked as he came in next, followed by the others in a big mass of angry testosterone.

"Look in the kitchen," Luke said.

"And the back deck," Joe added.

Blaine gave Tiffany a dark glare as he went past her to search the house. She covered her mouth with her hand, but her eyes danced with silent laughter.

Alex and Paul came in last, and Hope watched as Paul immediately sought her out in the group. Her insides quivered at the proprietary look on his face before he caught himself and seemed to remember he wasn't allowed to look at her that way anymore.

Hope felt the loss acutely, every part of her aching for him as he directed his gaze elsewhere.

Alex went directly to Jenny, who lit up at the sight of him.

Blaine came back into the living room and stood before Tiffany, hands on hips, his mouth tight with displeasure. "What gives, Tiffany?"

"I have no idea what you're talking about, Chief Taylor. My friends and I are having an innocent bachelorette party that's been invaded by men who weren't invited."

Adam held up a huge dildo for the others to see. "Innocent, huh?"

When the dildo began buzzing, Adam jerked with surprise, sending the dildo flying. The women lost it laughing. They screamed with hysterics that only made the men madder.

"*Where the hell are the strippers?*" Mac roared.

"Did you hire strippers?" Maddie asked Sydney, the two of them the picture of innocence.

"I didn't." To Erin, Sydney said, "Did you?"

"Nope. I wouldn't know where to find strippers."

"Don't look at me," Kara said as Dan glowered at her.

Blaine continued to glare at Tiffany while she continued to cry with silent laughter.

"Gentlemen," Joe said, his gaze fixed on Janey, "I believe we've been had."

"We've been *what*?" Mac asked, his face red with barely suppressed rage.

"*Had*, Mac," Joe said. "It's a prank. An evil, *evil* prank."

"A prank," Mac said, advancing toward Maddie, who backed up until she encountered a wall. "*A goddamned prank?*"

"Hi, honey," Maddie said with a goofy smile. "Did you boys have fun at your party?"

"No, we did not have fun, because we were *preoccupied by the thought of our women cavorting with male strippers!*"

"What strippers?" Maddie asked, batting her eyelashes at him.

Oh wow, Hope thought, trying not to laugh out loud at Maddie's innocent act, *she's good.*

Maddie hooked her hand around Mac's neck and brought him in close enough to whisper in his ear. Whatever she said had the desired effect. The tension leached from Mac's shoulders as he leaned into his wife's embrace.

"As long as you're all here," Sydney said, "we ought to combine these two parties."

"Is this a massive ploy to get us to do another of those stupid Jack-and-Jill thingies?" Evan asked.

"Not this time," Grace told her fiancé, patting his chest. "By the way, Syd, who won the pool?"

Sydney consulted the spreadsheet, checked her watch and declared Abby the winner. She handed over the bag of cash. "Maddie owes you two hundred smackers."

Abby clapped her hands in glee as she accepted the bag of cash and promptly handed it over to Jenny. "Buy dinner on the honeymoon on us— and Maddie."

"Wait," Adam said. "You guys were *betting* on us?"

"Maybe just a little." Abby went up on tiptoes to kiss Adam. "But we're so glad you're here now."

He scowled at her playfully. "Nicely played, my love."

Paul sat next to Hope on the sofa. "Can you believe all this?"

"It's pretty funny."

"They were going insane at our party. There was no stopping them from coming here."

"Did it ruin your plans?"

"Nah, I didn't have any plans other than feeding them, plying them with drinks and making sure Al has a great time."

With Jenny seated in his lap, Alex was laughing at something Erin was telling them—and nuzzling Jenny's neck between laughs.

"Mission accomplished."

Grant and Owen carried in coolers, and Evan followed them with guitars. They ended up on Luke and Syd's back deck with Owen and Evan playing for them while everyone sang along.

Sydney had created a cozy outdoor living space that included comfortable sofas and a fire pit. The moon shimmered on the surface of the ocean, and the island's raw beauty only added to Hope's melancholy. Ethan would be devastated to leave here, and so would she.

Paul appeared next to her with a glass of white wine that he offered her.

"I shouldn't," she said. "I'm driving."

"You can leave your car here, and I'll bring you to get it in the morning. I haven't had a thing to drink. Ethan is sleeping at Jonah's, and Mom will be asleep by the time we get home. You should take advantage of the opportunity to have some fun while you can."

Hope glanced up at him and couldn't help but notice the sadness that clung to him the same way it did her. She took the wine from him. "Thank you."

He sat next to her, the two of them separate even though they were right in the middle of the revelry.

She waited for him to say something, but he didn't. What else could be said? Though he talked to his brother and their friends, and though he laughed and participated in the party, his heart wasn't in it. She knew him well enough by now to be able to tell that.

Every so often, his leg would brush against hers, and she'd have to fight the urge to lean into him, to let him soothe the ache that only grew worse the longer she sat next to him. There might've been a million miles standing between them rather than half an inch.

"Hope?" he said, drawing her out of her thoughts. "Luke was asking if you like living on Gansett."

"Oh, sorry. Yes, I love it. My son does, too."

"Alex and Paul are lucky to have you," Luke said.

"It's been a pleasure to help out," Hope said, her throat closing. God, she was going to cry if she didn't get out of there right away. "Excuse me." She got up and left the deck, hearing Luke ask, "Was it something I said?" as she went.

Hope went into the hallway bathroom to splash cold water on her face, hoping it would help to calm emotions that were all over the place tonight. Patting her face with a hand towel, she studied herself in the mirror and decided she must not be fooling anyone with her so-called party face. Time to go home. At least there she could wallow in her misery without dragging anyone else down.

She opened the door to Paul standing in the hallway. He stepped into the bathroom and shut the door.

He overwhelmed the small space with his big frame. "Are you okay?"

"I-I…" She wanted to assure him she was fine, but she couldn't look at that handsome face and lie to him. "No," she said softly. "I'm a mess." Later she wouldn't be able to say if she reached for him or he reached for her. What did it matter when it felt so damned good to be in his arms again, to kiss him, to feel his arms around her, making her feel safe and cherished?

A knock on the bathroom door ended the moment.

They stared at each other, equally dazzled.

"Later," he said. "We'll talk later." He opened the door and walked out, leaving her stunned by the force of her attraction to him as well as the endless need for more.

Hope followed him to the hallway, where Adam McCarthy studied his phone, a sly smile on his face. "Sorry," she muttered.

"No worries."

Thankfully, the party was beginning to break up, and Alex asked Paul if he'd give them a ride home. Since she'd had two glasses of wine, she took Paul up on his offer to leave her car there until tomorrow. He held the door to his truck for her and waited until she was settled before he closed it.

Alex and Jenny climbed into the back, whispering and giggling like the happy newlyweds they were. The sounds of sloppy kissing and more giggling seemed extra loud to her, or maybe it was the silence hanging between her and Paul that made it seem so loud.

"Guess what Erin told me tonight," Jenny said.

"What's that?" Alex asked.

"Slim, who came to her rescue when she sprained her ankle, has been coming by to visit and asked her out."

"That's cool," Alex said.

"He's a good guy," Paul added.

"I'm glad you think so," Jenny said. "She deserves only the best."

"Drop us at our place," Alex said when they drove into the driveway at home. "If you don't mind staying with Mom."

"I don't mind." Paul pulled up to the dark hulk of Alex and Jenny's new house, and they fell out of the car, laughing as Alex scooped her up into his arms, whirled her around and carried her inside, calling over his shoulder, "Great time, bro. Thanks!"

Paul waited until they were safely inside before he backed out of their driveway and headed for home. When he killed the lights and shut off the engine, the darkness engulfed them. "Be with me tonight. No commitments, no promises. Just us taking what we both want."

She should say no. *More* wouldn't make the leaving any easier.

His hand found hers in the darkness. "Please."

The desperation she heard in that single word had her saying, "Yes."

"It's dark. Wait for me."

Her heart pounded and her chest tightened with the effort it took to draw air into her lungs. She shouldn't do this. She absolutely should not, but when he opened the door, took her hand and helped her out of the truck and then pressed her against it to kiss her senseless, she wasn't thinking about why she shouldn't. No, she was thinking about all the reasons she absolutely *should.*

Then he scooped her up the way Alex had done to Jenny, leaving Hope breathless from wanting him. He put her down on the porch. "I can't shock poor Mrs. Garfield by carrying you inside." Leaning in so his lips brushed against her ear, he added, "But I want to. I really want to."

Hope laughed at the salacious tone of his voice and let him guide her into the house, where Mrs. Garfield was on the sofa watching TV. As a retired nurse herself, she'd been a huge asset to the family.

"Hi there," she said. "Did you have a good time?"

"It was great," Paul said. "Alex and Jenny can now get married." He winked at Hope and then walked Mrs. Garfield to the door, waiting until she was in her car before he shut off the outside lights.

Hope loved being "in the know" that Alex and Jenny were already married. She loved being a part of everything that went on around here, even the difficult stuff with Marion. And she loved Paul. That much had become painfully apparent since she called it off with him. Sleeping with him tonight wasn't going to make anything better. In fact, it would probably make everything a whole lot worse.

But that certainly didn't stop her from taking the hand he offered. It didn't stop her from letting him lead her into his room.

"Give me one second to look in on Mom, and then I'm all yours."

All yours. Hope fairly swooned at the thought of such an incredible man being all hers, even if it was only for tonight. Alone in his room, it occurred to her that she could walk out of there and spare herself the agony that was sure to set in tomorrow. But she couldn't bring herself to take the first step that would lead to the safety of her own home.

He returned, leaving the door open so they could hear Marion if she got up. The night-light in the hallway made it possible for her to see the look of intent on his face as he approached her.

"You're so beautiful tonight," he whispered. "All the time, but tonight… You dazzled me."

"I like that word."

"It's a good word. It sums up rather perfectly how I feel about you." He leaned in to kiss her neck, setting off a chain reaction that registered in all her most important places, most particularly in her chest, where her heart beat erratically. "I couldn't take my eyes off you tonight. You might've been the only woman in the room."

"Paul," she said on a sigh, utterly charmed by his sweet words.

"The last couple of days have been torture. You're so close but so far away. I can't stand it."

"I'm sorry. I never meant to hurt you."

"You didn't. You're being smart and practical and wise when I want you to throw caution to the wind."

"I can't do that."

"I know," he said with a sigh of his own. He found the zipper on the back of her dress and drew it down slowly, his fingers brushing against the sensitive skin on her back as he went. The dress fell to her feet, leaving her in a strapless bra and skimpy panties.

Had she dressed hoping for this outcome to the evening? Not intentionally, but judging by the flare of desire in his eyes, he liked what he saw.

She began unbuttoning the dress shirt he'd worn with khaki shorts. The rest of their clothes fell away until they were both naked.

"Just give me this for one minute," he whispered, his arms tight around her.

Hope gave him what he needed, because she needed it just as badly.

Paul raised his head off her shoulder to kiss her, a soft, sweet caress that made her want so much more.

There was that word again—*more*. He always made her want more of him, and she'd begun to suspect that she'd never get enough. With his arms still tight around her, he eased her onto the bed and leaned over her. "I thought I'd memorized every detail, but I forgot a few."

"Like what?"

"This," he said, laying his finger over the mole on her breast. He replaced his finger with his tongue. "I don't want to forget that or the way you go crazy when I do this." With his thumbs on her hipbones, he pressed down.

She cried out, and her legs fell open.

Paul dropped to his knees next to the bed, his hands flat against her thighs.

"Paul... Wait..."

"I don't want to wait. I only got one little taste of you while we were away, and I kept thinking I didn't get nearly enough."

All the air left her body in one long exhale that he took as permission to proceed. Holding her open with his thumbs, he stroked her with his tongue until she was writhing on the bed and pulling his hair so hard, he worried he'd have bald spots. But that didn't stop him. He slid two fingers into her, going slowly to draw out the pleasure.

"Are you still sore?"

"No," she said, sounding breathless. Her legs trembled, and her internal muscles clamped down on his fingers.

Blowing on her clit, he said, "Mmm, so hot." He sucked on her clit, and she screamed as she came.

Paul stayed with her until she began to relax. Then he replaced his fingers with his cock and triggered a second wave. "Hope…"

She wrapped her arms around his neck and drew him into a kiss as he worked his way into her slowly.

He was so afraid to hurt her by driving in hard the way he wanted to.

Her hands moved down his back to cup his ass, pulling him toward her.

Groaning, he began to move in her while keeping his lips close to her ear. "Hope… You feel so good. This feels so good. Stay with me. Be with me." He kissed away the moisture that leaked from her eyes. "We'll figure it out together. Don't leave me."

A sob escaped from her lips as she continued to move with him.

"Do you feel how great it is, too?"

"Yes," she whispered. "God, *yes*."

"I can't let you go." He pressed into her, looking for the spot that had set her off before and knowing he'd found it when he felt the telltale tightening of her internal muscles. "Yes, sweetheart, come for me. Let me feel you."

Her release led to his, and he came down on top of her, gathering her in close to him. "Don't go, Hope. We'll make it work."

She shook her head. "I have to get another job."

"I'll take care of you and Ethan. You'll have everything you need."

"You're wonderful and sweet to want to do that, but I can't."

He wanted to scream with frustration. "What we have here doesn't come around every day."

"I certainly know that."

"We can't give up without a fight."

"We're not doing that. We're acknowledging that it can't go anywhere."

"What if I came with you?"

"You can't do that, Paul. Your life and your business are here."

"I don't want to be here if you and Ethan aren't here with me."

She caressed his face with both hands. "I wish things were different. You have no idea how much I wish that."

"I bet I do." He forced a smile for her benefit and withdrew from her. Lying on his back, he stared up at the ceiling as if he might find the answers there.

"I should go," she said after a long period of silence.

"Not yet." Paul turned on his side and put his arm around her. "Spend the night with me."

"It won't make anything better."

"Maybe not, but it'll make tonight better."

She turned into his embrace, her hand resting on his chest over his heart. "You have to know if I could have anything I wanted, it would be you."

"You can have me. We can have it all."

"I can't have you and a job, too. There're no jobs here for nurses. I have to go where the work is."

"There're other jobs here. Maybe you could find something else."

"I'm still digging out of the hole Carl put me in. I can't afford to take a pay cut."

Paul took hold of her hand. "I hate that it seems so hopeless."

"Ha. No pun intended."

"I don't want to be hopeless or Hope-less." As he played with her fingers, he tried to gather his thoughts. "In all the time I've lived here, I never looked forward to the day I could get out of here the way Alex and so many of the other kids we knew did. They all counted down the days until they could get the hell out. That was never me. But now, with the thought of all that water between where I am and where you are, I want out of here for the first time."

"I hate that I've caused that to happen."

"It's not your fault."

"I'm sorry it's worked out this way, but I'm not sorry it happened."

Paul pulled her in closer to him so he could kiss her. "I'm not sorry either."

CHAPTER 24

Sitting around the fire outside Seamus and Carolina's house, Big Mac took it upon himself to keep the fire fed since Seamus was preoccupied tonight.

"It's so good of you guys to come by to check on us," Carolina said.

"The bachelor and bachelorette parties ended a little prematurely," Big Mac said, "so we hoped we'd find you still up."

"It's such a wonderful thing you're doing for those boys," Linda said. "How are they?"

"They've gone back to school," Caro said. "Returning to their routine seems to be helping."

"Just like it did for Joe," Linda said.

"Yes."

Linda glanced at Big Mac. "We just want you to know that we're here for you like we were then. You're not in this alone. Everyone wants to help."

"It's so nice of you to say that," Caro said. "We'll take all the help we can get."

Seamus stood suddenly. "I'm going to get a beer. I'll grab one for you, too, Mac. Ladies?"

They demurred, and he walked toward the house.

"Poor guy is wound up," Caro said. "He's so afraid he's going to mess things up for the boys. I've tried to assure him he'll be great, but he's still stressed."

Big Mac got up. "I'll have a chat with him. See what I can do."

"Oh, Mac," Caro said. "Would you? That would help. I know it would."

He squeezed Caro's shoulder. "I'll do what I can." Big Mac went into the house and found Seamus in the kitchen, beer in hand, staring out into the darkness through the window over the kitchen sink. "Is that one for me?"

"Oh yeah, sorry." Seamus twisted the cap off and handed it to him.

"Here's to fatherhood," Big Mac said, raising his bottle to Seamus. "Best thing to ever happen to me."

Seamus touched his bottle to Big Mac's. "That's good to hear."

"It will be for you, too."

"Wasn't quite how I pictured it happening when I was growing up in Ireland."

"Ahhh, yes, plans. They make a mockery of us, don't they?"

"Indeed," Seamus said with a chuckle.

"I'm a big believer in things happening for a reason. There's a reason you ended up in this house next door to those boys."

"I thought that reason was Caro."

"She wasn't the only reason. They're part of the master plan, too."

Seamus took a swig from his beer. "Yes, I guess they are."

"You aren't having regrets about taking them in, are you?"

"No. God, no. Nothing like that."

"Then what is it? Something's nagging at you."

"It's the enormity of the responsibility." He rested a hand on his chest. "I feel like there's an elephant sitting right here when I think about how it's my job now to protect them and keep them safe. They like to be outside and to run wild, and when I think about all the ways they can get hurt… Are you *laughing* at me?"

Big Mac had tried to hold it back, but the laughter wouldn't be contained. "You think you're different from any other man who gets handed a little bundle of joy? We *all* feel that way, Seamus. Every one of us. It's called parenthood. The good news is the panic passes in time. You realize they aren't as breakable as you think they are at first."

"These guys aren't babies."

"No, they aren't, and you'll need to keep a close eye on them so they don't get hurt or find trouble. But that's the easy part. Wait until someone breaks their heart, or they leave home and don't come back for a good long while. That's worse." He put his hand on Seamus's shoulder. "One thing I know for sure, knowing you as

I do, is that they'll get one hundred fifty percent from you, and one day they'll look back with gratitude at the incredible stroke of luck that brought you into their lives."

"You think so?" Seamus asked, seeming to battle his emotions.

"I know so. Right now, the task before you seems monumental, and it is in many ways. But it'll also be the most fun you'll ever have in your life. And when they grow up and become your friends as well as your sons…" Big Mac's voice broke. "That's the ultimate joy."

"Thanks for this. Means a lot to me coming from you."

"You're not in this alone, Seamus. You and Caro have an entire island full of people who want to help make sure those boys are well loved. I love having kids over to the marina to go crabbing and out on the boat and lots of other fun stuff. You'll teach them how to drive the ferries and the best Irish swear words. You've got a lifetime worth of wisdom to share with them. It'll all be okay."

"I'm going to take your word for it."

"I'm rarely wrong about anything. Just ask my family."

"And they say I'm full of blarney," Seamus said with a laugh as he extended his hand to Big Mac. "Thank you."

Big Mac shook his hand. "My pleasure."

*

"You and I are in the biggest fight we've ever been in," Mac said to Maddie as he drove them home.

She covered her mouth to keep from laughing, because she knew he wouldn't appreciate that when he sounded genuinely pissed.

"If you laugh at me, I swear to God, Madeline…"

"What'll happen?"

"I'll take you to bed and spank your ass until it's hot pink."

"Mmm, can we do that even if I don't laugh at you?"

When his head spun around to look at her, he nearly drove off the road.

"Mac!"

He swerved the truck back into the lane and didn't say anything more as they drove the rest of the way home. When he took a fast right turn onto Sweet Meadow Farm Road, Maddie began to worry that he might be serious about that spanking. And why did her entire body go hot at the thought of it?

"I can't believe you let me think there were going to be strippers there when all along it was nothing but a prank."

"It was a good prank. You have to admit it."

"I'll admit no such thing. That'll just encourage you."

"Why are you really mad? Because I pulled one over on you, or because you think I'm interested in male strippers?"

Her adorable husband, who had an answer for everything, had nothing to say to that.

"Ah-ha! You don't even know why you're mad. And PS, you cost us two hundred bucks for being the first alpha beast to roar through the door tonight."

"Let's talk about you gambling on top of all your other sins. Here I thought I'd married such a nice girl, and it turns out she's a mean, prank-perpetrating gambler who drinks, too."

Maddie hiccupped loudly, which sent her into fits of laughter. "Those cosmos were *gooooood*."

"I couldn't even have fun with my friends tonight because I was so worried about strange men touching my wife. I hope you're happy."

She began to giggle again and couldn't stop.

"You're getting so spanked, it's not even funny."

"Oh please. You wouldn't dare."

"You don't think so?"

He brought the truck to a skidding stop and was out the driver's-side door before she could begin to process what he'd said. The passenger door flew open, and he reached for her, unbuckling her seat belt and hauling her over his shoulder.

"Mac! Stop it! You're going to make me puke!"

His hand came down on her ass with a sharp crack, sending heat scorching through her that gathered in a tight knot between her legs. *Whoa...*

"You did not just do that."

He did it again, and she had the same reaction. *Wow, this is going to be hot.* But of course she couldn't actually let him know she *liked* it when he went alpha on her. He'd be even more unlivable than he already was. He climbed the stairs to the deck, where he unlocked the door, walked inside, locked up and went straight upstairs to their room. The kids were spending the night with her mother and Ned, so they had the house all to themselves. Normally, that was something she looked forward to.

"Mac…" She landed on the bed with a bounce.

Easing her skirt up to her waist, he flipped her over and pushed a couple of pillows under her hips. He dragged her panties down to just under her cheeks and laid his hands on her bottom. "Say no."

"What?"

"If you don't want this, say no. Tell me not to, and I won't."

"I'm not saying no." She was too hot and bothered—and curious—to say anything other than yes.

His hand came down on her ass, making a loud cracking sound that echoed through the room. Then he rubbed the spot, sending heat from her bottom straight to her clit. Holy moly. He did it again and again and again, striking a different place each time, until she was on the verge of begging him to make her come.

"Tell me why you're getting a spanking," he said, his voice thick with desire.

"I was very naughty and lied to you about the strippers."

"That's right." Another spank.

Maddie's back bowed as she thrust her ass upward, hoping he'd take the hint and move things along. But he was in no rush.

His hand came down again, and the heat was nearly unbearable. "Don't forget how you also laughed at me."

"That, too."

"Are you sorry?"

"So, *so* sorry."

"You are not."

She began to laugh again, even though she burned for him. When she heard his zipper, she knew relief was on the way. She grasped handfuls of the comforter while she waited in breathless anticipation to see what he would do next.

He ran his finger from her backbone down to the crevice between her cheeks, stopping only when he encountered the evidence of her arousal. "Fuck," he growled. "Someone likes being spanked."

"Mmmm, I'll have to be bad more often."

"Don't you dare," he said as he pushed into her from behind, his fingers digging into her hips as he went at her hard and fast and so deep.

Maddie was already about to explode when he reached around to caress her clit, sending her screaming into an orgasm for the ages.

"Holy shit," he muttered, driving into her again before he let himself join her. "Just when I think it can't get any hotter…"

"It does. It's crazy. You're crazy."

"You make me that way."

"I can't believe you spanked me."

"I can't believe you liked it so much."

She grasped his hand, which was flat against her belly. "Only because it was you, and I knew you'd never really hurt me, even if it was the biggest fight ever."

"I wasn't really mad at you, Maddie. If I had been, I never would've touched you."

"I know," she said with a happy sigh. In her wildest dreams, she'd never imagined a love like this would happen to her. "I trust you more than anyone in this entire world."

"And I trust you, which is why I knew you'd never let strange men touch what's mine."

"No, I wouldn't, but it was fun to torture you a little."

"It was a good prank," he said begrudgingly.

Maddie laughed. "Best prank ever."

"You know what this means, though, don't you?"

"What?"

"Revenge, my sweet, is a dish best served cold." He nibbled on her shoulder and made her squirm.

"Will I get to spank you when you prank me?"

"We'll have to see about that."

"Ha! I knew it. Double-standard McCarthy strikes again."

Pushing his hips into her, he reminded her he was still embedded deep inside her, as if she needed the reminder. "You liked it."

"I loved it."

After a long, quiet moment, he said, "I've been thinking…"

"About?"

"The custody situation."

She nudged him. "Let me up so I can see you if we're going to talk serious stuff."

He withdrew from her, removed the pillows and helped her turn over.

Stretched out next to him on top of the bed, she slid her leg between his and put her arm around him. "What're you thinking?"

"They should go to Tiffany. Other than you and me and the grandparents, they spend the most time with her, and they're most comfortable with her."

"Are you sure?"

He nodded. "As long as we stipulate that my family gets full access, I'd be okay with them going to Tiffany and Blaine."

"They would be my first choice, too. Thank you for understanding."

"This isn't about me getting my way or picking my family over yours. It's about doing what's best for Thomas and Hailey. And this is what's best if the worst thing should happen."

"I hate to say this in light of very recent events, but I think you might be growing up, Mac."

"Shut up," he said, laughing. "That'll never happen."

She pushed herself up on an elbow and leaned in to kiss him. "Are we still in the biggest fight ever?"

"*Ever*. It's so big, it's epic." He shook his head. "Male strippers… And from what I hear, it was *your* idea to wind us up like puppets all week."

Maddie caressed his face, loving the scrape of his whiskers under her palm. "You're so easily wounded."

"The thought of you so much as looking at another guy makes me insane. I'm almost ashamed to admit how jealous I was."

"From the day you pushed me off my bike, I haven't so much as looked at anyone else. How could I when all I see is you?"

"Awww, that's very sweet." He cupped her tingling ass and pulled her over until she was on top of him. "But you're still in big trouble."

"Good," she said, smiling down at him. "I love your kind of trouble."

"And I love you, even when you're mean to me."

She was still laughing when he kissed her.

CHAPTER 25

As one of Jenny's bridesmaids, Erin insisted on helping Sydney clean up after the party.

"Luke will give you a ride home," Sydney said when they were finished.

"No need. I already called a cab."

"You didn't have to do that," Luke said. "I would've taken you."

"None of us should be driving tonight, so stay here with your lovely pregnant wife and enjoy the rest of your evening. It was a great party, Syd. Jenny loved it."

Sydney hugged her. "Thanks again for all your help."

A toot sounded outside as Erin gathered up her sweater, purse and the platter she'd brought. "My pleasure. I'll see you at the wedding, if not before."

"See you then."

Erin gave Sydney's dog, Buddy, a pat on the head as she went out the door to the waiting cab in the driveway. She smiled when she realized it was Ned Saunders, whom she'd met several times at gatherings with the McCarthy family.

"Hi, Ned," she said as she got into the backseat of the old woody station wagon. "You're working late tonight."

"Wanted to make sure everyone got home from the parties okay," he said. "Heard you gals pulled one over on the fellas."

"It was pretty funny. They were a hot mess."

Ned chuckled. "I can only imagine. Heard Mac was the worst."

"He was the first one through the door, so Maddie had to pay two hundred bucks to the pot."

"What pot?"

"Um, we might've bet on what time they'd crash."

Ned's laughter echoed through the small space. "That's downright mean a y'all."

"I know," Erin said with a sigh. "But it was so damned funny."

"Bet it was. Been thinkin' bout'cha last coupla days."

"You have? Why?"

"Happened to hear a little rumor 'bout a weddin' the other day. Thought it might be hittin' ya kinda hard, in light of everythin'."

"It's very kind of you to think of me," Erin said softly, touched by his thoughtfulness.

"Tough thing you and Jenny went through. Can't even imagine. Our Adam was in the city that day. Longest day a my life. Probably gonna be a tough week till the weddin'. Maybe a case of the blues after, but yer gonna be okay."

"That's good to know." She closed her eyes against the burn of tears. She'd about had it with the tears at this point.

"This island is known for its healin' powers." Ned smiled at her in the mirror. "Worked its wonders on Jenny. Bet it will fer you, too."

"It's already been very good for me. The people here are just the best people I've ever met. Yourself included."

"Aww, thanks, honey. Nice a ya ta say so." He pulled into the long driveway that led to the lighthouse.

Erin had left the gate unlocked so she could get back in, and he wouldn't let her get it for him. So she stayed put while he took care of the gate and then bounded back to the car.

"Looks like ya got a visitor," Ned said, driving slowly.

Erin's heart did a backflip when she realized Slim must've come by and had waited for her. "I think I might know who it is."

"Anyone I know?"

"Can you keep a secret?"

"Bartenders and cab drivers," Ned said, making her laugh when she remembered Slim saying the same thing about pilots and bartenders. "We're vaults."

"It's Slim Jackson. We've become friends, I guess you could say."

"Good guy. Ya couldn't ask fer better."

"I'll take that as a ringing endorsement, coming from you."

Ned pulled up to the lighthouse and put the car in park. "You take care of yerself these next few weeks. 'Tis okay to be a bit melancholy, but don't let it go too far. Ya hear?"

"I do," she said, smiling at him. "And I appreciate your kind words." With a twenty-dollar bill in hand, she reached over the seat.

"Yer money t'ain't no good here, honey."

"Thank you, Ned, for the ride and the words of wisdom." She leaned over the seat to kiss his cheek, leaving him flustered as she got out of the car, dragging her crutches behind her. She was about as over them as she was the tears.

Ned turned the cab around and left with a toot of the horn.

Waving to him, Erin dropped the crutches on the grass and hobbled over to the fire pit, where Slim had made himself right at home. "Fancy meeting you here," she said.

He got up to give her the chair and took a seat on the cooler, reaching for her injured foot to prop it up next to him. "Heard the festivities didn't turn out quite as planned tonight. Sorry to miss it. I had a late flight and just got back to the island half an hour ago."

"And you came right here?"

"Directly."

"How come?"

"Other than the fact that a very, *very* cute lighthouse keeper lives here?"

It had been a long time since any man had called her cute. The compliment made Erin's face heat up, which, thankfully, he couldn't see. The glow of the fire made them both look hot—particularly him. "Other than that."

"I figured tonight might be another of those tough nights for you. Thought I'd come by to check on you."

"That's exceptionally nice of you."

"I'm an exceptionally nice guy."

She laughed at that even as she suspected it was true. "Who doesn't lack for self-confidence."

"Only where you're concerned. Never quite certain where I stand with you."

"Your approval ratings are higher than ever right now."

"Yeah?" he asked, his face lighting up with glee.

She rolled her eyes. "Don't let one victory get you all full of yourself."

"Wouldn't dream of it." He tossed another log onto the fire and stoked it. "So was it a tough night?"

"It wasn't too bad, all things considered." She told him about the prank the girls had perpetrated, and enjoyed his ringing laughter at her description of the guys reacting to having been had. "Jenny is glowing with happiness, and the prank sort of took over the night when the guys crashed looking for strippers. Lots of laughs, good music, good food, good friends. It was fun."

"I'm glad you had a nice time."

"I just had a lovely chat with Ned on the way home. He said something that really resonated with me."

Slim got up from the cooler and opened it to retrieve the marshmallows Erin had in there. He affixed two of them to sticks and handed one to her along with a second marshmallow for later. "He's the best when you need advice. What'd he say?"

"That it's okay to be a little melancholy over the wedding, but I shouldn't let it get out of control. That wouldn't be good."

"No, it wouldn't. You've worked long and hard to get to where you are now."

"And where am I exactly?"

"You're in a place where you have good friends, lots of laughs, good food, good music," he said, quoting her words back to her. "You have a cool job, and you live in a lighthouse. What's better than that?"

"Not much." He didn't even know about the other job she had as an advice columnist to the lovelorn, ironic as that was since she hadn't had much of a love life to speak of in years. "So I was thinking…"

"About me?" he asked hopefully.

She threw her extra marshmallow at him.

"I'll take that as a no."

"I was thinking about Jenny's wedding. Her second wedding, I should say."

"What about it?"

"I'm allowed to bring a date."

"Is that right?"

"Uh-huh. You know of any single guys who might like to go to a fun wedding with me?"

His mouth fell open and snapped shut.

She had to hold back laughter that was straining to get out.

"I know this one guy," he said after a long pause. "He's kind of dashing in a roguish sort of way. Movie-star handsome, absurdly talented and very interested in spending more time with a certain cute lighthouse keeper."

"Movie-star handsome, roguish, absurdly talented... He sounds like a player."

"Nah, he's not. He's too much of a homebody to be a player, although he does enjoy a little *playing* on occasion. He's a one-woman kind of guy."

"Do you have his number?"

His marshmallow caught fire, and he blew on it until it was extinguished. "Umm, you do know I'm talking about me, right?"

"Oh," Erin said, feigning surprise while continuing to suppress the laughter. She'd laughed more with him than she had in years. "I thought it had to be someone else, because who describes himself as roguish, movie-star handsome and absurdly talented?"

"Ha!" he said with a grin that could only be described as roguish. "So I went a little far trying to sell myself as the perfect date for this important wedding of yours?"

"Little bit." She held her marshmallow over the fire until it was toasted to a golden brown. "But if you'd like to come with me..."

"I would. I'd like to. Very much so."

"Good," she said, smiling at him. "I should mention that my parents will be there. Just in case that makes you want to back out."

"It doesn't. I'm in. But it doesn't count as the dinner you promised me."

A shiver of excitement danced through her at the thought of spending more time with the dashingly roguish pilot.

*

The Saturday-night crowd at the Beachcomber had thinned out by the time Kevin McCarthy pulled up a barstool.

Chelsea came over to him, smiling warily. "Dr. McCarthy."

"Ms. Rose."

She raised a brow as she put a napkin down on the bar and placed an ice-cold light beer on it. "Glass?"

"Comes in one." The cold beer tasted good going down. "You gonna call my big brother on me tonight?"

"You gonna give me reason to?"

Kevin laughed at her saucy comeback. When she smiled at him, he realized how pretty she was. Her thick blonde hair was braided down her back. She wore little or no makeup, but she didn't need it, and though she was tall, she carried her height with an elegance to her movements that indicated dance training. The fact that she was far too young for him didn't keep him from noticing that she was a beautiful woman.

"Where're you coming from?" she asked.

"I was at my brother Frank's for dinner with my sons."

"How many boys do you have?"

"Two, Riley and Finn. I guess they count as men these days. They're twenty-five and twenty-seven."

"You don't look old enough to have kids that age."

"Had them young."

"Where's their mom?" she asked, taking a casual glance at the wedding ring he still wore.

He hadn't been able to bring himself to remove it. "That's kind of a long story."

As they talked, she'd been drying glasses out of the dishwasher and returning them to the shelves. "I'm here until one."

The open invitation to share wasn't lost on him. As someone who made a living listening to other people's problems, he rarely shared his own with anyone. But there was something about her that had him spilling the whole ugly story.

By the time he finished telling her about his wife leaving him for a younger guy, she'd discarded the dishtowel and he had her full attention.

"I'm so sorry, Kevin. That's awful." Without asking if he wanted it, she opened another beer for him and put it down on the bar. "That one's on me."

"Thank you."

"Had you guys been having problems?" she asked tentatively, as if she wasn't entirely sure she should ask.

"Not that I knew of. I was blindsided." He took a drink of the beer. "But with hindsight, I can see there were signs that I missed. Or chose to ignore. I don't know. She wasn't happy. I thought it was a phase that would pass. It had before." Sliding a finger through the condensation on the bottle, he said, "After the boys left home, we found ourselves without much to talk about. It happens. I see it a lot in my practice."

"It's a big change after years of focusing on your kids."

"It is, and we were guilty of making it all about the kids, to the exclusion of our relationship. We tried to get back on track. Went on a few vacations, spent time with friends. But it took effort that hadn't been necessary way back when."

"I think it says something for you that you can look back and see where the trouble was."

"Too bad I didn't realize how bad the trouble was before it was too late."

"You knew."

"I did?"

She nodded. "You said it took effort, that it wasn't easy the way it once had been. You had to be aware of that at the time."

"I was, but I never expected her to actually leave me for another guy. And what she said on the way out the door…"

"What did she say?"

"That life was too short to spend it with me."

"Ah," she said, shaking her head. "That was unnecessary. It's her loss. You know that, don't you?"

"You think she's saying that when she's getting busy with her young stud?"

"Is that the part that pisses you off the most? That he's younger?"

"Nah."

"You sure?"

"Kinda."

Her husky laugh warmed him on the inside the way a shot of whisky would. A low hum of desire took him by surprise. It'd been a long time since he'd felt anything resembling desire. "You're easy to talk to, Ms. Rose."

"Thank you, Dr. McCarthy."

"How do you know I'm a doctor anyway?"

"I asked your brother."

"Which one?"

"Mac. I saw him in the grocery store earlier today."

"And you asked him about me."

"I might've."

He was so out of practice with such things that Kevin wasn't sure he was reading this correctly. Was she flirting with him? "How come?"

"I thought you seemed troubled the other night. I asked if you were okay. We got to talking." She shrugged.

"And that's all it was? Some bartenderly concern?"

"Is that a word?"

"Answer the question."

"It might've been more than that."

Definitely flirting. He cocked his head to take a closer look at her pretty face. She never blinked.

"I'm sorry for what you've been through, but I'm not sorry you're single."

"Separated."

"Permanently and legally?"

"Heading that way."

"Are you planning to go back to her?"

"No."

"What if she shows up here and says it was all a big mistake?"

Kevin thought about that for a minute. "Even then." Permanent damage had been done, and there was no undoing that.

"Then that counts as single in my book."

"Does it now?"

"Yep." She gave him that look again, the one that couldn't be mistaken for anything other than interest. "I slept with your niece's husband once."

"Joe or Owen?

"Joe."

"Before he was her husband?"

"Yes! Years before."

"Okay."

"So that doesn't appall you?"

"Why should it? I assume you were both single and consenting."

"We were."

Kevin shrugged. "Sex happens."

"Does it?"

"That's been my experience."

"What do you think about it maybe happening tonight?"

For a moment, Kevin was rendered speechless. But then he recovered. "I'm fifty-two."

"Are you incapable?"

"No," he said with a laugh. "All the equipment works just fine, thank you, with no medication required. But I suspect I'm a hell of a lot older than you are."

"I'm thirty-six."

"That's sixteen years."

"A doctor who can also add." She fanned her face dramatically. "You don't find that every day."

She was cute and sexy and funny and lovely. And young. Too young for him, but he'd gone hard as stone at the thought of taking her to bed. The confident way in which she'd propositioned him was a huge turn-on. He was forever counseling his female patients to take control of their own sexuality. To find a woman who clearly owned her sexuality was incredibly hot.

"So what do you say, Doc? Would you like to come home with me tonight?"

He'd never once, in thirty years together, been unfaithful to Deb. But his marriage was over and she'd moved on with someone else. There was no reason he couldn't do the same. Under the bar, he slid the wedding ring off his finger and stashed it in his back pocket. "Yes, I believe I would."

CHAPTER 26

The final week before the wedding passed in a flurry of activity that left Paul's head spinning with details and emotions and despair so deep and so pervasive, he wondered if he'd ever recover from losing Hope and Ethan, not to mention the sudden and painful removal of his mother from her home.

David's phone calls on their behalf had yielded immediate results. A memory care facility on the mainland had an opening that had become available after a patient died. They could take Marion as soon as Paul and Alex could get her there. David had urged them not to say no, since it could be months before another spot would open up.

Paul and his brother had gone round and round about whether they should wait until after the wedding to move her, but in the end, they'd decided to go forth sooner rather than later. The wedding would be confusing to her, and as much as Alex wanted her there, he'd chosen to do what was best for her rather than him.

In a way, Paul was relieved that she wouldn't be there to potentially disrupt his brother's big day. As soon as he had that thought, he hated himself for it. But ever since she'd slapped Hope, Paul had found it more difficult to separate the illness from the mother he loved. Something had changed that day—the day that Hope became more important to him than his own mother.

During Marion's last few days at home, Hope packed her most treasured photos to send with her. She lovingly sewed nametags into Marion's clothing and made sure her medication was well organized for a smooth transition. In short, she did everything she could to make the move as easy for Alex and Paul as she could, and they would be eternally grateful to her.

They moved Marion on Wednesday, three days before Alex's wedding. In the end, she went somewhat quietly. Her confusion had gotten worse than ever in the last few days she'd been at home, and even though their hearts were breaking to know she'd probably never again return to the home she loved, they had no doubt anymore that they were doing what was best for her, even if it about killed them to actually do it.

Jenny and Hope had offered to come with them, but the brothers had declined their kind offer, wanting to see to the move themselves. They returned to the island six hours after they left.

As the ferry broached the breakwater in South Harbor, Alex said, "After spending years stressing out about this day, it was almost too easy." They stood at the rail and watched the town of Gansett come into view.

"I suppose it was easy because it was time."

"Maybe."

"Hopefully, Lizzie will get her rest home off the ground, and we can move her back to the island," Alex said.

"Mom might be better off to stay where she is if she's gotten used to it."

After a long pause, Alex said, "Dad would understand why we had to do this, wouldn't he?"

"Yeah, he would." Paul said what Alex wanted to hear, but he was no more certain of what their father would have to say about this than his brother was. As they'd made preparations for the move, Paul had tried not to think about what their father would think about it. He could only hope that George Martinez somehow knew that they'd done everything humanly possible to postpone the inevitable for as long as they could. Paul would never admit to anyone that he felt oddly relieved to have the weight of the responsibility for his mother's care off his shoulders and Alex's. Once again, he felt like shit for even having the thought.

"We did the best we could for a long time," Alex said.

"We certainly did. Longer than most people would have."

"And one of us will see her every week." They planned to take turns going to the mainland, and Marion's friends, including Daisy, had also promised to visit as often as they could. "Do you feel like shit for being relieved that it's not up to us anymore?"

"Total shit."

With Marion's move complete, Hope told Ethan that they'd be leaving Gansett after the wedding to move back to the mainland. Ethan didn't take the news well, lashing out at his mother, Paul, Alex and anyone who would listen to how unfair it was that he had to leave the best place he'd ever lived. Paul's heart broke all over again at realizing how devastated Ethan was to be leaving.

From his post on the back porch later that night, he could hear Hope arguing with Ethan, who was refusing to take a shower. Though it wasn't his place or his business, Paul got up from the step, crossed the yard and went up the stairs to the cabin, knocking on the door.

Looking frazzled, Hope came to the door. "Paul."

He gestured to the interior of the cabin. "May I?"

Wearily, she opened the door to admit him. He took a chance and put his hands on her shoulders and kissed her forehead. It was the first time he'd touched her in days, and it took everything he had to let his hands drop from her shoulders when all he wanted was to touch her everywhere. "Take a break. I got this."

Walking around the boxes she'd begun to pack, Paul went into Ethan's room, where the little guy was sitting on his bed, his arms crossed and his face set with fury. Paul's father would've said he was "bull-necking."

"What're you doing here?" Ethan asked sullenly.

"I heard the way you were talking to your mom, and I thought, that's not the way my buddy Ethan talks to his mom. My buddy Ethan is respectful and does what he's told."

"I'm not your buddy anymore. We're leaving."

"I know, and that totally sucks."

"Sucks is a bad word."

"How's stinks?" Paul asked as he sat at the foot of Ethan's bed, taking note of the Avengers comforter. "Is that better?"

His big eyes filled with tears as he shook his head. "I'm so mad at her."

"You're not being fair, Ethan. We hired her to take care of Mrs. Marion, and her illness got a lot worse, so she can't live here with us anymore."

"Why not?" he asked, his voice breaking. "Is my mom not a good enough nurse?"

"She's a great nurse, but there's only so much she or anyone can do to help Mrs. Marion."

"She doesn't remember things."

"No, she doesn't. Soon she's going to forget how to eat and breathe, which is going to be really, really scary. That's why she needs to live somewhere else, so they can help her when that happens."

"Is-is she going to die like Kyle and Jackson's mom did?"

"Eventually."

Ethan threw himself at Paul. "I don't want her to die."

Paul held him close. "Aww, buddy, I don't want that either. But everyone dies someday, and it's going to be better for Mrs. Marion to have more care than we can provide here, even with your mom doing her very, very best."

"Are you sad that your mom is leaving?"

"I'm so sad, and I'm sad that you and your mom are leaving, too."

"I don't want to go."

"I don't want you to go, but the good news is you can come back to visit any time you want."

"Won't be the same as living here."

"No, it won't, but I'll call you, and we'll see each other. I promise." Paul held Ethan while he cried out his frustrations. "Will you do something for me?"

Ethan nodded.

"Will you please mind your mom and do what she asks? This is hard for her, too, and arguing with you doesn't make it better for her. You don't want to make her sadder, do you?"

"No. She's so sad. Like she was when my dad got in trouble."

Paul felt like he'd been gut-punched. Good God, had it really come to that? "Everything is going to be okay. Now how about you take that shower your mom wants you to have?"

"Okay," Ethan said glumly.

Paul released him and waited until the bathroom door clicked shut behind Ethan before he got up to leave the room.

Hope was standing in the hallway, wiping away tears.

Drawn to her as powerfully as he'd ever been, he put his arms around her.

She rested her hands on his hips and her head on his shoulder.

He wanted to beg and plead with her. He wanted to remind her of how incredible they'd been together. But he didn't do any of those things. Rather, he only held her until the shower turned off. Though it was the hardest thing he'd ever done, he let her go.

"Thank you," she whispered.

"Sure." He left her with a small smile and got the hell out of there while he still could. Every part of him ached at the thought of losing them. For the first time, he began to give serious thought to leaving the business, his home, his brother, his life on Gansett to go wherever they were. "Motherfucker," he muttered to the dark house.

"What's that about?" Alex asked, flipping on a light.

The sudden light as well as the sound of his brother's voice startled Paul. "Nothing."

"Gotta be something to have you swearing like that."

"Nothing to be concerned about."

"Paul. Come on…"

"She's leaving. They're leaving, and I don't want them to."

"Assume you've said as much?"

"Yeah. For all the good it did."

"What exactly did you say?"

"I told her I wanted her and Ethan to stay, that I'd take care of them, that we'd figure it out. She said she has to work, that she's still in the hole from the shit her ex pulled."

"Hmm." Alex rubbed the scruff on his jaw that he'd grown in deference to Jenny's wishes for stubble at the wedding. Their father would've told him to shave his damned face.

"What does that mean? *Hmm?*"

"Did you happen to mention among those reasons you gave her to stay that you love her?"

"I… I… No, I didn't. I thought it was too soon."

Alex laughed. "She's over there packing to leave. Soon enough it's going to be too late."

Alex's words sent panic shooting directly to Paul's heart.

"I'm not telling you what to do, but if she's what you want—and I think she is—put it all out there, Paul."

He was right. Alex was one hundred percent right. "She said she'd never get married again."

"That was before she fell in love with you."

Hearing Alex say, in such a matter-of-fact way, that Hope was in love with him made him feel elated, until he remembered the many obstacles still standing in their way. "What if I ask her and she says no?"

"Then at least you won't have to spend the rest of your life wondering what might've happened if you went for it." Alex held up a finger. "Wait here."

Alex was gone long enough for Paul to break into a cold sweat. Was he really going to propose to her? And what if she did say no? What then? Alex's return interrupted his panic attack.

"Hold out your hand." Alex took Paul's hand and dropped the ring their father had given their mother for their twentieth anniversary into his palm. Then he closed Paul's hand around the ring and held it for a long moment. "Since Mom can't wear it anymore, she'd want you to have it."

It had become too big for her finger, and rather than take the chance that she might lose it, they'd convinced her to put it away for safekeeping—and told her that every time she asked about the ring.

"It doesn't feel right to give away something that belongs to Mom."

"Our mom, the one who loved and cared for us our entire lives, would want you to give that ring to the woman you love. Remember how much she hated waste of any kind? She can't have valuables where she is now, and she'd say it was wasteful to let it sit in a drawer somewhere waiting for her to die so it can go to you anyway."

Paul studied the gorgeous ring that had a two-carat diamond solitaire surrounded by smaller diamonds on either side of it. "Remember how much she loved this ring?"

"I remember how much she loved that he pulled off such a great surprise without her knowing a thing about it. She loved that even more than she loved the ring itself."

Paul smiled at the memory of the parents who'd been so hopelessly devoted to each other. He wanted that. He wanted what they'd had, what Alex and Jenny had. And he wanted it with Hope. "You're sure you don't mind if the ring goes to me? You're the oldest. It should be yours."

Alex swept away Paul's concerns with the wave of his hand. "I'm all set for rings, and besides, Mom has other jewelry that can go to Jenny someday. That ring is for Hope. It's what Mom would want. I know it."

"Thanks for this, for giving me the push I needed."

"Any time. I came over to get Jenny's phone charger, and I'm glad I came when I did. I hate to think of having to deal with you if you let those two get away."

Paul hated to think of that, too. "I'm going to wait until after the wedding and then I'll do it."

"I hope you get everything you want and deserve, Paul."

"Thank you—and thank you for coming home when I needed you."

Alex smiled and winked on his way to the door. "Turned out to be the best thing I ever did."

Long after Alex was gone to the new home he shared with Jenny, Paul stared at the ring in his hand, thinking about what he would say to Hope and hoping he could convince her to stay and make a life with him.

*

Jenny and Alex scored an absolutely glorious early October day for their long-awaited wedding. Over the last few days, Jenny's family had arrived from North Carolina and Toby's family had come from Pennsylvania. Meeting them had been among the more emotional moments for Alex, as he was well aware that their son's death had made his happily ever after possible. A gruesome thought to be certain.

However, he took his lead from them, and they'd chosen to focus on Jenny and her happiness rather than the sadness of the past. They were such happy, positive people, and Alex admired them greatly for having the fortitude to go on after their unimaginable loss. He also appreciated that they were genuinely thrilled for him and Jenny, and he could see that their acceptance of him and their marriage had filled her with joy.

He wanted her to be happy today. They'd both waited a long time to find each other, but after everything she'd been through, he wanted it to be particularly perfect for her. The only thing that wasn't perfect for him was that his beloved parents wouldn't be there. He liked to think his father was always watching over him and had no doubt that George would wholeheartedly approve of Jenny for him, and in her rare moments of lucidity over the last year, Alex hoped his mom had come to know how much he loved Jenny.

Alex waited with Paul and Evan McCarthy in the room provided for the groom's party at the Chesterfield. Paul was messing with his bow tie, so Alex went to offer his assistance. "Let me." He adjusted and straightened the tie and picked a spot of lint off the black tux. "There."

"Thanks."

"Why are you more nervous than I am?"

"You know why."

"So it's on for after?"

As his cheek pulsed with tension, Paul nodded.

"You know what you're gonna say?"

"Yeah."

"I hope it goes exactly the way you want it to."

"Me, too."

"Don't leave anything left unsaid, Paul. Put it all on the table."

"That's the plan."

Lizzie arrived with a white rose for Alex's lapel and burgundy roses for Paul and Evan. Thankfully, she took mercy on them and pinned them on, too.

"How's Jenny?" Alex asked.

"She's radiant."

That was exactly what he wanted to hear.

"Jared heard from his brother," Lizzie said. "He's agreed to come take a look at our fair island. No promises. Yet."

"That's great, Lizzie."

"I'm sorry we couldn't get it done in time to make a difference for your family. But maybe down the road…"

"Maybe so. No matter how the timing works out, it's a great thing you're doing. It's something we need here."

"Fingers crossed. Patience is not my forte, but Jared says if we ease Quinn into the idea, he's apt to bite."

"And if he doesn't, then I'm sure you'll find someone else."

Lizzie touched her earpiece and then smiled at Alex. "Show time."

CHAPTER 27

Surely this day has to be a dream, Jenny thought as she exchanged vows with Alex on the wide veranda behind the Chesterfield. *Because nothing could ever be this perfect and still be real.* Even though this ceremony was a mere formality, that didn't stop a tight knot of emotion from forming in her throat as Alex whispered, "Told ya so, it's all good" as promised and once again pledged to love and cherish her forever. She would never get tired of hearing those words or of the way his fierce brown eyes went soft with love when he said them. They lit the third candle for Toby, sharing a meaningful private smile as they paid tribute to the man she'd loved and lost, which only made her love Alex more than she already did.

Her family, Toby's family, Alex's friends and their Gansett Island family were all there to watch this time, which somehow made it that much more official.

With Sydney and Erin standing by her side, this wedding bore little resemblance to the one she'd planned so long ago. Then, her sisters would have been her attendants, but life and years had changed the dynamic between the three of them, and when it came time to choose attendants this time, there'd been no doubt about who she wanted standing with her today.

Sydney had been the first to reach out to her when she arrived on Gansett hoping for a fresh start. They had bonded initially over their shared experience with tragedy and loss, but their relationship had become a friendship Jenny treasured. They'd moved past that early common ground, with both of them finding a second chance at happily ever after while continuing to honor the ones they'd loved and lost.

And Erin… In the years since Toby's death, Erin had become a sister of Jenny's heart. She was thrilled to have Erin here on Gansett, especially today.

Having Toby's parents here had also made the day extra special. Knowing they were happy for her and that she had their love and support meant the world to her.

As the day unfolded with military precision thanks to Lizzie's unwavering attention to detail, Jenny thought of the secret she and Alex had decided to keep to themselves for the time being, until they were through the critical first trimester. But knowing their baby was part of the wedding made the day that much sweeter.

And when Alex gathered her into his arms to dance to the song they'd chosen to summarize their love, Jenny knew a moment of pure bliss as she danced to "At Last" with her gorgeous new husband.

"Happy?" he asked.

"That's not a big enough word to describe how I feel today. You?"

"Same. There are no words."

"I'm sorry your mom couldn't be here."

"I am, too, but it's for the best. She's getting what she needs, and we'll see her tomorrow." They were spending tonight in the honeymoon suite at the Beachcomber before heading for the mainland to see Marion on their way to a honeymoon in Hawaii.

He had, at some point in the last few days, come around to accepting the fact that it truly was in Marion's best interest to move her into the facility where she could receive more intense care. It pained them, however, that Marion's move had put Hope out of a job. They'd come to care for her and Ethan tremendously, and it would be hard to say good-bye to them when they left the island.

"I feel so sad for Hope," Jenny said, her gaze finding their new friend sitting at a table full of friends but seeming so painfully alone.

"Don't feel too sad," Alex said. "Paul's going to pop the question tonight."

"Oh my God! He is? Really?"

"Yep."

"Hmm."

"What?"

"It's just… What she said that day… How she'd never get married again. He heard her say that, right?"

"Yeah, he did, but he's going to ask her anyway."

"Why do I suddenly feel insanely nervous for him?"

"He's nervous enough for all of us."

"What if she says no?"

"Then we'll prop him up as best we can and get him through it."

"God, I hope she says yes."

"Me, too."

*

Paul took the microphone that Lizzie handed him and made a big production of clearing his throat to get the happy couple to stop kissing long enough for him to do his duty as best man. "If you crazy kids could come up for air for a few minutes, the best man has a few words he'd like to say."

Alex rolled his eyes and signaled for him to proceed.

"On behalf of Alex and Jenny, I'd like to welcome you to their wedding. It's a day we've all looked forward to since last summer, when Jenny and Alex met during the hottest stretch of weather we've had here in decades. They've been hot and bothered ever since." The line drew a big laugh, especially from the bride and groom. "And trust me, I know. I've had the misfortune of living right next door to them, and I've learned to sleep with headphones and music. Loud music." More laughs.

"All kidding aside, however, I've also had the unique perspective of knowing Alex before Jenny and after Jenny. I've got to say I much prefer post-Jenny to pre-Jenny, even if I've sacrificed quite a lot of sleep in the post-Jenny era." While everyone laughed, he sought out Hope, who watched him with a wistful look on her face that made him feel more optimistic about his plans for later. She looked so beautiful today in a clingy, sexy dark gold dress. He held her gaze as he said, "It's a rare thing, a miracle of sorts, for two people so incredibly well-suited to each other to find one another in this chaotic world, and it's even more special when they both deserve the kind of happiness Alex and Jenny have found together.

"Although our parents always loved me better than him," Paul said to more laughter, "they'd be delighted to welcome Jenny into the Martinez family, and on their behalf, I say to Jenny that the Martinez family is lucky to have you—and so is Alex. I love you both and wish you a lifetime of the kind of happiness you're sharing with all of us today." He raised his glass to them, and when he saw tears in their eyes, he decided he'd done his job. Then he shifted his gaze to Hope and caught her dabbing at her own eyes.

Alex stood and took the microphone from him. "Thank you, Paul, and for the record, Mom and Dad always loved *me* best. They frequently said they should've quit while they were ahead."

Paul punched his brother's arm and returned to his seat.

"I want to thank you all for being here today. Jenny and I are so thrilled to share our special day with you. I'm sure you must be wondering why there're bowls of tomatoes on your table. This was a little surprise I orchestrated for my lovely bride, who introduced herself to me by chucking tomatoes at me the day we met. It was true love from the second that first tomato hit me square in the back after my gang mower woke her up during last year's heat wave."

Jenny hid her face behind her hands as she shook with laughter.

"Don't let her fool you—that sweet exterior and soft Southern accent hide a steel magnolia on the inside, and she set the tone from the beginning by letting me know I wasn't going to get away with anything. She's been keeping me in line ever since, and I wouldn't have it any other way." He held up a flute of champagne. "To my beautiful wife, Jenny. Getting hit by your tomato was the best thing to ever happen to me. I love you forever."

As Jenny wiped up tears, the rest of the gathering laughed and clapped at Alex's story.

Paul had heard about the tomatoes many times before, but hearing it in this context made him more determined than ever to throw a few tomatoes of his own—if that was what it took—to convince Hope that the only place in this world she and Ethan belonged was with him. One way or the other, they were going to get their happily ever after.

*

Torture. That was the word Hope would use to describe the last few days as she packed up her belongings and Ethan's while searching for a new job that would take them away from Paul and the people who'd become like family to them. She'd had a promising second phone interview yesterday, and they were eager for her to come to the mainland to meet in person. She should be relieved to have a hot job prospect, but it had been a very long time since Hope had felt at home anywhere the way she did in her cozy cabin, across the yard from the Martinez house that had also begun to feel like home, and she had absolutely no desire to leave. So rather than feeling relieved, she felt despondent.

Paul and Alex had done the right thing to move Marion when they did. As a medical professional, Hope had fully supported their decision and had done everything she could to make it easier for them even as her heart broke into a million pieces at the implications for herself and Ethan. And Paul…

Other than the night he'd intervened with Ethan, Paul had respected her wishes and kept his distance. The more he stayed away, however, the harder it was for her to respect her own wishes. She lay awake night after night, fighting the desire to leave her bed and go to him. Only Ethan sleeping across the hall kept her where she belonged.

The sight of Paul in a tux today hadn't helped her resolve at all. Her mouth had watered at the first glance of him decked out in formal attire. He looked so sexy, and she wasn't the only woman in attendance who noticed. The punch of jealousy and the sharp sting of desire between her legs was a reminder that it would be a very long time—if ever—before she "got over" Paul Martinez.

She'd received the message he'd sent her in his speech loud and clear. What they'd found together didn't come around every day. She certainly knew that, but she'd like to think she'd learned from the mistakes of the past and couldn't gamble her future—or Ethan's—even for something as wonderful as what she had with Paul. She would never again allow herself to become financially dependent upon a man, no matter how much she loved him or suspected he loved her.

Her gaze took in the room full of happy people and found Ethan at a table with Seamus, Carolina, Kyle and Jackson. The three boys were giggling at something Seamus was saying to them, and her heart ached all over again at the thought of taking him away from his new friends. Ethan had thrived here, and having to tell him they were leaving had nearly killed her.

He'd been furious with her ever since, which had only made a difficult situation worse.

A tap on her shoulder had her spinning around to find Paul standing behind her, extending a hand to her. "Dance with me."

She noted that the request wasn't made in the form of a question but rather a plea. Powerless to resist him, she took his hand and let him lead her to the dance floor. Of course the song had to be Elvis Presley singing "Can't Help Falling in Love."

For the first time since the last time she'd been in his arms, the ache inside her subsided and the longing intensified.

"You look so incredibly sexy today," he whispered in her ear, setting off a whole other reaction.

"That wasn't the goal," she said with a nervous laugh.

"You're effortlessly sexy."

In all the years she'd been married, her husband had never said anything like that to her. Everything about this man was different from the man she'd married, but even knowing that, she couldn't seem to throw caution to the wind and forget the many lessons she'd learned the hard way.

She'd thought about his sweet offer many times during sleepless nights and had been tempted more than once to say to hell with lessons learned. What did they matter if it meant having to live without him? But then she'd remember what it had felt like to be desperate and alone and deeply in debt, and the fear would trump the desire every time.

"Ethan is spending the night with Seamus and Carolina," Paul whispered in her ear. "After the wedding, I need a few minutes of your time."

Surprised to hear of plans she'd known nothing about, she said, "Wait, since when is he staying with them?"

"Since I asked if he could. They were happy to have him. Seamus said he's good for the boys because he makes them laugh, and they need that right now."

"Why did you ask if he could stay there?"

"Because we need to talk, and I want you all to myself when we do."

Though every part of her wanted to hear what he had to say, her better judgment ruled the day. "It's not a good idea, Paul."

"How do you know that?" he asked, his dark eyes dancing with amusement. "You haven't heard what I have to say yet."

She shook her head. "I can't let this get any worse than it already is. These last couple of weeks…"

"I know, sweetheart. Believe me. I know. Give me tonight. Please?"

Her better judgment was going to have to get the hell out of the way, because there was no way she could deny him when he asked for something in that particular tone of voice. "Okay."

*

Erin had to work up the nerve, once her bridesmaid duties were officially finished, to take Slim over to meet her parents. Thankfully, her ankle had healed enough to forgo the crutches, but the high-heeled sandals would have to go soon because her ankle was beginning to ache.

"Mom, Dad, this is my friend Slim Jackson," she said, having practiced the introduction in her mind repeatedly in the last few days. "Slim, my parents, Mary Beth and Tom Barton."

"Such a pleasure to meet you," Slim said, full of the charm she'd come to expect from him. He looked amazing in a navy suit with a light blue shirt. His dark hair had been combed into submission, and she'd felt his sexy brown eyes on her all day while she tended to Jenny.

"I understand we have you to thank for rescuing Erin after she hurt her ankle," her dad said.

Erin had no doubt her parents would love Slim. He was their kind of guy—friendly, accomplished, easy to talk to. In many ways, he reminded her of Toby. He'd been less gregarious than Slim but no less charming.

"That was certainly no hardship," he said with a smile for her. They talked for a few minutes about Slim's work as a pilot. "Could I get you a drink?"

"That'd be nice," Mary Beth said. "White wine for me and a beer for Tom, please."

"For you?" he asked Erin.

"I'm good for now. Thanks."

"Be right back." He walked backward toward the bar. "Don't talk about me while I'm gone."

Erin rolled her eyes and laughed at him.

"Well," her mom said, taking a closer look at Erin. "What's this I see? A spark of true interest?"

"Perhaps," Erin said. "It's very new. Don't get too excited just yet."

"He's lovely," her mom said. "Handsome as all get-out, too."

"Is he? I hadn't noticed."

That made them both laugh, which warmed her heart. For many years after Toby died, she'd wondered if any of them would ever laugh again.

"I assume Slim is a nickname?" Mary Beth asked.

"It is, and you're not going to believe what his real name is."

"What?"

"Tobias Fitzgerald Jackson Junior."

"Oh," Mary Beth said, the single word sounding more like a gasp. "That's..."

"Crazy," Tom said softly.

"Isn't it?" Erin asked. "When he first told me... You're going to think it's silly, but..."

"You felt like our Toby might've sent him to you," Mary Beth said.

"Yes," Erin said, relieved that her mom got it. "I'd like to think such things are possible."

"So would we," Tom said, smiling at her. "Your brother would be pleased to see Jenny so happy, and he'd like your Slim."

"I'm glad you think Toby would've liked him, but he's not *my* Slim," Erin said. "We're friends. That's all."

"I guess we'll see about that, won't we?" Tom asked with a wink for his daughter.

Slim returned with drinks for her parents, which they accepted graciously.

"You two ought to go dance," Mary Beth said. "I love this song."

The DJ was playing "When a Man Loves a Woman."

"May I?" Slim asked with a gallant bow as he extended his arm to her.

"She'd love to," Mary Beth said.

"Honestly, Mother." Erin sent her parents a teasingly withering look and let Slim lead her to the dance floor. "Sorry about that."

"About what?" he asked as his arms came around her for the first time since he carried her into the lighthouse.

Erin had danced with plenty of men, but never before had she been so unsure of where to put her hands or why it seemed so difficult to get air to her lungs. God, he smelled good.

"You okay?"

"Um, sure. Why?

"You're kind of stiff."

She blew out a breath and tried to force herself to relax.

"It's okay," he said. "I'm used to it. I have that effect on women."

Erin poked his rock-hard abdomen, which made him laugh and helped her to relax. A little. Why did this moment feel so damned monumental? It was just a dance, for crying out loud.

"By the way, in case I forget to tell you later, that's the sexiest bridesmaid gown I've ever seen."

"I'm sure you've seen a lot of them."

"Most of them are hideous. That one is H-O-T."

"Thank you," she said, pleased and ridiculously aroused by his compliment. "My parents liked you."

"That's great to hear. They're nice people, and it's good of them to be here."

"They love Jenny like a daughter. They wouldn't have missed it."

Off to the side of the dance floor, her parents were having an animated conversation with Jenny's parents.

"Hard to think about how differently that relationship should've played out," Erin said, and then caught herself when she realized she'd said it out loud. In for a penny... "They should be sharing grandchildren by now."

He tightened his hold on her and touched his lips to her forehead, the simple gesture of comfort doing far more to soothe her than words ever could.

When she opened her eyes, she caught Jenny watching her with an astonished expression on her face.

Erin sent her a goofy grin that would ensure a flurry of texts from Hawaii.

"People are looking at us," he said in a conspiratorial whisper. "I think we're officially going public here. How do you feel about that?"

"I'm not sure what you mean," she said, playing for time to formulate a witty reply.

"You, me, dating, public, people knowing. Is that okay?"

"Oh, so now we're dating?"

"You asked me out today, didn't you? You agreed to go to dinner with me, didn't you? When I take you home later, you're probably going to want to kiss me, aren't you?"

Erin's system overheated at the thought of kissing him. "Don't count your chickens, my friend."

His low chuckle rumbled through his muscular body, but then he pulled her in even closer to him, and her mind went totally blank of all thoughts except for how much she hoped he'd carry through on that "threat."

CHAPTER 28

With his plans for later coming together, Paul endeavored to enjoy the day with friends and family who'd come from near and far to celebrate with Jenny and Alex. They ate and drank like kings and danced liked fools. The tuxedo jackets came off, the bow ties were removed, and the ladies kicked off their heels.

It was a blast. After the years of agony surrounding their mother's illness, Paul enjoyed a rare day without the many responsibilities that had weighed so heavily on him for such a long time.

Evan and Owen took over during the DJ's break and played a set that had everyone singing at the top of their lungs before Jenny and Alex once again took center stage for one last dance. They departed a few minutes later in a shower of rose petals and well wishes.

All in all, a perfect day, and one that Paul intended to make even better when he got Hope home. He'd quit drinking hours ago so he could drive her home and so he'd have his wits about him as he made his case to her. This was the most important thing he'd ever do, and he was determined to do it right. She deserved nothing less than his very best, and that was what she'd always get from him, if only he could convince her to let him try to make her happy.

Ethan had been thrilled to leave with the O'Gradys, and it was nice to see him smiling again.

"What a day," he said as he drove home with Hope in the passenger seat of his truck where he hoped to see her for the rest of his life.

"It was awesome," Hope said. "They're so happy."

He again noted the wistful tone of her voice. "Yes, they are."

"That was the most beautiful wedding I've ever been to, especially knowing what she's been through to get there."

"I know. It was so cool that Toby's parents were there, too. That meant a lot to her."

They fell silent for the rest of the ride home. Paul tried not to think about the tension he felt coming from her, but rather tried to stay focused on his plans—and his agenda. He brought his truck to a stop in the driveway outside the house and turned off the engine.

"Give me five minutes, and I'll be back to get you, okay?" He'd set everything up before he left.

"Oh, um, okay."

He loved that nervous little hitch in her voice. He loved that she had no idea what was about to happen. The only thing that could make this better was if he knew what her answer would be. But he'd chosen to have faith in what he felt for her and what he knew she felt for him, even if the words had never been spoken.

With a spring in his step, he bounded up the stairs and went inside to light the candles he'd bought at Tiffany's store with this moment in mind. In deference to the chill in the October air, he also lit the fire he'd laid earlier, hoping it would be cool enough for it.

Paul took a critical look at the room before he went back outside to help her out of the truck. He would've loved to pick her up and carry her inside, but he erred on the side of reserve so he wouldn't scare her off. He kept a light grip on her hand, though, as he led her up the stairs, letting her go ahead of him into the house.

She stopped right inside the door. "Paul... What... What's all this?"

"Come in, and I'll tell you." He helped her out of his tuxedo coat that she'd worn home and tossed it over a chair.

Though she curled her hand around his, he felt her reluctance in every step she took to the sofa, where they sat next to each other.

He turned to face her, and the wariness he saw in her expression had him aching for the suffering that had made it so difficult for her to trust him. *Here goes...*

Linking their fingers, he gazed into her eyes. "Remember when we talked about you and Ethan staying here, and I said I'd take care of you?"

She bit her lip and nodded. "I remember."

"It occurred to me afterward that I'd left out a few important details."

"What details?"

His heart pounded double time as he dropped to his knees before her.

She gasped. "Paul…"

"The most important detail that I forgot to mention is that I love you, Hope. I love you and I love Ethan, and I want you both in my life to stay. When I said I wanted to take care of you, I meant it, but I also understand how important it is to you to be independent financially and professionally. And that's why I think you should go forward with your plans to get a job on the mainland, but maybe a part-time job one or two days a week? We'll rent an apartment over there for when you have to work, as long as you come home to Ethan and me when your shift ends. I want to make this our home—and you can do anything you want to the house to make it your own. I want to raise Ethan as if he were my own. I want to have more babies with you. I want everything with you, and I swear to you—on my life and the lives of everyone I love—I will never be untrue to you. Will you marry me, Hope?"

Tears were sliding down her cheeks, and for the life of him, he couldn't tell if they were happy tears or sad tears.

"Hope?"

"You… You love me?"

He laughed softly. "Did you hear anything else I said after that?"

"I heard all of it." She wiped away the tears that continued to come.

From his pocket, he produced the ring he'd carried around all day like a talisman, hoping it would bring him luck.

"That's your mother's," she whispered.

"Alex gave it to me and told me to give it to you. He said our mom, the mom we knew and loved for so long, would want you to have it because she'd love you for me. She'd love us together."

Hope covered her mouth and shook her head.

Did that mean she was saying no? He honestly didn't know how he would cope if she turned him down. Gambling on the fact that he suspected she loved him as much as he loved her, he took hold of her left hand and slid the ring on her finger. "Well, look at that," he said reverently. "It fits like it was meant for you. My father gave my mother this ring on their twentieth anniversary. She loved it almost as much as she loved him. I want what they had, Hope. I want what Alex has with Jenny. And I want it with you. So will you please marry me?"

"Yes," she whispered, so softly that he thought for a second he was hearing things.

"You want to say that one more time so I can be sure I heard you right?"

"Yes, Paul," she said, smiling as the tears continued to roll down her cheeks. "I'll marry you."

Only then was he able to indulge in the first truly deep breath he'd taken all day. He gathered her into his arms and held on tight, thanking God and his father and anyone else who might've played even a small part in making sure this went his way—that it went *their* way.

"I love you, too," she said, breaking the silence. "And what you said..."

He tucked her hair behind her ear. "What did I say?"

"About me working and how you'll never be untrue... You can't possibly know what that means to me."

"I do know. I know *you*, and I know what matters to you, and I want to be what you want and need."

"You are. You already are."

He kissed her then the way he'd been dying to during the lonely nights when she'd been so close to him but so far away.

Her arms came around him as she returned the kiss, matching his desperation. They ended up on the sofa, him on top of her as the agony faded away, leaving only a lifetime of joy to look forward to. "Here we are again on the sofa where you first kissed me."

"You're never going to forget that, are you?"

Smiling, he said, "Nope." He stared at her gorgeous face because he could. "I'll always be thankful that you lost your mind and kissed me. It saved us a ton of time that we might've wasted pretending this wasn't happening."

"The first day we met, I thought, wow… *He's* going to be my boss?"

"Really?"

She nodded. "I had to remind myself to keep it professional. Until I forgot."

"Thank God for that." He kissed her again. "Alex said we've been eye-fucking each other since the day we met."

She dissolved into helpless laughter. "Your brother certainly has a way with words."

"That he does, but he's not wrong about how long I've wanted you, even if I tried to pretend otherwise because you worked for us." He tugged at her bodice. "How do we get this sexy dress off you?"

"Right over the top."

He pulled back to find the hem and pushed it up and over her head, leaving her in only a black strapless bra and skimpy panties. "Are you really going to marry me?"

"I really am."

"You said you'd never get married again."

"You've changed my mind about a lot of things." She got to work undoing the studs on his tuxedo shirt. "I've thought about this sexy body nonstop."

"Not being able to touch you was the purest form of torture I've ever experienced."

"Touch me now, Paul. Touch me every day for the rest of our lives."

"There's nothing I'd rather do."

EPILOGUE

Hope woke in Paul's arms at the stroke of six, as she did every day whether she needed to or not. Today she most definitely did not need to. Ethan was safe and happy with his friends, and she was engaged to Paul Martinez, who had kept her up half the night celebrating.

"We're going to have to do something about your early hours," he muttered without opening his eyes.

"Blame Ethan. It's all his fault."

"Speaking of Ethan, how early can we go over there and tell him the news?"

"We can't go there at six in the morning."

"Bet they're up."

"Too early."

"Eight?"

"That's more civilized."

"Whatever shall we do until then?" he asked, rolling onto his back and bringing her with him.

"Is this the kind of husband you're going to be?"

"What kind is that?"

"Insatiable."

He moved his hands from her hips to cup her breasts, running his thumbs over her nipples, which tightened instantly. "Is that going to be a problem for my wife?"

She shook her head. "I have no problems. Not anymore." Shifting her hips, she took him in slowly because that made him crazy, and she loved him that way. She loved knowing she did that to him.

"What're you thinking right now?"

"Other than how in the world am I going to keep up with this guy?"

Smiling, he said, "Other than that."

"I love knowing that if I go slow, it makes you crazy. I love knowing that if I do this," she said, squeezing her internal muscles, "you'll do that." Predictably, he gasped and got even harder inside her.

"And I love knowing if I do this," he said, stroking her clit, "you'll do that."

She came instantly, screaming from the pleasure that overtook her, leaving her trembling in his arms afterward.

"And I love the *hell* out of that."

Hope laughed at the dirty way he said the words. "I love the hell out of you, and I'm so glad I can finally tell you that."

"So am I, sweetheart."

*

Hope kept him well occupied until eight, when they took a shower together, laughing and teasing and kissing. He would've said he was fully sated until her sexy, naked body proved otherwise.

"I can't believe you're leaving me in this condition on the first day we're engaged," he said as he drove them to Seamus and Carolina's house.

"Sorry, but you broke me last night."

"I'll fix you later."

She smiled over at him, and the peaceful happy glow on her face filled him with the kind of contentment he'd never expected to find. Then she reached across the center console for his hand and made it even better. "I can't wait to tell Ethan."

"Neither can I."

They pulled into Seamus and Carolina's driveway, where Ethan was in the yard with Jackson, Kyle and their dog, playing with a soccer ball. When Ethan saw them, he let out a happy cry and ran for his mother. She scooped him up and peppered his face with kisses. "Are you guys having fun?"

"So much fun."

She put Ethan down and reached for Kyle and Jackson, who ran to her, too.

Her sweetness to the boys hit Paul right in the chest.

"I don't hafta go home yet, do I?" Ethan asked.

"Not quite, but Paul and I wanted to talk to you."

"Is something wrong?"

"No, baby." Hope gathered him into her arms again. "It's really good news. At least we hope you'll think so."

While Kyle and Jackson looked on, Paul squatted down so he could look Ethan in the eye. "How'd you like to stay here on Gansett?"

Ethan's big eyes widened with glee. "Really?" He looked up at his mom, who nodded. "So we don't hafta move away?"

"Last night, I asked your mom to marry me, and she said yes. Now I'm hoping you'll say yes, too, so you guys will get to stay here with me."

Ethan hurled himself at Paul, who managed to keep his balance as he hugged him.

"Should I take that as a yes?" Paul said, thrilled by Ethan's reaction.

"We really get to stay forever?" Ethan asked his mother.

"Yes, honey."

"And will you be my new dad?" he asked Paul.

The question hit him with the force of a gut punch. "If that's what you want," he said gruffly.

"It is." Ethan broke free of Paul's embrace. "Hey, you guys," he said to Jackson and Kyle, "me and my mom are gettin' married!"

Paul exchanged glances with Hope, her smile as wide as his. He held out his hand to help her up. As the boys ran inside to tell Seamus and Carolina the news, Paul hugged her. "I guess it's official now."

"No getting out of it."

He kissed her and then kept his arm around her as they followed the boys into the house. "No worries about that, sweetheart. I'm in." He stole one more kiss while he could. "I'm *all*-in."

AUTHOR'S NOTE

Wow, book 13, and it's still so much fun to write the Gansett Island Series! It's like a vacation for me to go back to Gansett! I can't thank you enough for continuing to show up for every new book—even when I make you wait ten long months. I look forward to every minute I get to spend on my fictional island with people who feel like family after writing them for so many years. If you'd like to chat about *Love After Dark* with other readers, please join the **Love After Dark Reader Group.**

I plan to keep writing Gansett books as long as you keep telling me you love them. If you do love them, help other readers discover the series by leaving a review at the retailer of your choice and/or Goodreads. And make sure to tell your friends that book 1, *Maid for Love,* is FREE!

Slim and Erin will headline the next full-length book, but I have a surprise for you before then (see below). Make sure you don't miss announcements about new books by joining my newsletter mailing list at marieforce.com (left side where it asks for your name and email address), subscribing to my blog and joining the **McCarthy Reader Group.**

I'm so blessed to work with a dedicated, fun group of women, including Julie Cupp, CMP, Lisa Cafferty, CPA, Holly Sullivan, Isabel Sullivan, Nikki Colquhoun, Cheryl Serra, Ashley Lopez and Courtney Lopes. Thank you all so much for everything you do for me every day. And thank you to my husband, Dan, who runs our lives so I can write as much as I do. Thank you to my amazing editorial team of Linda Ingmanson and Joyce Lamb, who make themselves available to me whenever I need them. Thank you, ladies! And a big thank-you to my beta readers Anne Woodall, Ronlyn Howe and Kara Conrad for always being willing to read for me when I need you! Special thanks to Sarah Spate Morrison, Family Nurse Practitioner, for keeping me straight on all things medical.

Julie's friends (and now my friends, too) Ashley and Bryan Lopez were such great sports about modeling for the cover of *Love After Dark*. I can't say enough about how much I love this cover that Ashley's twin sister, Courtney Lopes, designed after the photo shoot done by my photographer friend, Pam Sardinha, assisted by her husband, David, and Julie. What a family affair, and the end result is gorgeous, just like the couple who posed for us! Thanks, guys!

Love After Dark is part of our Read to Win promotion in which readers can take a quick 20-question quiz on the content of Love After Dark and be entered to win an all-expense paid trip for two to my 2016 Reader Weekend in Newport, RI. You'll have two other chances to win before the end of the year with the release of *Fatal Frenzy*, Fatal book 9, on September 15 and *It's Only Love*, Green Mountain, book 5, on November 3. Find all the details at marieforce.com/readtowin.

Most of all, I'm thankful for the readers who make this the most fun "job" I've ever had. Thank you so much for your support and enthusiasm for my books. Love you all! Keep reading to find out more about a very special Gansett Island novella coming later this year AND to view the cover of *You'll Be Mine*, Will and Cameron's Green Mountain wedding novella, which is out on October 20.

Turn the page to read chapter 1 of *Celebration After Dark*, a SURPRISE Gansett Island Novella, featuring Big Mac and Linda McCarthy, out on December 1!

xoxo

Marie

Special Announcement!

I'm very excited to announce here for the FIRST TIME that *Celebration After Dark*, a novella featuring Big Mac and Linda McCarthy's 40th Anniversary—with a look back on how their romance first began—will be released on Tuesday, December 1! Readers have been asking for Big Mac and Linda's story for years now, and I thought their anniversary was a great opportunity to get their story out there.

You'll also hear more from each of the five McCarthy kids in this new story, as well as updates on several other Gansett Island favorite couples. I've had so much fun writing this new Gansett Island story this summer, and I can't wait to get it out you. Have you wondered what winter is like on Gansett? Wonder no more! *Celebration After Dark* is out on December 1. Preorder your copy now to read the minute it's released!

CELEBRATION AFTER DARK
CHAPTER 1

Mac McCarthy Senior, known to all as Big Mac, woke on the morning of December twentieth to the distinctive sounds of winter on Gansett Island—howling wind, icy snow pinging against the windows and groaning beams in the house he'd called home for four decades. But today was not just any average winter day. On this day, forty years ago, he'd married the love of his life. Today was a day for celebration.

The kids were throwing a party later that Big Mac and Linda weren't supposed to know about. "Voodoo Mama," as the kids called her, knew everything they were up to, and she always had. She'd picked up on the scent of a party months ago, which was why they hadn't planned one for themselves. He had a few surprises of his own to mark the occasion that he couldn't wait to give her.

She slept curled up to him, the way she did every night. Even on the few occasions when they'd been at odds, she'd never failed to reach for him in her sleep. Their marriage had been filled with love and joy and five incredible kids who'd been the light of their lives. Each of them had found their soul mate in the last few years and were happily settled, which was the only thing their parents had ever truly wanted for them.

Nothing made Big Mac happier than seeing his kids happy and in love with people he would've hand-chosen for each of them. Mac with Maddie, Grant with Stephanie, Adam with Abby, Evan with Grace and Janey with Joe. All of them perfect matches in every way that mattered.

In addition to his own five, he'd been like a father to Luke Harris, the young man who'd worked for him at the marina since he was fourteen, who was now happily married to his first love, Sydney Donovan Harris, and had a baby on the way.

A few years ago, Big Mac had made Mac and Luke his partners in the marina, which had been one of the best things he'd ever done. It freed him up to relax a little while the two young guys put their considerable energy into steering the business into the modern era. Big Mac was more than happy to take a backseat to them. He had grandchildren to coddle and fish to catch and a wife to take traveling as he'd promised her he would once the kids were launched and the businesses were in good hands.

And then there was Mallory Vaughn, the woman who'd appeared earlier in the year with the life-changing news that she was the daughter he'd never known he had. Talk about shocking! But Linda had set the tone, accepting Mallory into their family and making sure her arrival didn't turn into a crisis for them. He'd never loved his gorgeous wife more than he had watching her welcome his daughter into their home and family.

The bedside clock read six twenty, which was far too early to wake Linda to begin the celebration. With nowhere to be for hours, they had the day to themselves before the party. That was plenty of time to shower her with the gifts he'd spent months organizing, among other things he wanted to do today.

He was kind of glad it was snowing. The men of the family had been spending every possible minute helping his son Mac and his nephew Shane with the addition to the home of Seamus and Carolina O'Grady, who'd recently taken in two young boys after their mother's tragic death. Everyone wanted to see the new family settled as soon as possible, and they were down to finish work on the addition. With the storm raging outside, he could justify a day off to spend with his wife.

In the meantime, he found his thoughts wandering back in time to the summer day when he first laid eyes on the woman who'd become his wife. He'd been home in Providence to close on the ramshackle marina that everyone had told him not to buy. His dad had been particularly vociferous in his objections.

"Your grandmother left you that money so you could make something of yourself, Mac," his father had said. "She'd be very disappointed to see you pissing it away on a hunk of junk in the middle of nowhere."

"I'm sorry you think so, Dad, but I've got a feeling about this place. With a little love and a lot of work, I think I can turn it into a goldmine."

"And how do you plan to *eat* while you're waiting to strike gold?"

"I've got my charter captain's license and feelers out all over the place. I'll find work. Don't worry." As long as he was near the water in some way or another, Mac was confident that he could make a living somehow.

Frank McCarthy Senior had shaken his head with disgust and dismay over the plans his middle son had made for his little corner of Gansett Island.

"Let him be, Frank," Mac's mother, Jane, had said. "He's got to make his own way the same way you made yours. Harping on him isn't going to change his mind, especially when he's signing the papers tomorrow."

Despite his mother's support, Mac had left his parents' home that day feeling dejected and scared for the first time since he'd fallen in love with the marina. What if his dad was right? What if he'd truly pissed away the nest egg his grandmother had left him on something that would never pay off?

As he drove the truck he'd bought in high school that was on its last legs to his brother Frank's place, he blasted Bruce Springsteen's new album "Born to Run" in the tape deck while his chest tightened with stress and panic. He'd wagered everything he had and then some on the marina, knowing it needed a load of work to make it presentable. He'd never been afraid of hard work and had been looking forward to getting on with it before his dad filled his head with worries.

Mac found a parking space two blocks from Frank's house, and after he shut off the engine, he sat there for a minute thinking it through from every angle. One of the lawyers Frank had interned with over the summer had been good enough to look over the contracts for the purchase of the marina and declared them sound. Mac had had the place surveyed, and even though it looked a little rough around the edges to the naked eye, it was structurally sound. He had financing in place for the portion not covered by his inheritance and had built in money for renovations.

It would take years to own the place free and clear, but he still had faith that eventually the investment of his time and money would pay off. And if it didn't? Well, he was a young guy with plenty of time to recover and find something else to do with his life.

He got out of the truck and walked to Frank's apartment, which occupied the first floor of a three-story Victorian. Frank was heading to law school at Brown in the fall and lived there with two other guys. The three of them were hosting this afternoon's party in the backyard. Mac was in bad need of some time with his big brother—not to mention a couple of cold ones.

Mac let himself into the apartment with the key Frank had given him so he could crash on the sofa rather than stay at home, where his mother would want him home by midnight and then sniff him, looking for telltale signs that he'd been drinking. It was easier to stay with Frank, who expected him to smell like beer because they usually drank it together.

"Mac!" Frank called from the kitchen. "Get in here and check out these wings that Brett made. They'll set your mouth on fire."

"And doesn't that sound like fun?"

Frank took a closer look at him. "What's with you?"

"Nothing."

Leaving the kitchen, Frank took him by the arm and steered him back the way he'd come. They went through the front door to the porch. "Let me ask again—what's with you?"

Mac hesitated, but only for a second because this was Frankie, his big brother and best friend. If anyone would tell it to him straight, it was Frank. "Am I making a huge mistake buying the marina?"

"*What?*"

"You heard me. Am I pissing away Grandma's money on something stupid?"

"Where's this shit coming from?"

"Something Dad said has me thinking. What if it's a total disaster, and I lose my shirt?"

"What if it's a huge success and you make millions? Have you considered that possibility?"

"Not really. I'd be perfectly satisfied to make a decent living from the place. I'm not looking for millions."

"Still, it's not outside the realm of possibility. People are saying Gansett is the next Martha's Vineyard. Sky's the limit, bro, and you're in on the ground floor."

"So you still think it's a good idea to buy the place?"

"If I didn't think so, I would've said so." Frank was the one person from his life in Providence who'd been out to the island to see the marina because Mac trusted his brother's instincts and wanted his opinion. "You've got your work cut out for you to undo years of neglect, but that's nothing you can't handle."

Frank's assurances helped to calm the wave of panic that had been growing since he left their parents' home earlier.

"You're going to sign those papers tomorrow and take the plunge, because if you don't, you'll spend the rest of your life wondering what might've happened if you had."

"That's very true."

"Sometimes you've just got to go for it, Mac, and let the chips fall where they will. Either it'll be a success or it won't, but the only failure here would be in not trying."

"Thanks, Frankie. That's exactly what I needed to hear."

"Dad means well. You know he does, but sometimes he spouts off without thinking. Don't let him fill your mind with doubts. This is what you want, Mac. Go for it."

"I'm going to."

"Good." Frank's gaze shifted to something in the street, and his smile lit up his face. "Here comes my girl, and she's brought friends. *Cute* friends."

Mac looked toward the street and saw JoAnn, Frank's girlfriend since high school, coming down the sidewalk with three other girls in tow. He immediately zeroed in on one of them. She was petite with long blonde hair, an arresting face and eyes that danced with glee at something one of her friends was saying.

Mac felt like he'd been sucker-punched watching her come closer.

"Earth to Mac," Frank said, drawing his attention off the blonde goddess.

"Wh-who is that?"

"Huh?"

"The blonde with JoAnn. Who is she?"

"That's her friend Linda from PC," he said, referring to Providence College.

"Introduce me."

"Um, okay…"

JoAnn came up the stairs and launched herself at Frankie, laying a wet, sloppy kiss on him. "God, this week was endless."

"For me, too, baby."

The two of them had been mad about each other from the moment they met in high school when Jo's family moved to the city. Frank had come home from the first day of school professing he'd met his future wife, and they'd been together ever since.

Keeping an arm around JoAnn, Frank said, "Ladies, this is my brother, Mac. Mac, meet Josie, Linda and Kathy."

Linda. Her name is Linda. Mac shook hands with all three women and then gave his full attention to the one in the middle, who stood out in the group of women like a shining star. He'd never been so bowled over by a girl—or a woman. She was all woman, but giggled like a girl with her friends as they made their way inside with JoAnn leading the way.

"Easy," Frank said, his hand on Mac's arm.

"How do you think Linda would feel about living on Gansett Island with an up-and-coming marina owner?"

Frank tossed his head back and laughed as hard as Mac had ever seen him laugh.

Too bad Mac had been serious.

"You don't do anything halfway, do you, Mac?"

"What's the point of doing something halfway?"

"Go easy so you don't scare her off. She'll think you're some sort of ax murderer if you ask her to come live on your remote island five minutes after you meet her."

"You can laugh all you want, Frankie, but that girl is going to live with me on my island. Mark my words."

"Good thing you're going to have a lawyer in the family. You're going to need me to defend you when she files charges against you."

Mac laughed at Frank's joke, but he suspected he'd need his brother to be his best man before he'd ever need his legal services.

*

Big Mac chuckled at the memory of that long-ago day. It had been ages since he'd thought about how his father had nearly talked him out of buying the marina—and what a mistake that would've been. He'd paid off the loan within five years and had gone on to make millions on the place, just as Frankie had predicted it might. Hadn't happened overnight, but the island had been featured on a TV show on East Coast destinations two years after he bought the marina, and nothing was ever the same after that.

And speaking of never the same... He was never the same after that day at Frank's house. That was the day his life really began, the day he met Linda.

Celebration After Dark is out on December 1, 2015! Preorder your copy today to read it on release day!

Turn the page to read Chapter 1 of **You'll Be Mine**, Will and Cameron's Green Mountain Wedding Novella, available in ebook format

October 20! Get it in Print NOW in *Ask Me Why* Anthology, available everywhere print book are sold.

Will Abbott and Cameron Murphy are finally ready to tie the knot— as long as family, friends and a love-struck moose don't get in the way.

You'll Be Mine
Chapter 1

Two days before her wedding to Will Abbott, Cameron Murphy shut off her laptop at exactly one forty-five in the afternoon and left it in the office she shared with her fiancé. She wouldn't need the computer for two weeks. The next time she returned to the office, he'd be her husband and they'd be back from their honeymoon.

Filled with giddy excitement, Cameron turned off the office light and closed the door behind her. Will was already gone for the day, running last-minute wedding errands while she finished up at work.

Their office manager, Mary, stood up and came around her desk to give Cameron a hug. "Enjoy every minute of this special time," she said, nearly reducing Cameron to tears.

"Thank you so much, Mary. I'll see you tomorrow night, right?" She was one of a few special friends invited to join the family for the rehearsal dinner Will's parents were throwing at the big red barn where Will and his siblings had been raised.

"Wouldn't miss it for the world."

"I'll see you then."

Cameron skipped down the stairs and into the store where she was greeted with more hugs and good wishes from the employees. While no one would mistake her little old nuptials for the royal wedding, it sort of had that feel to it. In Butler, Vermont, the Abbotts were royalty. With a family of ten children and businesses that employed numerous members of the local community, an Abbott wedding was big news.

She accepted a hug, a kiss, best wishes and a cider doughnut from Dottie, who ran the doughnut counter. After talking wedding plans with Dottie and the other ladies for a couple of minutes, Cameron took her doughnut to the store's front porch to enjoy it in relative peace. With only two days to go, she was no longer worried about fitting into her dress, so she took a seat on one of the rockers and ate her treat in guilt-free heaven.

She'd no sooner begun to relax than who should appear on a leisurely stroll down Elm Street but her very own stalker, Fred the Moose. Cameron sank deeper into the rocker, hoping Fred wouldn't notice her. In all her years of living in New York City and after scores of first dates, she'd never had an actual stalker—until she came to Vermont and slammed her MINI Cooper into Fred, the Butler town moose. Since then he'd taken such a keen interest in her that Will's dad, Lincoln, had recently concluded that Fred had a crush on her.

Fantastic. A moose with a crush. With her dad due at two, and Patrick Murphy always on time, the last thing she needed was yet another mooseast-rophy. Fortunately, Fred didn't see her sitting on the porch and continued on his merry way, leaving Cameron to breathe easier about Fred but not about her dad's impending arrival.

The thought of her billionaire businessman father in tiny Butler had provoked more nerves than anything else about the upcoming weekend. Marrying Will? No worries at all. Getting through the wedding? Who cared if it all went wrong? At the end of the day, she'd be married to Will. That was all that mattered. But bringing Patrick here to this place she now called home?

Cameron drew in a deep breath and blew it out. She hoped he wouldn't do or say something to make her feel less at home here, because she loved everything about Butler and her life with Will in Vermont. She'd experienced mud season—along with a late-season blast of snow—spring, summer and now the glorious autumn, which was, without a doubt, her favorite season so far.

How could she adequately describe the russet glow of the trees, the vivid blue skies, the bright sunny days and the chilly autumn nights spent snuggled up with Will in front of the woodstove? The apples, pumpkins, chrysanthemums, corn husks tied to porch rails, hay bales and cider. She loved it all, but she especially loved the scent of wood smoke in the air.

Cameron couldn't have asked for a better time of year to pitch a tent in their enormous yard and throw a great big party. All her favorite autumn touches would be incorporated into the wedding, and she couldn't wait to see it all come together on Saturday. At Will's suggestion, they'd hired a wedding planner to see to the myriad details because they were both so busy at work.

At first, Cameron had balked at the idea of hiring a stranger to plan the most important day of her life, but Regan had won her over at their first meeting and had quickly become essential to her. No way could Cameron have focused on the website she was building for the store and planned a wedding at the same time.

She glanced at her watch. Three minutes until two. Patrick would be here any second, probably in the town car he used to get around the city. Under no circumstances could she picture her dad driving himself six hours north to Vermont. Not when there were deals to be struck and money to be made. Time, he always said, was money.

He'd shocked the hell out of her when he told her he wanted to come up on Thursday so he could spend some time with her and Will before the madness began in earnest. Her dad would be sleeping in their loft tonight, and Will had already put her on notice that he would *not* have sex with her while her dad was in the house. She couldn't wait to break his resolve.

The thought of how she planned to accomplish that had her in giggles that died on her lips at the familiar *thump, thump, thump* sound that suddenly invaded the peaceful afternoon.

No way. No freaking way. He did not!

If this was what she thought it was, she'd have no choice but to kill him. Warily, she got up from her chair and ventured down the stairs to look up at the sky just as her father's big, black Sikorsky helicopter came swooping in on tiny Butler, bringing cars and people to a halt on Elm Street.

One woman let out an ear-piercing scream and dove for some nearby bushes.

Equal parts amused and aggravated, Cameron took off jogging toward the town common, the one space nearby where the bird could land unencumbered. As she went, she realized she should've expected him to make an entrance. Didn't he always?

Nolan and Skeeter were outside the garage looking up when she went by.

"What the hell was that?" asked Nolan, who would be her brother-in-law after the wedding. He was married to Will's sister Hannah, who'd become Cameron's close friend since she had moved to Butler.

"Just my dad coming to town."

"Jumping Jehoshaphat!" Skeeter said. "Thought it was the end of the world."

"Nope, just Patrick Murphy coming to what he considers the end of the earth. Gotta run. See you later."

"Bye, Cam," Nolan said.

"I assume that's with you," Lucas Abbott said, gesturing toward the town common with his thumb, as Cameron trotted past his woodworking barn.

"You'd be correct."

"That thing is righteous. Does he give rides?"

"I'll be sure to ask him."

"Nice."

Cameron sort of hated that everyone in town would know her pedigree after her father's auspicious arrival. Maybe they already knew. In fact, they probably did. The Butler gossip grapevine was nothing short of astonishing. If the people in town knew who she was, or who her father was, no one made a thing of it. After this, they probably would, which saddened her. She loved her low-key, under-the-radar life in Butler and wouldn't change a thing about it.

But she also loved her dad, and after thirty years as his daughter, she should certainly be accustomed to the grandiose way he did things. She got to the field just as he was emerging from the gigantic black bird with the gold PME lettering on the side: Patrick Murphy Enterprises. Those initials were as familiar to Cameron as her own because they'd always been part of her life.

Hoping to regain her breath and her composure, she came to a stop about twenty yards from the landing site and waited for him to come to her—by himself. That was interesting, as she'd expected his girlfriend-slash-housekeeper Lena to be with him.

With her hands on her hips, Cameron watched him exchange a few words with the pilot before shaking his hand, grabbing a suitcase and garment bag as well as his ever-present messenger bag, which he slung over his shoulder. Wait until he experienced Butler Wi-Fi, or the lack thereof.

He was tall with dark blond hair, piercing blue eyes and a smile on his handsome face, and as he walked to Cameron, her heart softened toward him, as it always did, no matter how outrageous he might be.

She took the garment bag from him and lifted her cheek to receive his kiss. "Always gotta make an entrance, don't you?"

"What's that supposed to mean?"

"The *bird*, Dad. You scared the hell out of everyone. They thought we were being attacked."

He looked completely baffled. "I told you I'd be here at two."

"I was watching for a car, not a chopper."

Recoiling from the very idea, he said, "I didn't have six hours to sit in traffic on the Taconic. As it is, my ass is numb after ninety minutes in the chopper."

"We do have airports in Vermont, you know."

"We checked on that. Closest one that could take the Lear is in Burlington, which is more than two hours from here. Time—"

"Is money," she said with a sigh. "I know."

"Besides, you're taking the Lear to Fiji, and for the record, I'd like to point out it wasn't my idea to move you out to the bumfuck of nowhere."

Cameron laughed at his colorful wording. "This is *not* the bumfuck of nowhere. This," she said, with a dramatic sweep of her arm, "is the lovely, magnificent town of Butler, Vermont."

"It's as charming as I recall from the last time I was here for Linc's wedding."

"Are you being sarcastic?"

"Me? Sarcastic?"

"I thought Lena was coming with you."

"Yeah, about that . . . We've kind of cooled it."

"Is she still working for you?" Cameron had spoken to her recently and hadn't heard that she was no longer in Patrick's employ.

"Oh, yeah. It's all good."

Cameron was certainly used to the way women came and went in her father's life. She'd learned not to get attached to any of them. They didn't stick around long enough to make it worth her while. "Well, it's great to see you and to have you here. I know it's not what you're used to, but I think you'll enjoy it."

He stopped walking and turned to her. "You're here. That's all I need to enjoy myself, honey."

Cameron let the garment bag flop over her arm so she could hug him. "Thank you so much for coming, Dad."

He wrapped his arms around her. "Happy to be anywhere you are."

They stashed Patrick's bags in Cameron's black SUV. "Where'd you get this beast?"

"Will insisted I trade the MINI for something built for Vermont winters. I don't love it, but as I haven't survived a winter here yet, I'll take his word for it."

"So this is the store, huh?"

"Yep."

"Show me around."

"You really want to see it?"

"I really do."

She took Patrick's hand, eager to introduce him to all her new friends. "Right this way."

He followed her up the stairs to the porch and into the Green Mountain Country Store in all its glory.

"Wow." Patrick took a look around and glanced up at the vintage bicycle fastened to one of the wooden beams above the store. "I feel like I just stepped into an episode of *Little House on the Prairie*."

"Isn't it amazing? I'll never forget the first time I came in here. It was like I'd been transported or something." She looked up at him as he took in the barrels full of peanuts and iced bottles of Coke and products from a bygone era, a simpler time, hoping he'd see the magic she saw every time she came through the doors to the store. "That's dumb, right?"

"Not at all. It's quite something. I'm wondering, though, how in the name of hell you build a website for a place like this."

Cameron laughed. "Slowly and painstakingly."

"I can't wait to see how you've captured it."

She tugged on his hand. "Come meet Dottie and have a cider doughnut."

"Oh, I don't think—"

"You have to! Your visit won't be complete without one." She led him back to the doughnut counter where Dottie was pulling a fresh batch from the oven. "Perfect timing. Dottie, this is my dad, Patrick, and he's in bad need of a doughnut."

Dottie wiped her hands on a towel before reaching across the counter to shake Patrick's hand. "So nice to meet you, Patrick. We're all very big fans of your daughter."

"As am I."

"Can I get one of those for him?"

"Of course! Another for you, sweetie?"

"Absolutely not! I've got a dress to fit into on Saturday, so don't tempt me." To Patrick, Cameron added, "Dottie is the devil when it comes to these doughnuts."

"Why, thank you," Dottie said with a proud smile as she handed over a piping-hot doughnut to Patrick.

Both women watched expectantly as he took a bite.

His blue eyes lit up. "Holy Moses, that's good."

"*Right?*" Cameron said, pleased by his obvious pleasure. "I limit myself to two a week, or I wouldn't fit through the doors around here. Come on upstairs and check out the office. See you later, Dottie."

"Bye, Cam. Nice to meet you, Patrick."

"You, too."

He followed her through the store, stopping to look at various items as they went.

"That's Hannah's jewelry," Cameron said of the pieces that had stopped him for a closer look. "She's Will's older sister, twin to Hunter, who's the company CFO."

"She does beautiful work."

"I know! I'm a huge fan. I have a couple of her bracelets. Helps to have friends in high places."

"I'm glad you're making friends here."

They proceeded up the stairs to the offices on the second floor. "So many friends. And now Lucy's here a lot, too, which makes it even better."

"Back so soon?" Mary asked when they arrived in the reception area. "I didn't think I'd see you here again for at least two weeks."

"I wanted you to meet my dad, Patrick."

Mary came around her desk to shake his hand. "So nice to meet Cameron's dad. We adore her here."

"So I'm hearing. Nice to meet you, too."

"This is our office." Cameron opened the door and turned on the lights so her dad could see her workspace.

"*Our* office?"

"Mine and Will's."

"You two *share* an office? They didn't give you one of your own?"

"We tried," Mary said. "Those kids are inseparable."

Cameron blushed and shrugged. "What she said. Besides, if I'm in another office, how am I supposed to play footsie with him during the day?"

"Ugh," Patrick said with a grunt of laughter. "TMI. I'd go crazy sharing office space with anyone, especially such a small one."

"Not everyone can have an acre in the sky to call their own," Cameron said disdainfully.

He tweaked her nose. "It's not a full acre, and I do need my elbow room."

"You're a spoiled, pampered brat, and we all know it."

Mary laughed at their sparring.

"Don't listen to her, Mary," Patrick said with a wink, which had Mary blushing to the roots of her brown hair. "We all know who the spoiled brat is here."

"Yeah, and it's not me."

"I'm afraid I have to side with your daughter, Patrick. There's nothing spoiled about her. She works harder than all of us put together."

"Thank you, Mary. I'll make sure Hunter hears about your fifty percent raise."

They left Mary laughing as they went back downstairs.

"What's her story?" Patrick asked.

"Who, Mary?"

"Yeah. She's adorable."

"Dad . . . Don't. She's a really nice person. Leave her alone. She wouldn't stand a chance against your brand of charm."

"Why can't I have a little fun while I'm in town?"

Cameron stopped on the landing and turned to him. "She's off-limits. I mean that."

"Don't be so touchy, Cam." He kissed her cheek and proceeded ahead of her into the store.

She watched him go with a growing sense of unease. She'd be watching him this weekend and keeping him far, far away from Mary—and all the other single women in Butler.

You'll Be Mine is out in ebook format on October 20, 2015! Get it in print NOW in the Ask Me Why Anthology, available everywhere print book are sold.

WHO'S WHO ON GANSETT ISALND?

Updated through Kisses After Dark, Book 12. May contain spoilers for those who haven't read all the books.

The McCarthy Family

"Big Mac" and Linda McCarthy, owners of McCarthy's Gansett Island Marina and McCarthy's Gansett Island Inn, are parents to:

- Mac McCarthy Jr., who is married to Maddie Chester McCarthy and father to Thomas and Hailey McCarthy
- Grant McCarthy, screenwriter, engaged to Stephanie Logan, owner of Stephanie's Bistro
- Adam McCarthy, computer geek, engaged to Abby Callahan, owner of Abby's Attic
- Evan McCarthy, owner of Island Breeze Records, engaged to Grace Ryan, owner of Ryan's Pharmacy
- Janey McCarthy Cantrell, married to Joe Cantrell, owner of the Gansett Island Ferry Company; mother of P.J. Cantrell
- Mallory Vaughn, daughter of Big Mac McCarthy and Diana Vaughn

Judge Frank McCarthy, brother to "Big Mac" McCarthy, father to:

- Laura McCarthy Lawry, cousin to Mac, Grant, Adam, Evan and Janey; married to Owen Lawry, mother of Holden Newsome
- Shane McCarthy, cousin to Mac, Grant, Adam, Evan and Janey; brother to Laura Lawry; engaged to Katie Lawry

Dr. Kevin McCarthy, brother to Big Mac and Frank McCarthy; psychiatrist

- Deb McCarthy, estranged wife of Kevin McCarthy; mother of Riley and Finn McCarthy
- Riley McCarthy, son of Kevin and Deb McCarthy
- Finn McCarthy, son of Kevin and Deb McCarthy

McCarthy Friends & Family

Owen Lawry, musician and best friend of Evan McCarthy; married to Laura McCarthy Lawry

Luke Harris, co-owner of McCarthys Gansett Island Marina and married to Sydney Donovan

Sydney Donovan, interior decorator, married to Luke Harris

Ned Saunders, best friend to Big Mac McCarthy; married to Francine Chester Saunders, mother of Maddie McCarthy and Tiffany Taylor

Francine Chester Saunders, mother of Maddie McCarthy and Tiffany Taylor; married to Ned Saunders

Tiffany Taylor, sister to Maddie McCarthy, daughter of Francine Saunders, mother to Ashleigh Sturgil; married to Police Chief Blaine Taylor

Blaine Taylor, Gansett Island police chief, married to Tiffany Taylor

Bobby Chester, estranged father of Maddie McCarthy and Tiffany Taylor, ex-husband of Francine Saunders

Jim Sturgil, ex-husband of Tiffany Taylor, father to Ashleigh Sturgil

Seamus O'Grady, manager of the Gansett Island Ferry Company; married to Carolina Cantrell

Carolina Cantrell O'Grady, mother of Joe Cantrell, married to Seamus O'Grady

Lisa Chandler, neighbor to Seamus and Carolina Cantrell

Kyle Chandler, son of Lisa

Jackson Chandler, son of Lisa

Dan Torrington, celebrity lawyer and friend to Grant McCarthy, engaged to Kara Ballard

Kara Ballard, operator of Ballard's Launch Service, engaged to Dan Torrington

Abby Callahan, owner of Abby's Attic, former girlfriend of Grant McCarthy, engaged to Adam McCarthy

Dr. Cal Maitland, former island doctor and ex-fiancé of Abby Callahan

Charlie Grandchamp, stepfather of Stephanie Logan, engaged to Sarah Lawry

Sarah Lawry, mother of Owen Lawry, engaged to Charlie Grandchamp

Mark Lawry, father of Owen Lawry; estranged husband of Sarah Lawry

Katie Lawry, sister of Owen Lawry; daughter of Sarah Lawry; twin to Julia; engaged to Shane McCarthy

Julia Lawry, sister of Owen Lawry; daughter of Sarah Lawry; twin to Katie

Slim Jackson, Gansett Island pilot

Dr. David Lawrence, Gansett Island doctor, former fiancé of Janey McCarthy Cantrell; dating Daisy Babson

Daisy Babson, friend of Maddie McCarthy's, housekeeping manager at McCarthy's Gansett Island Inn; dating Dr. David Lawrence

Jenny Wilks, lighthouse keeper; engaged to Alex Martinez

Alex Martinez, co-owner of Martinez Lawn & Garden; fiancé of Jenny Wilks

Paul Martinez, co-owner of Martinez Lawn & Garden; member of Gansett Town Council

Marion Martinez, mother of Paul and Alex Martinez

Hope Russell, nurse to Marion Martinez, mother of Ethan Russell

Ethan Russell, son of Hope Russell

Jared James, resident billionaire, co-owner of The Chesterfield; married to Lizzie James

Elisabeth "Lizzie" James, co-owner of The Chesterfield; married to Jared James

Erin Barton, lighthouse keeper

Mason Johns, island fire chief

Truck Henry, Daisy Babson's abusive ex-boyfriend

Victoria Stevens, Gansett Island midwife; dating Shannon O'Grady

Shannon O'Grady, cousin of Seamus O'Grady; dating Victoria Stevens

Rebecca, owner of the South Harbor Diner

Chelsea Rose, bartender at the Beachcomber

Doc Potter, island veterinarian

Chloe Dennis, owner of the Curl Up and Dye Salon

The Children of Gansett Island

- Thomas McCarthy, son of Maddie McCarthy; adopted son of Mac McCarthy
- Hailey McCarthy, daughter of Maddie and Mac McCarthy
- Ashleigh Sturgil, daughter of Tiffany Taylor and Jim Sturgil
- Holden Newsome, son of Laura McCarthy and her ex-husband, Justin Newsome
- P.J. Cantrell, son of Joe and Janey Cantrell

OTHER TITLES BY MARIE FORCE

The Treading Water Series

10th Anniversary Treading Water Boxed Set (ebook)

Book 1: Treading Water

Book 2: Marking Time

Book 3: Starting Over

Book 4: Coming Home

The Green Mountain Series

Book 1: All You Need Is Love

Book 2: I Want to Hold Your Hand

Book 3: I Saw Her Standing There

Book 4: And I Love Her

Novella: You'll Be Mine in the Ask Me Why Anthology

Book 5: It's Only Love (November 3, 2015)

Single Titles

The Single Titles Boxed Set

Georgia on My Mind

True North

The Fall

Everyone Loves a Hero

Love at First Flight

Line of Scrimmage

Books from M. S. Force
The Erotic Quantum Trilogy

Book 1: Virtuous

Book 2: Valorous

Book 3: Victorious

Romantic Suspense Novels Available from Marie Force

The Fatal Series

One Night With You, A Fatal Series Prequel Novella

Book 1: Fatal Affair

Book 2: Fatal Justice

Book 3: Fatal Consequences

Book 3.5: Fatal Destiny The Wedding Novella

Book 4: Fatal Flaw

Book 5: Fatal Deception

Book 6: Fatal Mistake

Book 7: Fatal Jeopardy

Book 8: Fatal Scandal

Book 9: Fatal Frenzy (September 15, 2015)

Single Title

The Wreck

ABOUT THE AUTHOR

With more than 4 million books sold, **Marie Force** is the *New York Times, USA Today* and *Wall Street Journal* bestselling, award-winning author of more than 40 contemporary romances. Her *New York Times* bestselling self-published Gansett Island Series has sold 2 million e-books since *Maid for Love* was released in 2011. She is also the author of the *New York Times* bestselling Fatal Series from Harlequin's Carina Press, as well as the *New York Times* bestselling Green Mountain Series from Berkley, among other books and series. Marie's new erotic Quantum Trilogy was released under the name of M.S. Force in April 2015, and all three books were *New York Times* and *USA Today* bestsellers. The trilogy is now set to become a series.

While her husband was in the Navy, Marie lived in Spain, Maryland and Florida, and she is now settled in her home state of Rhode Island. She is the mother of two teenagers and two feisty dogs, Brandy and Louie.

Join Marie's mailing list for news about new books and upcoming appearances in your area. Follow her on Twitter @marieforce and on Facebook. Join one of Marie's many reader groups. Contact Marie at *marie@marieforce.com*. Subscribe to my new blog to hear the latest and greatest news, including giveaways and other great prizes. Go to the blog website and enter your email address on the upper right-hand side.

CPSIA information can be obtained at www.ICGtesting.com
Printed in the USA
LVOW06s1558290915

456190LV00003B/501/P